Devil's Despair

Sirena Robinson

Supposed Crimes LLC • Matthews, North Carolina

Published in the United States.
Supposed Crimes LLC
Matthews, North Carolina

First Edition

ISBN: 978-1-938108-59-4

www.supposedcrimes.com

This book is typeset in Goudy Old Style,
licensed by Ascender Corporation.

Books in This Series

Devil's Dilemma
Devil's Despair
Devil's Redemption
Devil's Salvation
Nephilim Rising
Nephil's Destruction

Acknowledgements

To my wonderful betas, Amy and Adrian: without you, this novel would be full of sentences starting with conjunctions, random commas, and amusing misspellings. You have helped make it readable. Thank you for all your hard work.

Prologue

"That was a really scary story."

Amaya sat up in her bed, her curly hair frizzy from being asleep. She turned on the lamp and studied the man in the white suit that stood next to her window. "Are Mommy and Daddy gone again?"

Gabriel smiled reassuringly. "I don't want you to worry. They're always back when you wake up, aren't they?"

"Most of the time," she agreed readily, tossing back the blankets to join him at the window. "Uncle Gabe, what do they do?"

"They keep people safe. Your parents are good people, and they have very important work that they have to do. Sometimes, that work takes them away from here and from you. When that happens, it's very important that they know you're safe, so they ask me to stay and watch over you." He laid a hand on her head. "One of these days you'll understand."

"I'm nine and five-sixths now, you know. I'm practically a grown up."

Amused, Gabriel chuckled. "Practically isn't actually, muppet. Back into bed now. I don't need your mother mad at me because you've had no sleep for school tomorrow."

"What they don't know won't hurt them."

"Yes, but if you're yawning through your lessons, they'll know, now won't they?"

Knowing when she was beaten, Amaya looked up at him with hopeful eyes. "Will you tell me another story at least? You always tell me a story when you watch me."

"Get into bed." He followed her to the bed and sat next to her, leaning against the wall with his legs stretched out in front of him. "What story would you like?"

"Did Griffin really die? In the last story, at the end, she died."

"Yes, she really died. She did a very important thing, and without her sacrifice, you would never have been born. She was a special woman, and we should always remember what she did."

"What happened after that?"

"A lot happened after that. Is that the story you want?"

"Will you tell me about how my parents got married? I don't even know their names. Just Mom and Dad. They say it's too dangerous."

Gabriel adjusted the blanket so that it covered Amaya's shoulders. "They're wise in that. These times are very uncertain, and your parents play a very important part. You'll know all you need to know when you're old enough to understand."

"Can you at least tell me how they met?"

He chuckled softly. "There is a lot that happened between the Choosing and when your parents were married. Don't you want to know that story first?"

Amaya huffed a sigh and crossed her arms over her chest. "Do I have much of a choice?"

"Not if you want a story."

"Then it'll have to do, won't it?"

Gabriel ruffled her hair. "Remind me again how you humans begin your stories? 'A long time ago, in a galaxy far, far away'—is that right?"

Despite herself, the child giggled. "Once upon a time."

"That's it. Once upon a time, several months before the Choosing, it became clear to Lucifer that he was going to lose. The Chosen was going to Choose Heaven, and the Angels would walk the Earth for a million years. Because Lucifer is not known for playing fair, he decided he needed to have a plan to find another way to get free from Hell. He convened his Devils, and his demons, and they all tried to come up with a way. Finally, Beelzebub figured it out. Do you have any idea what he figured out?"

"What?"

"Well, think about it. What's the one thing God can't interfere with?"

"Free will."

"Right. And who has free will?"

"People." Amaya scrunched her nose, thinking hard. Finally, she jumped in the bed with excitement. "He found a person that could let him out!"

"Very close. Remember, in Genesis, in the beginning, God created the Heavens and the Earth. He didn't create Hell until after the Battle. When He created Hell, He made it below Earth—far, far below so that no human could ever get there without being sent there. Now, I don't want you to think it's somewhere on Earth, or in Earth, because it's much more complex than that, but all you need to know is that to access Hell—to send people there and for demons to have access to Earth—there had to be a door. One door to let souls in after they die, and one door to let demons and Devils out. Lucifer was the only Devil that could never leave Hell. On each of these doors, God placed guards—magic protections that would keep Lucifer from leaving and that would control how many got out. In order to defeat the Choosing, Lucifer would need to find people who would, and who could, break them free."

"Why would anyone want to let him out?"

"Because they didn't know any better. Lucifer is very charming and very persuasive. Most people are easily swayed. Beelzebub spent ten years scouring the globe, finding every worshipper of Lucifer and rallying them. He found witches, warlocks, and creatures of Hell, like werewolves and vampires. Remember what they are?"

"People bitten by Hell hounds who die with the venom in their systems and those who die with demon blood in them."

"Exactly right. He found them all, or at least all of them that wanted Lucifer out, and he gathered them together. The ones that survived the Choosing—that weren't killed when it happened—came together and started working magic—spells, potions, sacrifices, and rituals. Powerful, dark magic that they pulled out of the bowels of Hell and manipulated into what they needed it to be. It took six months, but eventually, they cracked the locks, and demons poured out onto Earth. More than ever had before. Devils, too, and hounds. They broke the rules and found a way around the Choosing. God was enraged. He wanted to start the End of Days immediately. Some of the Angels, those who had been involved with the Choosing, who had seen what Griffin went through, what the cost of her Choice had been, begged God to reconsider and to allow them time to find a way to stop it. He gave them fifty human years."

"That's a long time!"

"Not to God. It's the blink of an eye. Do you know what they did?"

Amaya looked at him through dark eyes too wise for her years. "We both know you've never told me this one before."

Gabriel chuckled. "Very well. They brought together six very special people. Six people from across time, who were the best at what they could do. Together, they would have to close the door, and then they would have to cast the demons back into Hell. To do this, they would have to do several things. First, they would need to seal it shut by spilling upon it the blood of the first vampire, the one who first rose, a hybrid of demon and human. Then, they would need to seal it shut by killing the warlock who opened the Gate in the first place. Last, they would have to destroy the Gate to keep any demons from escaping back to Earth until the thousand millennia won by Heaven in the Choosing had elapsed."

"Who were the six?"

"Two were those who were termed the Lost. They should have fought for the other side, by nature of their very existence."

"Gage and Alaria."

"Very good. Then, there would be two fighters. One a Warrior, the other a Hunter by birthright, born to slay vampires. He would be strong and agile, with a touch of magic, and the ability to sense demon blood."

"Braxton. The Warrior is Braxton, isn't it?"

"Yes. Lastly, there would be two witches. One, a Healer, who could take into herself the pain of another and make them whole again. She would also be a direct descendant of the Chosen. The other was the most powerful witch who had ever lived. They would bring together Time—past, present and future. They would come together into one circle, without beginning and without end."

"How did they destroy the Gate?"

Gabriel smiled. "That's another story for another night. The first part of this story is a while before that. Tonight I'll tell you about how they stopped the purge and kept more demons from coming out of the Gates."

Amaya sighed. "Fine. You never tell me the story I want to hear. What happened after Griffin died?"

Gabriel stroked a hand over her hair. "I thought that was the story I'm getting ready to tell you."

"No, I mean right after. Did Alaria get her wish? Is she human? What happened to Braxton and Gage?"

"Can't you wait for that to be revealed in this story?"

Amaya shook her head so vehemently that her hair smacked her in the face. "No! That's part of the last story. I want you to tell me what happened right after the Choosing before you start something new."

"I think we might have time for that as well."

She grinned and wrapped her arms around his waist. "How does it start?"

"It starts as all good stories start. Once upon a time..."

Chapter One

January 1st, 2030 - The Choosing Place

BRAXTON REGAINED consciousness slowly, his head pounding from crashing into the wall. He managed to open one eye, then the other, and force himself to roll onto his back. He blinked rapidly when blood dripped into his eyes and swiped at it with one hand when the blinking did nothing more than make it burn worse. When he managed to lift his head, he saw Gage sitting in the last pew, looking banged up but in one piece. Gage saw him stir and climbed to his feet, crossing the room and offering a hand to pull the other man up. Braxton was only mildly embarrassed when his knee wouldn't hold him, and he had to lean heavily on the vampire. He looked around the chapel, taking in the broken wood and the debris littering the floor.

"Where is she?"

"Over here."

Alaria's voice surprised him, and he focused on her sitting on the floor, leaning against the wall at the front of the sanctuary. Her face was bruising in an array of colors, and her legs were stretched out in front of her. He followed her gaze to where Griffin lay, eyes open and glassy, the knife sticking out of her chest and a pool of slowly congealing blood still warm underneath her. Tears made Braxton's throat feel thick, but he held them back.

He tested his knee once again and found that it held his weight. Walking across the room, his eyes never wavering, he stared at her body, tears making his vision fuzzy. "She did it."

Gage chuckled. "Did you ever doubt that she would?"

Braxton thought about that for a minute and shook his head. "Actually, no, I didn't." He stooped next to Griffin's body, brushed her hair back from her face and pulled the knife from her chest. It was covered in blood and bits of flesh. He let the knife fall from his fingers and clatter to the floor. "You did good, baby." He laid his hand over her eyes, closing them for what would be the final time. He looked up and addressed Gage and Alaria. "I want to take her home to bury her."

Alaria struggled to her feet, groaning when every bone in her body ached and screamed. Her gait was unsteady as she walked to him, and the pain she felt was clearly evident from the expression on her face. "Give me a few more minutes, and I'll take us all back." She coughed. "I just need to work up the energy to teleport. Keeping Azazel off of her took a lot out of me."

Braxton walked to the Devil and pressed two fingers to her throat, just below her chin and to the right. "I don't think so, Alaria."

"Why not?"

He reached down, took her hand, placed her fingers where his had been, and watched as the truth dawned on her. "Because your heart is beating."

Her breath came whooshing out as she suddenly realized she needed to breathe. Her heart pounded in her chest, and she felt it beat beneath her fingertips. She held her breath and heard her blood rushing through her veins. Her face split into a smile, and without thinking, she tossed her arms around Braxton's neck in an enthusiastic hug, knocking him back several steps as he struggled to keep his balance. "I'm human! Son of a bitch, He did it!"

"Did you doubt our Father?" As he spoke, Gabriel appeared in a flash of light, looking as perfectly put together as always. "Or was it Griffin you doubted?"

"I never doubted Griffin." Alaria offered him a grin. "Where the fuck have you been? You missed the whole damn thing."

His gaze was dark and his expression wry. "Azazel attempted to chain me to his rock. He managed to get one of his shackles on me without getting stuck in the traps. Given that those shackles are made to hold any supernatural creature, they are effective on Angels, and it took a while to get out." Gabriel looked among the three. "Are you all that survived?"

Gage nodded. "Yeah. Everyone else is dead. I checked."

"I had hoped that more would survive. I'll take you home to your family, Braxton, and return you to wherever you wish to go, Gage. Alaria..." His voice trailed off for a moment. "...I'm not sure what I should do with you."

Braxton tried to lift Griffin's body but found that he was too weak.

Understanding, Gage stepped in, lifting Griffin easily. Her hair fell over one of his arms, stained red with blood and hanging more than halfway to the floor. Alaria wrapped her arm around Braxton to support part of his weight, and they hobbled toward the Angel together.

Braxton cleared his throat to get Gabriel's attention. "How was she when she died? Was she in pain?"

Gabriel smiled as he reached out to touch each of them. "She died a hero." He laid a hand on Braxton's shoulder. "It's time to go home. Important things are getting ready to happen."

Braxton adjusted his tie in the mirror, his eyes skating over the yellowing bruises on his face. He glanced up when he heard a knock at the door. "Come in!"

Alaria's face appeared in the mirror as she stepped through. "Your mother says that it is time to go. Father Dooley is waiting for us at the cemetery." She shuddered. "I don't quite understand your need to bury your dead in a box. It's morbid."

Braxton lifted one of his eyebrows. "You're one of us now, y'know."

"I'll never bury someone in a box." She reached out and straightened his tie. "Are you ready for this?"

"As ready as you can be to bury your wife."

Alaria stepped back to survey her work. "Are the feelings fading?"

He nodded. "I'm not sure I want them to. It's so bizarre. I loved her so much and hated it. Not because of her, but because I knew, deep down, that it was never real. Now that she's gone, and the feelings are starting to fade, and I have confirmation that God interfered, I cling to those feelings as hard as I can because I don't want to forget them and let her go."

"I'm sure that's normal, given the circumstances." She smoothed her hands over her black skirt. "We should leave. Your mother makes me nervous."

Braxton couldn't stop the grin that split his face. "She's terrifying. You don't want to piss her off." He laid a hand on her back to lead her down the stairs, out the door, and into his car. His parents and sister were already in his father's car, which was parked directly behind his. "How are you doing?"

She shook her head. "Today is about you. I'm fine."

"You wake up screaming every single night. That's not fine." He glanced at her as he pulled away from the curb. "You wake the whole house shrieking and then refuse to talk about it. I can't help you if you won't tell me what's going on."

"You're already doing too much by letting me stay with you and arranging for a human identity and paperwork."

"Just tell me what you're having nightmares about."

Alaria sighed. "Things I've done to people. Let's just say that the guilt of five million years of torturing people can be a bit overwhelming at times. It's manifesting in my dreams."

They rode in silence for several minutes. As he turned into the cemetery, Braxton cleared his throat and spoke. "I think you should go stay with Gage for a while. He has some experience with what you're going through. He could help you."

Her voice was small and soft. "If he can help, I'll go."

Braxton parked the car. "I'll call him tomorrow. I'll go with you to help you settle in."

She shook her head. "You don't have to do that." She waited while he rounded the car to open her door. "Seriously, Brax, I'm fine."

"I'm going. Live with it." He cast a glance at the empty grave, the casket and the five chairs sitting next to it. "After this, I'm going to get so drunk I won't be able to drive for three days."

Alaria smiled wryly. "I've never been drunk, actually."

"Want to come?"

"Sure."

He again laid his hand on her back and guided her through the headstones to their seats. "Good." He smiled at Father Dooley and sat between Alaria and Sam. Sam reached over and twined her fingers with his. She squeezed them tightly before speaking.

"I'll be the designated driver."

Alaria's eyebrows shot up. "How the hell did you know what we're planning?"

Sam chuckled. "I have bat ears. Brax can attest to that."

Braxton looked serious. "She can hear you whispering on the phone from three doors down, I swear to God."

Father Dooley cleared his throat and waited for the small group to fall silent before speaking. "We have gathered here today not to mourn the loss of Griffin but to celebrate her life and what she has given to us all." He paused to look around. "She gave love, she gave friendship, and she gave life. Because of her, we all have futures. That is not something to mourn—it is something to be glad of." He cleared his throat and opened a slim book. "I will start with a reading from the Book of Wisdom.

"'The souls of the righteous are in the hands of God, and no torment will ever touch them. In the eyes of the foolish they seemed to have died and their departure was thought to be a disaster, and their going from us to be their destruction; but they are at peace. For though in the sight of others they were punished, their hope is full of immortality. Having been disciplined a little, they will receive great good, because God tested them and found them worthy of Himself; like gold in the furnace He tried them, and like a sacrificial burnt offering He accepted them. In the time of their visitation they will shine forth, and will run like sparks through the stubble. They will govern nations and rule over peoples, and the Lord will reign over them forever. Those who trust in Him will understand truth, and the faithful will abide with Him in love, because grace and mercy are upon His holy ones, and He watches over His elect.'

"Griffin was chosen by God for a purpose, and she fulfilled her task with dignity and with grace. She is rejoicing in Heaven with Angels, while we reap the benefits of her sacrifice. She has given us a world without evil, a world without demons. For the first time since God cast out Lucifer, the world will be at peace. Griffin embraced her mission with determination and faith, and she never wavered from her goal. I will conclude with a reading of the twenty-third Psalm.

"'The Lord is my Shepherd; I shall not want. He maketh me to lie down in green pastures: He leadeth me beside the still waters. He restoreth my soul: He leadeth me in the paths of righteousness for His name' sake. Yea, though I walk through the valley of the shadow of death, I will fear no evil: For thou art with me; Thy rod and thy staff, they comfort me. Thou preparest a table before me in the presence of mine enemies; Thou anointest my head with oil; My cup runneth over. Surely goodness and mercy shall follow me all the days of my life, and I will dwell in the House of the Lord forever.'" Father Dooley bowed his head. "Let us pray.

"Our Heavenly Father, we have gathered here today in your presence, to thank you for the life of Griffin. We mourn her loss and grieve her absence. We know that she is in a better place and that she is safe in your arms. We rejoice in her life and in the sacrifice she made to ensure that there is a future for us. Never has one person done so much for so many at so great a cost since your son, Jesus Christ, died upon the cross. We thank you for her life and celebrate her and you. You promised us in Genesis that 'By the sweat of your brow you will eat your food until you return to the ground, since from it you were taken; for dust you are and to dust you will return.' We return Griffin to the ground today and praise you for the glory that was her life. In sure and certain hope of the resurrection to eternal life through our Lord, Jesus Christ, we commend Griffin to the Almighty God. We commit her body to the ground—earth to earth, ashes to ashes, dust to dust. 'The Lord bless her and keep her, the Lord maketh his face to shine upon her and be gracious unto her and give her peace.' In the name of God the Father, God the Son, and God the Holy Ghost, Amen."

Father Dooley crossed to the podium set up and plucked a rosebud from a vase. He handed it to Braxton, then chose four more for Alaria, Sam, Allen and Miranda before taking one for himself. The workers from the funeral home approached the grave when he motioned to them, and the casket was slowly lowered into the ground. One by one, the five present threw in a flower and a handful of dirt. Father Dooley hugged each as they walked by, tears shining in his eyes.

Braxton kept going. He couldn't stay, didn't have the strength. He felt Sam beside him, her arm around him and her protruding belly brushing against him. Alaria was on her other side, staring stonily ahead and staunchly ignoring the physical evidence of her emotions dripping down her cheeks. They walked together toward his car. As Alaria climbed into the backseat, she uttered three words.

"Drunk sounds good."

Braxton slipped into the passenger's seat, leaving Sam to drive. He echoed the sentiment. "Drunk sounds good."

Chapter Two

February, 2087 - New York City

"Jesus Christ, it's cold out there!" Greer Dawson slammed the door behind her and starting moving through the crowd toward the bar. The man behind the bar threw up a hand in a friendly wave and put a glass on the worn wood before she even sidled up to it.

"Cold out there?"

"It's February, and we're in New York. What do you think?" She unwound her scarf and shrugged off her coat. "What've ya got today?"

"Jim and Dave brought me a couple barrels of homemade wine. It tastes pretty decent. They got ahold of some apples about to rot and bought them to turn into booze."

"Lemme try that then." She slid onto the stool, her well-worn jeans stretching tight over her thighs as she moved. "Training was brutal today. I could use a couple drinks before curfew."

Damon Mackenzie looked at the clock on the wall as he filled the glass he'd placed in front of her with pink wine. "It's only seven. We have to be in the barracks by eleven. Plenty of time."

"I hate winter. We can't be outside until it's light, and then we only have a few hours when it's not either too dark or too cold." Greer took a drink of the wine and swished it around her mouth for several seconds. "This is pretty damn good." She looked around at the crowd. "Do you need me to help serve or something?"

Damon shook his head. "I've got it. You've worked all day."

Greer rolled her eyes and finished her drink in a single gulp. "So did you, boss man." She hopped off the stool and ducked under the counter to join him behind the bar. "Give me a tray. I can serve."

Damon swatted her butt with the towel he kept draped over his shoulder to clean up spills. "Do you ever take no for an answer?"

"You know me well enough to know the answer to that." She took the apron he held out and tied it on.

"I could always order you to cease and desist."

Greer bumped him with one hip on her way out into the crowd. She threw a careless smile over one shoulder. "We're off duty, Captain. I don't have to do a damn thing you tell me."

Damon grinned as he turned to pour moonshine into a glass for a man at the bar. "That woman'll be the death of me yet."

The man shook his head and sipped his drink contemplatively. "It wouldn't be so bad if you were tappin' her. Piece of ass like that around here? Damn." He whistled appreciatively. "I wouldn't mind getting a taste."

Damon's eyes darkened slightly, and the smile faded until his lips pressed tightly together. "She's like my sister. You watch what you say." When the man didn't respond, Damon turned to serve another customer, turning back to whisk the crumpled bills on the counter into the creaky old register. He looked around for Greer and saw her talking animatedly with a group of men in uniforms, her curly blonde hair swept up in a messy bun, tendrils falling around her face. Even through the din of the bar, he could hear her laugh.

She turned and caught his eye, her gaze conveying curiosity. Something about his expression must have concerned her because within seconds he felt the familiar pressure against his mind of her seeking access. Before he could even think about it, he felt his mind open up and allowed her to slip inside.

"What's wrong?"

"Just a customer saying things he shouldn't say."

"I don't need you to protect me, Damon. I can take care of myself."

"I never said you couldn't. And notice that I'm not brawling with him, so it's not like I'm jumping to your defense. I just wish you'd be more careful."

Greer chuckled, both in his head and out loud. *"Dude, I'm serving homemade beer and moonshine to a bar full of people, some of whom I work with every day. I don't think I'm in a ton of danger here."* Her voice softened. *"I know you feel responsible for me, but seriously, I'm a grown up. Knock it off."*

"I'm responsible for our entire squad. Don't take it personally."

Greer broke the connection. The older brother complex Damon had going on was damned annoying. Fifteen years they'd known one another, and he was still trying to protect her the same way he had at twelve when he'd rescued her from the demon trying to possess her.

Not that she hadn't returned the favor five years later when she'd brought him back after he'd nearly drowned in the Hudson River. Even still she could remember the panic rising in her throat as they'd careened over the bridge and into the icy water below and the jarring force of the impact that had blinded her for several heart stopping seconds. She shivered involuntarily, still able to feel the water seeping through her clothes.

Damon had been unconscious and hurt badly. His airbag had failed to go off when they hit, but Greer had struggled, fighting the nylon of the seatbelt viciously, until finally, it had given way and she'd been able to lunge across the Jeep to get to Damon.

His skin had been so cold. Icy and clammy. Dead. The minutes of towing him back to shore had been the scariest of her whole life to that point. She clearly remembered the chunks of ice she'd shoved away from them and the frothy, sluggish water that tried to drag them both down. It had seemed like eternity before she'd heaved his limp weight from the river and up onto the rocky shore.

She remembered the moon, full and bright, making everything glow. She could still feel how raw her throat had been from screaming for help and the feel of his chest under her hands as she did CPR. Finally, when her head had cleared and she'd been able to think, she'd placed her hands on his chest, reached into herself, and done what she had been born to do. She had healed him, taken his pain into herself, and used her own energy to reach deep within him to find the dying embers of life. She'd breathed her own breath into his lungs and fanned those embers back into flame.

Greer was startled back into the present when the alarms started going off. Deafening, wailing alarms that echoed through the night and drowned out any other noise. The tray she'd been holding in her arms dropped to the floor. Alcohol and glass sprayed her feet and legs. She whirled, searching the crowd. Already the men in uniform were charging through the throng of panicked people, their guns at the ready.

She was jostled and bumped as people ran by in a panic. Most wore crosses around their necks: a meager form of protection against the horrors their world had to offer them. Others, like Greer and Damon, had thirteen tiny tattoos across their shoulders, a deeper protection against possession.

Damon locked down the bar. He secured all but the front door, salting them and quickly painting protection symbols on the walls. He had already tucked a pistol in the waistband of his jeans. Greer ran past him into the back room and came back with their emergency packs and her own weapon.

"We have to get to the locker room. If we're under attack, we need to get our equipment."

"I know. It's going to be pandemonium out there." He shouldered one of the packs and then paused to help Greer fasten her Kevlar vest. "Stay close and move fast."

She grinned as they wound their way through the now empty bar. "This isn't my first rodeo, cowboy. I can keep up."

To say it was chaos would have been a horrific understatement. The streets flooded with civilians—workers rushing back from their shifts, patrons of the few bars and restaurants in the strip, and others who had been out for less legal reasons—all panicking and trying to get home. People from all walks of life shared the tunnels, all going different places. When the alarms went off—blaring and echoing through the city, bouncing off buildings and shrieking in warning—they all shared the same goal. Get off the street.

Everyone, that is, except the soldiers. They had been trained to defend against attacks. Equally deadly with guns, swords, stakes and spells, they would charge into the fray, go to the entrances of the city, and fight to the death to keep the monsters at bay.

Greer and Damon wound their way through the masses as quickly as they could. They flashed their ID cards at the guards to the barracks and bolted down the long hallway to their locker room. The rest of the team had already assembled and were going through the motions of readying for war.

Greer didn't even notice that she was in a room with nine men. Her shoes pinged off a locker as she kicked them from her feet. Denim hit the ground with a soft whoosh, soon to be joined by the crumpled up form of her shirt. In five seconds, she twisted her arms behind her back and released the clasps on her bra.

She spun the dial on the lock that secured her locker quickly and without even needing to look at it. She heard the telltale snick that told her she'd gotten it right and dropped the lock on the floor carelessly. She yanked her sports bra on over her bare breasts and then shimmied into the black cargos they had all been assigned. Next came the black wife-beater, then the long sleeved black button-up shirt, followed by her bulletproof vest and her boots. She scraped her hair off her face, secured it with an elastic band and a thick fabric headband that served to keep any fly-aways from falling into her eyes. She yanked on the fingerless gloves that protected her hands, strapped her walkie-talkie to her arm, and fastened the straps to her pack across her chest.

Damon had already entered the code for the weapons locker, and it swung open to reveal their choices. Each pack contained Holy Water, stakes, a silver dagger, salt and protective bundles of herbs. They also carried several clips of ammunition on their utility belts, which strapped across their hips. Each one held a different type of ammo. Silver for the werewolves. Wooden bullets in case they were fighting vampires. Salt-crusted hollow-points if it was demons they were after. Finally, they carried regular bullets for the Familiars they could face.

Greer shoved three clips of each type of bullet into the pockets on her belt and bent to strap her pistol to her ankle where it joined a wicked looking buck knife. A second pistol was tucked into her waistband against the small of her back and secured with a snap into her belt. Lastly, she plucked a combat rifle off of the wall and checked to make sure it was loaded.

"We don't know what we're facing yet." Damon addressed the team, his voice calm and steady. "We've dealt with anything this world has to throw at us before, and we've lived to tell about it. I know we don't normally do this, but this is the first time in years that the demons have attacked a city. This isn't our typical recon and supply mission. We must keep them from getting inside the city. Martinez, you take three men and go to the South entrance. Isaacs, you take three and head to the West entrance. Dawson, you're coming with me to HQ. We need to find out what's going on, and then we'll split from there. I'll join you at the South. Dawson will head west." He clapped his hands once. "Let's go!"

Greer jogged to keep up with Damon's longer stride, her heart pounding in her chest and her gun lifted to her shoulder but aimed down until she needed it. If she needed it. God, she prayed she didn't need it.

Three blocks before they got to headquarters, they could hear gunshots and screams. Damon exchanged a dark look with the guard manning the door as they entered. There were half a dozen men in the room, all huddled around a bank of grainy screens as they tried to see what was going on through the fifty-year-old cameras they had placed around the city.

"Familiars. A fucking army of them. There's got to be a couple hundred demons to be controlling this many of them. The doors are uncompromised, but our men can only take on so many of them. Patrols say there are groups of vampires heading in, and one patrol caught sight of a pack of wolves coming this direction."

Damon and Greer looked at each other, a plethora of emotions passing between them in one glance. Damon was the one who spoke. "Have you been in contact with any other cities? Is this widespread?"

"It's just us. The settlement in Newark is sending three hundred soldiers to help. Boston is mobilizing six hundred."

"That's less than a thousand reinforcements." Greer gestured to the screen. "It looks like there are ten thousand Familiars out there."

"At least." General Hammond nodded grimly. "They're scared that they'll be next. No one wants to part with a lot of their fighters when they don't know if a herd of Familiars might only be fifteen minutes away from their Gates. The colony in Washington D.C. has told us that they have a fleet of nine jets left that they're willing to send up with three bombs each. That could take out a significant chunk of the Familiars on the surface. We'd still have to fight our way through the ones in the tunnels, but that's the downside of living in the subway system." He sighed deeply, looking at Damon and Greer. "I need you two to get out there and start getting the buses ready to evacuate if that's what we need to do. I'm telling D.C. to send the bombs. We're gonna have a panicked crowd on our hands, and you're going to have to deal with it. I can't spare soldiers from the entrances or the tunnels."

Damon nodded. "Yes, sir. My men are stationed at both entrances. I can keep in contact with them. I'll radio in if there are any breaches."

"Very good. Dismissed."

Greer waited until they were back out into the now mostly empty streets before speaking. "Damon, they're after something. We haven't had an attack like this in years. Not since Philadelphia fell."

"I know."

No one knew how it had happened, why it had happened, or even what exactly had happened until it was too late. The Hell Gate had burst open and demons had poured out, bringing with them other creatures from the depths of Hell. Vampires, werewolves, shape shifters—and then there were the Devils: the elite, the leaders; strong and vicious. The world hadn't stood a chance.

Within ten years, most of Europe, Africa and South America had collapsed into chaos. The United States had lasted another eight years before the government collapsed in on itself. Australia had been the last continent to fall in 2052. By 2060, none of the major cities were left. Regional governments and militias had cropped up, moving people underground, building structures and housing, and forming armies. They'd started to fight back.

"What do you think it is?"

Damon spared her a dark look. "I'm not that psychic."

Greer couldn't help the smile that slipped over her mouth. "You have an opinion about everything."

"Not about this, I don't." He shoved open the heavy metal door to the garages to expose the lines of old yellow school buses. "Can you believe kids used to ride these things to school?"

"Way back when they actually had schools." Greer picked up a clipboard and started checking the inventory of fuel, her pencil moving quickly over the paper as she did the math. "Now we just have basic stuff until they're old enough to work at something."

"What's the range on these things?"

"Sixty gallon tanks, twelve miles to the gallon means we can go a bit over seven hundred miles straight on a full tank. We have a hundred and fifteen buses and..." She squinted at the paper, trying to work the math "...about fourteen thousand gallons of diesel right now. Which means we could fill each twice, and that doesn't account for the fuel currently in them."

Damon sighed deeply. "It's going to take hours for the two of us to fuel up and load these by ourselves."

"Then we'd might as well get started." Greer lifted onto her tiptoes and snagged the keys to the fork lift. "Open up the back doors to these things. I'll start loading in the extra barrels."

Before either of them could take a single step, the entire garage shook as the first of twenty-seven bombs dropped onto the wreckage of New York City. Debris fell from the ceiling; several of the diesel drums toppled over and rolled across the floor. When the second bomb rocked the garage, chunks of concrete fell from the ceiling.

Damon grabbed Greer around the waist and tossed her onto the ground, rolling with her under one of the buses, his much larger body pressing her into the cold cement. The din from the explosion was so loud that neither could hear anything else. He touched a finger to her forehead, then slipped into her mind.

"We have to get out of here. This place isn't going to hold up to another twenty-

five bombs. It's going to fall in on itself. There isn't going to be any evacuation because we're all going to be dead."

Greer shook her head violently. "We can't just leave everyone! It's suicide to leave the city without the rest of the team."

Damon gripped her chin and turned her head so that he could meet her eyes. His voice was urgent inside her mind. *"This structure is going to collapse. We have no idea what the tunnels look like heading back into the main part of the city. They could be gone already. Or they could be fine and the other teams are evacuating out the main entrances. I am telling you that there is no choice. If we do not leave, we will die."*

Greer searched his eyes for any sign that he was less than completely sure about what he had said. When she found none, she spoke slowly. *"We'll have to move fast to get to the doors. Once we get to them, there is no telling what's on the other side."*

Damon reached into his bag and pulled out two grenades. *"You hit the lever to open the doors, and I'll toss these out. I have two explosive and three smoke grenades. Once they go off, we run together. Keep hold of my hand so we don't get separated."*

"Okay." She waited until the room stopped shaking from the third bomb. *"Let's go!"*

Greer rolled, her arms tucked tight against her body, and sprang to her feet lithely. She didn't have to look to know that Damon was right behind her. She flattened herself against the far wall and slapped the button that would open the tall sliding doors.

Damon methodically threw each of his grenades. One smoke, followed by a regular grenade, followed by another pair. He saved the last smoke grenade in case of an emergency. Hearts pounding, they waited until all four had gone off before they charged through the door. Damon grabbed Greer's hand in his own, holding it tightly as they darted into the unknown.

The Familiars were clumsy and stupid, completely at the mercy of their demonic masters. Damon battled his way through them brutally, using his hands as often as he used his weapon. Greer took a more discerning approach. She pulled her hand loose, darted up the side of one of the slopes that encased the dirt road leading to the surface, and picked them off one by one. Her aim was sharp and true, and her hands remained steady on her weapon as she squeezed the trigger over and over again.

She saw the red dots so indicative of a laser sight trying to find its target. She screamed, her voice hoarse and rough. Damon turned to look at her, his face splattered with blood from the Familiars he had killed. Panicking and unable to calm herself enough to use their psychic link, Greer scrambled down the hill, desperate to reach him in time.

The dots settled on his head and chest. Damon looked down, his eyes registering what was happening a split second before two shots rang out through the night. Instead of the impact of the bullets that would have ended his life, Greer, her smaller body moving as fast as it could, slammed into him with enough force to send him flying backward, hitting the dirt with a sickening smack.

The impact made his head rattle and his bones ache. Greer was still and heavy on top of him. He rolled her onto the ground, her blonde hair spilling out of its bonds to obscure her face. He shoved it back, desperately pressing his ear to her mouth, the sound of her shallow breathing an instant relief.

Reassured that she was alive, he spared a moment to look around and swore under his breath when he saw Familiars wobbling through the still lingering fog from the smoke grenades. Blood, sticky and warm, seeped from Greer's prone body, pooling beneath her in a much larger quantity than he was comfortable with. Knowing that he had no choice, Damon slung her pack across his back, draped her weapon over his shoulder and gathered Greer in his arms, lifting her and cradling her against his chest, her curly hair streaming over his arm. With one furtive look around, he did the only thing he could. He ran.

Chapter Three

BEING OUTSIDE at night was dangerous. Damon was keenly aware of that fact as he ran through the streets of the once vibrant city of New York. He dodged burned out cars and piles of debris and avoided going toward any gunfire that he heard.

The problem with being outside wasn't just that there were vampires, Hell hounds and werewolves. There were also people. People who refused to join one of the settlements. They were generally violent, desperate people. Most became vampire food. Those who didn't were nearly as dangerous as the monsters.

He knew he had to get Greer off the street. She was still bleeding—her shirt and pants both soaked with the blood that poured from her. The scent would attract the monsters. If they were somehow lucky enough not to get caught by vampires, the odds of making it through the night without getting caught by gang members or mercenaries were slim to none.

Greer stirred in his arms, her eyes fluttering as she regained consciousness. A low groan rumbled in her chest as the pain speared through her. Damon shifted his grip on her to press her face into his chest, muffling the sound. When her eyes shot open with panic in them as she gained consciousness, he shushed her.

"It's not safe yet—you have to be quiet."

Understanding dawned in her eyes, and she reached out to lay her fingertips against his jaw, the physical contact helping her forge the connection that was as easy as breathing when she was healthy. Alarmingly weak, her voice filled his mind.

"What happened?"

"You were shot. Twice, I think. I'm not sure yet. I have to get us someplace safe so that we can figure out what the hell we're doing."

"The city?"

Damon looked down, and his eyes told her everything she needed to know. Tears blurred her vision, burning as she struggled to hold them in. He climbed over a pile of trash and wood and found an entrance to a garden level apartment that was down a half flight of stairs. The windows had bars on them, and the door was still in one piece.

"Can you stand for me to pick this lock?"

Greer nodded, and he carefully placed her on her feet. The searing, burning pain that shot through her right hip told her exactly where she'd been shot, and she leaned heavily against the brick wall, lifting up her leg to ease the pressure.

Damon crouched in front of the door, a penlight clenched between his teeth to illuminate the knob. His hands were graceful and confident as he worked the lock-pick. After thirty tense seconds, the lock turned with a quiet click and the door swung open. He looked over his shoulder to make sure Greer was still standing and ducked inside to check that there was nothing inside that shouldn't be.

Within three minutes he was back. He wrapped one arm around Greer's waist, then bent his knees to loop his other arm under her knees, lifting her easily to carry her inside. He kicked the door closed and carried her swiftly to the back of the apartment and a bedroom that looked as if it had been frozen in time.

The bed was still made. Clothes still hung in the closet. Damon laid her on the bed and left her briefly to secure the apartment the best that he could. By the time he came back into the room, Greer had managed to kick her feet free from her boots and peel off her vest and long-sleeved shirt.

"Hip and shoulder. Shoulder looks like it went all the way through. It's messy. I can't tell what my hip looks like yet."

Damon sat on the bed next to her and shrugged off his own gear. "You're in no shape to try and heal yourself right now. You've lost too much blood."

Greer winced when he moved the strap of her tank top to inspect the damage the bullet had done to her shoulder. "Since when do fucking Familiars fire guns, anyway?"

Damon shrugged. "There's still a lot that we don't know about them. Maybe it was a demon. Maybe the demon was only controlling one or two so it could do it better, or maybe it was a human. We know there are some that work with the demons. It could be one of a million things. It doesn't matter now. We need to get you patched up as much as we can. Some food and sleep and you'll be able to manage something."

"It's gonna have to be one or the other. I can't do both."

He nodded. "I know. It's got to be the shoulder. You need to be able to shoot."

Greer gritted her teeth against the pain as Damon used his knife to slice her tank away from her body so that she didn't have to lift her arms over her head. "If the city fell, the closest base is in Boston. That's a walk that will take at least two weeks. I have to be able to walk."

"I can help you."

She laughed at that. "You're beastly, Damon, but even you can't carry a hundred-fifty in packs and drag another hundred-fifty in me for a few hundred miles."

"We can try and find a vehicle."

"Yeah, and we both know that fuel is an unknown at best. The roads are deadly at night and not much better during the day. We'd have to find something that offered some protection. There's no guarantee."

Damon dumped his pack out on the floor and rifled through the contents. "We'll deal with that later. I'm going to have to clean you up some." He poked at her shoulder, inspecting the seeping, jagged wound. Greer gritted her teeth and fisted her hands to keep from crying out. He used his knife to cut off the strap to her sports bra and ripped open an alcohol wipe. "This is going to hurt."

It did hurt. By the time Damon was done cleaning the wound, front and back, Greer was sobbing silently, tears streaming down her face. When her teeth sank into her lips and blood mingled with the tears, Damon knew that he would have to do something. He sat back and took her hands in his.

"This is just going to get worse. The scent of that will attract vamps. I need to stitch it closed. Probably sew up your hip, too." He leaned over to pick up the first aid kid. "You aren't going to be able to stay quiet for all of that. You're doing great right now, but it's going to hurt a lot worse. If you start screaming, we're not going to be alone for long, and we don't have the ammo to hold them off, especially not if we have to walk to Boston. We need to conserve our resources as much as possible."

"Knock me out." Greer's voice was steady and sure, leaving no room for questioning. "It's the only choice." She obligingly lifted her hips for him to remove her pants when he unbuckled them and tugged on the blood soaked fabric. "Leave the hip open. I'll be able to heal it once I've had some sleep and food. If you stitch it and then I try, it'll make it harder."

Damon smiled. "I'd rather not have you mess up my embroidery to begin with." He rifled through the first aid kit, looking for something that he could use to sedate her. When he found nothing, he knew that the only other option was an unpleasant one. He felt the pressure of his pistol against the small of his back and stood, crossing into the adjoining bathroom to check for any pain medication or sedatives. Finding nothing, he reluctantly went back into the bedroom.

Greer sat against the headboard. Her attention was focused on the wound on her hip. Damon knew immediately that he would never have another opportunity to do what needed to be done. He crossed the room to the bed, his hand closing around the gun. In one smooth motion, he whirled and smashed the butt of the gun into Greer's temple. Soundlessly, her eyes rolled back in her head, and she crumbled to the side, unconscious before she hit the mattress.

Knowing that he had to work quickly, Damon shrugged out of his long-sleeved shirt and set about his task. He found a large mixing bowl in the kitchen and two gallon jugs full of water in a closet he imagined had once been a pantry. There were still towels folded in the bathroom, which he used to clean the blood from Greer's bruised skin.

Sewing skin wasn't easy. It was thick, almost rubbery, and gave resistance unlike any fabric. The needle didn't go through smoothly, and the line of black stitches stuck out glaringly against her shoulder. The flesh was angry and red, puckering up as it was wrenched together by the thread.

The exit was larger than the entrance and took triple the amount of stitches. He cleaned the wound on her hip meticulously, picking out dirt and fibers. The bullet was embedded in the bone, and he knew that trying to push it out would deplete her tenuous energy stores. Sweat beaded on his forehead as he carefully sanitized his utility knife by holding the blade over the flame of a lighter until it glowed red.

If skin was hard to stitch, it was easier to cut than it should have been. The razor sharp blade of his knife sliced through her flesh as if it was made of butter. The white of her hipbone was a stark contrast against the deep red of blood and the pewter grey of the perfectly round bullet buried deep within it.

The sound the blade made as it collided with bone was like a metallic twang, as if he'd flicked a cymbal with a fingernail. Digging the bullet out reminded him of the sound of a mortar and pestle grinding against one another. When he finally held the projectile in his palm, he was struck by how something so tiny could do so much damage. It didn't matter how many times he saw it, the wreckage left in the wake of a bullet always made him a little nauseous.

He bandaged her hip with gauze and tape. Her hair was matted with dried blood, and her remaining clothing was in tatters. Gently, Damon washed the blood from her skin and painstakingly rinsed her hair. It took both gallons of the water that he'd found before her blonde locks lost the sticky red hue.

Finally, he stripped off her ruined clothes and dug through their bags to find something else to put on her. He finally settled on the extra shirt that he had packed in his bag. It buttoned in the front, which made it easier for him to put it on her, and was both baggy and long, covering her body from shoulder to thigh.

His job done, Damon tucked blankets around Greer to keep her warm, pulled a chair into the bedroom and dropped into it to wait for her to wake up.

For the second time in the same night, Greer found herself regaining consciousness. Her head felt as if it had been split open, and her whole body ached with cold and pain in equal shares. She groaned as she became aware of herself and struggled to peel her eyelids open.

The room was almost pitch black, save for a flashlight Damon had set in the middle of the floor. The man in question sat in a chair, cleaning their weapons. When he saw her eyes open, he smiled and set aside the project.

"How do you feel?"

"Like I was hit in the head with a gun."

"Then you feel about right." He stood and crossed the room to perch on the mattress next to her. "I got the bullet out of your hip and stitched up your shoulder. Your clothes are destroyed, but I think the stuff in that closet might fit you."

"How has this place not been raided?"

"It's below street level with an alley entrance. I'm sure that there are actually a lot of places like this. Demons aren't exactly worried about stealing clothes, and there aren't enough people left to hit them all."

"At least not yet. It'll get bad, Damon. The cities that are left—they'll be attacked now." Greer carefully and gently shifted her legs around to place her feet on the floor. "They won't stop until they kill us all."

"They can't kill us all." He helped her to her feet, supporting most of her weight as they moved from the bedroom into the kitchen to try and find some food. "As horrible as that is to say, at least the vamps need us for food. Demons can't exist here without humans to host them, and they can't have their Familiars without having us."

"How many do you think are left?"

"People? I don't know. If I had to guess, at last half the world is gone." He cast her a smile. "Chin up, Dawson. We're still alive, and we're still fighting." He eased her into a chair and started rifling through cabinets. Within a couple minutes, he turned up three cans of fruit cocktail, one can of chicken noodle soup, and a box of pop tarts. Greer used her toe to open the pantry, which yielded a box a saltine crackers, some breakfast bars, a case of soda, and a half dozen cans of black beans.

"Well, with the MREs we both have, if we're careful, this might be enough for a week."

"Maybe. We only have ten MREs total, five in each pack. We're going to be burning a shit ton of calories walking to Boston in the middle of the winter. If we're lucky, we can scavenge on our way, too, so this is a good start." Damon pulled out his Swiss army knife and opened up a can of the fruit. "We'll split this and have a pop tart. You can have the soup, too, to give you the energy you'll need to heal."

Greer ignored the guilt she felt at using more than her share of their resources but knew that he was right. She needed the food to heal her hip, and leaving it injured would be more of a strain on their journey than the extra food she needed to make sure she could heal it.

They ate in relative silence, the flashlight their only source of light. The cold was oppressive, and Greer's teeth began to chatter halfway through the meal. Damon went on a search for more blankets and turned up two in the second bedroom, which he tucked around her shoulders and draped over her legs.

Once she had finished the soup, Damon tossed the cans in the sink and opened them each a can of soda. "Let's get you back to the bed so that we can get this hip taken care of and get some sleep."

Greer held up her arms to let him pull her up. She leaned against him so that he could help her walk, her teeth gritted against the pain and her face pale and drawn. Just getting back into the bed was a hassle. Her hip rebelled against every movement she made, and her shoulder screamed with its own form of pain from the hole in it.

Once she was settled, she leaned back against the pillows and took several deep breaths to help alleviate the pain. "Okay, let's do this." She moved the tail of the shirt so that there was nothing lying on her skin. She'd once healed her jeans into a cut on her knee when she was twelve years old. Pulling denim out of skin was extraordinarily unpleasant. "I can't promise I'll be able to stay quiet. Once I start, it's hard for me to stay cognizant of what's going on. With someone else I can, but when it's me it's a lot harder."

Damon nodded. "I'll keep you quiet." He squeezed her hand reassuringly. "Just do what you need to do, Greer. I'll handle it."

He was prepared for her eyes going blank, for them changing from blue to white. He was even prepared for the way her body arched and stiffened. When a cry tore from her lips, he laid a hand over her mouth to muffle the sound.

There was something magical about watching her literally heal herself. She'd explained it to him once, shortly after she'd saved his life. It was like reaching into someone and finding their pain. She took it into herself and used her own energy to transform it into something else, something whole. Bones would heal, muscle would reknit, skin would seal and form a perfect pink barrier over what had been a wound.

He'd seen bullets back themselves out of a man. Broken legs had straightened as the bones realigned. Once she was done, she'd always been a bit tired and had needed to eat. Healing herself, however, was a completely different experience. Her energy stores were already depleted and her body was already weak. Taking her own injury deeper into herself multiplied the pain almost exponentially. Greer conjectured that the pain was payment for using her gift on herself instead of on others.

Blood seeped from her hip as she concentrated on the wound. Damon snagged a towel from the floor and tucked it under her to absorb it. Her body jerked, almost in a seizure, and her teeth ground so loudly that he could hear them.

After fifteen agonizing minutes, there was a perfect circle of pink, soft skin where there had been a bullet hole only moments earlier. Greer collapsed to the mattress, her body going limp. Tears seeped from her eyes, and her forehead was drenched in sweat, a product of the exertion she had been putting out.

Damon gathered her in his arms, lifting her upper body to lay in his lap, his hands framing her face as he waited for her to open her eyes. When she did, they were filled with pain and fear. He lifted her and tucked her head in the curve of his neck and murmured nonsense words of comfort. She sobbed into his neck, her muscles quivering and her hands gripping his arms.

"Are you okay?"

Greer nodded into his shoulder. When she spoke, her voice was little more than a whisper. "No matter how many times I have to do that, I'm never exactly prepared for how bad it hurts when I use it on myself." She shivered and pulled back, desperate to end the moment and return to their normal state. "It's cold in here. Let's see if any of those clothes will fit me."

She limped to the closet, still favoring her right hip, but able to support her own weight. She checked the sizes on the pants and found that they would be a tad big, but they would work. She opened and closed the drawers of the dresser, found a tank top that would fit, and grinned when she found thick wool socks.

"These'll come in handy." She tossed the socks onto the bed and then checked the tag on a bra. "I'm about three cup sizes too big for these. Is my extra bra ruined?"

Damon snagged her pack and unzipped the front pocket. "Nope." He tossed her the scrap of fabric and followed it with a pair of plain black boy shorts. "You even have clean underwear."

Unashamed of her body and completely comfortable with Damon, Greer unbuttoned the shirt she'd been dressed in and gently eased it down her left arm, trying to avoid the line of black stitches on both sides of her shoulder. After it took her three tries to step into her underwear using only one arm, she glared at Damon, who was watching her from the chair, one leg crossed casually across the other, a huge grin on his face.

"This isn't funny."

"No, it is." Damon climbed to his feet. "I suppose I could help you." He dug through the drawers and found a pair of sweatpants. "Put your hand on my shoulder." He bent down, guided one foot in, and then the other. He reached his arm around her body and guided the sweats up her legs and thighs. He tied the drawstring at her waist to keep them from sliding back down. "Do you want to wear the bra now or save it for in the morning?"

Something about the sight of Damon Mackenzie on his knees tying her sweatpants set butterflies fluttering in her stomach. It was a reaction that she had never before associated with her commanding officer and one that she wasn't entirely sure she cared for.

Never before had she been conscious of him looking at her. Living in the barracks as one of very few female soldiers had her constantly seeing naked men and men seeing her naked. It was a product of the environment they lived in. It had been uncomfortable and uneasy at first, but after ten years, it was like second nature. Until now.

"Greer?"

Damon's voice was soft and shook her from her thoughts. She felt herself blushing and prayed he couldn't see the flush in the dim light from their flashlight. She cleared her throat. "Now. My arm will just be more sore in the morning. I'd like to minimize the pain all I can."

"No problem. Let me see if I can find you a sweater to put on. It's damned cold tonight." He picked up the light and shined the beam on the closet. He slid hangers over the rack until he found a thick knit fisherman's sweater. It looked like it may have belonged to a man, but it would keep her warm, despite being a bit baggy. "I tried to radio back to the city while you were out. All I could get was static. No one is picking up on any channels. I checked with the HQ in D.C., and they said all bombs were dropped but their pilots are reporting that it looked as if both entrances had been breached."

"It's gone, then."

"Most likely. D.C. said we're welcome there, though it's farther. I got someone at Boston, but their commander is out on a run. They're supposed to radio back sometime tomorrow to let us know if we can head that direction."

"Is it safe to stay here past sunrise?"

He shook his head and laid the sweater on the back of the chair before he stooped to pick up the thick cotton sports bra. "No. We'll have to move and find new shelter. I wouldn't want to stay any place on the surface more than one night. If we don't hear from Boston before dawn, I say we should head to Washington. The difference in distance isn't enough to warrant sticking around here another day." He turned the garment around in his hands, trying to figure out the best way to put it on her. "How the hell does this thing work?"

Greer couldn't help but laugh. "I think you've taken enough of those off in your years, Mackenzie."

"Those mostly had snaps in the back. This straps you down and holds you in. The ones I'm used to made breasts look more appetizing than this thing does."

"Thanks."

Picking up on the sarcasm in her tone, Damon grinned again. "Hey, I didn't say yours weren't great, too." He glanced down at her breasts, which were full, soft, milky globes of flesh positioned high on her chest and adorned with dusky tips.

"I didn't ask your opinion on my chest." She blushed even deeper. "Let's just get this over with. It's getting embarrassing."

"Okay, let's get your arms through, and then I'll take it over your head." He held the bra against her stomach and helped her loop her injured arm through. As he began to slide it into place over her breasts, the pad of his thumb brushed against one tightly beaded nipple. When a slight whimper tore its way from her throat, they both froze.

Chapter Four

Damon unfroze first. He efficiently yanked the bra over her head, and into place and stepped back. Greer's eyes were shut, and her face was bright red from humiliation. He grabbed the sweater from the chair and put it on her. She refused to open her eyes while he finished dressing her.

"Greer—"

"Shut up. I don't want to talk about it."

"I'm sorry."

Her eyes snapped open, and she saw the sheepish look on Damon's face. "Sorry for what?"

"I didn't mean to touch you. I wasn't trying to cop a feel or anything. It was an accident. You don't have to be embarrassed."

Greer blushed an even deeper red, her face resembling a tomato. She leaned against the dresser, her eyes darting around the room, settling everywhere except on Damon. It took him the better part of two minutes to notice. When he did, realization dawned in his eyes.

"You aren't upset that I touched you. You're upset that you liked it." He ran his eyes over her face. "It's okay, Greer." He took a step toward her, reached out, and laid his fingertips against her cheek. "I liked it, too." He took another step. "You don't need to be embarrassed. We've been friends too long for you to be embarrassed about anything around me."

Greer wasn't prepared for the way her heart pounded in her chest or the way her breath caught in her throat. When he glided his fingers down the curve of her neck, he ignited little fires beneath her skin. "This is weird."

Damon smiled. "Yeah, it is. Bad weird?"

She shook her head. "Just weird. I've known you since I was twelve years old, and in sixteen years, we've never gone here."

"You've never really almost died before. Even in the river, it was only ever me that was in danger of not surviving."

She closed her eyes and let her face turn into his hand. "That's what this is. We got scared and we're friends and we love each other and it's all getting mixed up. Add in me being naked, and we've got this."

"Maybe. Do you want to stop?"

Greer opened her eyes and tipped her head back to look into his icy blue eyes. "I should, but I don't."

"It doesn't have to change anything."

"I don't want anything to change. I want us to stay exactly like we are." Greer lifted one hand and let her fingers slide through his pitch black hair. "We might wake up in the morning and wish this hadn't ever happened."

"Then perhaps you should stop acting like sophomoric teenagers and begin acting like the trained soldiers I was hoping that you would be."

Greer and Damon sprang apart, Damon shoving her behind him with one arm and grabbing his gun with the other. He leveled it at the man that had appeared with nothing more than a whisper, his fingers steady on the trigger. "Who are you? What do you want? How did you get in here?"

The man in the white suit lifted one blond eyebrow. "My name is Gabriel, and I am an Angel of the Lord. I've come here to request your assistance. Your demonic protections and herbs offer no deterrence against Angels."

"Angels don't exist."

Gabriel laughed. "Why is it that you humans always doubt our existence? You live in a world infested with the creatures of Hell, and yet you doubt that there are Angels?" He shook his head in apparent disbelief. "The Choosing has been for nothing."

"The Choosing?" Greer eased out from behind Damon, her curiosity piqued. "What's the Choosing?"

"It was supposed to be a great time in human history. Demons were to be banished from the Earth for a million years. She Chose God. Lucifer managed to find a warlock and some witches to open a Hell Gate to let them all back out. They were only gone from the Earth for a few of your months before the Gates opened and Hell spilled forth."

Damon lowered the barrel of his weapon a fraction of an inch. "We don't have a clue what you're talking about."

Gabriel looked to Greer. "Your grandmother was the Chosen. Griffin Javensen. She gave her life to keep your reality from happening. Your father was adopted."

"How did you know that?"

"I told you, Greer Dawson. I am an Angel of the Lord." He turned to Damon. "You are from Hunter blood. You can sense demon blood. Use the abilities you were born with and reassure yourself that I am not a demon."

"I knew that the second I realized you were here." Damon shifted the gun slightly. "What I don't have is an Angel detector. Give me one reason I shouldn't shoot you."

"Your bullets will bounce off of me, and I don't think any of us would enjoy the company of the creatures that would be attracted by those gunshots." Gabriel walked idly into the kitchen and sat at the table. He held up one hand and set a fire burning in the living room fireplace. "I'll answer the questions that you have."

"Why are you here?" Greer followed him into the kitchen and sat down, curiosity getting the better of her. "What do you want?"

"I want your help. The time has come to stop the purge." Gabriel gestured for Damon to sit as well. "Fifty-seven human years ago, there was an event in your history that should have changed the course of your world. Lucifer out-maneuvered us, and he used free will to manipulate humans into springing the Gates back open after they were closed. God wanted to destroy Earth."

"Why didn't He?"

"Because I begged Him not to. He has given me half a human century to fix the problem. I've come up with a way to do just that."

"You just said this happened almost sixty years ago."

"That I did, my boy. Time, to an Angel, is as fluid as a river. I can move through it with a thought. This is the future. Neither of you have been born yet. This world does not yet exist. I have come forward through time because the two of you possess the skills that I require."

"What skills?"

"You're a Healer, Greer, and Damon, you are a Hunter. Throughout time, Healers and Hunters have gravitated toward one another. When brought together, they share a psychic link. You make each other stronger. Tell me, had either of you shared a mind before the night he nearly drowned?"

Greer and Damon exchanged a look. Damon spoke. "We assumed it was a product of the experience. Greer thought she brought me back to life and that maybe she left a little of herself behind."

"That's partially accurate. You were not meant to die, though your heart did stop beating. The link was forged because your true nature recognized its counterpart. You were meant to work together. As a descendent of the Chosen, you are important to stopping the purge. Because you are her Hunter, you are also important, Damon. Those two facts required me to travel through time in order to fetch you."

"What do you want us to do?"

"I want for you to return to the present with me and fight to close the Hell Gate. If you don't succeed in doing so, your world will end seven years before we reach this day."

"How do we do that?"

"That will be revealed to you in stages. The first task will be to stop the purge. To do that, you will need to kill Laelia. She is the first vampire, and the strongest of them all. She is working with a Sorcerer, Garrick, who was the one who figured out how to open the Gate. Do not be fooled. She has considerable power of her own, as she is feeding on witches to absorb some of their magic through drinking their blood. You will work with four others. Two will be the Lost. Those who, by virtue of existence, should be fighting for the other side. There will also be a powerful witch and a Warrior. Together, the six of you will complete three tasks. At the end, if you succeed, it will take one last act, in order to rid Earth of demons forever. If you succeed, this reality will never exist."

Damon leaned back in his chair and stared at the Angel. "That's a tall order."

"It is. Greer has been chosen for this by nature of birth. You are chosen because you are in the undesirable position of being the first human of Hunter descent that she Healed."

A frown settled across Damon's face. "It's not an undesirable position. Not to me. Greer saved my life. She's my best friend."

"Regardless, being connected to her in such a manner has placed you in this position. I need for the two of you to decide whether or not you're going to help."

Greer gestured to the front door with her good arm. "What choice do we have? The human race is a half-breath from being wiped out. If we can stop that, we have to do it." She looked at Damon. "There's no other option."

"How do we know you're telling the truth?"

"You don't. You'll have to trust, believe, and have faith."

"Where would we be going?"

Gabriel chuckled. "I haven't a sense of your dates and times. However, I believe that you would be returning to 2030. Over a half century before the time in which we are in at this moment."

"The other four? Do they know we're coming?"

"Not as yet. The witch will be brought forward from the past when she is needed. Bringing someone with as much power as she has is draining, even for an Angel. The other three exist in the present. They will know why you are there when you arrive."

Damon looked at Greer intently, searching her eyes. When she didn't waver, he lifted his hands in a sign of surrender. "Okay, then. I've never time-traveled before."

Gabriel stood. "Good. Gather what you'll need. The shorter the amount of time I spend here, the safer you'll be. I don't doubt that your return will be sensed by your enemies. You should be prepared to fight. I will send you to where you need to go, but my involvement in the tasks before you will be limited. I am a guide, not a companion. You may not take any technology that doesn't exist in that time. If it does not exist in the present, it will not exist there when you return."

"We don't exist in your present."

"You're meant to exist. If you succeed, the technology may not. Go, now, and gather what you wish to take."

Damon spent five minutes packing their bags and strapping on his own gear. Then he helped Greer into her vest and laced her boots. He used strips of a towel to form a sling for her arm and tied her pack onto her back, padding the straps with towels so that it didn't rub her stitches.

"Are you sure you want to do this?"

Greer looked up at him, her eyes clearly conveying her concern. "What choice do we have? He's telling us that the world is literally going to end if we don't."

"He's also telling us that the world was going to end and your grandmother stopped it and now they need us to stop it. What's to say that he doesn't come after your grandchildren for the same thing?"

"We've known about the Warriors since the demons got loose. They're practically the only reason humanity has lasted as long as it has. Who's to say this isn't a constant struggle and it's just our turn to pick it up? Maybe this will be the last time. Maybe it won't. Who are we to decide when the world ends? I don't want to die. I don't want you to die." She shrugged. "I don't think we have much of a choice. I don't think we could live with ourselves if we didn't at least try."

"I want to know more about what happened."

"Yeah, I'm with you there. Hopefully, the other four aren't as in the dark as we are."

Damon sighed deeply. "If this was just me, I'd have told him no, but I can't let you go alone, especially not with your shoulder the way that it is."

She looked up at him, his hands still on the straps of her pack, adjusting them so that they were snug against the towels. "This is pretty scary stuff."

"We'll do it together. Honestly, the thing that makes me the most nervous is not taking our guns. We're going to go into whatever it is we're being dropped into with nothing but stakes and holy water."

"We'll manage. There will be weapons wherever we're going." Her rich brown eyes met his clear blue ones, and she reached out to cover his fingers with her own. "We'll handle whatever they throw at us. We both know we have to do this. There isn't any other choice."

"I know." Damon tucked her hair behind her ears. "About earlier—"

Greer shook her head. "Not now. Let's talk about it when we're safe and warm. I don't want either of us to do something now that we'll regret later. There's a lot going on right now, and we're both all mixed up. We nearly died, the city is gone, and now this."

"You're probably exactly right." He ran his hand over her hair. "What would have happened if the Angel hadn't popped in when he did?"

She flushed deep red. "I don't know."

"Yes, you do." He slid his hand around to the back of her neck, and he drew her forward until she was pressed against his chest. He towered over her by eight or nine inches and was big enough that she felt dwarfed when he wrapped his other arm around her waist. "Tell me no."

Her voice was a whisper, unsure and shaky. "No."

"I don't believe you."

His mouth closed over hers, warm and firm. Fire simmered just below the surface, and both yearned to explore it. Damon's fingers rubbed the back of her neck as he kissed her. He angled her head back so that he could slip his tongue between her lips.

Her taste flooded him. Sweet and rich and all Greer. He groaned and dragged her closer, plunged deeper. Her good arm lifted to wrap around his neck, and she opened her mouth to tangle her tongue with his.

He pulled back from her before the kiss could get out of control. He braced his forehead against hers, their breath mingling. Greer's eyes were still closed, and her arm was still wrapped around his neck. He slowly took a step back and straightened, his eyes clouded with some emotion even he couldn't quite put his finger on.

"Well, that definitely gives us something to think about." He shook his head to clear it. "We should go."

"Yeah, let's get this show on the road."

They left the bedroom and joined Gabriel in the kitchen. The Angel was still sitting at the table, one leg crossed over the other and his hands folded on his knee. He rose when he saw them and dusted imaginary lint from his pristine suit.

"I will not be accompanying you, nor do I know what sort of situation you will be going into. Two of your group are residing in Ireland for the moment, and I am arranging for you to be placed within close proximity to them. I've no doubt that they will know you've arrived and will fill you in on the rest of the details." He reached out and touched both Damon and Greer's foreheads. "Yours is a Godly mission, and win or lose, your reward will be great in Heaven. I wish you luck."

With that, Gabriel snapped his fingers almost carelessly and sent Damon and Greer spiraling through both space and time.

Chapter Five

August 12th, 2030 - County Clare, Ireland

IT WAS WARM when they landed. Damon stumbled two steps to get his balance after being dropped unceremoniously onto a stone platform that appeared to be in the middle of the woods. He turned in a slow circle, taking in their surroundings. Greer appeared next to him, her face pale from fear.

"Half of me wondered if he wasn't going to just kill us." She glanced around the clearing and looked down at herself. "Our fucking packs are gone."

"Guess he wasn't lying about not bringing things back." He stooped down and yanked a black backpack from beneath the altar. "Though someone was looking out for us." He unzipped it and found half a dozen stakes, two half-gallon containers filled with what he assumed was Holy Water, a machete, two semi-automatic pistols with four clips, and two pouches of salt.

"It's something, at least." Greer scanned the woods, the hair on the back of her neck standing up. "I don't think we're the only ones here."

"Vampires—a dozen."

She knew better than to question his ability to sense how many there were. "That's a lot to take on with stakes."

"We have a machete. Great for taking off heads." He peered into the woods, trying to see their adversaries. "They're armed, but not with guns. Swords, I think. Damn. Did the fucking vampires time travel, too?"

Greer shook her head in disbelief. "At this point I don't know if I would doubt it. We just came fifty years back in time and went from New York City to the middle of Ireland in less than thirty seconds."

"Do you remember how to fight vamps? It's been a while since we went up against them."

That much was true. Most of the creatures they fought were Familiars and demons. Vampires could only come out at night, so humans had quickly learned to stay inside when the sun wasn't out. It had been more than three years since their last skirmish with any.

"Stake through the heart or take off the head. Crosses are useless, Holy Water just burns, and garlic just gives them bad breath." She used the knife that had been strapped to her thigh to cut the makeshift sling away from her arm.

"If they're young, they might still be in the throes of blood lust. If they are, letting yourself get bitten is a strategy. The taste and smell drives them crazy. If they're older, the last thing in the world you want is for them to get their teeth in you. It will not end well for you."

"How can you tell?"

"You can't, but I can." Damon tossed a stake in the air and caught it handily. "Here they come."

Greer had time for one breath before the vampires burst out of the forest. She did a quick count. Twelve. Briefly, she let herself wonder how Damon had been so sure about the number. Shaking off the thought, she gripped her stake hard in her good hand and dug in her heels to brace for the impact of a vampire barreling toward her at full speed.

The first one was huge and outweighed her by a solid hundred and fifty pounds. He carried a sword, had eyes that glowed red, and his teeth were long and sharp. Greer was ready for him. She dropped her shoulder at the last minute and slammed it into the vampire's stomach, using his own momentum against him to throw him over her shoulder.

He landed on his back with a thud loud enough that the forest floor shook. She rolled to her feet and leaped onto the monster, gripping the stake in both hands. With a yell, she drove it into his chest and through his heart. In an instant, what had been a man became a pile of dust as it dissolved into what it should have become after the human died.

Before Greer could climb to her feet, she was grabbed from behind by one of the other vampires. She managed to grab the sword the one she'd killed had been carrying and swung it wildly, trying to hit anything that she could. The blade made contact with a third, slicing open his abdomen so that his intestines spilled out onto the dirt in a gleaming, wet mass.

She thrashed and struggled, using all four limbs. She screamed when she felt fangs sink into her neck, the burning pain nearly more than she could handle. The sword clattered to the ground, and she fastened both hands on his head and dug her fingernails into his eyeballs.

The first thing she noticed, oddly enough, was the feel of them. Eyeballs had a very unique consistency. They were slick and warm with a ridge where the iris was. When her nails pressed through the surface, they popped like boils, seeping a warm, slimy liquid that coated her fingers and dripped down his face.

The vampire dropped Greer to cover his face with his hands. She used the few seconds she had to grab the sword she'd dropped. Hefting the unwieldy weapon, she lifted it and sliced. The muscles in the neck and vertebrae of the spine gave her more resistance than she'd thought they would. It felt a little like hacking through a hard plastic package with a butter knife.

Finally, the head dropped to the ground, its face in a horrific scowl before it dissolved. Greer didn't have even a moment to breathe before there were two more upon her. She scrambled to her feet, her eyes darting around to do a count. Seven left. One was bleeding on the ground, its intestines in its hands, four battled Damon, and two were facing her.

The impact of the fall to the ground had split her incision open. Blood ran freely down her arm. It was her dominant hand, so she knew that she had no choice but to use it. She tested the weight in her hand, backing up to keep distance between her and her adversaries. She used her right hand to unbuckle her belt and took ten seconds to use the leather to lash the sword to her hand so that she wouldn't drop it.

"You can't even hold your weapon steady, but yet you somehow think that you can defeat me?"

She wiped blood from her eyes with her left hand and wondered briefly how it got there. "I've killed two of your buddies so far."

"Newborns compared to me." He smiled. "I've been alive since before my home country invaded the Americas."

Almost three hundred years. She chose not to say anything. Instead, she lifted her weapon an inch higher and planted her heels in the dirt. Her gaze never wavered from the vampire in front of her. With a roar, he charged.

The clash of metal sent sparks flying. Greer had only wielded a sword a handful of times, and she knew she was far from talented with a blade. She gripped the handle in both hands and swung it with controlled abandon to block his slashes.

The vampire's blade hit true once, slicing deep into Greer's thigh and striking bone. The force of the slash threw her off balance, and she tumbled to the ground, her ankle turning painfully on a rock as she fell.

Panicking, she clawed at the sword to loosen the lashing holding it to her arm. She kicked her one good foot to scoot her body back from him. She felt a stick beneath her back and froze. Slowly, her mind racing, she moved inch by inch until the fingers of her injured arm were brushing against the wood. The vampire advanced on her slowly, twirling his sword like a baton. He squatted next to her and grabbed her chin in his hand.

"Garrick told me that you'd be hard to kill. The six the Angel picked to save this sorry excuse for a world can only do it together. Kill you and the problem is solved." He leaned close to her ear, his fangs fully extended. "I've only gotten to eat a few Healers in my day. Hopefully, your blood will be just as sweet and rich as I remember."

Greer slowly unbuckled her utility knife from her pants. Once she had a firm grip on the handle, she reared up with a scream and drove it into the side of the vampire's neck. The beast grabbed her by her throat and lifted her off the ground. Her fingers grappled for and found the stick that had been beneath her.

"You stupid girl." He yanked the knife from his throat. "Steel doesn't kill vampires."

If his hand hadn't been closing off her air supply, she would have said something smart and pithy. Instead, she settled for using every bit of her strength to ram the stick in her hand into his chest. She knew the moment that it hit his heart from both the look on his face and the fact that she was falling and could breathe.

She hit the ground on her already sore ankle, and both felt, and heard, it snap as she landed. Her head smacked the ground hard enough to rattle her brain. She knew in that moment that she was done. She had nothing more to give—no more fight.

Instead of a vampire's, the face that appeared above her was Damon's. He was covered in blood and still holding a sword, but he was alive. She stared up at him, unsure if she could speak and scared to try. She felt pressure on her brain and opened the door to let him in.

"Are you okay?"

"I don't think I can actually talk."

Damon went to the pack he'd dropped somewhere in the midst of the battle. He dug through it and pulled out a bottle of water. He dropped to the ground next to her and lifted her upper body to give her a drink. She swallowed desperately, the cool water a welcome relief to her sore and bruised throat.

"You killed nine vampires." Her voice was weak and squeaky. "How in the hell did you kill nine vampires?"

"Hunter blood, I guess. I've always been pretty good at playing Buffy the Vampire Slayer."

"Who?"

Damon laughed. "Never mind. Early twenty-first century pop culture reference. My grandmother had the DVDs." He scanned the forest. "I don't sense any more of them, but we aren't safe here. Can you walk?"

Greer lifted her shoulders in a shrug. "We'll find out. Help me up."

Damon gripped both of her elbows and lifted her to her feet. Her ankle was swelling rapidly and her thigh was pouring blood down her leg. She used her knife to cut one sleeve from her shirt to tie around her thigh in an attempt to stop the blood flow. She managed to take a few steps before nodding to Damon.

"We'll have to take it slow. My boot is tight enough that it's keeping my ankle in place. I think I'll be able to hop well enough to make it."

He picked up the machete and headed into the woods. "Watch your step. It's darker in here than in that clearing, but we need the cover until morning."

The forest was nearly black, with only slivers of silvery moonlight breaking through the thick canopy of vegetation. The ground was littered with brush, logs and vines that made walking silently difficult. Damon was uninjured, so he moved much faster than Greer, even when he was making an effort to slow down.

She struggled to keep up, pushing herself to the limits of her body and beyond. Every step sent bolts of searing pain up both legs, one from the ankle and the other from the thigh. Her shoulder burned from the reopened wound, and her head pounded from the headache that formed behind her eyes. Already, there was a thick black bruise winding its way around her throat.

As they walked, her clothes dried stiff with blood, mud and sweat. The heat was oppressive, the air thick and humid. Both Damon and Greer knew it was going to rain. That knowledge spurred both to move faster and push harder, trying to find shelter before the skies split open and unleashed their fury.

Thunder rumbled in the distance and lightning illuminated the forest in brief spurts when Greer's body rebelled against her. She tripped over a root and went sprawling, hitting the dirt with bone crunching force. The landing was enough to set everything bleeding again and quickly soaking through the makeshift bandage on her thigh.

"Damon." Her voice was whispery, but she knew he would hear it. It only took him twenty seconds to backtrack on the trail to her position. He crouched next to her, concerned.

"Are you okay?"

"I need a break."

In the ten years that they had been serving together, he could not remember one single time that Greer had ever asked for a break. That fact alone sent a bolt of fear rocketing through him. He dropped the pack to the ground and crouched next to her, the only light from their one flashlight.

"We need to get you inside somewhere. What is the most pressing problem?"

Greer laughed, the sound bitter and fearful. "I don't know. I think my ankle is broken. My thigh is split wide open. The stitches on my shoulder didn't hold, so I'm bleeding there again, and my hip broke open. Add to that, I think my windpipe is nearly crushed, and I know I have a concussion." Tears flooded her eyes, and her breathing became shallow. "I'm going to die!"

Damon cupped her face in his big hands and forced her to meet his gaze. "Listen to me, Greer Dawson. You are NOT going to die. You're hurt, and it's bad, but we're safe and we're together and that's all that matters. We came here for a mission, and I'll be damned if I let you check out before we even get started." He efficiently unlaced her boots and pulled them off of her feet. "Now suck it up and help me figure out what we need to do here."

Greer took several trembling breaths to clear her head. When he looked at her, his eyebrows lifted questioningly, she nodded. "We need to wrap my ankle. A splint would be best. I'm going to have to go barefoot because now that it's out of my boot, there's no way in hell that we're going to be able to cram it back in."

"That's an easy fix. I can splint you with some sticks and a few strips of fabric off that sweater. Tell me about your thigh."

"It's bad. It needs to be wrapped good to stop the bleeding. I couldn't even try to heal it right now. If we had some gauze, I'd say we should pack it and then wrap a bandage over it."

"We can handle that, too. I'll put that sling back on your shoulder and then you should be good." He shined the light around the woods. "I think I hear a stream over that way. Let's get you to it so that we can clean up a bit and get this taken care of. If we take too long, we're going to get rained on, and that's the last thing we need."

Damon lifted her as if she were a child and carried her swiftly to the happily babbling creek. He placed her gently on a large rock and used his knife to cut away her blood-stained sweater. He tossed the fabric into a damp pile and took off his own button up to leave himself clad in a wife beater. He washed the dirt and blood out of his shirt and cut it into strips of fabric.

It only took him a couple minutes to hack some young branches off of a tree and split them in half to use on either side of her ankle as a splint. Greer dug her nails into the dirt next to her and bit into her lip until blood bloomed on her pale skin in a meager defense against the scream that threatened to burst out of her as he straightened her foot to splint and wrap it.

"You holding up?"

Damon's voice was enough to puncture her pain-induced haze. She shook her head to clear it. "I'm still alive."

"That's a hell of a lot better than the alternative." He shifted to go through the pile of sweater pieces and washed out one chunk until there was no dirt or blood. "We don't have gauze, but we do have this thick stuff from your sweater. It's the best we can do right now. I'm going to pack your thigh with it and then tie some of my shirt around your leg. It's going to hurt like hell."

"What doesn't hurt like hell right now?" She managed a half laugh. "I've gotten beaten more in the past twenty-four hours than in the past three years put together."

"It's certainly not a night we'll ever forget." He used the knife to slice off the leg of her pants, leaving her bare from the thigh down to her ankle. "Try not to scream."

Greer sucked in a breath and held it until her lungs burned and black spots flitted around the perimeter of her vision. Tears flooded her eyes as Damon stuffed strips of fabric into the wound. She bit down on her lip, the salty tang of blood blossoming on her tongue. After two heart-stopping minutes, he sat back on his haunches and surveyed his work.

"Hopefully that'll hold for a while. I'm going to sling your arm to protect that shoulder, and then we'll get moving. I'll carry you for the first bit."

"You're not going to carry me." Greer snorted at the prospect. "If I'm going, it's going to be on my own two feet."

"Don't try to be heroic. We lost our packs. The one that was waiting for us is maybe fifteen pounds. If I get you settled on my back, it'll only be twenty pounds more than our two packs." He went back to the creek to fill up the canteen, handed it to her, and then refilled it when it came back empty. "We have to get inside somewhere before this storm hits. There isn't time to argue about it."

Greer tried to walk. She valiantly took three steps before her splinted ankle gave out and she went sprawling. She caught herself on her hands and knees and barely restrained the scream of pain. Damon bent and slipped an arm around her, lifting her to her feet almost effortlessly.

"Ready to stop trying to be a hero?"

"I hate you."

Damon laughed as he helped her climb onto his back. "I love you, too."

He carried her for nearly a half an hour before he heard hooves. He clicked the flashlight off and bent to help Greer onto her feet. He pressed a finger to her lips so that she would be quiet and unbuckled his knife from his belt.

Damon slipped through the brush to the path they had been traveling parallel to. He reached out with his mind and probed Greer, slipping inside easily.

"*Two people on horseback. One is a vampire.*"

"*The other?*"

Damon's distress was palpable. "*I'm not sure. Not a vamp, but not human, either.*"

"*Another Angel?*"

"*No. It's different than Gabriel. I don't know what it is. Not a Familiar and not a demon.*"

Greer's panic rose up in an all-consuming wave. "*Devil.*"

They had only ever come into contact with one Devil. Six of his squad hadn't come away from the encounter. Damon listened intently, using all of his senses to determine what it was that was coming toward them. After several moments of crushing silence, he shook his head.

"*No. It has a heartbeat.*"

The relief was instant. Greer took a deep breath and let it out in short bursts. "*What do we do?*"

"*Wait until they've gone and hope that the vampire doesn't smell us.*"

Damon risked them hearing the low hiss of the zipper on the bag as he unzipped it to remove a stake. When the hoof beats stopped on the path directly across from his position, his heart pounded in his chest. He gripped the stake tightly in one hand, the knife in the other, ready to fight whatever came at him.

It was a fight that never came.

"We know you're in there. We're not here to hurt you." The voice was male, strong, and clear. "Come on out so we can tend to your injuries."

A second voice floated toward them, musical and female. "Gabriel sent us for you. We would be your Lost."

Chapter Six

Damon froze the moment the voices penetrated the forest. Greer looked at him with trepidation and curiosity in her eyes, waiting for him to make the decision. He spent ten seconds thinking through the possible outcomes before he expelled a breath he hadn't realized he was holding and called back to the strangers.

"We're armed. Just leave us alone. We're not interested in a fight."

Within a moment, the man's voice floated to them once more. "I'm not after fighting you, Damon. If I was, you'd be dead already. Now, the way I see it, you have two choices. The female in there with you is losing blood faster than she can replace it. I can smell it. You can take your chances and try to find help or you can let us tend her injuries and give you a safe bed. She'll end up dead if you leave and dead if I'm not who I say I am. If what I'm telling you is true, then you're ahead because you'll be safe and alive. Do the math and carry her on out here."

Greer leaned against a tree and stared at Damon through pain-hazed eyes. "They're right."

Damon sighed deeply. "I damn well know they're right. I just haven't worked myself around to handing you over to a vampire and whatever the hell that other thing is out there."

"I'm human—same as you—more or less."

Damon laughed bitterly. "It's the less that bothers me."

Greer gritted her teeth and righted herself. "We're coming out."

She managed ten steps before she tripped on a root and went sprawling. Before Damon could grab her, the vampire caught her arms in his hands and righted her gently, holding her by the biceps until she was steady and standing in the clearing. He stepped back and offered a smile.

"I'm Gage Windsor, and this is Alaria. You'd be Damon Mackenzie and Greer Dawson. Gabriel told us to expect you."

Alaria sneered. "Stupid Angel and his dramatics. Gave us a whole ten minutes' notice before telling us you'd been dropped into the middle of a fucking battle. Another hour's warning and we'd have been there waiting for you." She took stock of Greer with a practiced eye. "She'll live if we get her back to the house soon. She'll need to do her Healer mojo, but she'll live."

"What are you?"

Alaria laughed. "Straight to the point. Okay. I am a human. I have a heartbeat, blood, feelings—everything that you do. I used to be a Devil. Before that, I was an Angel."

Damon grabbed Greer by the wrist and dragged her behind him. "There is no past tense to Devil."

Gage made a noise in his throat. "You couldn't wait until we had them settled in?" He turned to Damon. "I know there's a lot you don't understand, and I promise you that I'll explain everything to you both. The most important thing is to get her inside before she either dies or we get more unwelcome company. Your arrival has attracted enough notice without us standing in the woods and announcing our presence to everything else out here. I don't know what it's worth, but you've my word that no harm will come to you or your companion."

Greer peeked out from behind Damon. "Gabriel told us that there would be two that should fight for the other side. Unless he sent us here to die, I think it's pretty clear that these are the two that we're supposed to meet." She took one step to the side. "The longer we stand here, the more likely it is that other things will find us. It's not like we could stop them from taking us anyway, so let's just go."

Annoyed, Damon nodded. "Okay." He glanced up at the inky black sky. "Damned Angel. You could make this whole thing easier if you just appeared and told us these two aren't going to eat us."

Alaria smiled and swung up into the saddle. "That's Gabe for ya. He does like things dramatic. Gage will ride with me and the two of you can take the other horse. We're only about thirty minutes from his estate, but it's all wooded."

Damon took the reins to the second mount and gestured to Greer. "I'll give you a leg up."

Greer studied the horse and measured the distance with her eyes. "I can't get up there."

Without a word, Gage grabbed Greer around the waist and easily lifted her above his head to deposit her on the horse. Before Damon could even form an objection, Gage was on his own horse and nudging the large animal down the trail. Five seconds later, his voice floated back down to Damon.

"Unless you want to be lost with a horse in this storm, I suggest you get on the beast and follow us."

Damon swung into the saddle behind Greer. He reached around her to take the reins and dug his heel into the horse's side. No one said a word until Greer collapsed against Damon's chest, her head lolling to the side and her body going limp. Almost before Damon could panic, Gage spoke, his voice soft.

"She passed out. Her heartbeat is steady."

Damon pressed his fingers to her throat to feel the pulse for himself. "Why isn't the smell of the blood driving you mad?"

Gage chuckled. "Not all vampires are ravening beasts. I'll grant you that most are and that it's very few who ever escape the bloodlust completely. I got mine under control several centuries ago."

"How old are you?"

"Almost fourteen hundred years."

"I've never heard of a vamp that old."

"Most aren't. Other than Laelia, who is the first vampire, I'm the oldest. I believe my closest competitor will close out his first millennium sometime this century. Not sure when."

Damon shook his head and shifted his eyes to Alaria. "You were a Devil? How did you become human?"

Alaria chuckled. "The short answer is I made a deal to get my humanity. I'd prefer not to tell the long of it twice, so we'll wait until your companion is back in the land of the conscious." She looked over her shoulder at him. "How did you get dragged into this mess?"

"Gabriel told us that Greer is the granddaughter of the Chosen and that she's a Healer. Apparently, whenever there is a true Healer, there is a Hunter. I'm the unlucky bastard that got that role."

Gage snorted. "You'd no sooner let her do this without you than you'd cut off your right arm. I didn't think there were any true Hunter lines left."

"There aren't many. We're pretty few and far between. Most got absorbed into the Warrior lines."

Alaria laughed again. "They loved the idea of Warriors who could sense vampire and demon blood, and there were so few of you that it made it easy to breed you into theirs. Warriors chose to hunt and Hunters were born into it. Eventually, the lines got so blurred between who was which that I'm surprised Gabe managed to find one of each."

"There were a couple who kept it pretty pure. Some Warriors believed that being able to sense demons was a crutch and made Hunters lazy. Some Hunters thought breeding with Warriors would water down the bloodlines." Damon shifted Greer in his arms and addressed Gage. "What do you eat?"

"Blood, like every other vampire that wants to keep surviving." Gage shook his head when Damon started to draw back on the reins. "Drinking blood doesn't mean I eat people. In my centuries, I've managed to amass quite a fortune. I pay a handsome price to buy blood. Not nearly as tasty as out of the vein, but it sustains me and doesn't offend the more moral among us." He slid off his mount and landed lithely, reaching up to help Alaria down.

Damon tried to gather Greer in his arms but found his seat on the horse not steady enough for the amount of movement required. He struggled for several seconds before seriously considering just jumping off and hoping for the best. Finally, he gave in and looked down at Gage, who had been standing next to the horse, patiently waiting for him to hand down Greer.

"One drop gets in your mouth and I'll turn you into a pile of dust."

Gage cocked one eyebrow as he took Greer from the other man. "Son, if I wanted her blood, you'd both be bone dry and dead. I know you don't trust me, and I think a lot more of you for that than if you did, but the fact remains that we are on the same team and we are going to have to deal with one another. You can get on board with that sooner or later. I suggest the former, since it'll make this easier for everyone involved."

Before Damon could respond, Gage carried Greer into the house, leaving the door open for Damon to follow him. He followed the vampire into the sprawling mansion and up a sweeping staircase. Gage ducked into a bedroom and laid Greer on the bed.

"Don't touch her."

Gage shrugged. "Suit yourself. Alaria can help you clean her up and bandage her wounds. I'll have some blood sent up to give her a transfusion if you'll tell me her type."

"B positive." Damon unsheathed his knife and began efficiently slicing the ruined bits of fabric from Greer. Alaria slipped in quietly, a bowl of hot water and a stack of towels balanced on a tray. She disappeared as quickly as she'd appeared and was back with a tray of medical supplies almost before he noticed she was gone.

"She'll be fine."

"I know." Damon bent his head over his work, sweat rolling down his forehead as he gently washed dried blood and dirt from her bruised skin. "I've never known of a Devil wanting to become human again."

"What makes you think there were ever more that did?"

"Point taken."

"I suppose the fact that you've never heard of me means that I'm either dead, or I managed to stay off their radar. Given that we're about to battle head to head with the forces of Hell...I suspect the former."

"Why are you involved in this?"

Alaria made a noise in her throat as she considered how to answer. She turned a sponge over in her hand and began washing Greer's hair. "Because Gabriel asked me to."

"That doesn't seem like a very good reason."

"Gabe and I were companions for many years. I owe him a favor or two. He asked, and I'll do it. Because he wants me too, because I don't want the world to end just after I get to be a part of it, and because I have a goddamn soul now, and it's the right thing to do."

Damon shook his head as he began bandaging the various cuts. "A Devil with a conscience. The world is going batshit crazy."

Alaria laughed. "Yes, it is." She stood. "I'll set up the transfusion in the room next door. These sheets are soaked and the last thing she needs is to catch pneumonia on top of everything else."

It wasn't Damon, or any other person, that woke Greer. It wasn't sunlight streaming through the window or the cool dark of night descending upon it. It was her body betraying her—her gift forcing itself from her, making her heal herself.

She woke up screaming.

The pain was all-consuming and completely encompassing. She clawed at the bandages, tearing them away from her skin. Bones popped and shifted and blood seeped from the day old wounds. Her eyes rolled back in her head, and her body arched off the bed, nearly bending in half. Her nails bit into her palms in a pitiful attempt to distract her mind from the pain of healing itself.

Damon and Gage barreled through the door at nearly the same moment, both having flown down the hall at the first scream. Damon leaped onto the bed with her, gripping her hand in one of his, his other hand going to her face to stroke her hair back off of her sweaty skin.

Shallow screams tore from her throat, one after the other. Sweat poured from her skin, dampening the sheets beneath her and making her skin slick and cold.

It was over as quickly as it began. She went still and silent, her body sinking back down to the mattress and her eyes closing. Damon pressed his fingers to her neck, relief flooding him when he felt her heartbeat against his fingertips, strong and slow. Her breathing deepened and slowed, becoming the even, rhythmic inhalations of a thick, restorative sleep.

Gage dropped into the bedside chair. "What the hell was that?"

Damon slipped off of the bed and sank to the carpet, leaning against the wall. "That was scaring ten years off my life is what that was." He shook his head. "She healed herself. If I had to guess, I'd say she didn't realize she was doing it. There's still a lot we don't understand about her gifts. What we do know is that it takes a thousand times more out of her if she uses it on herself than if she uses it on someone else."

"You're telling me that her body did that on its own, without her controlling it?"

"If I had to wager a guess, yeah, that's what happened."

"Well, that's just fantastic. A fuckin' Healer who doesn't know how to work her own abilities."

Damon chuckled wryly. "Be honest. She's not here because she's a Healer. There are plenty of those. She's here because her grandmother was your Chosen and because she's a highly trained soldier."

"No, if I had to wager my own guess in this situation, she's a Healer because of Griffin. She has no choice in her participation in this." Gage sighed wearily as he stood. "I can only hope her end isn't as tragic and useless as that of her grandmother."

Damon's head snapped up. "What are you talking about?"

Gage's brows knit together. "You don't know?"

"I had a two minute conversation with Gabriel and got dropped into the middle of a war. No, I don't know, but you had better start explaining."

"Greer's grandmother is dead. She sacrificed herself in the Choosing. Had to kill herself for the privilege of getting to make that choice." He rubbed his hands over his face. "Before you get your panties in a twist, I know nothing of any deaths being required this time around."

Damon leaned his head back against the wall. "At this point, I don't think there's anything that would surprise me. One day the world is normal and the next there are demons flooding it. One minute I'm talking to my best friend and the next an Angel is asking us to time travel. I'm sitting in the kind of house that hasn't existed for fifty years, having a conversation with a vampire. No, I don't think there's anything left to throw at me."

"What happened? With the Hell Gate, I mean."

Damon shook his head. "No one knows exactly. In 2030, sometime in late summer, maybe August, weird news stories started trickling out of Europe. By September, there were demons everywhere. It only took ten years for Europe, Africa and South America to collapse. Eighteen years for the United States. By 2060, there weren't any cities left. All the people went underground to escape. We built towns in subway systems, bunkers, whatever we could find. Old coal mines, the basements of buildings, anything at all. We've been fighting them ever since."

"Has Gabriel told you what you need to do?"

"He said the first part is to stop the Purge. We have to kill Laelia, whoever that is."

"She's the one who turned me into a vampire." Gage went to the window to look out. "That's a story for another day. Get some rest. I know there are a lot of questions we're going to want to ask one another once the young lady is awake."

Damon waited until Gage was pulling the door closed before he spoke. "Just one thing. Why are you in on this? Do you have a choice, or were you drafted like we were?"

"There isn't ever much of a choice when dealing with Gabriel. He finds a way to make you do what he wants, but inasmuch as anyone ever gets to choose, I decided to be a part of this."

"Why?"

Gage smiled wistfully. "Because I was not made a vampire by my own choice. I've never turned anyone, and I don't believe in taking humanity away so carelessly. I'm a monster, and I've accepted that. The things I've done—well, I know I'll burn for them. If I can keep one human from living the existence that I have had to, all of this is worth it." He shook his head. "Besides, I might be the only one strong enough to kill that bitch."

Chapter Seven

August 13th, 2030 - Ireland

WHEN GREER woke the next morning, her body was aching and her head was pounding. She gritted her teeth against the pain and forced her eyes to open. The light streaming in through the curtains was bright and cheery, and just the sight of a sunny morning pissed her off. She rolled to her side and sat up, sucking in a breath when her whole body rebelled. She wanted nothing more than to lie back down and forget about getting out of bed, but neither her bladder nor the grime on her teeth would allow it.

Resigned to agony, she placed her feet on the floor and pushed herself onto them. Her knees buckled, and she pitched forward, catching herself on the dresser to keep from falling flat on her face. She groaned at the jarring stop and bit her tongue.

The taste of blood bloomed in her mouth and a wave of nausea rose from her empty stomach at the taste. Deciding the most pressing need was brushing her teeth, she forced her knees to be steady and limped into the bathroom.

Someone had laid out towels, a brand new toothbrush, a tube of toothpaste, a hairbrush and an array of toiletries. Neatly folded on the counter were a pair of sweatpants, socks and a t-shirt. Grateful, she tore open the toothbrush package and squeezed toothpaste out.

The minty flavor overcame the taste of morning breath and blood as she scrubbed her teeth enthusiastically. She would have continued had she not gotten a glimpse of herself in the mirror above the sink. With a gasp, her hands went to her face and the toothbrush clattered against the porcelain of the sink.

Both of her eyes were black. There was a bruise on one cheekbone and a cut above her eyebrow. Her chin was scraped and there was a thick purple band wrapping around her neck.

As quickly as she could, she stripped off her clothes to survey the damage. She saw a thick pink scar where the slice on her thigh had been. Two puckered patches of skin marked the bullet wound on her shoulder. A third told her where she'd been shot in the hip. One ankle was black and blue but the bones had been straightened and put into their proper place.

She'd healed herself and had no memory of it. Greer sat down onto the lid of the toilet as that sank in. She'd never been able to heal more than one injury on herself before, but there were four distinct instances of her having used her gift within a short period of time.

Contemplating what that might mean, she stepped into the massive shower and turned on the hot spray. The water loosened the tightness in her muscles and eased the pain. She leaned her head against the cool tiles and let the water pound against her back.

Fifteen minutes later, dressed, and with her hair tied back in a long ponytail, she descended the stairs. Each step was exceedingly more difficult. Her breaths were shallow and fast, and she closed her eyes as she gripped the railing to try and make the wave of dizziness dissipate. She knew she needed to eat to replace the fuel that she had used healing herself. If she didn't make it to the kitchen soon, she was going to pass out.

Her muscles trembled from the effort of staying upright and her chest burned from exertion. She attempted one more step, knowing that there were only five left and she had no other choice. Her vision swarmed with black dots, and she missed the step, pitching forward and tumbling down the last few. Her mind had time to brace for the impact of the slate floor at the bottom of the steps in anticipation of hitting. Before her body could slam into them, she was scooped up and cradled against someone.

"Easy there. I've got you." Gage shifted her so that one of her arms was around his neck and her feet were on the floor. "You should have called. One of us would have helped you down."

Greer bit back a snarky response. "Where's Damon?"

"I'm right here." Damon hurried across the room and took her other arm, shifting the burden of her weight onto him. Gage stepped back, respecting the boundaries being set. "I'm not quite as fast as a fucking vampire."

Greer made a feeble attempt to laugh. "Not many are." She looked around the room, her gaze settling on Alaria, who had come into the room after Damon. "I feel like I'm a sideshow or something. Stop staring at me!"

Alaria giggled. "Well, looking like you do, we could put you in the circus as a clown. All the pretty colors."

Greer found herself fighting a smile. She glared at the other woman and then swung her gaze to Damon. "I need food."

Damon started moving toward what Greer prayed was the kitchen. "Coming right up."

He settled her at the table in the breakfast nook and began rifling through cabinets. Alaria slipped in behind him and took the lid off a pot on the stove. Greer's mouth nearly watered at the aromatic smell of the beef stew. Thirty seconds later, three bowls of the stew, thick slices of bread and glasses of milk were on the table. Alaria spared a slight smile for Greer.

"All men are the same. They never look at what's right in front of them."

"I knew it was there. I'm not entirely sure it isn't poisoned."

Gage leaned against the doorframe. "You'll come to trust us. We're in this for the same reasons you are."

"I seriously doubt that."

The vampire's smile was sharp and dangerous. "That's right. You're here for a girl. We're here because we want to save the world. You tell me which of us has the more pure intentions." He leveled a glare at Damon. "I've tolerated your pissy attitude for the better part of three days waiting for her to come back to herself. I understand this is hard and that you're confused and that you've been put into a situation that you don't want to be in, but we are all on the same side, and the snark is not appreciated. Lay off it. We're on the same side. I get that you're hardwired to hate vampires, and Alaria isn't exactly a loveable type of woman, but if we wanted to hurt you, you'd be dead a thousand times over."

Damon bristled. "I don't know who you think you are, talking to me that way, but it's going to stop. You're a vampire—a monster. You eat people to stay alive, and I don't even want to know how many people have died by your hand."

"Not as many as by yours, I'd bet. How many Familiars have you slaughtered, Damon? How many people have you picked off through a sniper's scope?"

"That's different."

Gage nodded. "Oh, it's different, all right. You're fighting a war. You make a choice every time you squeeze the trigger. You decide to take a life. Vampires have the defense of needing blood to survive. We come back with bloodlust. Most don't ever break out of it. Imagine how much easier it would be to kill if you needed to do it to survive. If their death ensured your survival in a basic, immediate way. Then you tell me about how you're so morally superior to me. I accept what I am and what I've done. I fought to become more than what I was made to be. Don't judge something you don't understand."

Greer cleared her throat. "I think that's enough." She let her eyes drift over each of the three faces. "They're right. They could have killed us both a hundred times by now. Obviously, we're where we're supposed to be, and we need to work together. From what I can tell, that's the only way that we're going to survive." She reached out and covered Damon's hand with her own. "I know you didn't want to do this, and I know the situation sucks, but we have to trust them."

Alaria leaned back in her chair. "As much as I hate to agree with anyone, Greer is right. We're stuck with each other for the foreseeable future, so we need to make the best of it. Stupid Gabe brought you guys back in August, so there's no way we're stopping the Hell Gate from opening. All we can do is work toward stopping the demons from getting out."

"I'm not entirely sure why it is that the first step is to stop the flow of demons rather than seal the Gate shut."

Alaria cleared her throat. "I can answer that for you. When the Gate opens, it's like breaking a dam. Before you can repair the damage, you have to stop the flood. Stopping the purge is putting a band-aid on it. We're basically inserting a temporary barrier that will let us kill Garrick and close the Gate." She paused to take a bite of her stew. "Gage, it's time to go get Braxton."

Damon lifted his eyebrows. "Who is Braxton?"

Gage took in a breath he didn't need and expelled it forcefully. "Braxton is a Warrior. He was brought into the Choosing by Gabriel. He and Griffin were involved with one another."

Alaria laughed. "Involved? He married her. She was his wife. He knew she was going to die, but when Gabe told us that Lucifer had found a way around the Choosing to get demons out, he...broke. He's back in the States."

"He's not in a good place, but he's one of the six, so we have to get him back to where he needs to be."

Greer dropped her spoon into her bowl and offered a smile as Damon rose to refill it. "What do you mean, not in a good place?"

Gage exchanged a look with Alaria before he spoke. "He's depressed. He's torn up about Griffin basically dying for nothing. He loved her."

"No, he thinks he loved her. We both know the Angels manipulated his feelings, and so does he. That's what's bugging him so damn bad. Trying to figure out what was real and what wasn't. He's the best Warrior you'd ever want to meet, and a good guy on top of it. First human I got fond of." Alaria sighed. "Regardless, he's part of this and we're going to need him."

Damon held up a hand. "You're telling me that part of our group is a mentally disturbed, depressed widower who is off pouting? We're supposed to trust our lives to him?" He looked at Greer in disbelief. "A vampire with a heart of gold, a former Devil, and a lunatic. We'd be better off going back home!"

Gage chuckled. "I can't disagree with anything that you've said. We still don't know who the sixth person is going to be, and we're in a bad situation. Braxton is a Warrior. He's capable of anything you're capable of, and he will get his head on straight and get in the game. It's what he does. Alaria is going to make sure of that."

Alaria snorted into her glass of milk. "Why do I have to be the one to go get his sorry ass?"

"Because you understand what he's going through better than I do. You knew Griffin better and you were involved in the whole of it. I came in at the very end as hired muscle."

She conceded the point with a sigh. "Get your plane here, then. I'll head out in a day or two." She shook her head. "I never thought I'd step foot in Pennsylvania again."

"How are you feeling?"

Greer looked up from the book she was idly flipping through to see Gage standing in the doorway to the library. "Sore and tired, but a lot stronger than earlier." She closed the book. "You have more books in this one room than I've ever seen in my whole life."

Gage perched on the couch near her feet. "Is there anything that you need? I know you must still be in a lot of pain."

Greer shook her head. "I'm really feeling pretty good." She looked at him pointedly. "Does Damon know you're down here?"

"I haven't the foggiest idea. Do you answer to him?"

"No. We're friends, and he's protective of me. We've lost so much in the past few days...our whole city fell to Familiars, and we both nearly died. He's the only reason that I'm alive."

"Have you ever known the world to be anything other than overrun by demons?"

She shook her head again. "By the time I was born, it was getting bad. We'd started to fight back and had taken back a few small towns. Warriors were leading raids on demonic strongholds, and there were some government-like factions popping up. My parents were killed when I was ten. My dad went out on a supply run and came back possessed. I got away while he was killing my mom. We'd been living in an abandoned factory, down in the basement.

"I lasted eighteen months on my own. I squatted in basements and churches, found a few people who would take me in for a night or two. When I was twelve, I got caught by a demon. It was trying to possess me. I had gotten the anti-possession tattoos when I was six, but one or two had gotten damaged over time. It was trying to force its way into me when Damon and his father found me. He was seventeen and had just joined the militia. They killed the demon and took me back with them."

"It can't be easy, Damon leaving his parents."

"They're dead." Greer shifted on the couch. "Everyone we've ever known is dead. When the city fell, everyone died. Another city sent planes with bombs to try and kill the Familiars before they got into the tunnels. What we didn't know was how structurally unsound the tunnels had become. If they weren't killed by Familiars, they were killed by the collapses. I nearly got crushed by debris in the garages."

"For what it's worth, I wish that there was a way for us to stop it before they get out."

Her voice was small and uncharacteristically timid. "Me too."

Gage patted her knee. "I didn't come in here to make you feel bad. I came to see if you might have a word with Damon. He seems to listen to you."

Suspicious, she quirked an eyebrow. "What do you want?"

"We won't survive if we don't work together. I know he doesn't trust us. In the position that the two of you are in, I can't say that I would be any different, but the fact remains that all we have is each other. Braxton will be able to ease a lot of your apprehension. He's a Warrior. Quite frankly, he's the best Warrior that has ever lived. If Gabriel ever showed up when he could actually be useful, he could tell you a lot that you need to know. I would like for Damon to work with us. We need to train, talk and figure out a plan of action, and we need to do it together. Do you think you could do that?"

Greer thought about it for a long minute before nodding. "I can do that."

Chapter Eight

DAMON WAS IN the gym in the basement. Greer knew before she got to the bottom of the stairs that he was not in a good mood. The unmistakable sound of balled fists colliding with a punching bag drifted up the steps and warned her of his attitude. Sighing, Greer squared her shoulders and finished the climb down.

Damon looked up when he heard her close the door but kept punching the hanging bag. His face was coated in a sheen of sweat and his shirt was soaked with it. His breath came in short gasps, and his muscles were screaming for a break. Instead of giving his body what it needed, he pressed onward.

"Damon."

"I'm busy."

"I want to talk to you."

Damon shrugged. "So talk."

"Why are you mad at me?"

He bounced back a half-step. "I'm not mad at you. I'm pissed at the situation. I never imagined saving the world would entail living with a vampire and a Devil."

"That's kind of what I wanted to talk to you about." Greer lowered herself to the floor and leaned against the wall. "We need to make some decisions about what we're doing."

Damon drained half a bottle of water in one gulp. "Do we actually get to make those decisions, or are they getting made for us? We got had, Greer. We got lured into helping, and now we're sixty years in the past, and the odds are that neither of us is going to survive. We don't know who the sixth person is, this Braxton person sounds like he's out of his fucking mind, and then the vampire slips and tells me that 'Oh yeah, this is the second time we've tried this, and the first time Greer's grandmother had to stab herself in the fucking heart'!" He angrily screwed the cap back on.

"I don't know how we let ourselves get conned into helping with this because the only thing we are going to get out of it is killed."

Greer winced at the anger in his voice and leaned her head against the wall with her eyes closed tightly. "We knew it would be dangerous."

"You've already almost died twice—once saving my life. I won't let you kill yourself like your grandmother did. I won't stand for it. I'll hog-tie you and go hide somewhere if I have to, but we are not going down that road."

Greer laughed incredulously. "You think I would honestly kill myself? Damon, give me a little credit. I can handle this. I wasn't at a hundred percent when we came back here. If I had been, I wouldn't be nearly so pathetic now. I will get through this, and so will you. I know you don't trust Gage or Alaria, but I think you need to revisit that."

He looked at her as if she'd sprouted a second head. "Why the fuck would I do that?"

Frustrated, Greer plowed her hands through her hair and tugged sharply on it. "Because a frickin' Angel sent us here, and Angels don't send people into traps."

Damon toweled off his face and squatted in front of her. "How do we know that, though? We didn't even know Angels existed until three days ago. We've been fighting this war for five decades and they just now decide to show their faces? How much confidence are we supposed to have in Gabriel? He could be a traitor, or he could want the world to end. For all we know, he could be Satan."

Greer spoke slowly as if she were addressing a small child. "They could have killed us both by now. As much as you might hate it, Gabriel hasn't told us one single thing that hasn't been true. The fact is that we're here and we have to try. We know how bad it is in the future. There aren't demons and vampires and Hell hounds and Familiars everywhere here! We can walk outside without a weapon. If there is even a slim chance that we can keep things from becoming what they are in our time, then we have to do it. Maybe our parents won't be dead, or our friends, or everyone we've ever known! We have a chance to change our present by helping change their future, Damon. If we have to fight for that chance, I'm willing to do it. I've fought for a whole hell of a lot less."

Damon threw the bottle of water and watched it bounce off the wall as he stalked the length of the room. "Maybe we'll die trying! Or maybe we'll just disappear because something will change and we'll never be born!" He threw out his arms and walked backward several steps.

"Wouldn't that be fun?"

"Gabriel said we're meant to exist." Greer's voice was soothing. She heaved herself to her feet, took several seconds to catch her breath, and then crossed the mat to stand in front of him. "I know you didn't ask for this. You're here because of who my grandmother is. You're the unlucky bastard who was the first actual Hunter I crossed. If you don't want to stay, I'll understand, but I have to at least try to make this work." She lifted her shoulders in a helpless shrug. "I want you with me, of course, but I understand if you can't."

Damon deflated and let out a sigh. He reached out and touched his fingertips to her cheek. "If you stay, I stay. There's no way in hell I could live with myself if I let you do this without me."

"We have to work with them."

Another sigh, this one followed with a low growl of displeasure. "I know. I don't like it, but I know."

"Neither of them has tried anything, and Alaria is human now. That has to ease your worries somewhat."

"The only thing that would ease my concerns is if we all get through this whole damn thing alive." He stooped to pick up the crunched remains of his plastic water bottle. "I think I'm all talked out about this for tonight, babe. I'm gonna go shower and go to bed. Do you need help up the stairs?"

Greer looked at the steep staircase with trepidation in her eyes. She hadn't considered that she would need to go back up the stairs when she had come down them. Even getting down had taken her the lion's share of five minutes. It would likely take her several times that to go back up. Regardless of how much better she felt, the truth was that she was still as weak as a kitten.

Reluctantly, she nodded. "I don't know if I could make it up those stairs and then the stairs to go to bed, too."

Damon grinned and crossed in front of her. "You might get a little sweaty, but hop on."

With a lot of help, Greer hooked her legs around his waist and heaved herself onto his back. Easily, Damon ascended the stairs to the main floor and then the second flight to the level where the bedrooms were. At the top, he bent his knees and stooped to let her slide off his back. Once her feet were on the floor, they walked together down the hall toward the rooms they had been put in, which connected with a bathroom.

"I know you're still sore, but we need to start working your muscles some. If you feel up to it, we'll at least go for a walk in the morning and do some light weights. Nothing too intense, because you need to heal, but enough to keep you in fighting shape."

Greer opened her door. "Sounds like a plan. I know I've only been awake a few hours, but I feel like I could fall over asleep." She offered a smile. "I'll see you in the morning."

She shut the door and leaned against it for a moment before taking a deep breath and crossing the room to the window. The moon was big and full against an inky black sky dotted with stars. It was the first time she could remember ever having seen the moon without being scared to be exposed at night.

It was that feeling that told her she could do what she had been brought back to do. She'd lived her whole life scared. Scared of demons, Devils, and Familiars. Vampires ruled the night, and Hell hounds roamed the streets freely, waiting for their next meal to come out. The world was a cruel, deadly place in her time. Here, it was a bit gentler, and not nearly as scary. Yet. If they lost...Greer shook her head to clear the thought from it. She wouldn't let that happen. She wouldn't let it become what her present was.

It had lost everything that had once made it beautiful. No one could appreciate a moonlit night, or a sunset, without debilitating fear. She leaned her head against the windowpane and watched her breath fog up the glass each time she exhaled.

She heard the water start in the bathroom and Damon moving around. The curtain rustled as he got into the shower. Unwittingly, she thought of the singular kiss that they had shared. Her stomach clenched with excitement and anticipation as she remembered how she had felt. Sighing, she pushed off the wall and headed toward the bathroom. Those feelings were something they probably needed to discuss.

She knocked with one knuckle before twisting the door knob and poking her head in. "Can I come in?"

Damon stuck his head out from behind the curtain. "If you only have to pee, sure. Anything else and you can wait."

She laughed as she closed the door and sat on the closed toilet. "I just wanted to talk to you about something for a minute."

"Shoot." His head disappeared back into the shower stall.

"Before the Angel zapped us back in time, what happened in that apartment, I thought we maybe should talk about it."

"You're blushing really hard right now, aren't you?"

Greer laid her palm on her face and felt the burn of her skin. "Probably." She took a deep breath. "Doesn't change the fact that it's a conversation we need to have."

His head popped out again. "For some reason you decided to have this conversation when I'm naked and wet?" He wiggled his eyebrows playfully and crooked one finger at her. "Does that mean you wanna join me?"

Her face flaming and an unexpected knot of desire forming in her belly, Greer snapped at him. "Could you take this seriously, please?"

Damon laughed from behind the curtain. "I am. Seriously, you and I have known each other for sixteen years. We're not suddenly going to stop being who we are with each other because I kissed you. I don't want to go there if anything is going to change that."

"You want to go there then?"

"Stop trying to read between the lines." The water shut off and his arm burst through the curtains to snag a towel from the hook. "You can be such a girl sometimes."

"I am a girl." Greer wrinkled her nose when he shook his hair and water droplets splattered on her face. He stepped out of the shower with the towel knotted around his waist and went to the sink. "I don't think it was an unreasonable question."

"Stand up." Damon took three steps to stand in front of her. She gaped up at him.

"Why?"

"Just do it, Greer." He held out a hand and pulled her to her feet. "What do you feel?"

Her brows knitted in confusion. "What do you mean?"

"Right now, this second. What are you feeling?"

"Tired and annoyed that you're not talking to me."

He tugged on her arm and turned so that she was pinned between the sink and him. He grabbed her hips and lifted her onto the sink, stepping between her legs so that he was merely inches from her. "Just because I'm not saying what you want to hear doesn't mean I'm not participating in the conversation." He placed his hands very deliberately on either side of her legs. "How do you feel now?"

Greer lifted her eyebrows and tried to ignore the heat coming off of his body and the speed at which her heart beat. She waited several beats to make sure her voice was steady and neutral. "What are you trying to get at?"

"Do I really have to spell it out for you?"

Annoyance overriding the other emotions, Greer glared at him. "Apparently."

Damon leaned forward until his nose was a centimeter from touching her neck. He breathed deeply and inhaled the scent of her skin, then let his breath, damp and hot, skim over her as he exhaled. "How do you feel?" He nudged her neck with his nose. "Is your heart racing?" His hands lightly ran up her thighs to grasp her hips, and he pressed his lips to her throat to feel her pulse racing. "Do you feel hot?" He jerked her forward, just a little bit roughly, until her hips were anchored against his and the fabric of the towel was dangerously close to slipping down his body. "Is your blood pounding in your ears?" He scraped his teeth over her skin. "Are you wet?"

Greer's eyes were closed. She concentrated on her breathing, trying to keep it even. Her skin was flaming, and it was all she could do not to gasp for breath at the onslaught of his questions and the proximity of his next-to-naked body.

He brushed his lips over her collarbone so lightly that all she felt was the promise of contact. Her whole body shuddered in a shiver of anticipation. He let one of her hips go and reached up to flick one of her nipples through her shirt. The tightly beaded flesh was clearly visible through the thin fabric, and he rubbed it gently with his finger. A bolt of desire shot through her.

"How do you feel?" He lifted his head so that his eyes bored into her, hot and intense. When she didn't answer, he stepped back. She was immediately cold from the loss of his body heat. Her eyes snapped open, and she stared at him with a mixture of want, need, and confusion. He shrugged carelessly and opened the door to his bedroom. "Until you can answer that question, this goes no further. Think about it, Greer. Let me know when you decide what you want."

Chapter Nine

GREER WAS STILL muttering about Damon when she slipped into bed fifteen minutes later. She ached from her still-healing injuries and was so tired she could barely keep her eyes open. She punched her pillow twice out of frustration before settling down on it and stared stonily at the ceiling. Within five minutes, her mind drifted, and her eyes fell shut. She floated into sleep and dropped off the cliff of consciousness and into a dream.

"Where am I?"

A redhead wearing a long flowing gown smiled and spread her arms to encompass the meadow in which they stood. "This is what is known as the dream plane."

Greer turned in a slow circle and took in the lush grass and hillside dotted with trees. "Who are you?"

"I'm the sixth member of your group. Gabriel came to me last evening and requested that I reach out and initiate contact with one of you. Your mind was the easiest for me to access."

"Why didn't he just come to me himself?"

"This isn't something that he wanted to get involved in. He felt that it was important that you know the first part of your task will occur largely without my involvement. I will be brought forth when I am needed. My appearance in your time would prematurely alert Lucifer and Garrick. Without me, it is possible that you could kill the vampire Laelia and patch the Hell Gate without their immediate knowledge."

"You're the witch?"

"There are many names." The woman smiled again and began to walk. Greer cast a furtive glance around and then followed. "I possess magic. You call it witch. In my time we were called Priestesses. Some call us Sorceress, others call us Wiccans. The list goes on."

"Where are you from?"

"I am a Priestess at the temple of Athena in Greece. I have known from a very young age that I was to be called away from my home and into a future from which I could not return."

Greer scoffed. "At least you had notice. Damn Angel just appeared a few days ago and told us we had to leave." She thought for a moment. "How do you speak English if you're from Greece? Shouldn't you speak Greek?"

The woman smiled. "You're right. I should, and do, speak Greek. I've been trained since I was very young that this was to be my path, and I was given the gift of languages." She shifted the conversation back to Greer. "You're from the future, then?"

"Yeah, about three thousand years into the future from you if I'm remembering right."

"I was asked to make sure that your group knows that there is danger coming. You are not safe, nor will you be until the three tasks are completed. Laelia is strong, and she has many followers. She is not yet working with Garrick, but that may be the conclusion if they determine their chances of survival are greater together than apart. His magic is strong. He is seeking to release Lucifer. Even in your time, Lucifer remained chained to Hell. If that were to change, there would be no survival for humanity."

"How is he still stuck there when everything else is out?"

"His binds were placed upon him by God. The others were bound by Angels. It takes much more power to break the will of God than of Angels."

"Can it be done?"

"Yes. His chains grow weaker with each passing day. That is not to be your focus this moment. You must concentrate on the task at hand. You must find Laelia and spill her life's blood upon the entrance to the Hell Gate. It will act as a temporary patch on the flow of demons. Those on Earth can return to Hell, but none in Hell can get out. In the second task, my task, we will close the Gates."

"Won't that trap the demons already on Earth here?"

"That is an unfortunate reality. In the third task, we will banish all the other Devils and demons from Earth."

"How?"

"That's not the concern right now."

Greer sighed in frustration. "You can't tell me something like that and then not finish the story." She looked around again and noticed that the sky was rapidly darkening. Thunder rumbled in the distance and lightning speared through the clouds. Something wasn't right. "What's going on?"

"My entrance to the dream plane has been detected. Garrick is watching me. You cannot remain here any longer. Return to your bed and tell my message to the others in your group. Do not concern yourself with any except the first task."

The woman seized Greer's hand and dragged her back down the path toward the spot where she had first appeared. Her grip was strong and firm, but Greer managed to pull away from it. She planted her feet firmly.

"How do we banish the other demons back to Hell?"

The woman looked around nervously. "It requires that the roots of the wings that the Devils had be carved from their backs. Once that is done, there are other spells and rituals that will need to be completed before they can be cast out."

Greer shook her head. "One of those original fallen is Alaria. She's human now. What will that mean?"

"I don't know. I am not an expert in this. I know only what Gabriel has told me. I'm sure that he is aware of the situation. Concentrate on the first task, Greer. You cannot complete the other two without first accomplishing this one." She jumped when a crack of lightning lit up the hillside. "You must go now. There is no more time to dally. If he sees you here, your life will be in incredible danger. I am not a Dreamweaver. My power is limited here. His is not. Go now, before he has forced his way in."

Before Greer could even open her mouth to speak, she jerked awake in her bed, sunlight streaming through the curtains and birds chirping happily outside the window. Someone had brought in a stack of jeans and shirts and laid them on the dresser. On top of them was a pack of plain cotton underwear and two bras.

She felt stronger as soon as she got out of bed. Her leg was still sore, and her shoulder twinged when she lifted her arms over her head, but she felt almost back to normal. One more day of rest and she would be ready to jump back in.

She showered briskly and headed downstairs. It felt good not to have to take a break halfway down to catch her breath before attempting the rest. Her thighs were burning when she stepped off the last step, and the prospect of going back up was still slightly daunting, but she was relatively sure she could manage it.

Alaria, Gage, and Damon were all in the kitchen. Gage was drinking something out of a coffee cup, and the other two were devouring scrambled eggs and toast. Gage waved for her to sit and scooped another serving out of a pan on the stove.

"How'd you sleep?"

Greer lifted one shoulder. "Fine. I had weird dreams, though."

Alaria's head lifted from her plate. "Dreams about what?"

"A woman in some field. She said she was the sixth."

Gage sat down at the table. "You're going to need to tell us everything about the dream."

Greer looked between the vampire and former Devil anxiously. "Why? It was just a dream."

Damon laid his hand over hers gently. "Sometimes dreams aren't dreams. Seers can get glimpses into the future occasionally. Dreamweavers are witches or warlocks that have the ability to create a dream world and bring someone else into it. Some witches are powerful enough to access that dream plane, though they aren't strong enough to use much of their powers there."

"How do you know all this? In fifteen years you've never told me any of this, and suddenly you're a fucking encyclopedia Britannica on all things supernatural?"

A flicker of hurt flashed in his eyes, but he shook it off. "There are some things I thought I was better off keeping to myself."

Gage motioned with his hand to bring the attention back to himself. "This isn't the time for bickering. Greer, if you would, please tell us what happened. Spare no detail. Anything could be important."

"She said Gabriel sent her to me."

Alaria snorted. "Of course he did. That damn Angel never did know the meaning of subtle." She finished the last of her coffee. "Go on, then. Tell us what revelations Gabriel had for us."

Painstakingly, Greer spent the next forty minutes being grilled about every word she had exchanged with the strange woman. Gage and Alaria took turns peppering her with questions about everything from where they'd been to what they'd been wearing. She did her best to answer everything but found that a lot of the details were fuzzy. Finally, Gage patted her arm sympathetically and rose from the table.

"That's enough. Sometimes the images get hazy. Your brain has never experienced the dream plane before, so it doesn't know quite what to make of it. When an Angel or a Devil takes you there, your brain somehow realizes that it's real, but it's different when it's another human doing the summoning. I think the power is weaker, maybe."

Damon leaned back in the chair and crossed one leg over the other. "That raises the question, what do we do now? We obviously need to find this Laelia and kill her."

"That's not as easy as you might think it is. Laelia hasn't surfaced in more than three hundred years." Gage took in a breath he didn't need and expelled it quickly. "She managed to seriously piss off Lilith back around the Revolutionary War. They got into a pissing contest over a warlock. It was not pretty, and Laelia barely survived. She hasn't been seen since."

"How do we know she's even still alive then?" Greer absent-mindedly speared a piece of egg and nibbled on it. "I mean, isn't it possible that someone offed her in the last quarter millennium?"

"I would know." Gage's voice was confident. When both Damon and Greer looked at him, confused, he shook his head and continued. "She made me into a vampire. I would know if she was dead because we're connected by a sire-bond."

The question spilled out so fast Greer couldn't have stopped it had her life depended on it. "What's a sire-bond?"

"To make a vampire, a demon or Devil must feed their blood to a human as they are dying. The blood transforms the person into something else—a vampire. It's almost a hybrid of human and demon. Vampires pass that along each time they create a new vamp. It's gotten watered down over the generations, and vampires now are nothing like what they used to be. For the first few generations, we inherited some demonic powers. Teleportation, a measure of magic, that sort of thing. It's been bled out over thousands of years, but Laelia got it all. She was the original vampire, and her magic is very strong. When she passed that on to me, it created a bond between the two of us. Not something strong enough that she could find out where we are or I, her, but enough that I would probably know if she was dead."

Alaria sighed. "The problem is, if she knows we're after her, there's nothing stopping her from making a fucking army of super powerful vampires."

"She'll find out. She is not one that should be underestimated." Gage leaned against the wall casually. "Once she does, she'll seek out Garrick, if she hasn't already, and they'll work together. It's in her best interest to work with Lucifer instead of hiding on her own and hoping she gets lucky."

Damon cleared his throat. "Fascinating as this is, that still doesn't answer the question of what the fuck we do right now. I, for one, am getting tired of sitting around talking when we could be doing something. Every minute that we keep blowing smoke is another demon that's escaping from Hell, another Hell hound that's come back, or another vampire that's back on Earth." He looked at Gage. "You don't need to tell us what real vampires are. When the Gates opened, every supernatural creature that was ever sent to Hell got a second chance. Including all the original vampires—all the ones sired by demons and Devils—that had ever been killed. Our world was literally flooded with monsters."

Greer nodded. "It was bad. I have a question. I thought demons could already come and go from Hell?"

Alaria smiled. "Some could. Demons are human souls that have been twisted into something else. They're trapped until a Devil lets them out. We were cast out by God and into the pit. Lilith managed to wriggle out of that. The rest of us were stuck for a good long while until we could break loose. We have the ability to possess bodies like demons, and most did since it was easier than breaking out our bodies. The body I'm in is actually what we call a vessel. A human who was born looking exactly the way we did when we were Angels. It calls to us. I suspect we have Lilith to thank for that, but it's beside the point. Once we Devils were out, we could release a certain number of demons under our control. The number of demons or Devils on Earth at any time were roughly ten percent of the number down there. There are hundreds of Devils that were lesser Angels that never managed to break out. Hell was new. It wasn't something God ever intended to create, and it wasn't perfect. We found the holes."

"What happens to your bodies when you possess someone else?"

Alaria laughed. "I know it sounds complicated. We could dissolve ourselves into our essence and force it into a human. We were still there, all the little pieces, just inside someone else. When we found our vessel, it became permanent, and we gave up the right to possess people unless we wanted to lose it." She shuddered. "I hated sharing a body."

"What happened to the person who was in that body before?" Greer's eyes were wide with a mixture of trepidation and curiosity.

Alaria pondered that for a moment. "I really don't know. There was never anyone in here with me, so I guess it died." She shook her head. "We're getting off track again." She turned her gaze to Damon. "To answer your question, we go get Braxton. I'm leaving tonight for Philly."

Chapter Ten

August 14th, 2030 - Philadelphia, Pennsylvania
ALARIA STEPPED off the ramp of the airplane regally, as comfortable in heels as any other woman would have been in sneakers. A purse was draped over one arm, and she held a small carry-on in the other hand. She noticed the glances she was getting from both men and women and chuckled under her breath.

She briskly weaved through the throng of people in the airport and hopped on the escalator to descend into the baggage claim area. Since she hadn't checked any luggage, she passed straight through and pushed through the revolving door that led to the exit. As promised, there was a sleek, black car parked at the curb. The driver tipped his hat in her direction and opened the door.

Once she was settled into the seat and the driver had slipped behind the wheel, he glanced at her in the rearview mirror. "Where to, ma'am?"

"Seven-fifty-nine Montrose."

The drive out to the apartment building in which Braxton lived was long and annoying. Traffic was horrid, horns honked constantly, and the car was bumper-to-bumper with other vehicles almost the entire drive.

After nearly an hour, the driver pulled up to the curb, and Alaria slid out. "Don't bother waiting. I'll call if I need you again."

There was no doorman. Instead, there was a panel with buttons and names scrawled above them. Not wanting to spend time convincing Braxton to open the door, she began methodically pushing them until someone buzzed her in. Ignoring the elevator, she dashed up the stairs to the third floor.

She watched the numbers change until she found the right door and knocked sharply. "Braxton! Open up."

A voice sounded from inside. "Go away, Alaria."

Alaria shook her head even though she knew he couldn't see her. She opened her purse and withdrew a lock pick kit. Within twenty seconds, the deadbolt turned and the door swung open. The scene that awaited had her torn between gagging and running.

The apartment was dark, with not a single light on. There were pizza boxes and Chinese containers covering every available surface. Empty beer and liquor bottles littered the floor and the entire apartment smelled like garbage that had been sitting in a locked car for two weeks. She wondered briefly if it was even safe to breathe the air before stepping over the threshold and into the pit.

"Love what you've done with the place."

Braxton Winslow sat in a recliner, wearing worn jeans and a black shirt, with his feet bare. His face was covered with a week old beard and his hair was hanging into his face. He pushed the footstool in on the recliner and leveled a glare at her.

"Whatever you've come to say or do, I'm not interested in hearing it. Go away and leave me be."

"I'm not nice, Brax. I'm not going to coddle you here. Get off your ass, get dressed and get packed. We have a job to do."

"I don't want coddling. I don't want you here. Go. Away."

Alaria went to the window and drew open the curtains to let light stream in. "This place is disgusting."

"I know."

"Do you ever clean it?"

"When I can't take the smell anymore."

Her lips quirked into what threatened to be a smile. "It's getting close, don't ya think?"

"Another three or four days, I think." Braxton heaved himself to his feet. "I'm not helping."

"We both know that's a lie."

"No, it's not. I gave everything to the Choosing. I watched the woman I loved drive a knife into her heart and give up her life to save the world. Three months later, some stupid coven springs the Gates and lets all the fucking creepy-crawlies out again. Her death was for nothing." He glared at her again. "You're living the life Griffin should have had."

Alaria snarled. "Don't try to put me on a guilt trip. She was going to die. If I hadn't helped, she'd have been dead way before the Choosing."

"She could have asked for her own life."

"Yeah, if she'd have gotten there alive. Do you really think she would have?"

He jerked open the refrigerator to withdraw a beer. "We'll never know. She died to save this pathetic excuse for a world."

"You sitting here refusing to help is making that sacrifice for nothing. She's in Heaven, Braxton. She has no clue who we are or that we ever existed. She still exists, just not here." Alaria reached out and took the bottle from him. "I know you miss her."

"You don't know shit."

She touched his hand with her fingertips. "I liked her, too. She was special. For everything I put her through, everything Hell sent at her, she fought until the end. She'd still be fighting if she was here."

"She's not here."

"She died for you, for her son, for Sam, and for the rest of your family. She knew what was going to happen, and she did what had to be done. She could have run away or refused to do it, but she didn't. She was brave and strong. She would want you to finish this. We have to pick up where she left off."

For a moment, tears welled in Braxton's eyes. He dashed them away angrily. "Who sent you, anyway? Gabriel or Gage?"

"I don't answer to them."

"You sure as shit didn't come here on your own."

"Give me a little credit. I want the world to keep on spinning. Being human does me no good if the world ends before I get to live my life."

"Then it's about you being selfish again. You only ever want what's good for you."

"I'm not apologizing for that. I know the score. I might die doing this, but I'll die for sure if I don't. That doesn't leave me much choice."

"You're doing this because you have the hots for Gabe."

Annoyed, Alaria fought to keep her voice level. She wrenched open a cabinet and yanked out a trash bag. "Don't comment on things you know nothing about."

"I know enough."

"Griffin's granddaughter is pretty pleasant. The man who came with her is a different story, though. I've never met anyone more suspicious in my whole life."

Braxton blinked several times rapidly. "What the hell are you talking about?"

"Just making small-talk while I clean up a bit." She began gathering beer bottles. "You should really recycle these. Anyway, her name is Greer, and she's twenty-eight. Gabe brought her back here from the future. She's a militia soldier. In her world, people live underground in subway tunnels and basements. Before Gabe pulled her out, her whole city got wiped out by Familiars. She and this Damon guy were the only survivors that we know of. She's a Healer. A real, honest-to-God Healer. Not like Allen, who just has a hand with medicine. She can back a bullet out of a bone with nothing other than her mind."

"What are you trying to do, Alaria?"

She sat the bag on the floor and crossed the room to stand in front of him. "I'm trying to make you see what is at risk. Griffin didn't die for nothing. The world is still here. Yeah, Lucifer cheated, and it sucks. Did you really expect that he wouldn't? Griffin died to help save the world. We just have to finish what she started. We owe that to her."

"Did you know?"

It was Alaria's turn to blink rapidly from confusion. "Did I know what?"

"That he was planning this. Did you know about it?"

Sympathy stirred in her, and she smiled gently. "No, I didn't know."

"Why should I believe you?"

"Because I'm telling you the truth." Alaria looked pained. "He wouldn't have told me. I was given the Choosing as a trial. He knew I fought for different reasons, and he didn't trust me as much as the others. I'm not sure Beelzebub and Lilith knew until the last few months. I didn't know, Braxton. Gabe told me they were trying, but Michael was supposed to be dealing with it. Griffin not Choosing would have made the Gates weaker, and it would be worse."

Braxton laughed bitterly. "They let her die as a stopgap."

Alaria couldn't argue. "Kinda, yeah."

"I should say fuck it, and let them clean up their own mess."

"We probably all should. Gabriel fought with us—so did Michael. Gage nearly died. Your sister lost her husband. We owe it to ourselves to keep Greer's reality from becoming ours."

He looked around his apartment and stalked back to the fridge. "How long did you tell Gage it would take you to convince me?"

"Two hours. I bet him five hundred dollars I could get it done within that time. He thought it would take until tomorrow."

"That damn vampire has too much money anyway."

Alaria smiled. "Go grab a shower. I'll see what food there is in here to make for dinner."

Braxton barked a laugh as he slammed the fridge shut and headed for his bedroom. "There's nothing but spoiled milk and questionable eggs in here. We'll have to go out."

She looked around the mess again and swore under her breath before raising her voice so he could hear her from the bathroom. "How about I borrow some sweats and we scrub this place while we wait for delivery?"

Braxton's muffled voice floated back. "I don't have any clean."

"Out it is."

"How long has it been since you've seen daylight?"

Braxton thought about that as he and Alaria weaved through the crowd of people downtown on a Saturday evening. "I think I went grocery shopping sometime last week." He took her elbow to help her walk on a grate in her heels, absently tucking it into the crook of his arm as they walked. "How are you adjusting to everything? It's been what? Three months since you went to stay with Gage?"

Alaria nodded. "It's been hard. I won't lie about that. One of the problems with having a soul is that I get to feel guilty for everything I did. I can't even remember all of the things I have to feel guilty about. I thought it would crush me."

"Was Gage able to help?"

"Well, I'm standing here and not balled up in a corner crying—so yeah, he did a good job helping me work through it." She bumped a man passing them and threw an apology over her shoulder. "Anyway, we're still trying to figure out what I can do."

"What do you mean?"

"Not everything went away when I got a heartbeat. I can still teleport, though not very far, and I can access the dream plane, though I have no power there. It's like I kept the light version of all my powers. I'm as strong as Gage is, and I can still conjure my whip and dagger, though we suspect they don't carry as much of a punch as they used to. I feel pain a lot more, and I need sleep, which is new, but being able to taste food is amazing. I've gained ten pounds since I became human." She looked up at his now clean-shaven face. "How are you?"

"I was fine until Gabe told us about the backup plan. Well, not fine, but dealing. She's gone, and she isn't ever coming back, and that has been hard to deal with. I feel guilty because even after I married her, she was still coming second. I'm afraid that I never really knew who she was. I knew that she was Chosen, but I didn't know her favorite color or her favorite food."

Alaria's voice was small and unsure, two traits Braxton hadn't ever before associated with her. "Blue and spaghetti."

"You knew her better than I did." He averted his eyes from hers, as if he was afraid to let her see the moisture coating them. Alaria smiled gently.

"Probably."

"I think the worst thing is having all these feelings and knowing that they aren't all mine. I was used, and I knew it while it was happening, but getting to the Choosing was so damned important that I played along. I'm paying for it now."

"It'll get better. It'll fade. Grief doesn't last forever."

"Logically, I know that. But right now, it feels like I let her die for nothing."

"You didn't let her die. She would be dead no matter what." Alaria pulled him into a restaurant. "I'm in the mood for red meat."

For the first time all day, Braxton grinned and swept out his arm. "Ladies first." He held the door while she entered, frowning for a brief moment while he battled the grief back down. Alaria looked over her shoulder and he forced himself to smile again and followed her to the booth.

They had almost made it back to Braxton's apartment, their arms loaded down with bags of cleaning supplies and Braxton carrying a tub of laundry detergent when the hair on the back of Alaria's neck rose ominously. She cast a look at Braxton and knew from the set of his jaw that he had also realized they were being followed. His voice was a tense whisper when he spoke.

"Seven behind and three ahead." Braxton laid a hand on Alaria's back to guide her.

"Four demons, four vampires and two werewolves."

"We don't have the right weapons."

Alaria nodded. "I know. Fight or run?"

"I have one gun with two clips. That'll take care of the demons. Any chance you can conjure yourself a stake or a sword?"

"I can do a sword. That leaves the wolves."

"Chopping their heads off will work."

"If they don't rip me to pieces first. Any chance those bullets are silver?"

"Salt crusted. I've been concerned about demons, not dogs."

Alaria sighed bitterly. "There's the bright side. No Hellhounds." She grabbed his elbow and jerked him sideways into a dark alley. "We need to be as far away from people as we can."

The footfalls behind them picked up speed. "They're not trying to be sneaky anymore." Braxton glanced over his shoulder and saw them rushing toward him. "Time's up. We've got to fight."

Alaria nodded. "We need to stay close. This is gonna be touch and go."

"Go for the wolves first."

"On it."

With a loud crack, Alaria disappeared from the alley and reappeared thirty feet ahead, dressed in the red and black leather she'd favored as a Devil. In her hand was a gleaming sword with a razor's edge. Within seconds, the men standing in front of her transformed—their bones popped out of place and snapped as they reformed. Hair sprouted all over their bodies. Their teeth lengthened and sharpened into points, glistening with saliva.

They snarled viciously, their eyes glowing green in the moonlight. Their hair was long and wiry and their claws were thick and black. Saliva dripped from their canines and they flexed their paws menacingly. Alaria lifted her sword and held it in front of her body. She was ready for a battle.

They came at her fast and in unison. She ducked, swept her leg out and sent one skidding into the wall. Her blade flashed as she used the sword to block the assault from the wolf. Sparks flew as metal met claw. Gunshots rang out behind her, and she knew Braxton was picking off the demons.

The sword cut through flesh with a thwack, and a paw landed on the pavement, severed from the leg it had once been attached to. The wolf yelped and screamed. Blood sprayed the brick in a black gleaming mist. Alaria charged, her body twirling with the swipe of the sword. She lifted the weapon above her head to give her more leverage. She planted her heels securely and drove the blade downward, spearing it through the chest of the wolf flying at her.

The momentum of the wolf carried it over her, and she leaped back-ward, twisting in the air to land in a crouch, the body of the beast landing three feet away from her, the sword sticking out of it. Alaria wiped blood from her brow and sauntered over to the remains of the werewolf. With a glance at the other wolf, who was running at her at full speed, she gripped the handle and yanked.

One swipe was all it took to end a life. She slashed violently, and blood sprayed down on her head as one half of the werewolf landed on either side of her. She cast a surveying look around the alley and counted three other bodies from the demons Braxton had killed.

The vampires were circling. Vampires were ruthless, but mostly, they were smart. She knew they'd been waiting to see if the other creatures would kill them before they entered the fray. She twirled the sword cockily and grinned.

"Bring it on, boys."

The vampires burst into action as one cohesive bloc. They barreled toward her, fangs bared, their growls echoing between the buildings. She managed to catch one as it crashed into her, the blade slicing deeply into his thigh and glinting off the bone.

Two more caught her by the arms and lifted her off her feet. Her heart pounded in her chest, panic rising into her throat. It was a living thing, with claws and teeth as dangerous as any creature present in the alley. Her back slammed into the brick with a force that sloshed her brain against her skull.

One of the monsters pressed his body against hers. He had the gall to rub on her, jutting his horrendous erection into her belly. He leaned down and sniffed at her neck hungrily. Without warning, his tongue sprang from his head and licked her sweaty skin.

"I wonder what former Devil blood tastes like." His teeth scraped her skin. Blood pooled in the shallow puncture and one drop ran down her shoulder. He lapped at it like a kitten would milk and hummed when the taste exploded in his mouth. "Delicious."

Alaria jutted her chin up and spat in his face. "Go to hell."

"I'll take you with me."

His teeth sank into the soft flesh of her neck. Alaria could feel blood flowing out of her veins. A searing pain spread from the bite and radiated outward until her whole body was frozen from agony. She tried to struggle, but without her demonic strength, the best she could do was wiggle her legs. In a hand-to-hand fight, she could have easily taken him, but being pinned against the wall gave the vampire the advantage.

The vampire burst into dust, and the blade of her sword slashed dangerously close to Alaria's nose. Before either she, or the other three vampires, could make sense of what had happened, Braxton chopped off the head of the second. The other two had the good sense to run. Braxton debated briefly on whether or not he should pursue them before hefting Alaria to her feet and supporting her weight against his side.

"We need to get you cleaned up."

Alaria pressed her hand to the wound in her neck. "We can't go back to your apartment."

"The airport's probably out, too. We need to get out of the city." He glanced around at the debris of the bags they had carried. He chuckled. "The laundry detergent survived."

Alaria laughed weakly. "We're gonna need it." She sagged against him. "I need a drink."

Braxton perked up and hauled her toward a car parked on the street. "I think I can manage that."

Chapter Eleven

THE HOTEL WAS dingy and small, but there would hopefully be two beds and running water. Braxton had swapped out cars twice in the last six hours as they worked their way south. Finally, he'd darted off the highway and into the parking lot of a motel that looked like the rooms rented by the hour.

Alaria still held a wad of cloth to the bite on her neck. It had long ago been soaked through with blood, and her skin was pale and clammy. Once Braxton had the room key in his hand, he opened her door and lugged her out of the car. He wrapped his arm around her waist and pulled hers around his shoulders.

She leaned heavily against him, barely able to support her own weight. He fumbled to get the key in the lock, missing twice before jamming it in the slot and waiting impatiently until the light flashed green and the door swung open. He flipped the light switch and shook his head when one bare light bulb in the ceiling was all that came on. He glanced into the bathroom as he dragged Alaria toward the bed and saw that both the sink and tub were red with rust. Maybe hoping for running water was being too optimistic.

"I'm going to call Gage and figure out what the hell I need to do to fix this damn bite." He laid her on the bed and dug his phone from his pocket. Before he could start dialing, closed her eyes.

"Don't let me die. That's what you do. People survive vampire bites all the time, Brax. I'm just weak from losing blood. If I die, I'll turn."

Braxton waved her words aside and focused on the phone pressed to his ear. Gage picked up on the third ring. "Well, look who's joining the land of the living. How the hell are ya, Brax?"

"We were attacked. Alaria's been bitten by a vampire."

Gage's voice was immediately serious. "Is she still alive?"

"Yeah, she's still kickin'." Braxton looked at her, sprawled on the bed with a wadded up bloody rag pressed to her neck. "Bitching at me as always."

"You'll need to clean the bite and boil out any residual venom. If it stays in the wound, it'll continue to make the infection worse. There's nothing you can do about what's already in her blood stream. She'll need a couple days to heal, but she should be fine. Her immune system will fight it off. Keep her warm and make sure she eats a lot. She'll need the energy. Vampire bites aren't fatal, Brax. You know that."

"Most people don't survive them. I've killed vamps, but I don't normally treat the victims."

"Most people don't survive because young vampires can't stop eating once they get their fangs in someone." Gage's voice was dry and humorless. "If she's breathing and has blood left in her body, she'll be just fine. Where are you?"

"Somewhere in Virginia. We've been driving for a few hours."

"I'll send my plane wherever you want it so that you can get back. I can have a car wherever you need it to pick you up."

Braxton glanced at Alaria and then around the room. "It'll be sometime tomorrow. I'm going to get her cleaned up and get some food in her. After that, I'll look at a map and figure out where we could meet the plane. It'll need to be a local airport or some field somewhere. I'm not taking the risk of a major airport. Not until we know who's after us."

"My guess is Laelia. She knows the circle is coming together and she may have thought that you were still alone and an easy target. Take you out and the rest of us can't do what we're supposed to do."

Braxton nodded out of habit, then shook his head when he realized he was only on the phone. "Okay, well, we'll be careful, then." He started to hang up, staring at the phone for several seconds before changing his mind and pressing it to his ear again. "Umm, Alaria said something about one of the people from the future being Griffin's granddaughter?"

Gage sighed. "Yeah. Her name's Greer Dawson. You'll like her."

Braxton closed his eyes against a flood of pain. "Does she look like her?"

Gage's voice conveyed sympathy but not even a trace of pity. "A little. The coloring is similar and the eyes are close, but she's definitely her own person. She's a soldier."

Braxton shook his head to clear it. "Okay, I'm gonna go. We'll be back in Ireland soon."

"Be careful. If Laelia's after you, you're not safe. Keep your guard up. Call if you need transport."

The men hung up at the same time; neither felt the need for pleasantries and goodbyes. Braxton turned his attention to the woman on the bed. "I need to go stock up on supplies. I saw a supermarket an exit back. Are you okay here?"

"I'll be fine. I'm just going to lay here." Alaria peeled open her eyes and offered him a smile. "Bring back food, if you would. Burgers and fries, maybe some soda."

"I'll grab you some clothes, too." He paused at the door. "I have to ask. How did you magically switch to your old getup?" He gestured to the skin tight black leather pants and the red bustier. "I thought that went away when you turned human."

"I thought the same thing. I don't know how it works. I'm not sure Gabe even knows how it works. All I can tell you is that when I conjure a weapon, I look like this. I go back to my original Devil form. I can peel them off, burn them, cut them to ribbons, whatever, and the next time I make a sword, I'll be back in them." She leaned further into the pillows. "I'm some freak-of-nature human/Devil hybrid, I swear to Satan."

Braxton chuckled. "Better than all Devil."

"Bullshit. I get the worst of being a human. PMS and bloating and sore boobs, and then I still have to wear this getup and battle vampires like I'm Buffy!"

Braxton snorted. "Okay, Buffy, stay here and try not to fight any more creatures until I get back."

It took him forty minutes to buy clothes for them both and the supplies to clean out Alaria's neck and to get a bag of greasy burgers from a diner. He knew they had to restock on weapons and ammunition. He had only six bullets left, and the one sword was all Alaria had.

When he opened the door to the motel room, he found Alaria wrapped in a towel and standing in the bathroom with her hair tied up in a knot and blood crusted on her neck and shoulder. She glanced back at him when he came in.

"I couldn't take it anymore. The smell of the blood was making me sick to my stomach."

Braxton dropped the bags onto the bed. "Can you wash it off or do you need help?"

Alaria craned her neck to look at the wound. "I can handle this part of it." She grabbed a washcloth and held it under the trickle of water coming from the faucet. "We need to find a gun store and a church. We need salt, herbs, Holy Water, everything."

"I know. It's four in the morning, so we're gonna have to wait a few hours. Once you've had some sleep, I'll try to figure out where we can meet Gage's plane."

"We're sitting ducks right now, Brax. If they find us between now and then, we're dead."

"There's nothing to be done about it right this second. I'll stay up to watch while you log a few hours, and then we'll switch."

"Did you bring salt?"

"Yeah. Salt, lavender, and some herbs they had in the grocery store."

"Enough for protection bundles?"

"Rudimentary ones, but they'll do the job. Rosemary, sage, lavender, that sort of thing."

"It'll work well enough." She rinsed the cloth and dabbed at her neck some more. "Make them up, and we'll both get some sleep. Vampires can't come in without an invitation, we'll hear wolves a mile away, and the hounds can't get through the salt and herbs."

Braxton watched her clean her neck with halfhearted interest. The wound was jagged and deep and likely should have been sutured shut. "That's gonna leave a gnarly scar."

"Two inches over and he'd have ripped out my throat." She dropped the cloth into the sink and padded out into the main part of the room. "How do you want me?"

Braxton blinked rapidly. His brain struggled to make sense of the words. His pants became suddenly uncomfortable as he waded through very explicit images and back into reality. "What?"

Alaria chuckled. "Get your mind out of the gutter. Gage said you need to boil out the infection. Do I need to lay down, stand in the bathroom, what?"

"Bathroom. We don't want to get the beds wet with the hydrogen peroxide."

He followed her back into the bathroom, a brown bottle in one hand and a first aid kit in the other. The first splash of peroxide was cold and burned as it flooded the wound on her neck. Bubbles boiled up as it ate through any beginnings of infection. Yellow pus drained out of the bite. Amazed at how quickly a vampire bite became infected, Braxton wiped the mess away with a towel before pouring more peroxide on the wound.

Once it stopped bubbling, he unscrewed the cap on a bottle of rubbing alcohol and poured a generous amount over the flesh. Alaria bit back a scream and grabbed the sink with both hands. The porcelain cracked and shattered under the force of her grip. They both jumped back from the shards. Braxton's eyes were wide and his eyebrows nearly met his hairline.

"How the hell did you do that?"

Alaria looked up at him with pain still evident across her face. "I told you. I don't think I'm totally human."

He looked at the broken sink and back to her face. "That's a concern for another day." He opened the first aid kit and pulled out a roll of gauze. "Let's get that thing covered up."

He coated the entire side of her neck with antibiotic ointment before covering it with gauze and tape. That done, he tossed her the sweatpants and tank top he'd bought and waited on his bed until she was changed before ducking into the bathroom to change into clean sweats and a t-shirt. By the time he came out of the bathroom, she had torn into the bag of food and was chewing a huge bite of cheeseburger.

"This is awesome."

Braxton flopped on the second bed and unwrapped his own sandwich. "Good."

Alaria chewed thoughtfully for several seconds before speaking again. "I think it's good."

He looked at her blankly. "What?"

"That you got a hard-on earlier." She laughed at his shocked look. "Bear with me here. I wasn't propositioning you. I just mean that if you were really as tied up on Griffin as you think you are, you wouldn't have thought I meant sex when I asked that question." She took another bite, chewed, and swallowed. "I know you think you loved her, and I believe in some way that you did, but I also think that all your feelings are being magnified by whatever it is Gabe did to make you fall for her. I really believe that you're not grieving for her as much as you're depressed that, for all intents and purposes, everything we went through was for nothing at all."

Braxton sighed. "I don't know why I am still surprised by anything that comes out of your mouth. When they turned you into a human, they didn't install a filter between your brain and your mouth." He leaned back until he was laying down, his sandwich all but forgotten. "I miss her. I feel guilty about her dying and guilty that I didn't know her better. I loved her, and I grieve that loss, but I can handle that. It's the guilt that makes it hard."

"Regardless, if you can think about sex with someone else, even someone as shockingly inappropriate as me, it means you're starting to move on."

"I'm not thinking about sex with you." He closed his eyes in a meager defense to the conversation. "I do not want to talk about this."

"Okay." She rubbed at the bandage. "This thing itches. Did you put anything on it that would make it itch?"

Concerned, Braxton sat up and shook his head. "No." He stood up and crossed to the side of her bed. "Let me see."

Gently, he peeled off the bandage. Beneath the gauze, her skin was covered by a white and pink scar, but any trace of the injury was gone. He ran his fingers over the new skin, his brows knit together in confusion.

"What is it?"

"It's gone. The bite. You have a scar, but the bite is healed up."

Alaria jumped from the bed and dashed into the bathroom. She danced over the shards of porcelain they hadn't bothered to clean up and turned her head to look at her neck. "What the hell?"

"I don't know how this is possible without a Healer."

Alaria turned, her eyes full of trepidation. Her hand was still pressed to the side of her neck. She moved forward until their toes were almost touching. She looked up and met his gaze. "What am I?"

Braxton met her eyes in the mirror, their faces showing identical expressions of fear and trepidation. He took two breaths to calm his nerves, then lifted his hand to press three fingers against her throat. Her heartbeat was strong and steady, pounding reassuringly against his hand. He left them there several seconds too long before dropping his arm.

"You have a heartbeat. I've seen you bleed. You eat, you sleep, you feel emotions. As far as we know, anything that can kill me would kill you, too. Far as I can tell, you're a real girl, Pinocchio."

Alaria stared at him blankly. "What the hell is Pinocchio?"

Braxton laughed and the tension in the room shattered. "Old cartoon." He gripped her hips and lifted her over the shattered sink easily. "Everything will look brighter in the morning. Let's get some sleep and reassess then. For what it's worth, I think it's really likely that God, or Gabe, or whomever actually made you human again, knew what was happening and let you keep some of your abilities to help out." He plodded back into the bedroom and tossed himself onto the mattress. "We both need to get some sleep."

Alaria nodded, her worries not completely abated. She slipped between the sheets in her bed and stared at the ceiling blankly. "Brax?"

He turned his head to look at her. "Yeah?"

"I miss her, too."

He offered a small smile and then became very interested in a crack in the ceiling. "I know you do."

Chapter Twelve

August 16th, 2030 - Ireland

"Jab. Cross. Hook. Uppercut." Gage called out punches as Greer and Damon sparred. Both were drenched in sweat and breathing heavily. Greer's hips rotated as she swung her whole body into the movements in order to pack more force into each punch. Damon blocked them with mirroring actions.

He lashed out with his leg, trying to catch her off-guard, and she jumped over the appendage before landing nimbly on her feet. She swung in an arch, and her boot made contact with the side of his head a split second before he grabbed her ankle in both hands and twisted. He used her momentum against her and spun her whole body, propelling her face down into the thick rubber mat below.

Before she could move, his knee was in her back, and he twisted her arms behind her body painfully, pinning her down under his weight. She pounded her forehead into the mat out of frustration.

"Give."

The pressure on her spine immediately went away. She rolled over and held out a hand to let Damon pull her to her feet. Gage tossed them each a bottle of water and a towel. Greer wiped her forehead with the back of one hand and braced her elbows on her knees.

Gage patted her head gently. "You're doing great. You've got a lot of muscle tone and strength to get back. How is your thigh holding up?"

"It's fine. It's my fucking shoulder that's the problem." She rotated her arm and the cartilage ground. "It pops every time I lift it over my head."

Damon toweled himself off and bent to stretch his hamstrings. "You need more strength training. If you can strengthen the muscles around the joint, it'll help shore it up."

"I don't have time to lift a lot of weights. I need to build endurance and range of motion to get back."

Gage cleared his throat. "You're doing great, Greer. Keep doing what you're doing. It's not going to be completely better overnight. This is the first day you've hit the mat. It's a really awesome first effort."

Greer drained her water and tossed the bottle into the trashcan. "We have no idea how long we have before we're going to have to fight. Alaria was attacked yesterday, for God's sake. We need to be ready."

Damon reached out and pushed a strand of her hair behind her ear. "We'll be ready. Pushing yourself to the breaking point isn't doing anyone any good."

Greer swatted at his hand and yanked at the towel around her neck in frustration. "I don't need the two of you telling me what to do!" She glared at them both. "Go back to hating each other or something."

She stormed back into the house, her gait angry and her shoulders rigid. Gage whistled softly, his eyebrows lifted in an expression of wonder. "She's a firecracker, that one."

Damon laughed. "You have no idea."

"I don't envy you, son. I like my women a little bit more accommodating."

"So do I."

Gage slapped Damon's shoulder in a gesture of support. "Good luck. I bet she's a hell of a handful."

Damon shook his head. "Hold up. Greer and I are friends. We're not like that."

The vampire shook his head and started into the house. "Keep tellin' yourself that."

Damon rolled his eyes and followed. "It is possible to be friends with a woman, y'know."

Gage snorted. "No, it's not." He chuckled. "I'm fourteen hundred years old. I have never seen it actually work where a man and a woman can be friends and no one gets their panties in a twist." He held open the door to the house for Damon and then followed him inside. "Besides, you and the feisty one are closer to combusting than any 'friends' I've ever seen." Gage made air quotes with his fingers, and Damon could barely control the bubble of laughter that rose in his chest.

The laughter slid back down his throat when they turned the corner into the living room and found Greer pinned to the wall. The man holding her by the throat turned around and grinned at Gage.

"Hello, Gage. Nice to see you again."

Gage surveyed the situation, his entire demeanor oozing boredom. "Ariander. I see they let you out again. Miranda will be quite disappointed."

"That Warrior bitch couldn't hold me for long. As soon as Beelzebub found out I had useful information, he let me out. When I found out about what's going on and how that damned Angel is interfering again, I knew that I had to act. The way I hear it, if I kill one of you six, you won't be strong enough to close the Gates. I also hear that there's a spot open to the left of Lucifer. Killing the circle might just earn me that throne."

Gage snorted with laughter. "You really think so? You're a demon. You were human. You're no better to Lucifer than I am. He'll never let you into the throne room."

Ariander's grip on Greer's throat tightened, and the Healer took on a blue tint. Still, Gage didn't look panicked. Damon tensed behind him, his muscles coiled like those of a caged animal, ready to attack.

"If you kill her," Gage said nonchalantly as he took three steps sideways, "I'll bring her back as a vampire."

Damon's head whipped to the side. "She's not going to die!"

Gage chuckled. "I'd think not, but on the off chance she does, it's not going to be the end of things. I'll bring her back." Out of the sight of either the demon or the Hunter, Gage snagged the handle of a dagger on one of the shelves and eased it into the palm of his hand. "What's your endgame, Ariander? You want to let every single demon in Hell walk the Earth? What happens in fifty years when there are no humans left?"

Ariander brought Greer around to his front. He wrapped his forearm around her throat and the other around her waist. "I'll tear her throat out with my teeth. There won't be anything left to turn."

Gage lifted one eyebrow. "How long do you think you'll last between when you sink your teeth into her flesh and I rip your head off your shoulders? I move as fast as you do. I'd be willing to wager you don't even get a good bite before you're back in the Lake." He tapped his finger to his chin inquisitively. "I doubt they'll be so keen to let you out this time."

Ariander smiled dangerously. "Your mistake, vampire, is in thinking I came alone. Your house is surrounded. I brought a half dozen werewolves and twice that many vampires with me."

"I know." Gage slid a glance to Damon and almost imperceptibly shifted his head to the right. Damon looked and saw Alaria and a man he'd never before met in the kitchen. Both were armed. "I'm not concerned about a pack of hairy dogs. You should know better than to bring vampires after me. I'm older than they are. Stronger, too. Do you remember who my sire is?"

"How could I forget? Laelia, the cold-as-ice bitch that is the key to this whole damned thing. Here's the thing. Beelzebub found Laelia two months ago. She's been making us more fodder for the cannons. All those vamps out there have the same sire you do. Which means, in case you haven't caught up, they're just as strong as you."

Gage looked unconcerned. "Two months isn't enough time to be in control of the bloodlust enough to be as strong as I am." He shrugged. "It's of no concern. I'm getting really tired of this." He looked at Damon. "Aren't you a little sick of Ariander?"

"I could do without him."

Greer looked at Damon intensely and without a word, reached out and pushed into his mind. "*Get ready. I can flip him. Is Gage ready with that knife?*"

Damon looked at Gage and saw the knife gripped tightly in his fist. "*Yeah. He's ready. Be careful. This guy is dangerous.*"

"*He's just a demon. We've got bigger problems than one demon.*"

Greer shifted slightly and lifted her foot. She slammed it down into Ariander's instep and grabbed the arm around her neck with both of her hands. She dug her nails into his flesh and bent, rolling to the ground and flipping him over her head. The hand he had on her hip fisted, and she felt her flesh tear as they landed.

She elbowed him in the nose and sank her teeth into his arm to free herself. She'd barely rolled to her feet before Gage pounced. He leaped across the room in one motion and drove the knife into Ariander's chest. He screamed and clawed at the knife, trying to wrench it from his chest. His eyes flashed from black to red to white. With a roar, the silver and black smoke poured from his mouth and blasted a hole in the roof as it dissipated.

Greer rubbed her throat. "What was on that knife?"

"It's been salt-crusted and forged in Holy Water. It won't anchor him to the pit the same way an exorcism will, but it forces him out and he has to find a new body, which can take a while. In battle, that's about the best you can hope for." Gage went to the window and looked out. "We need to get ready. Follow me."

He led them through the first floor and into his office, striding to the armoire and opening the doors to reveal a menagerie of weapons. A short sword and a pistol hung next to one another on the shelf. Gage withdrew both, tucking them in his waistband. Slowly, he turned and surveyed the other four.

"Who's the best shot?"

Greer's hand shot up. "I was the sniper for our squad."

Gage plucked down a high-powered rifle and handed her three separate clips. "Blue is for demons. They're salt-crusted and forged in Holy Water. Red is for vampires. They're wooden bullets. Hit the heart. Green is for werewolves. Those are silver rounds. There's a ladder up to the roof on the third floor. Get up there."

Greer grabbed the ammunition and ran from the room. Damon noticed drops of blood on the floor but didn't have an opportunity to dwell on them before Gage shoved a gun and sword into his hands. Alaria had already conjured herself a whip and dagger, and the other man was loading a clip into his gun. He glanced at Damon before they headed through the door.

"I'm Braxton, by the way."

Damon chuckled. "Damon. Nice to meet you." He twirled the sword. "Ready to kick some ass?"

Braxton lifted his gun. "Let's go."

Damon strode through the door with purpose. The yard was lit with Gage's outside lights, and there was a line of vampires standing fifty yards from the house. He heard the footfalls of the wolves circling them, just out of sight. Fifteen seconds before the vampires reached them, Greer's first shot cracked through the night and a vampire burst into dust.

That one shot signaled the start of the battle. Damon swung his sword and sliced through the throng of vampires charging him. A dozen was a horrible underestimation of the number of creatures in Gage's back yard.

Within seconds, he was surrounded. His blade slashed through the mob. He felt a back slam against his own and looked back to see Alaria pressed against him. She viciously wielded her weapons, and together, they carved their way through the vampires. Alaria reached out and grabbed his arm, using his leverage to swing her body up and around so that she could drive her dagger into the heart of the first werewolf that came at them. Before the second reached Gage, another shot rang out and it dropped.

Slowly, they drove the masses back. Gage efficiently worked his way through the vampires, using his hands and fangs in equal shares. Blood ran down his face, and he forcefully ripped a vampire's head off his shoulders, tossing it carelessly aside before it dissolved.

There was a flash of white light as Gabriel appeared. He brandished a sword, and his wings were spread out behind him. He struck out with the sword, lightning shooting from its tip and destroying anything it touched. Within a matter of seconds, the yard was covered in smoking remains. Gabriel sheathed his sword and glanced around to make sure everyone was present"There has been more movement than anticipated from your enemies."

Alaria snorted. "Way to state the obvious. What do we do about it?" She dropped her whip and dagger and let them both disappear.

"Laelia is still escaping detection." Gabriel sighed deeply. "Each day more demons spill from Hell upon the Earth. It will come to the notice of humans within the next month. Michael is laying down the lives of a legion of Angels trying to stem the flow. The Host of Heaven cannot take much more defeat before we are too weak."

Gage whistled. "We need to find that bitch and rip her head off. Where is the opening to Hell?"

"It is in the middle of some place you refer to as Colorado. There is a cave that extends deep within the Earth. Within the cave is a Gate. It is heavily guarded by demons. The demons are under the control of Lilith, Azazel and Abalam."

Alaria's eyes widened slightly. "Abalam is one nasty son of a bitch. He works with Abaddon, who was the Gate keeper. Abaddon was in charge of bringing souls to Abalam when they came through. Abaddon and Abalam were two of the Archangels. Abalam worked under Michael as one of the warrior Angels. Since the Fall, He's never left Hell." She met Gabriel's gaze. "Are you telling me he's out?"

Gabriel nodded. "He's out."

Damon cleared his throat. "Who is Abalam?"

Alaria answered. "He's a Devil that was in charge of torturing souls that came in to Hell. He never left Hell, just played with souls and was happy. He knows more ways to torture you that you can ever imagine. He's not like Lilith and Azazel in strength, but I wouldn't recommend underestimating him. Demons and Devils feed on pain. The more pain surrounding us, the stronger they are."

Gabriel took over the explanation. "When souls are tortured long enough, they eventually become demons. It takes thousands of years. He's been producing demons since the Fall. On Earth, we're afraid that he is torturing those who may know where you five are."

Braxton's eyes widened. "My parents and Sam."

Gabriel held up a hand. "Don't worry about your family. Your parents, Samantha, and your niece have been placed under the protection of Angels. They are safe and will remain protected until this is over."

"Where are they?"

"I think it's best if all you know is that they are safe and being cared for. That way you can't give up information that they might want about them."

Braxton started to object before nodding in resignation. "Just make sure they're safe."

"I will personally check on them daily." Gabriel walked with them back toward the house. He nodded to Greer, who had made her way down from the roof. "Your marksmanship skills are impressive."

Greer grinned. "Thanks. I've had tons of practice." She looked at Damon, who was covered in blood and dust. "You need a shower."

"I'm going. Yell if anything else happens."

Gage gathered weapons from everyone. "I'm going to put these away and begin some more research into Laelia and her whereabouts. Knowing where the Gate is located is important, but we have to have her blood to stop the purge."

Alaria glanced at Gabriel, her stomach knotting from nerves. Her emotions were much more potent since she'd been made human, and he stole her breath every time he entered the room. "Greer, could you give us a minute?"

Greer rubbed her side absentmindedly. "Yeah, I'm gonna go wash up, too. I'm nasty from sparring and then that damn demon. Night."

Alaria murmured a response as Greer ascended the stairs before turning to face Gabriel. "It's been a while since you've dropped in."

Gabriel dropped heavily onto the couch. "The battle is fierce, Alaria. The loss of life is astounding. Humans, Angels, demons. Everyone is losing many. I fear no one will survive this."

"We're doing all we can."

"I know. You're still only five. I haven't been given the okay to bring the witch forward. I'm keeping watch over her as well. She's in danger as long as she's alone. If Garrick was to learn her identity, he would send someone to kill her before she comes forward. Even as powerful as she is, there is a lot that must happen before she will have the strength to defeat that damned Warlock."

Alaria perched next to him on the cushion. "We'll stop it. There isn't any other choice. I won't stand for being human just to watch the world end before I have a chance to live in it."

Gabriel reached out and tucked a strand of her hair behind her ear, his fingers lingering just a moment longer than necessary. "I know you'll stop this bloodshed. I have faith in you." He leaned back into the couch and smiled when she curled up next to him, drawing her legs underneath her and tucking her head against his shoulder. "You know this can't continue, Alaria."

She looked up at him. "Have you been punished?"

"We both know it's only a matter of time. He will find out."

"I know. What is He going to do to you?"

Gabriel laughed. "I haven't the slightest idea. I don't believe any Angel has ever fallen as far as I."

"Michael banged Lilith."

"While they were both Angels."

Alaria snorted. "That's what you think." She held one of his hands in both of hers. "I know this won't last. That it can't. I want to be human, and you want to be an Angel. That's a void no one could cross. I don't know how I feel, or how you feel, or what this even is." She grinned. "The sex was hot."

"I've nothing to compare it to."

She laughed softly. "Trust me, it was hot."

"It should not happen again. It was the heat of battle and the fear for our lives, and it led to heightened emotions that we acted upon irresponsibly. There is no future in this, Alaria."

Alaria tipped her head back and studied the ceiling. "Do we have a future at all? I know it's the same argument, but what are the odds we all survive this?"

"Slim."

"If we're going to die anyway, what's the harm in enjoying each other while we can?"

"Because you're human now, and as such, your emotions are more volatile and more tangible than they were while you were either a Devil or an Angel. This is going to feel more real to you. The odds of you becoming more attached than is prudent are high. I'm not sure we could avoid some emotional entanglement that would only jeopardize us both."

"I'm not completely human."

Gabe didn't even bother to argue. "It could not be done. You will have a human lifespan, but you could not be separated from some of your abilities."

Alaria smiled when she noticed him playing with the ends of her hair. "I know you, Gabe. If you were ending things with me, you'd be long gone by now. You don't want to stop any more than I do."

"I've been purposely avoiding you."

"I know. You have to. You're here now, though. Do you have anywhere else to be?"

"Not until your morning when I check in on Braxton's family."

"Will you stay with me?"

"I told you that what happened between us the night before the Choosing should not happen again. Allowing ourselves to continue down this path will mean nothing but pain."

"I know that. We're going to break each other's hearts." She rose to her knees and framed his face with her hands. "This isn't a fairy tale. We aren't magically going to end up together at the end of the story. All we have is tonight." She leaned forward and caught his bottom lip between her teeth, sucking it into her mouth before kissing him hard. "I want you, Gabe. For tonight, for as long as we have. I don't have any illusions about riding off into the sunset and living happily ever after. Happily ever after doesn't exist."

"We can avoid a good measure of the pain by not continuing to engage in the activities in which we engaged before."

"It's called sex." She pressed her chest against his and lowered her mouth to his ear. "If God didn't want you to have sex, why on Earth did He give you a penis?"

Taken aback, Gabriel coughed. "I don't presume to have insight into the mind of God. Were I to wager a guess, I assume so that we look familiar to humans in order to minimize their fear of us."

"Or maybe it's so you could experience human behaviors in order to understand them better." She slid off his lap and held out a hand. "Both times you said this shouldn't happen again. Not once did you say it wouldn't."

Gabriel looked at the offered hand and wavered, struggling mightily between what he should do and what he wanted to do. He knew continuing any relationship with the former Devil was a bad idea but couldn't stop the onslaught of the memories of her wrapped around him, hot and wet. Neither could he stop the reaction his body had to the visions.

"This is a bad idea."

Alaria smiled. "I know. Let's do it anyway." She brought both her hands to the bodice of the leather bustier she hadn't yet changed out of. Slowly, she pulled the laces and began loosening them. She slid it down her body, revealing her tanned flesh one inch at a time. "What we did last time is a small little taste of what sex can be." She dropped the garment onto his lap. "It can be hot, slow, sweet, hard, or whatever you want it to be. I can ride you like a pony or you can take me against the wall." She bent over and grabbed both of his hands to pull him to his feet. "We both know if you were leaving, you'd be gone already. Put a lid on the fight you've got going on with yourself and take me to bed."

Gabriel let her guide him down the hall, one hand in hers, the other still holding her bustier. She led him down the stairs to the room she kept in the basement, adjacent to the gym. She turned on the lamp with a flick of her wrist and closed the door, turning the lock. The small snick as the deadbolt slid into place sounded as loud as a gunshot in the silence of the room.

"I don't know what to do."

Alaria chuckled. "Whatever feels good." She slid his suit jacket off his shoulders. "You can start by taking your clothes off." She shimmied out of her leather pants and kicked off the heels. "Seriously, get naked."

Gabriel's movements were efficient. He unbuttoned his shirt, folded it, and laid it on her dresser before doing the same with his pants. He folded his socks and laid them inside his shoes before placing his shoes neatly on top of the pants. Naked, his engorged penis irrefutable proof of his desire, he faced Alaria.

"Now what?"

Alaria grabbed his hand and pushed him onto the bed. "Gabe, just go with it. If it feels good, it's fine. There isn't some step-by-step manual. You figured out what to do the last time."

Gabriel flushed deep red. "It was the heat of the moment."

She smiled wickedly. "This moment is about to get pretty fucking heated."

Before he could respond, she dropped to her knees and licked him from base to tip. He groaned loudly, and his hands tangled in her hair of their own volition. She took him in her mouth, surrounding him with wetness and heat and using her teeth to lightly scrape the sensitive skin, and sucked strongly, her tongue swirling around the sensitive head. She hummed when his hips lurched upward and wrapped her hand around the base, sliding it up and down while sucking.

Gabriel's eyes closed tightly, and he gripped her hair tighter. She slid her mouth up and down, her hot tongue running over and around him. Moments before he would have exploded from orgasm, she released him with a smacking sound and stood. She stepped between his legs and straddled him, bringing their chests together.

"Did that feel good?"

Gabriel was still breathing heavily. "I've never felt anything like it." He stroked her face with the back of his hand. "Is it possible for you to feel the way you just made me feel?"

Alaria hummed. "I enjoy this just as much as you."

"I want to make you feel that. Tell me how."

Alaria discovered then that there was nothing sexier than a man demanding to know what she liked. She slid back several inches to separate their bodies some. "There are a couple different ways."

"Tell me."

She slipped from his lap to join him on the mattress. Once they were lying side by side, she took his hand in hers and placed it on her breast. "Touch me here."

He gently massaged the globe of flesh, his skin slightly rough against her sensitive nipple. When he scraped his nail over the point, she sucked in a shallow breath and a moan escaped her. He rubbed the nipple with the pad of his thumb, his other hand emulating the motion on her other breast.

"May I taste your skin as you did mine?"

It took several heartbeats for his question to penetrate the fog. When it did, a knot of desire formed deep within her from the thought of his mouth on her. When she spoke, her voice was a whisper. "Please."

"Please, what?"

"Use your mouth."

Gabriel leaned down and touched the tip of his tongue to her dusky nipple. A shot of pleasure bolted through her, and she gasped. He glanced up at her. "Do you not like it?"

Alaria shook her head. "No, I like it. I like it a lot."

Encouraged by her response, he licked her flesh again before drawing it into his mouth to suck. His tongue was warm and soft against the beaded point. When her hands fisted in his hair, he sucked harder and found himself chuckling when she lifted her back and pressed herself into his mouth.

His voice was deep and low when he lifted his head to speak. "Where else do you like being touched?"

Alaria grabbed his hand and directed it between her legs. "There."

Gabriel used his thumb to rub where she was wet. Her knees bent, and her legs fell open, leaving her exposed to his touch. Hesitantly, he allowed one long, elegant finger to slip inside her. "Like this?"

She groaned. "Exactly like that."

Imitating the back and forth movement that she had used on him, he slid the digit against her wet skin. When he found her clit with his thumb, he pressed against it, then began rubbing when her hips bucked against his hand.

He studied her reactions and adjusted his ministrations to meet her needs. Her fingers wrapped around his wrist, and her other hand fisted in the sheet. Her head thrashed on the pillow, and her entire body became flushed with color and sweat.

"Alaria?"

Her eyes snapped open, and she stared up at him. "What?"

He looked sheepish and curious, all at the same time. "Would it be okay if I tasted you as you did me?"

Her eyes rolled back in her head as she spoke. "Yes."

His breath was warm on her inner thighs. He pressed a kiss to each leg before he gently touched her with the tip of his tongue, his movements as hesitant as they had been when he had licked her nipple. She grabbed his hair and yanked, pressing his face against her. He answered the demand and licked her again, his tongue probing her body and his mouth moving against her.

It was more than she could take. The feel of his tongue and mouth, of his hands on her hips, every sensation was magnified from when she'd been a Devil. The pleasure was stronger, and the desire hotter. She felt her climax rising like a tidal wave and fiercely battled it back down. He paid attention to her movements, and when she began pushing his head, he immediately stopped and sat back.

"Did I cause you pain?"

Alaria was gasping for breath. "Oh my God, no." She grabbed his face and kissed him deeply, her tongue tangling with his. She wrenched herself back. "I want you inside of me, and I want you now." She rose to her knees and turned so that her back was against his chest. "You won't hurt me. I want you to take me hard and fast until we both want to scream." She pulled his arms around her. "I'm going to be on my hands and knees and you're going to fuck me."

She leaned forward and arched her hips back toward him. His hands slid down to her hips, and he kneaded her flesh with his fingers. Slowly, he probed her entrance, sliding into her inch by inch. By the time he was buried in her, she was nearly sobbing from want. Slowly, he stroked out and back in, and they both groaned. Gaining confidence that he wasn't hurting her, Gabriel thrust again, a bit harder. Her resulting pant made his stomach knot.

He drove into her, spearing her flesh with his own and pushing her closer to the edge of ecstasy with every thrust. When she begged for more, he gave it to her, his hips surging. He leaned over her and gripped the head-board, the change in angle pushing him deeper. Her muscles contracted around him, signaling to him that she was on the verge. Without any con-scious thought, acting solely on instinct, Gabriel slowed his thrusting and slid into her gently, reaching around her body to press against her where she needed friction the most. With a muffled curse and a ragged groan, she toppled into orgasm, her body clenching around him. He thrust twice more before his own climax ripped out of him, and he jerked her hips against his as he came.

It took three minutes before Alaria could find words to speak. She glanced over at Gabriel, who lay next to her on the bed, his chest still heav-ing as he tried to catch his breath. "Are you going to freak out on me this time?"

Gabriel couldn't help the laugh that forced its way from him. "No. This was a much more conscious act than before." He rolled onto his side to face her. "Did I give you pleasure?"

"You have no idea." She snuggled into his arms and pressed a kiss to his chest. "Will you stay?" She yawned and yanked the blanket over them with one hand.

"I've no need for sleep as you do."

"That's okay. Just pretend for a while. When you get horny again, just wake me up. I'll take you for a ride you'll never forget."

Gabriel ran his hand over her hair and settled into the pillows. "Sleep well."

Chapter Thirteen

Greer closed the door to her room and kicked off her boots. Her muscles ached from sparring with Damon, and her shoulders were knotted with tension left over from the attack. She bent to peel off her socks and dropped them carelessly into the hamper. She grabbed a t-shirt and yoga pants from her dresser and walked into the bathroom.

Damon was at the sink, a towel slung low on his hips. He wiped steam off the mirror and inspected a cut on his face from where a blade had nicked him. He glanced over his shoulder when she came in.

"Shower's all yours."

Not in a mood to be around him, Greer sighed. "You should put clothes on."

"Why?"

"Because I don't want to look at you half-naked."

Damon grinned and pulled the knot in the towel loose, letting it pool around his feet. "There. Now I'm totally naked. Better?"

Greer shook her head and fought a laugh. "You're goofy."

"And you're in a foul-ass mood. What's going on?"

She yanked her shirt over her head. "I'm not at fighting weight yet. Things are picking up, and a fucking war is coming. I need to be battle ready." She unbuckled her belt and dropped it to the floor. "You're not helping me get there."

Damon snorted. "No. I'm not helping you hurt yourself by pushing too hard. It takes as long as it takes."

"The world is about to end! We are the only people that can stop it, and I'm dragging us down! Every day that I'm not up to par is another day that demons are wriggling out through that damn Gate and getting loose."

Damon had focused on something else. He waved her words aside. "Why didn't you tell me you're hurt?"

She looked down and saw claw marks on her side, still red and oozing blood. "Ariander got his nails in me when I flipped him. It's fine." She brushed him aside when he reached for her and stepped to the side. "Leave it alone."

He grabbed her and lifted her onto the sink, bending to inspect the damage. "They're not too deep, but you're full of grime. It needs to be cleaned."

"I'm getting in the shower. I'll clean it." She batted his hands away when he tried to pull apart the edges of the wound to look down into it. "You're like a mother hen, always hovering over me. I'm fine."

Damon captured both of her hands in one of his and held them tightly. He opened the cabinet under the sink with the other hand and yanked out a first aid kit and a bottle of hydrogen peroxide. "Just hold still and let me clean the damn thing." He unscrewed the lid of the peroxide and poured a stream onto her stomach. It soaked into her fatigues and the wound bubbled with white foam. Her breath hissed out between her teeth, and her fingers bit into the sink.

"Damn you, Damon."

"It'll feel better in a minute." He leaned down and blew on the marks, his breath cool and soothing. "At least I used the peroxide and not the alcohol." He patted her thighs and stepped back. "Hop in the shower and I'll slather on some ointment once you're dry."

Greer was still muttering under her breath by the time she had shimmied out of her pants and underwear and unsnapped her bra to let it drop to the floor. She jerked the shower curtain shut with an annoyed flick of her wrist and turned on a stream of hot water. Damon retreated to his room to dress and then returned, clad in sweats and a wife-beater. He busied himself gathering her clothes from the floor and depositing them in the hamper, then grabbed a towel from the closet and slung it over the shower rod so that she would have it when she was done. Satisfied, he sat on the sink to wait.

Ten minutes later, when he heard the distinctive sound of her squeezing shampoo into her hand for the fourth time, he broke the silence. "Your hair isn't that dirty."

Her sigh was frustrated and louder than necessary. "I got blood in it from Ariander. It's the black goopy demon blood. It's fucking nasty."

"It doesn't take four tries to get it out. You're just trying to stay in there until I give up and go to bed."

"What's your point?" She stuck her head around the curtain. "We spend way too much time in the bathroom together." She held out a strand of her hair to let him see that it was still coated in demon blood. "Satisfied?" She leveled a glare at him. "You act like I'm twelve and trying to avoid a boy. Just go to bed, Damon. I'll put the goop on it when I get out. Now, please let me finish getting this blood out of my hair in peace."

Damon jumped off the sink and wrapped her in the shower curtain, trapping her arms in the plastic and letting only her head and shoulders stick out. "I don't know, babe. I think you look pretty damn good covered in guts."

Greer shoved at his shoulder with her own, not at all amused by his actions. "It's blood, not guts, and don't call me babe. Let me go, Damon."

He lowered his head and breathed in the scent of shampoo and body wash. "You smell good." He nuzzled her skin with his nose. "I wonder how you taste."

"Don't you dare—" Greer's words slipped back in her throat as he nipped her shoulder with his teeth, then soothed the bite with a lap of his tongue. Her knees almost collapsed, and she leaned against him heavily. "Oh, God."

Damon hummed. "I thought so." He slid his mouth up her shoulder to the gentle slope of her neck and the line of her jaw. Her eyes rolled back in her head and her lids drifted shut. "I seem to remember you tasting even better...right...here."

His mouth closed over hers, warm and firm. His tongue darted in and out of her mouth, keeping her wondering how he was going to go about kissing her. She tried to struggle, to push him away and yell at him. She wanted to call him all the names that flitted through her brain in the split second between when she'd realized his intentions and when his arms had closed around her.

Her arms somehow freed themselves from the shower curtain and snaked around him, sliding over the muscles and kneading his back as she gripped it with her fingers. Her mouth opened and moved against his. She pressed against him feverishly, the water still beating down against her back, soaking Damon's arms and creating steam that enveloped them and filled the room, making it hot and even harder to breathe.

It was wrong. She was mad at him. The timing was off and there were a million very good reasons she should not have been in the shower kissing Damon. Or kissing Damon anywhere, for that matter. But there she was, being plundered by him and enjoying every single second of the sensual assault.

He eased back from her with several light kisses, his eyes clouded with desire, and the evidence of it anchored against her belly. "Do you wanna come out or do you want me to come in?"

There was a world of meaning in the question and no room for saying no. Greer looked up into his face, into the eyes of the man she'd known most of her life, and damned them both. "Get in here."

Before he could move even one muscle, there was a brisk knock at the door and Braxton's voice came through the wood. "Damon, can you come out here a minute? I need to speak with you."

Damon swore and dropped his head to Greer's shoulder before calling back. "I'll be right there." He stepped back. "Do not put clothes on."

He strode into his room, stopped to adjust his pants, and opened the door. Braxton was leaning against the railing overlooking the first level. "Sorry to drop by after a night like tonight, but I need to talk to you about a couple of things. Do you mind if we go into the study?"

Damon shrugged. "Lead the way."

Braxton headed up the stairs to the third floor. "Thanks." He held open a door and waved Damon in ahead of him before flipping on the light and closing the door. "I heard Greer getting in the shower, so I'll let you repeat everything to her, but there're going to be a few things happening pretty quickly after tonight."

Interest piqued, Damon dropped into one of the chairs. "Like what?"

"Gage thinks it's best if we move, and after tonight, I'm inclined to agree. He has a smaller estate in Scotland which is better protected magically. As long as you're amenable, we'll be moving there tomorrow."

"That's fine." He studied Braxton's face. "That's not why you called me up here."

"No, it's not. Or not all of it, anyway. Alaria and I are leaving as soon as we're settled to do some reconnaissance on the Gate. We'll likely be gone a week or two. It'll take us a few days to travel and it's a hell of a hike to get to where we need to go. There's no way to access it by plane or car without drawing attention."

"No offense, but you just got here. I don't exactly need to get prepared for you leaving again."

"Gage is leaving to talk to some contacts he has that may be able to help us get a location on Laelia. We need to find out where she is as fast as we can so that we stand a chance of stopping this purge before it gets much worse. How much time does Greer need to get back into shape?"

"She'll be there by the time you get back. She's just recovering from injuries. She was hurt pretty bad when Gabriel brought us back." Damon held up a hand. "Why doesn't the Angel just drop you off where you need to go?"

"He won't do that. He's very hands off." Braxton looked at the door ruefully. "Well, he's hands off of everything except Alaria."

Damon's eyes widened. "Gabriel and Alaria?"

Braxton reached for a bottle of the whiskey Gage kept on the shelf. "Yeah. I made the mistake of going downstairs to cool off and saw them go into her room. I couldn't get out of there fast enough."

"How does that even work?"

"It won't, not long term, anyway. I'm not sure how they managed to end up there now, honestly. I didn't see it coming. They'll both end up hurt." He drained the glass and poured a second. "I guess they know what they're doing. Regardless, it's none of my business." He finished the second drink and stood. "Would you let Greer know to get ready in the morning? The faster we leave here the better off we'll be."

"Sure. No problem."

"Are you sure you're comfortable being left alone?"

"It's no big deal. We can handle ourselves." Damon followed Braxton out of the room and back down the stairs. "I'm gonna turn in if that's all you need."

Braxton nodded. "Get a good night's sleep. I'll see you both in the morning." He waited until Damon had disappeared into his room before heading down the hall to his own bed.

Damon closed the door and immediately went back into the bathroom. The shower was empty and the clothes Greer had placed on the counter were gone. He reached for the doorknob to open the door to her room and twisted. It was locked.

Sighing, he hit his head against the wall twice in frustration before retreating to his own bed, damning Braxton Winslow to a thousand deaths with every step.

Chapter Fourteen

August 17th, 2030 - Ireland

"ARE YOU SURE we should be leaving again? We just got here." Alaria folded jeans and stuffed them in a duffel bag, her back turned to Braxton.

"We need to get eyes on this Gate. Get an idea of how many demons are there, how many Devils, and what collateral damage we might be looking at if we charge it." Braxton leaned against her door frame, his hands in his front pockets and his ankles crossed. "We're the best bet for getting in and out. Gage is trying to get coordinates on Laelia and the other two are still trying to figure out how to do this."

"I'm not suggesting we send someone else. Only that we might want to think about leaving so soon after the last attack. One thing we know for sure is that we're better off together than we are splitting up. I don't want them to get killed because we're off trying to be heroes."

Braxton closed the door and crossed the room to face her. "Is this about not wanting to leave Greer and Damon, or is it about not wanting to leave the little love nest you have going with our resident Archangel?"

Alaria's hands stilled on the zipper to her bag. She sat down on the bed. "It's not what you think it is."

"What do I think it is?"

"We aren't together. We aren't a couple. There's no future in it. It's just—"

"Just what, Alaria?"

"Just for now." Her voice was little more than a whisper.

Braxton sat down next to her and took her hand in one of his. "I'm an expert in just for now. You know this is going to end badly."

She nodded. "Yeah, it is. I can't help it, Brax. We waited for so long, and it just combusted a few months ago."

"This has been going on for months?"

"Technically, but there's only been twice. The night before the battle, and last night, which is the one I assume you know about."

"You're going to get hurt."

"I know."

He squeezed her fingers. "Hey, it could be worse. He could be dying in a few months."

Alaria felt her heart constrict at Braxton's words. "We're not so different after all, are we?"

Braxton shook his head. "No, I don't think we are." He patted her knee. "You have a choice. I didn't. You can walk away from this and spare both of you a lot of heartache. Or you can jump in headfirst and hope it doesn't implode." He sighed deeply. "You dragged me out of my funk. I promise to do the same when this ends badly for you, and it will end badly."

"I want to take your advice, Brax. In a lot of ways, I feel like you must have felt. There was so much history and so many pent-up emotions that it had to ignite at some point. I'm going to enjoy it while I can."

"What happens if God finds out?"

"I don't know." Alaria stared at her hands. "Nothing good. Gabe would be severely punished. There's nothing He can do to me—I have free will. Gabe doesn't, and being with me would be a direct violation."

Braxton stood and opened the door. "It's something for you to think about. I'm not going to try to tell you what to do. It would be a waste of my breath and your time. Just be careful. We need your head in the game." He paused before disappearing around the corner. "If you need to talk, you can talk to me. We're in this together, no matter what."

Alaria smiled tightly and waited until his footsteps had retreated down the hall before she collapsed on the bed. For the first time since the day she'd joined Lucifer, she allowed herself to cry.

Greer set her glass down a little harder than necessary and gaped at Braxton. "What the hell do you mean you're gallivanting off into the middle of nowhere with Alaria to try and find the Gate without us?"

Braxton lifted his eyebrows in amusement and looked at Damon. "Is she always so dense?"

Damon reached over and ruffled Greer's hair. "Only when she hasn't had enough sleep. Or food. Or sex. So, yeah, pretty much all the time. Ow!" He rubbed his shin where Greer kicked him. "She packs a hell of a punch though."

"In all seriousness, we need to find out how much manpower is on that Gate. The five of us have had no time to work together. We need to get in quietly and get out quietly. We aren't going there to make a scene and get into a fight. The two of us would get killed if we did. We need to do some recon, come back here, and train for what we're facing."

Damon risked the wrath of Greer again. "Besides, you need a few more days to train before you're ready for any hand-to-hand." He winced when her boot collided with his shin for the second time in a five-minute span.

"I'm fine! How many times do I have to tell you that?"

Braxton cleared his throat. "It's my call, Greer. You aren't ready, and you stay here."

Her eyes flashed with anger and she slammed her fist on the table. "I don't know who you think you are, but it isn't my boss! I don't need some bossy, mentally unstable Warrior telling me how to do my job. You may have gotten away with it before, but it's not going to be that way this time." She rose to her feet and went toe to toe with the much larger man. "I am not some wilting flower that needs to be coddled and kept from danger. I am a soldier. I have been fighting to survive in a world filled with nightmares since I was thirteen years old. I have killed as many demons as you have, if not more. I do not need protecting!"

Instead of getting angry, Braxton's face split into a wide grin. "You're just like her."

Frustrated and pissed, Greer blinked rapidly. "What the hell are you talking about?"

"Griffin. You're just like her. The spunk and the feistiness." He laid a hand on her shoulder. "You're right. I'm not the boss. But I'm right, too. We aren't working as a team yet, and we're going to have to figure out how to do that before we can go into that cave. Alaria and I have worked together before, just like you and Damon have. The difference is that we're both healthy. Like it or not, you still have a few days of training before you're up to par."

Greer shrugged off his hand and stalked around the kitchen to place the island between them. "I don't care how much you think I look like your dead wife. I'm not her, and I don't need protecting. I'm the only one who will decide whether or not I'm fine."

Braxton's expression softened. "Let's look at this another way. Where did you live?"

"New York. Why?"

"Did you ever leave New York?"

"No."

"Do you know much about what's going on in 2030?"

Greer shook her head reluctantly. "No."

"And do you have any idea how to find your way around Colorado?"

Her face flushed red and she again shook her head. "No."

"I do. Which means I go. Alaria goes because if she has to, she can teleport us out at least far enough to run. Once we know what we need to know, we're coming back here and we're plotting out a course of action. One thing that's very clear is that there are six of us in this and we all need to be working together to succeed. Until Gabriel decides to bring us our sixth, we have to make do with what we have. When we go in, we're all going in together. Don't worry about that."

Sufficiently put in her place, Greer deflated and sank back down onto the barstool. Damon pushed her cup of coffee and bowl of cereal across the island to her without a word. She glared at him before picking up her spoon and cramming Cheerios into her mouth. Braxton stared into his own cup of coffee and inclined his head in acknowledgment to Gage, who had just entered the room.

"When will you be back?" Greer's voice was small and not nearly so forceful.

"Two weeks tops. I've looked at the map, and the best way in is going to be a two-or-three-day hike. That means six days round trip, plus a day or two spying. We'll keep it as tight as we can."

Gage poured a bag of blood into a glass and stuck it in the microwave. "I'm delaying my trip until you've returned. I don't think it's prudent for us to be spread out so much. I've considered moving us to my Las Vegas residence, but I don't think that's the best course since the protections are so much more concentrated here. My mother was an extremely powerful witch and her bones are buried underneath the house. As long as they remain, the protections she placed will stay intact. Short of Devil's magic or Angelic help, there's nothing in existence that's stronger."

Alaria descended the stairs, her hair in a ponytail and wearing jeans and sneakers. She had a duffel bag over one shoulder and a jacket draped over one arm. Braxton met her eyes and smiled reassuringly. She joined the others at the table and took Gage's offered cup of coffee gratefully.

"Thanks."

"You look like you need it. Rough night?"

Braxton snorted into his cup. Alaria glared at him before answering Gage. "I didn't get much sleep."

"Try to sleep on the jet. It's going to be a rough couple of weeks and you'll need all the rest you can get. It's a long flight. You should take advantage of it."

Alaria gulped coffee. "I'll do my best. We'll need supplies of stakes, Holy Water and ammo. We're going to be carrying heavy when we head in."

"The jet is stocked with everything you'll need. Plenty of protein bars and water purification tablets. There's abundant water along your route, so that will lighten your load somewhat. I'm sending the ammo geared toward wolves, vamps, and demons and plenty of stakes and Holy Water."

Braxton nodded. "We'll manage. We're gearing to head in, find out what we need to know and get out as fast as possible. No unnecessary risks, but we need to be prepared for anything we might encounter."

Gage looked at Braxton sternly. "Solely reconnaissance. I know you, Winslow. You think you're some cowboy. Don't do anything stupid this time. Wait until I'm there to save your ass."

Braxton accepted Gage's proffered hand. "I've saved yours a time or two, old man." He glanced back at Alaria. "Ready?"

She slid off the barstool and shouldered her bag again. "As I'll ever be. Let's get this show on the road."

Braxton led her to the front door and into the waiting car. They climbed into the vehicle and Braxton pounded on the divider to let the driver know he could go. Once the car began the trek to the airport, he leaned back against the seat and studied the former Devil.

"Nervous?"

She laughed. "I'm only about to waltz into the cave where Azazel and Lilith are and let them find out for sure that I'm not dead and make myself the most hunted person on Earth. What's there to be nervous about?"

He patted her leg. "That's my girl."

Chapter Fifteen

August 17th, 2030 - Wyoming

SAM PACED. She walked the length of the house the Angels had taken her to over and over again. Her parents sat at the table, nursing cups of coffee, and two Angels stood guard on either side of the door. Her daughter, Finley, was sleeping in the playpen set up in the living room. After watching her pace for nearly an hour, Miranda cleared her throat.

"Sam, honey, come and sit down. There's no reason for you to be pacing."

"I want Gabriel to come back and tell me what the hell is going on. This was supposed to be over! Griffin Chose! She died!" She stomped to the Angels and poked one in the chest. "That was supposed to be the end of it, and now, eight months later, I'm getting jerked from my bed in the middle of the night and squirrelled away like some chest of treasure because the Hell Gate is open! And these clowns won't tell me what the fuck is happening and why in God's name they're keeping me here instead of taking me to my brother where I might actually be able to help!"

"This is not your task, Samantha." Gabriel appeared with a burst of light and immediately addressed the woman. "This is where you are safest, and it is where you will stay."

Sam redirected her fury at Gabriel. "What about free will? Isn't this interfering with it?"

"Not technically. I believe this would fit your definition of kidnapping. Now, were I to make you think you wanted to be here, that would be interrupting free will." He sat down at the table and glanced at Allen and Miranda. "It's nice to see you again. Have you found the accommodations to your liking?"

Allen answered. "The place is fine. We just want to know what's going on and why we're here. You didn't give us much when you brought us."

"I'll answer your questions. During the last weeks of the Choosing,

Lucifer developed a secondary plan. He used a warlock and a coven of witches to weave a spell strong enough to break the locks on the door to Hell. We tried to stop them, but since they are human, there was not much we could do. God would not approve the use of lethal force and there were only so many reinforcements we could place on the door. It opened four weeks ago."

Sam sank into a chair. "All the more reason that I need to be there. I'm a Warrior."

"You are not under protection because we doubt your ability to be an important part in stopping the flow of demons. You are here because you are hunted. Azazel has ordered his legions to seek out anyone with information about your brother and the others involved in this. Were they to find you, they would use you against Braxton. I cannot allow that to happen. You are here to protect him. He cannot be distracted by the trials facing him."

"He's doing this alone?" Miranda bounced her leg anxiously.

Gabriel smiled reassuringly. "Braxton is in good company, Miranda. Alaria is fighting with him, as is Gage. I have brought two soldiers back from the future in order to help and I will be adding a witch once I am given clearance to do so. Greer is Griffin's granddaughter, and Damon is a Hunter."

Allen whistled. "How did you find a true Hunter? Most of those lines have married into the Warrior lines."

"Most does not mean all. These six that I am forging together will perform three tasks in order to keep Hell from spilling out upon the Earth. Should they fail, the future Greer and Damon have experienced will come to fruition. We must stop that." He glanced back to the Angels at the door. "Raphael and Uriel will guard you until I deem it safe for you to leave. If you should need anything at all, ask them and they will make sure you receive it without delay."

"When can I see my brother?"

"I don't know. There is much for them to do, and their focus cannot be divided. I need you to trust me, Samantha. I will keep an eye on your brother and do my best to ensure that no harm befalls him. I cannot guarantee that he will live. I cannot even guarantee you that I will survive this battle, but what I can promise is that I would give my life for those fighting to preserve this world. I will lay down the life of every Angel in Heaven to make sure that we are successful."

Sam knew the Angel was telling the truth. There was no doubt in his voice and no room for argument. She nodded slowly. "You'll keep us updated, then? So we know what's going on?"

"I will check on you daily and speak to you routinely, though the conversations are not likely to be each day. I will not have the time to do so. Do you have further questions before I leave you?"

Allen cleared his throat. "Just let Brax know that we're safe and that we love him. We'll do whatever we have to in order to keep him as safe as possible."

"I'll relay the message." He turned to the Angels. "Neither of you are to leave your posts, not even for a moment. If they require something, hail one of the lesser Angels to fetch it. I want them under protection from now until you are relieved. Do you understand?"

One of the men, the one Gabriel had referred to as Raphael, nodded sternly. "Yes, sir."

"Uriel?"

"I understand, sir."

Without a response, Gabriel disappeared. Sam sprang to her feet and stalked to the window. "I can't believe this. I could be helping!"

Miranda smiled in mild amusement. "You heard Gabriel, sweetheart. We just have to hope your brother gets through this okay."

"How are the two of you so calm?"

Allen rose to refill his cup. "Years and years of practice. Braxton can handle whatever they throw at him. You have other priorities now, Sam. You have to focus on Finley and keeping her safe. You have a daughter to raise. Your job isn't to save the world. You did that once already."

Sam cast a loving glance to her sleeping daughter and felt the wave of grief for her husband that always accompanied it. "She looks so much like her daddy. He died for this world. It's the least I can do to make sure it still exists for her to grow up in."

Miranda stood and crossed the room to envelop her daughter in a hug. "Your job is to stay here with her. She needs her mommy. You did your part. It's time to let Braxton do his." She ran a hand over Sam's hair. "Besides, this old woman's heart can only take one child in danger at a time."

The Angels near the door looked at one another in alarm. Raphael unsheathed his sword. "There is activity outside."

Allen sat down his cup. "Who?"

Sam looked out the window again and cursed. "Not who, what. I see Lilith. Who's with her?"

Uriel peered out the peephole. "Abaddon."

"The Gatekeeper? Why in Hell is he here?"

Raphael surveyed the situation. "I suspect his presence is because there is no longer a Gate to keep. He is a very powerful Devil."

"What do we do?" Miranda rushed to the playpen and picked up the sleeping baby, cradling her granddaughter in her arms.

"You wait here. Uriel and I will dispatch the threat."

Sam looked around. "Something isn't right. It's too obvious." She looked at her mother. "Get Finley upstairs." She opened the hall closet and pulled out her shotgun. Allen withdrew a pistol from his duffel bag and pressed it into Miranda's hand.

"Go, Mandy. Keep the baby quiet."

The two Angels rushed out the door and charged at the two Devils. Sam watched in horror as many more demons materialized. She opened her mouth to yell at her parents to run for the car when a hand clamped over it.

Azazel held Sam tightly against his chest, easily overpowering her. "Hello, Samantha. How nice to see you again. Allen, always a pleasure. Where's your lovely wife and granddaughter?"

Allen stayed stonily silent. Azazel clucked his tongue in displeasure and eased his hand from Sam's mouth to her throat.

"You son of a bitch."

"That's not a very nice way to talk to the man who is now controlling whether you live or die." He smiled at Lilith, who had walked into the house, Uriel's head in her hand. "That was fast, sister."

"They weren't very good. It's been far too long since anyone gave them a good fight." She laid the head on the table and brushed her hands off. "Did you know that Devils are the only ones who can kill Angels? Rip out their essence and they dissipate into nothing. It's right about where a human heart would be. I prefer to drag it out through the neck. Nice and bloody that way."

Sam lunged against Azazel's arms when the third Devil dragged Miranda down the stairs. Finley was nowhere to be seen. "Let her go!"

Lilith clapped her hands. "The whole family's here. Isn't this fun, Abaddon?"

The other Devil, wearing black leather from heat to foot, shook his head. "Let's do what we came to and get back. Abalam is waiting for the humans."

"I don't answer to Abalam!" Lilith screeched loudly and tugged on her hair in annoyance. "I don't answer to anyone. I'll take all the time I want. Which one of the humans do you want?"

Abaddon surveyed the three. "Probably the young one. The other two are too old to hold up to his techniques. We wouldn't want them dying before we get the information we need." He glanced to Azazel. "Kill them."

Lilith pursed her lips and tapped one finger against them. "What of the child?"

Sam struggled again, kicking and biting anything that she could reach. "You monster! You leave my baby alone!"

Lilith giggled. "I've never had a daughter. Perhaps I'll take her and raise her myself. She'll need a mommy after you're dead."

Abaddon sighed deeply. "Just leave the whelp here. She'll starve to death in a few days."

Lilith glared at him. "I want to take it!" She disappeared and then reappeared with a sharp crack, now holding Finley in her arms. "I ripped your daddy's heart from his chest." She ran a finger down the baby's cheek. "You're going to be my baby now."

Azazel shook his head. "Which one are we taking back?"

Abaddon walked among Allen, Miranda and Sam. He peered into their eyes and sniffed their necks. When Miranda whimpered and flinched away, he licked her neck and ran one fingernail down her throat, the sharp point piercing the skin and drawing a thin line of blood.

"She's too weak."

"She killed Ariander." Lilith cooed to the infant. "She's stronger than you think."

"That was almost two of her decades ago. She's old and weak."

Azazel gritted his teeth, grinding them against each other. "It's his call, Lilith. Abalam only wants one. If it's not that one, kill her and move on."

Abaddon smiled at Miranda. "I'll let you choose how you die."

Miranda drew her shoulders back and spat in his face. "Go to hell, you Devil bastard."

"You first, darling."

Abaddon gripped Miranda's head in his hands. Sam threw herself against Azazel, and Allen charged across the room only to be thrown back by an invisible wall Lilith threw up with a careless toss of her hand. Miranda met her daughter's eyes.

"You survive, Samantha. I love you both. Kill the bas—"

The word was cut off with one jerk of Abaddon's hands. Her neck snapped with a sharp crack, and her body collapsed heavily to the ground in a limp pile. Azazel gripped Sam by the nape of the neck and dragged her to the side.

"Her death will alert Gabriel. Pick between these two and let's get out of here."

Abaddon strode across the room and smelled Allen and then nuzzled his nose into Sam's neck. He glanced between them several times. "This choice isn't easy. They're both strong and tough." He looked to Lilith. "Are you taking the child?"

Lilith was rocking from foot to foot, the baby cradled in her arms. "Yes."

"Abalam will want the mother. I'll take her."

"No!" Sam's scream was desperate and shrill. Her knees buckled and tears spilled from her eyes. "Leave him alone! Don't you touch him!" She sank her teeth into Azazel's hand when he tried to cover her mouth. "No! No!"

Azazel forced her mouth shut and clamped his hand over it. "Get it over with, Abaddon."

Abaddon leaned over until his nose was nearly touching Allen's. "Any last words, Dr. Winslow?"

Allen met Sam's eyes, tears filling his. "It's okay, Sammy girl. Get through this. Brax'll come for you. I love you." He closed his eyes. Abaddon lashed out and kicked Allen's knee, breaking it. He dropped to his knees, a muffled scream tearing from his lips. The Devil clenched his hand and twirled the sword that appeared.

"This is a Warrior's death." Abaddon gripped the sword in both hands and slashed once. The blade cut through Allen's neck with ease. There was a horrible half-second delay between the line of blood appearing on the skin and the head sliding off and falling to the floor with a thump. Sam's knees collapsed, and she sagged against Azazel. A heartbeat later, Allen's body slumped over and fell as a pool of dark red blood spread out from his neck.

Without a word, the three Devils disappeared, taking Sam and her baby with them. Sam was dizzy from the trip and fell flat when she was abruptly dropped. She scrambled to her feet, stumbling three steps before she gained her balance. She turned in a slow circle, taking in her surroundings. Her throat closed from terror, and her heart pounded in her chest.

They were in a cave. She was surrounded by demons and Devils. There were people chained to the wall, bound hand and foot by shackles. Hell hounds paced the perimeter, and their growls filled the cavern. A man wearing worn-in jeans and a polo walked over, his face suspiciously friendly. He held out a hand.

"Welcome to Hell. I'm Abalam. You are?"

Azazel shoved her toward the man. "This is Samantha. She's the Warrior's sister. If anyone knows where he is, it's gonna be her."

Abalam grinned. "Fantastic! I've got your room all set up for you. Follow me, please." He led her down one of the cave's off-shoots and into another chamber. A chair sat in the middle, anchored to the floor with a metal plate and with cuffs to hold her at the wrists and the ankles. In one corner were a twin mattress and a tray containing a plastic cup of water and a sandwich.

Sam took in all in with a sinking feeling in her gut. "What's this for?"

"This is what I like to call my information station." Abalam reached out and patted the chair proudly. "You'll come to know and loathe it soon enough. I wanted to introduce you to the place so that you can make an informed decision about how this is going to go." He lifted his brows when Lilith appeared holding the baby. "What in Lucifer's name is that?"

She cradled it protectively. "It's a baby." Lilith grinned viciously. "Her baby."

Abalam quirked his brow at Sam. "You have a child?"

She nodded silently, her gaze locked onto Finley.

"Male or female?"

Sam's voice was a whisper. "She's a girl."

"How old?"

"Six months."

Abalam clapped his hands. "You're getting the hang of this. I ask the questions, and you answer the questions. If you lie, or refuse to answer, I have to make you see why you should not do that. I have a certain skill set that is extremely useful in eliciting information out of people." He glared at Lilith. "Even I have standards. That's a potential soul. You'll not harm it."

Lilith growled and bared her teeth. "It's mine!"

"No, it's not. Lucifer placed me in charge until he's done digging Beelzebub out of the Lake. Until big brother gets back, you answer to me."

"Beelzebub is dead! That blonde bitch stabbed him with the Jesus knife!"

Abalam sighed. "We're not certain of his fate as of yet. Lucifer has gone into the Lake to see if he can be retrieved. Besides, if it's determined that he really is dead, you'll answer to me permanently."

Lilith snarled that time. "I answer to no one other than Lucifer!"

"Who has said you answer to me." He looked at her mildly. "That's really the end of the discussion."

"You've never been as powerful as me, Abalam."

"No, no I haven't. Raw power means nothing in this." He took two steps toward Lilith. "Would you like to take a turn in the chair?"

Lilith shook her head. "You wouldn't dare."

"Oh, I would dare. If you won't learn your place, I'll teach it to you. You will not harm that child or you will answer to me. Figure out how to keep it alive until I decide what to do with it."

Sensing that Abalam was truthful about not hurting Finley, Sam blurted, "She needs milk. I'm still nursing. If you won't let me feed her, she has to have formula. You'll need diapers to keep her clean."

Abalam smiled brightly at Sam. "Good girl! Volunteering information. Let's practice some more. How often does she need to eat?"

"Every three or four hours."

"Will she need anything other than milk?"

"She eats some jarred baby food now, but not much yet. She can get by on just milk if she needs to."

"Fabulous. You produce her nutrition?"

"Yes."

"When was she last fed?"

"It's been a little more than two hours."

He turned to Lilith. "Leave the child with her mother until you have found the supplies necessary to adequately care for it." He looked back to Sam. "I need to know where your brother is and who is with him. If you give me that information, you may go free with your child. If you do not provide that information, I will use my skills to drag it out of you and this will be the last time you see your daughter. If I determine you do not know what I need, you are of no use to me and you will be killed. Do you understand?"

Sam nodded. "Yes."

"I'm going to leave you to consider your options. I'll return in two hours to begin."

Chapter Sixteen

Gabriel was hailed into a garden. Michael greeted him with a handshake and a smile before sweeping out his arm. "Walk with me, brother. We have much to discuss."

"I need to check on the human family of the Warrior. I gave my word I would check on them each morning."

"That is one of the things that I wish to discuss with you. First, I want to talk about our formerly Fallen, now human sister."

"What of her?"

Michael drew to a stop and looked at Gabriel sympathetically. "I know you, Gabriel. I know about the meeting with her before the battle, and I know what has happened in the last few human months."

Gabriel dropped his head in shame. "I have failed."

"You have not failed any more than I have failed or as countless others amongst us have failed. We are not immune to the emotions of humans. We are not closed off to their desires. I didn't bring you here to lecture you or to worry you. I brought you here because we are brothers and because I care for you."

"Does He know?"

"No. He only knows what He wishes to know. I believe that He would agree anything that leads to the casting out of the Devils is a price worth paying. I do not believe that you will be punished."

"I don't care about the punishment. I've been punished over Alaria before."

"Our Father can be vengeful, and her betrayal hurt Him worse than most others. Your punishment was unfair. Gabe, I worry about how you will recover from this." Michael looked sad for a moment. "I still feel pangs because of Lilith, and she is further gone than even perhaps Lucifer."

"I know this will bring pain. I seem helpless to turn her down."

"Do you feel love for her?"

Gabriel shrugged his shoulders. "I don't know what love feels like. I feel things I've never experienced before. I am fond of her, I enjoy remembering when we were companions and the physical aspect of it is indescribable. I don't know if it is love."

"Is there anything that I could do to help you? I want for you to come through this as intact as possible. I fear for you, Gabriel."

"I fear for both of us. Alaria's emotions are much more tangible now that she has humanity. I fear she will feel love and that I will harm her when our dalliance has to end."

"Don't insult you or her by calling it a dalliance. You've circled this with that woman for millions of years. It's the conclusion that should have occurred long ago, but it will have to end eventually."

"I know." Gabriel clenched his hands at his sides in frustration. "I never intended for this to happen, Michael."

Michael sighed again. "I fear that there is more at play than either you or I are aware of."

"What do you mean?"

"There has been no input from Father on the course of things since He allowed you the half-century to correct the failings of the Choosing. I know that He normally leaves these things to the Host, but He has been absent and quiet."

"I've wondered about that myself. What do you suspect?"

"I'm not sure yet. Just be careful, brother. For the moment, we're on our own." He held out his hand and brought a bench up out of the moss. "Sit. There is one more matter of which we must speak."

Gabriel perched on the bench and waited while Michael settled next to him. "What is it?"

"Uriel and Raphael are dead. Their essence has been ripped from them. Braxton's parents were executed."

Gabriel surged to his feet, his wings spreading wide behind him. "When? How long have you known? Why was I not notified? I should have known the second they died!"

"I discovered it only moments before I called you here. The Angel of Death was called to retrieve the souls. He found Uriel and Raphael when he arrived. He came straight to me to inform me of the murders."

"Samantha and the infant?" He paced in the clearing, his steps short and staccato and his face taut with worry.

Michael stood to place his hand on Gabriel's shoulder. "Were not found there. They have been taken. I've dispatched a squad of Angels to locate them. We'll find her, brother. Death assures me that she is still alive, as is the child. As long as they are still breathing, we will be looking."

Gabriel set his mouth in a thin line. "Who is responsible?"

"Azazel, Lilith, and Abaddon."

"He took them to Abalam. If Abaddon was involved, they went to Abalam."

"We do not know where Abalam is."

Gabriel disappeared, his voice lingering behind him. "You might not. But I do."

Sam spat out blood. Her mouth was swollen and her tongue felt heavy and foreign in her mouth. Blood dripped off her fingers and pooled on the floor. There were shallow slices covering her body. One eye was swollen shut and both her big toenails had been ripped off.

Abalam picked up a scalpel and crossed the room to stand behind her. He touched the point to the tattoos covering her back. He brushed her hair off her neck and twisted it into a knot on the top of her head, securing it with a clip.

"You've been most tiresome with your refusal to give me the information I need." He used one hand to tighten her skin before digging the edge of the scalpel into the ink lines. "I'm left no other option but to carve these off your back and let a demon possess you."

"They'll never get my memories." She spat again, spit mixing with blood in a gleaming wet glob. "I'm a fucking Warrior, you Devil bastard. I know how to fight them out."

"Then I'll kill you and let them get at them that way. I'm going to ask you again. Where is your brother?" He dug the scalpel deeper and sliced downward, then up in an arc. He peeled off a chunk of flesh and tossed it onto a metal tray. Blood streamed out of Sam's back. He grabbed a rag and wiped it away.

"I don't know!" Sam's voice was a breathless scream. Tears mingled with the blood on her face from the wounds he had inflicted upon her.

Abalam circled so she could see him. "I'm beginning to believe that you don't know where he is. You say it with such conviction I'm not sure you could be lying to me." He tapped his index fingers against his lips. "Let me change tactics a bit. I'm sure you have some information I could use in that delightful little brain of yours. Who is with your brother?"

Sam gritted her teeth and closed her eyes. She concentrated on an image of Finley. She forced her mind to take her back to the look on Finn's face the day they'd found out about the baby. She slowed her breathing and felt her heart rate go back down. She deliberately opened her eyes and locked them onto Abalam.

"I don't know."

The Devil perused his tray of devices. "This is getting tiresome, Samantha. I believe you don't know where he is, so I'm going to stop asking that question. If you have nothing useful to me, I'm going to have to cut our game short and kill you. I don't want to do that. If you tell me one of the people helping your brother, I'll give you thirty minutes with your child."

The prospect of getting to see Finley even one final time had Sam sobbing. She took a gasping breath. "Gabriel."

Abalam sighed. "I asked for that, I suppose." He sat the scalpel on the tray. "We both know that wasn't the preferred information when I asked that question, though it is, technically, correct." He snapped his fingers and released the shackles on her hands and feet. "We'll resume in thirty minutes."

Sam grabbed Finley the moment a demon brought her in and cradled her against her chest. The baby was sleeping soundly, and Sam sobbed silently as she stared into the face of her daughter. She knew unequivocally that she would never see her child again. She tipped her head back to stare at the ceiling, her lips moving in a silent, desperate prayer that God would take care of her baby.

Her throat raw and thick with tears, Sam coughed and hummed. Finley cooed in her sleep and snuggled into her mother's chest. Sam tightened her grip on the baby and began to sing the lullaby she always used to put her daughter to sleep. Blood was drying in her hair, and her whole body ached and burned from pain. In that moment, with her daughter sleeping peacefully in her arms, she let it all fade away and concentrated on her last moments with the daughter she had carried and birthed.

"I love you, baby girl. I know you won't remember me, but you need to know how much you were loved. I won't get to see you grow up, get married, or have babies of your own." She pressed a kiss to the soft skin on Finley's cheek. "Your Daddy and I were so excited when we found out you were coming. You are wanted, and you are loved." She choked back a sob.

"I'll always watch over you, Finley. Braxton will come for you. I know he will. He'll love you for me. Just be happy, my love."

For the next twenty minutes, Sam did not move, and she did not speak. She rocked back and forth, tears streaming down her face as she cherished each second until Abalam returned. She knew when he did that her life would be over. In those last minutes, the only thing that mattered was memorizing every pore on her daughter's face.

Much too soon, the Devil opened the door and strode in. He smiled brightly and took the baby from her arms. She screamed and tried to hold onto the infant, but he was much too strong. She fell out of the chair and onto the floor. She tried to stand, but her legs wouldn't hold her and she sprawled again. She crawled, dragging herself across the floor, desperate for one more minute, one more second, with her child. She stretched her arm out, sobs tearing from her throat as she reached for Finley. Abalam stooped next to her and lowered the now crying baby so that Sam could press her face against Finley's chest. He leaned forward and pressed his lips to her ear. "Tell me what I need to know, and you have my word that you can walk out of here with your child and that no harm will come to either of you."

Sam cried harder. That was the one thing she knew she couldn't do. Her choice was not whether or not she was going to die. It was whether or not she was going to take everyone with Braxton out with her. She rolled onto her back and stared at the ceiling. She blinked twice before Abalam appeared in her field of vision again.

"Do you want to die, Samantha?"

"My husband is dead. My parents are dead. We both know that the only way I'm leaving this cave is in a bag."

"I don't know that. I know that I have questions and you have answers. If you give me those answers when I give you my questions, I will let you go. Don't you want to see her grow up?" He looked at the baby. "See her get married? Have grandchildren? Do you have so little regard for your own life that you would deny me simple words?"

Sam's brain was getting foggy from both pain and blood loss. She shook her head to clear it and opened her mouth. No words came out. She coughed and tried again. "Why do you need to know who's with him?"

Abalam shrugged. "Let's chalk it up to idle curiosity. I like to know my enemy. If I know who I'm facing, I can develop a more effective strategy. Just tell me their names, Samantha, and leave this place."

"I don't know them all."

Abalam smiled and handed the baby off to another demon. "There's a girl. Some information I actually believe. Telling me that you don't know them all leads me to the inevitable assumption that you know some of them. Tell me their names."

Sam closed her eyes tightly and took a deep breath. "Sadie. Elizabeth. Jacob. Michael. Adam, Eve, Abraham, Noah, Lot, Joseph, Mary, Matthew, Mark, Luke, John." She was still spouting off random names when Abalam dragged her into the chair and strapped her down. The chanting turned to yelps when the scalpel sliced into her flesh. Her shrieks echoed throughout the cavern. Eventually, not even the demons could tell when one cry ended and the next began.

Several hours later, they turned from the screams of the tortured to the screams of the dying.

Chapter Seventeen

ALARIA POKED the fire absently with a stick. Braxton breathed heavily next to her. He was wrapped in a sleeping bag, and his head rested on a balled up sweatshirt. She would keep watch for the first four hours of the night and then sleep for four hours before they began their trek again.

Colorado was a beautiful place. The trees stood tall above them and their surroundings were wild and gorgeous. They'd passed many streams and Lakes on their journey. They'd even spent two memorable hours trying to avoid shooting a bear that had stumbled upon them.

Alaria's head jerked to the side, and she smiled as Gabriel appeared. She heaved herself to her aching feet and crossed the clearing to him. "I thought it was dangerous for you to be here when we're heading to the Gate."

Gabriel reached out and took her hands. "I've failed." He dropped to his knees and wrapped his arms around her, pressing his face into her stomach. Worried and confused, Alaria wrapped her arms around his head and held him. Sobs tore from the Angel, and his tears soaked through her shirt and scalded her skin. She stroked his hair, murmuring words of comfort.

"What's happened, Gabe?" She whispered the question once he had stilled and his shoulders were no longer shaking. "What's going on?"

"I promised Braxton that I would care for his family. I placed them in the care of Uriel and Raphael. They were guarded. Lilith and Azazel and Abaddon killed my brothers and Braxton's parents. They've taken Samantha and her child to Abalam. Michael swears to me that they are still alive, though we do not know for how much longer."

Alaria closed her eyes and took three deep breaths before talking. "Where did they take her?"

"To the Gate. I've come to transport you and Braxton as close as I can get. I believe it will only take you approximately an hour to finish the walk once I drop you off. There are protections on the Gate that keep me from getting too close. If I were to brush against them, the Devils would be alerted of my presence." He wiped his face and sat on the ground, dirt smearing his normally pristine white suit. "I gave him my word and I have failed."

"We need to wake him up and tell him." She glanced at Braxton, still sleeping deeply. "I think I should be the one."

Gabriel nodded in agreement. "I'll stay right here."

Alaria bent down and pressed her mouth to his in a kiss. "It's okay, Gabe. I know you did your best." She stroked her hand down his face and straightened. "Brax will know that, too."

She squatted next to Braxton's sleeping form and laid her hand on his shoulder. His eyes snapped open and he sat up. "My turn?"

Alaria dropped all the way to the ground and laid her hand on his leg. "No. Something's happened."

Alert, Braxton looked around nervously. "What's wrong?"

"Gabriel is here. He's brought some bad news."

Braxton caught sight of Gabriel sitting on the ground, his eyes red and swollen. He rubbed his hands over his face and through his hair. "Who's dead?"

"It's not that simple. He's going to transport us to the edge of the protections the Devils have on the Gate. They have your sister and niece."

Braxton surged to his feet, his eyes snapping with anger. "They were supposed to be protected! Dammit! How the hell did this happen?"

Alaria jumped up and grabbed his hands. "They killed the Angels protecting them. Two Angels are dead. They killed your parents, and they took Sam and Finley. We have to get to them before they're dead, too."

He strode to Gabriel, his voice low and angry. "You promised me you would take care of them! You swore to me that they were safe!"

Gabriel climbed to his feet slowly. "I did. I've failed you. I checked on them yesterday morning. I spoke with them all and reassured them about you. All was as it should have been. An hour ago, Michael hailed me to his garden. He'd been informed by the Angel of Death that your parents had been killed. He found the remains of Uriel and Raphael in the cabin. I don't know how they found the cabin."

Braxton paced back and forth. "You're sure Sam and Finley are alive?"

"For the moment, yes."

"What were you doing?"

Gabriel blinked. "I'm not sure I know what you mean."

Braxton glared between Alaria and Gabriel. "I mean, were you fucking her when my parents were being murdered?"

Gabriel hung his head. "No. I was checking on the sixth member of your group and seeking permission to bring her forward. I swear to you, Braxton, this was not due to my recent...slips in appropriate behavior."

Alaria huffed. "He has no business asking that to begin with." She turned her gaze to Braxton. "You damn well knew the answer before you asked it. You're just being mean because you're hurt. He saw them yesterday morning, which is when you and I were getting ready to leave. I haven't been out of your sight since. I know you're hurting, and I know you're mad, but there's no reason to be mean. We're all doing the best we can. Now, set it aside, and let's get your sister back."

Braxton's gaze dropped to the ground. He knew she was right. He took several moments and battled back waves of grief and rage. He had to concentrate on the present. There would be time to mourn after Sam was safe. He battled down the emotions and forced himself to focus.

"Okay, we need a plan."

Gabriel spoke. "I'm going to transport you as close as I can. It will be an hour's hike from there. I'll brush against the barrier at other points to distract them and draw their attention. You must remove the protections. Once they are down, Michael will lead a squad in to fight the demons."

Alaria began packing their bags. "Are the Devils there?"

"We don't know. Abalam will be there. Beyond that, I can't say for sure."

Braxton shouldered his pack. "Let's get a move on."

Gabriel reached out and touched a hand to each of them. With a jolt, they were jerked through space. In the span of a heartbeat, they were standing hundreds of miles away from where they had been.

"Remember, get rid of those protections." Gabriel disappeared, leaving Braxton and Alaria alone. She hiked her pack higher on her back.

"Let's get this show on the road."

They ran through the woods, their footfalls muffled by the lush carpet of pine needles. They charged up the side of the hill, racing against time as they tried to get to Sam before she was killed. By the time they reached the top of the hill and peered over it, they were both sweating and breathing heavily.

Alaria stretched out on her stomach and glanced over the edge. The mouth of the cave was wide and flanked by two demons. She ducked back down and slid to Braxton, who was bracing his back against the hill and digging through their bags.

"What's it look like?"

"Two demons on the outside. I don't know how many on the inside." They both cringed when screams reached their ears. "Sam's still alive."

"For now." He loaded a clip into his pistol. "Did you see any other monsters? Vamps, wolves, hounds?"

"There'll be hounds." She began assembling a rifle. "Do you have a plan?"

"Kill them all."

"That's not a plan. That's a suicide mission."

"Do you have anything better?"

Alaria smiled grimly. "We wait until the lesser demons flood out to go after Gabe. You head to the top and start painting me some Devil's traps to keep them from jumping ship. I head down that hill and draw them out into the open. You pick them off from up above as they come out of the cave. Seeing me alive will be enough of a shock that it'll buy you a few seconds to get off some shots. Far as I'm aware, they have no idea what happened to me after the Choosing."

Braxton took the rifle and the can of spray paint she held out to him. "The angle might be okay to get some shots off, but it's going make it awfully dangerous for you."

"Give me a better option."

Braxton scrambled up the hill and stuck his head over. "I wish I could." He slipped back down to her. "You're going to have to pull them pretty far out into that clearing."

"I'll do my part. Just make damn sure you do yours." She slapped his shoulder. "I'm going to make my way around to the bottom. Get up there and get those symbols painted." She slung her bag over her shoulder. "Signal me when you're ready."

Braxton shouldered the rifle and offered her a rakish grin. "Don't die."

She smiled. "You don't die either."

As quietly as she could, Alaria slipped and slid down the hill and snuck through the brush around to the edge of the forest in front of the clearing. She crouched in the bushes, her eyes trained to the top of the cave. She could barely make out Braxton's form moving up the hill. She saw him pull out a knife and scrape at something—presumably the Angel protections—before shaking the can of spray paint and spraying Devil's traps on the ground. When she saw him wave his arms once before dropping to his stomach, she knew it was time.

She stood and clenched her fist. Her jeans and sweatshirt were exchanged for the black leather pants and red bustier. She wrapped her fingers around her whip and battled back the nerves. Heart pounding in her chest, she stepped into the clearing.

"Hello, boys. How nice to see you again." She smiled sharply at the demons guarding the entrance. "Would one of you be so kind as to run inside and have all my brothers and sisters come out to talk to me?"

The demons exchanged a look. One had the nerve to speak. "Alaria."

"In the flesh. Go on, now, scoot." She waved her hand at him. "I've things to discuss with creatures far above your pay grade."

A man came out of the cave, flanked by Hell hounds. Several other demons fell into line behind him. He quirked a brow at Alaria. "Well, as I live and don't breathe. Alaria is still alive. Where have you been, darling?" He put his hands on his hips. "Is that a heartbeat I hear?"

Alaria chuckled. "Ariander, you son of a bitch. I wish Griffin would have used that knife on you. You're more problems than you're worth and you never seem to die."

"What can I say? I'm slippery." He gestured to the hounds, and they sat on either side of him. "You have a lot of nerve coming here."

"Maybe I got bored with this human thing. I need to talk to whoever is in charge."

"He's busy." Ariander smiled as screams filled the air. "Abalam has a guest. You know how much he likes his guests."

Alaria's stomach clenched. She took three steps back and was relieved when the demons stepped toward her. "Then get Lilith or Azazel. I'll settle for Abaddon if I have to."

"They're busy right now. Lilith and Azazel are helping Laelia, and Abaddon is following a lead with Garrick. I'm sure you know Laelia and Garrick."

"I know them. What're they up to?"

Ariander bared his teeth. "Oh, nothing important. Just wiping out the pests that are humans."

"You used to be one, if I remember correctly."

"A cruel twist of fate. This is what I was always meant to be."

Alaria circled Ariander. "Funny. I remember you screaming for God and your mommy and mercy when Abalam had your soul up on his rack. He carved you to pieces for a hundred thousand years before he warped you enough to turn you into a demon. You were always a monster. Baby rapist."

The crowd of demons had grown larger. Alaria's heart pounded faster in her chest. Ariander advanced on her, his face twisted into a frightening snarl. His eyes turned black, and he reached for her. His fingers never made contact. Braxton's first bullet rang through the night and hit Ariander in the skull. Blood and bits of brain flew out. The demons charged.

Alaria fought like a madwoman. She kicked and spun, her whip in one hand and a dagger in the other. Her hair whirled behind her. She drove her elbow into the nose of one demon before dropping to the ground and rolling in order to avoid becoming dog food. The hound pounced.

Alaria thrashed, trying desperately to avoid the razor sharp teeth. Her heart sank when she felt those teeth close on her shoulder. She screamed and sank the dagger to its hilt in the hounds' neck. With a yell, she forced it off of her and rolled to her feet.

Over and over again, Braxton pulled the trigger and ended a life. Demons dropped from his bullets, and the clearing was foggy from the lingering demonic essence that was forced from the bodies. A roar of thunder rolled through the forest, and Michael descended into the clearing, his wings spread behind him and a dozen Angels surrounding him. He batted the demons away with his wings and leveled a dark look at Alaria.

"Get inside and find Samantha. Time is short for saving her."

Alaria dashed into the cave. Several demons were stuck in traps, courtesy of Braxton. She dodged them quickly, following the sounds of screams. She used her knife twice to kill stray demons and finally pushed into the chamber where Sam was.

Sam was strapped into an exam chair. She was bleeding from wounds too numerous to count. Her wrists were raw, and bone was peeking through the torn skin. Her feet were bare, she was missing two toes, and chunks of skin had been torn from her back.

Abalam sighed when the door opened. "I told you I was not to be disturbed. Can you not see that I have a guest?"

"I don't rightly care."

The Devil turned around, his eyes darkening when he realized who had entered his chamber. "You have a lot of nerve coming here. Are all my demons dead?"

"Mostly. Michael brought some friends with him once we got through your Angel wards."

"You're one of the ones helping her brother, then?"

"I suppose I am."

Abalam placed his scalpel on the tray very carefully. "You'll have to forgive me. My plans for the day did not include battling Michael and company." He looked down at himself. "I believe it's time for me to leave."

He tipped his head back and opened his mouth. Alaria, her feet planted solidly on the cave floor, began chanting in Latin. Her eyes darkened as she tapped into the small measure of magic she possessed. Wind whipped through her hair and the black smoke that was Abalam trying to leave his body was crammed back down the throat. Still chanting, she carefully drew a trap in the blood on the floor and pushed him into it.

"You bitch."

Alaria chuckled. "Is that the best you can do?" She crossed the room to Sam. "Do us both a favor and shut the fuck up." She grasped Sam's face in both her hands. "Braxton's here. He'll be here in just a minute."

"Finley."

"I'll find her as soon as Braxton gets here."

"I'm here." Braxton dashed through the door and went straight to his sister. "Oh my God." He snatched the keys to the shackles from the tray and freed her hands and feet. She fell forward into his arms. "Sammy, my God."

Sam coughed. "I'm dead, Brax."

"No. No, we have a Healer." He looked at Alaria. "Can you get Gabriel?"

There was a rustling as Gabriel appeared. "No need for her to call. I'm here." He knelt next to Sam. "I'm sorry, child. I do not have the power to heal you."

"Get Greer." Alaria brought over a container of water. "Here, Brax, get her to drink. I'm going to go find that baby."

Gabriel stood. "Braxton, may I speak to you for a moment?"

Sam's laugh was strangled. "No need to whisper. I know I'm dead, Gabriel. Your Healer can't possibly heal me."

"You haven't met Greer. She's Griffin's granddaughter. She's got power, Sam. She can do it. If anyone can, it's Greer." Braxton glared at Gabriel. "Get her! For the love of God, go get Greer!"

Gabriel disappeared with a flash of light. Alaria came back in, cradling

Finley in her arms. "Sam, I found the baby. She's fine." She dropped to her knees next to Sam, holding Finley out so that Sam could see her.

"I thought I'd never see her again." Sam coughed and blood splattered against the baby's cheek. "Brax, Mom and Dad are gone."

"I know." He ran his hand over her hair and settled her against his chest. "It's okay. We're going to get through this together."

"I—only have a few minutes." She looked at Abalam. "He knew I was almost dead. I didn't tell him anything."

"I know, little sister. I know you never would."

Sam tried to lift her hand to touch the baby but didn't have the strength. Alaria laid Finley on her mother's chest. "Brax—the baby, I want you to raise her."

Braxton looked at Finley with fear in his eyes. "Sam…"

"Don't. You're my brother. I know you can't now." She coughed again and her breaths got even shallower. "When this is over, you promise me you'll raise her for me. Tell her about me and about her daddy." Tears slipped down her face silently. "Tell her that we loved her. Tell her that every day." She looked at Alaria. "You'll help him?"

Alaria gripped Sam's hand and squeezed. "We'll take care of your little girl, Sam."

"It's getting harder to stay awake." She laughed bitterly. "I always wondered how I'd die. I never thought it would be getting tortured by a Devil bastard." She took a shaky breath. "I want to sleep."

Braxton's own tears fell, making tracks down his cheeks. "Don't do that, Sammy. I can't do this alone. Don't leave me."

Sam shook her head. "You aren't alone." She looked at Alaria. "She's here, Brax. She's one of us. You'll do this together." Her eyes were barely open. "I just want to sleep. Just for a little while."

When her eyes closed all the way and her breaths became almost non-existent, Braxton laid his head on his sister's and sobbed.

Chapter Eighteen

August 18th, 2030 · Scotland
"Damon, I don't want to talk about it." Greer set her glass down with a crack and glared at him. "We have other things to worry about right now aside from your libido."

Damon chuckled as he rounded the island. "This isn't about sex, Greer. I'm not that shallow. We need to talk about what's going on and how we're going to proceed."

"I don't want to talk about it. I want to finish getting into shape and get on with the whole point of being here." She sighed deeply. "We can't worry about whatever it is that's starting up between us."

Damon snagged her around the waist and pulled her against him. "Listen to me for thirty seconds. We cannot stop living. We still have to eat, and sleep, and do a lot of things. We can't let our lives get lost in this mess we've gotten wrapped up in. We have to keep living, Greer. There's nothing wrong with this."

Greer batted at his hands. "Damon, I don't want to jump into something. We have to keep our priorities straight. If we get our heads clouded with something else, people could end up dead." She leaned her head on his chest and breathed in his scent. "This isn't about whether or not I want to—it's about keeping our heads clear and making sure that everyone comes through this in one piece." She straightened and pulled away. "I can't risk the lives of anyone over something that might turn out to just be hormones." She lifted onto her tiptoes and pressed a kiss to his cheek. "I'm going to bed. Alone."

She headed up the stairs and into her room, closing the door securely behind her. She changed into shorts and a tank and slipped between the sheets. She pulled the quilt up over her shoulder and stretched to turn off the lamp. Within a matter of minutes, her breathing deepened and she sank into sleep.

The redheaded woman was again waiting for her. Greer looked around, her skin chilled from the brisk breeze. "What am I doing here?"

"I've brought you here to discuss with you some things that are going on and are concerning."

"Like what?"

"Laelia is mobilizing forces. There is a demon who is named Javal. He has the ability to move through time as Angels do. He is gathering forces in my time to attempt to stop me from coming forward. I've been calling for Gabriel, but he does not answer."

Greer dropped onto a rock. "There have been some difficulties here. There was an attack, and two of our group are out trying to find some information on the forces guarding the Hell Gate. We've been split up, and Gabriel has been pulling double duty. They've moved Braxton's family into safekeeping so that they won't get dragged into this."

"There's a lot that we have to do. Garrick grows stronger every day. He is channeling his power into Laelia and Javal. They feed on witches from all corners of time in order to make themselves stronger. Azazel and Lilith are working with them. You are going to have to battle Hell to get that Gate closed. I think it is time that I come forward through time and join you."

"Can you do that?"

"I'm not sure. Gabriel was certain that my presence would hinder the completion of the first task. Having me here splits their attention and requires Javal continuing to try and get to me. If I come forward, they will all be focused on stopping us. Though without me there, I question whether or not you will have enough power to fight a battle on as many fronts as you are being forced to."

Greer ran her hands through her hair. "I'm not sure what to do. How can I help you?"

"I don't think that you can." The woman sat next to her. "This has become more complicated than I had hoped it would get. I never thought it would be easy, but I had assumed there wouldn't be problems in getting me forward in time with the rest of you. It would appear that I've grossly underestimated the amount of power that Hell has on its side."

"I wish there was something I could do."

"As do I." She sighed deeply. "There are many trials ahead of us. The sooner I can get to everyone else, the better off we'll all be. My power will add to your protections." The woman sprang to her feet. "It's time for you to leave. Javal is here. He must have entered the plane on the remnants of my opening."

The sky darkened with clouds and thunder rolled across the field. Greer stood and turned around, searching the space for signs of another person. By the time she had made a complete rotation there was a slick man wearing khakis and a polo standing in the field. His black hair was a little too long and was hanging in his face. He smiled when she gasped and jumped back a step.

"Greer, get out of here. I'll hold him off as long as I can." The woman stepped in front of Greer, her long white dress billowing around her legs and her hair streaming out behind her in the wind.

Greer shook her head. "No. I'm not going anywhere. I'm a soldier. I can handle myself."

The man held out a hand. "Nice to meet you, Greer. I'm Javal. I'm the one who's going to kill you tonight."

His eyes flashed with power, and he tossed out one arm, throwing the redhead to the side. She sent back a stream of power, and he brushed it away. He clenched his hand and lifted her off the ground with a beam of magic, holding her immobilized and still.

"Give it up, Aradia. You're incredibly powerful but it doesn't translate to the dream plane very well."

Aradia gasped. "Greer, listen to me! He only has the power that you give him. If you believe he can't hurt you, he can't. Don't let him hurt you."

Greer drew up her fists to protect her face, one leg slightly in front of the other to give her more balance and her shoulders squared. "You can't hurt me."

Javal smiled. "I most certainly can. I want to chat with you first, though. How is it that you got sucked into this mess, Greer?"

"Let Aradia go."

"Focus on what I'm asking you, dear. You're not calling the shots in this conversation. Every breath you take is because I allow it. I could rip you to shreds before you could so much as open your mouth to scream."

Aradia fought to get loose from the invisible force holding her back. "I could kill you a hundred times, Javal. Haven't you the guts to face me while we're awake?"

The demon turned his head to acknowledge her. "Aradia, love, do shut up. I'm talking to Greer for the moment." He reached out and ran one finger down Greer's face, his nail slicing into the skin. Greer jumped back from the contact, her fingers moving to her face to wipe away the blood. Javal chuckled. "She doesn't truly believe I can't hurt her." He stuck his finger in his mouth and licked away the blood. "Healer blood is so sweet."

Aradia was gasping for breath. "He can't kill me here. He isn't strong enough. Get out of here while you still can!"

Greer shook her head. "I won't leave you."

Javal wagged his finger at Aradia. "I asked you nicely to shut up." He wiggled his finger and her lips clapped closed. "I won't ask again." He turned to Greer. "Where were we? Oh, yes. I was about to describe to you how I'm going to kill you." He sat down on the rock where Greer had sat and crossed his legs. "First, I'm going to fuck you. I'll make you like it, of course. Then, I'm going to tear your throat out. I'll rip your heart up through the hole in your neck, and you might have enough life in you to watch me take a bite of it before you die. Finally, once you're dead, I'm going to bathe in your blood." He smiled. "Doesn't that sound fun?"

Aradia's eyes had turned white. She tossed her head back and her lips were moving, though no words were coming out. Greer studied the witch for a moment before addressing Javal. "You have to come and get me first, you jackass. This is the coward's way out, coming after me in my dreams. I bet it's because you can't find me in the real world."

Javal advanced on her, backing her toward the edge of the cliff. He grabbed her by her throat and lifted her off the ground. "Let us get one thing straight, little girl. I am the most powerful demon alive. I could find you no matter where you are. I followed Aradia here because it was convenient and because I like convenience. Much simpler for me to kill you right here and now then have to fight my way in to that house Gage has you ensconced in." He lifted one hand, watching in delight as Greer's eyes widened with horror as his nails lengthened into talons. "If I kill you, I kill this damned circle and the Hell Gate stays open." He clicked his claws together. "I just really hope this death translates into the real world."

There was a flash of white hot pain as Javal plunged his hand into her chest. She felt her skin rip and her bone break from the force. For an instant, she could feel his fingers wrapped around her heart, could feel it beat in his hand once, twice, three times, before he ripped. She had one image of his arm, bloodied to the elbow, and his hand clenched around her heart before Aradia was free. The witch sent out a stream of magic so powerful it sent Greer careening through time and space to crash back into her own body.

She woke herself screaming. Before her eyes were even open, Damon had charged into the room through the bathroom and Gage had crashed through the door. She looked down at herself in horror and screamed even louder when she saw her tank top soaked with blood. In that instant, she couldn't breathe. She gasped and choked, her heart beating so fast it threatened to burst. Through the pain, she had a moment of clarity and felt relief knowing that the pounding organ was still securely inside her chest.

Damon leaped onto the bed and pressed his hands to the wound. Blood soaked her shirt, the sheets, and into the mattress. He met her terrified eyes with his. "Heal, Greer! Heal yourself! If you don't do it, you'll die!"

Gage was there within a heartbeat. He bared his fangs and sliced into his wrist, pressing it to her lips. His blood, thick and bitter, ran down her throat before Damon could so much as open his mouth to object. She coughed and gasped, trying to spit out the blood. Gage held a hand over her mouth until she swallowed.

"If she dies, she'll come back. I know you don't want to consider that, but this is bad."

Greer wrapped her hands around Damon's wrists. Her eyes betrayed her fear, and she opened and closed her mouth several times, trying to talk. She clawed at him, her nails breaking skin and drawing blood. Damon leaned down and braced his forehead against hers, his hands pressing against the gaping wound as hard as possible.

"Listen to me. You have to heal. If you don't, you're going to die. There's a fucking hole in your chest."

"Help."

The word was a whisper. Her face was pale and blood poured between Damon's fingers. He pushed harder. "Tell me what you need."

He felt her mind reach out and had barely allowed her entrance before she was charging through the door. She wrapped her mind around his, entwining their thoughts. He saw the demon, felt his sternum crack and break as a hand forced its way through. He heard and felt the sickening sensation of having an organ torn from the body.

She pushed through all of his barriers. Damon wasn't entirely sure she even consciously knew what she was doing. He saw her hands start to glow, and they left his arms to press against her chest. He felt a ripping sensation in his own chest and looked down to see blood seeping through the fabric of his shirt. He grabbed his chest, feeling for the extent of the injury.

He watched the stark white of her bones come back together. It knit itself, forming ribs and sternum—bones interspersed with the creamy beige of cartilage. Muscle stretched over it, the red, white and purple fibers weaving together. Next came blood vessels. The broken ends came together and blood began flowing through them. Finally, came the skin. Layer by layer, her skin healed. What started out as completely transparent gradually darkened and thickened until the wound closed and there was no evidence of the hole aside from a pool of blood and a thick pink scar. Damon looked down at himself and discovered that a matching scar had appeared on his chest.

Greer retreated from his mind incrementally. She felt her chest with her fingertips. Gage dropped into the chair next to the bed. Damon grabbed her face and turned it so that she was looking directly at him.

"What the hell happened? Who did this to you?"

Greer coughed. "Javal."

Gage swore. "Fucking asshole demon. He would have to be involved in this. There are protections on this place. Did he get in here?"

"Dream plane. The witch took me there. She's afraid that Gabriel isn't bringing her forward and that she's needed. She wants me to talk to him and convince him to bring her. She's going to try to find a way to get around him. We were talking and it got dark and stormy. He was strong. Aradia told me that he didn't have power unless I let him, but I guess I didn't really believe her. I tried to protect her, but he was too strong. He literally ripped my heart out. Aradia got loose just in time. She did something and sent me back. I guess not all of the dream injury made it through."

Gage nodded. "It never does unless you die. She must have sent you back just in time." He stood up. "I'm going to add some extra protections to the house. I'll bring up some herb bundles to put in your pillows. It'll keep them from bringing you into the dream plane." He paused at the door. "Do you need anything, Greer?"

She looked down at herself. "A shower and some clean sheets."

Gage chuckled. "The mattress will have to be replaced. There's another guest room across the hall. I'll take care of the mess in the morning."

Damon grabbed Greer under her arms and lifted her. Her knees buckled and she sagged heavily against him. He wrapped one arm around her waist and held her up. "How do you feel?"

Greer glared at him, her face pale and drawn. "Like a demon ripped my fucking heart out."

He lowered her onto the lid of the toilet. "I want to show you something." He pulled his shirt over his head. "I have a scar, too. When you healed, you reached into me somehow and my chest split open."

Greer reached out and laid her fingertips against the puckered skin. "I was dying." Her eyebrows drew together. "It was too bad for me to heal myself. When I went into your head, I think I must have borrowed some of your strength."

"How did this happen, though?" He gestured to the scar.

She let her hand drop to her lap. "I wish I could tell you. I don't know. Maybe it had something to do with our mental link. You shared your energy, and I shared my pain. It was too much for me, so I was able to pass some of it along to you through our link." She looked up at him. "I'm sorry."

Damon shook his head. "Don't you ever apologize for doing what you had to do in order to survive." He squatted in front of her. "Let's get you cleaned up."

Chapter Nineteen

DAMON DREW Greer's shirt over her head gently. He reached into the shower and turned on the water, sticking his hand under the spray to check the temperature. He supported her weight while she stepped out of her shorts and helped her climb into the spacious shower.

"Can you handle this on your own or do you need help?"

She tried to stand on her own and nearly fell. Embarrassed, she crossed her arms over her naked breasts. "I think I need help."

Damon stripped off his clothes and stepped in. "No big deal. I need to get the blood off anyway." He helped her maneuver under the water. Blood streamed out of her hair and stained the tiles. He kept one arm around her waist for stability and used the other to help rinse her hair. He grabbed a loofa and squeezed soap into it. Gently, he scrubbed the blood from her skin.

Greer lifted her hand and traced the scratches in Damon's arms where her nails had broken through his skin. "I'm sorry I hurt you."

Damon pulled her into a hug. "Don't you dare apologize to me." He pressed a kiss to her wet hair. "I thought I lost you, Greer. When I saw you and the blood and that fucking hole in your chest, I thought you were gone."

"Gage was going to bring me back." She offered a wry smile. "I'm glad I'm not a vampire."

Serious, Damon tipped her chin up until she met his eyes. "It would be better than you being dead." He dropped the loofa onto the floor of the shower. "Can you wait here while I get towels?"

She nodded. "I'm feeling a little steadier, I think." She waited, shivering, while Damon dashed across the room and grabbed three towels from the closet. He wrapped one around his waist and brought the other two back to her. He carefully wrapped one around her body and used the other to wind around her hair. He helped her step out and gently lowered her back to the lid of the toilet.

"I'll get you some clothes." He went into his room and returned with one of his button down shirts. He held it until she slipped her arms inside and then buttoned it. He disappeared momentarily before returning in sweatpants and a t-shirt. "I'll help you to bed."

Greer let him lift her onto her feet. "Damon..." she trailed off sheepishly.

"What is it?"

"Do you think...I mean...would it be okay if I stayed with you? I don't feel like being alone quite yet."

Damon led her into his room. "You don't have to be alone." He nudged her onto the edge of the bed and waited patiently for her to slide her legs under the blankets before he flipped off the light and slid into the bed next to her. He smiled in the dark when her hand slipped into his and squeezed her fingers. "Try to get some sleep. You need it."

Greer was silent for several minutes. When she spoke again, her voice was a low whisper. "Damon?"

He turned his head to look at her. "Yeah?"

"Is my heart still beating?"

Damon rolled onto his side and propped himself up on one elbow. He reached out with the other hand and laid it on her chest. Her heart beat rhythmically against his fingers. "Your heart is still beating." He smiled when her fingers covered his. "Can't you feel it?"

"I just wanted to make sure." She rolled to face him, her hand pressing against his to keep it where it was on her chest. "I thought I was going to die."

Damon rubbed his thumb over her scar. "So did I."

"It made me realize something." She took a deep breath and tightened her fingers around his. "You're right about what you said earlier. We can't stop having lives. We have to have something to go back to when this is all over, and we can't let this be everything to us." Her voice was thick with tears. "When I was dying, do you know what I thought?"

"What did you think?"

"You're all I have. You're my family, Damon. We've been everything to each other for the last decade. And I thought I was going to die without giving in to what we both want." She blinked back tears. "I don't want to die without knowing what it's like to be with you."

Damon felt tears well in his eyes and leaned forward to touch their foreheads together. "I don't want you to do anything that you're not a hundred percent sure about. I never want you to regret anything that we do together."

Greer shook her head. "I won't regret it. I'm sure. I thought I could avoid it, that it would go away or that we'd get over it. I don't want that. I don't want to get over it or avoid it. I want you. I want to see what this is. I don't want to spend another day without knowing what it's like to be with you."

"I don't want to hurt you. You're so weak."

"I'm not that weak." She began slipping the buttons on her shirt from their holes. "You won't hurt me. Make love to me, Damon."

He brought her closer until she was pressed solidly against his body. Gently, he took her mouth with his. Her lips were soft and parted to accept the kiss. She laid one hand against his cheek and very timidly flicked her tongue against his lips. With a low groan, he deepened the kiss and delved into her mouth.

He wrapped his arms around her, his hands sliding beneath the shirt to knead her muscles. His palms slid over her skin and down to her ass. He gripped her solidly and she lifted her leg to wrap it around his hip.

Breathless, Greer broke the kiss and sat up, rising to her knees. She finished unbuttoning the shirt and slipped it from her shoulders, tossing the fabric to the floor next to the bed. Moonlight streamed through the curtains and her skin glowed in the ethereal light.

Damon rose to face her. He laid his hands on her waist and dipped his head to kiss her neck. He nipped the curve of her shoulder and soothed the slight sting with a lap of his tongue. Her head rolled to the side and he devoured her skin. One hand slid up the side of her body to cup her breast, his fingers gliding over her skin to the hardened peak. He pulled back several inches and held both her breasts in his hands, their weight feeling glorious in his grasp.

"Do you even know how beautiful you are?"

Before she could answer, he dipped his head and licked her nipple. He drew the point into his mouth, sucking gently and rubbing his tongue over it. He massaged her other breast with his fingers, his thumb stroking her nipple gently. Her head fell back and her hair streamed over her shoulders, her face twisted in an expression of pleasure. He lowered her gently to the mattress and used one hand to part her thighs.

He probed her entrance with his middle finger. She was wet and hot.

He pressed his thumb against her clit and rubbed gently. She sucked in a gasping breath and fisted her hands in his hair. Damon released her nipple with a slight pop and met her eyes, his burning hot from passion.

"I've wanted to do this to you since that night we left the city. I wanted to toss you down on that fucking mattress and bury myself in you time and again until we were too exhausted to do it anymore." He nuzzled her neck with his nose. "Now that I've tasted your skin, I don't know how we ever kept from doing this for as long as we did."

Greer didn't answer. She couldn't. Her toes curled on the mattress and her hips lifted, pressing harder against his hand. He rubbed faster, providing friction and pressure. Her fingers gripped the sheets on either side of her body and her eyes closed on a sigh. He slid down her body slowly, trailing hot kisses over her ribs. He traced the line of her scar gently, his lips soft on her skin. He nuzzled the curve of her belly, and scraped his teeth over her hip playfully. When she jumped and a whimper escaped her, he rubbed his nose against her inner thigh.

His breath was moist and warm and she held hers in anticipation. He pressed a kiss to her, and her thighs fell open, exposing her completely to his gaze and touch. Without warning, he licked her. His tongue was soft and hot, and her hips leaped off the bed at his touch. He gripped her hips in his hands and buried his face between her thighs.

Greer's thighs tightened on his head, her hands went to his hair and tangled there, and her back arched slightly, pushing her harder against him. She was panting and gasping as he stabbed his tongue into her, the waves of pleasure almost too much to bear. His name was a low moan on her lips as she begged him to both stop and keep going at the same time.

Damon felt her muscles tense. He rubbed his tongue on that hard bundle of nerves that was the key to her ecstasy. Her whole body was wound tight with tension. Slowly, his hands traveled up her body until they cupped her breasts. He rubbed his thumbs over her nipples as he used his tongue to penetrate her. He felt her climax nearing as her muscles clenched and released. He spurred her on with his mouth and hands. In an instant, she flew apart, a ragged groan bursting from her as her orgasm rolled through her.

Her chest was heaving as she tried to catch her breath. Damon inconspicuously wiped his mouth on the sheet before laying down next to her and drawing her into his arms. She reached between their bodies, her fingers sliding inside his pants and brushing against the velvety hardness of his erection. Before she could wrap her hand around him, he reached down and twined their fingers, bringing her knuckles to his lips.

"Don't. I want you to enjoy tonight."

Greer blinked rapidly. "That was amazing, Damon. I don't want it to be over."

He kissed her deeply. "It's far from over." He rolled to the edge of the bed and opened the nightstand drawer. He pulled out a box of condoms and removed one. Greer's eyes widened.

"Where in the world did you get those?" She snatched it out of his hands. "A box of those cost a weeks' rations!"

Damon leaned back into the pillows. "Not here. Remember, this is before everything collapsed. These are about fifty cents apiece." He took it back and ripped it open. "If you're done ogling, I'm going to put it on now."

Greer giggled. "Do you even know how?"

He glared at her. "I have used a condom before, babe."

She giggled as he efficiently stripped off his clothes and rolled the condom on over his erection. He grabbed her hips and dragged her across the bed until she was under him. "I always wondered how you didn't have an army of little Mackenzies running around."

She lifted her legs to wrap around him. She jumped and shivered when she felt the tip of his penis probe her. He gripped her hip in one hand and used the other to guide himself. Inch by delicious inch he sank into her, until finally, he was buried inside. She squirmed and groaned.

"My God, that's good." She leaned up and kissed him, wrapping her arms around his shoulders. "We should have done this years ago."

He silenced her with another kiss. He withdrew from her body until only the very tip penetrated her before sinking back in until their bodies were anchored together. She was wet and hot and surrounded him like a fist. His hips pumped, driving himself into her in long, hard thrusts that made her eyes cross. She lifted her own hips to drive him deeper, her hands gripping his back desperately.

"Damon..." His name was a ragged whisper. "I want...I need..."

Damon sank his teeth into her earlobe and soothed the sting with his tongue. "What do you need, baby? Tell me." He nuzzled her neck. "You're so wet, so damn hot. I could do this for days." He slid out and back in, enjoying the slippery slide into her each time he thrust. "Tell me what you need to make you soar."

"More. Don't stop."

He laughed, the sound low and raunchy. "I'm not about to stop." He slowed his pace so that he was rocking his hips against hers to give her clitoral stimulation. "Do you want it slow like that?" He sped up the thrusts until he was pounding into her. "Or do you want it hard and fast?"

White-hot pleasure speared through her as he spoke. She planted her feet on the mattress and let her thighs fall open so that he had better access to her body. He leaned down and licked one of her nipples before sucking it into his mouth. He rolled it between his teeth, applying pressure just short of pain. He rubbed his tongue over the point, and Greer wondered briefly if it was possible to die from sex.

"How do you want it, Greer?" He lifted his head from her breast to meet her eyes. Sweat beaded on his forehead as he stroked into her. The veins on his neck had started to pop out from effort to hold himself back. She could feel his penis twitch when he held himself still, waiting for her to tell him her desires. She propped herself up on her elbows and nuzzled her face into the side of his neck until her lips were pressed against his ear.

"I want you to take me like you wanted to that night in the apartment. Finish what we started."

Damon lifted one of her legs and wrapped it around his hip, his hand sprawling on her thigh. He slid the other arm beneath her and crushed her against his body. His eyes bore into her, hot and bright. He leaned down and took her mouth in a searing kiss.

"Hold on."

He drove himself into her over and over again, spearing into her, his flesh hard and unyielding where hers was soft and supple. Every stroke took her closer to the edge, and she pushed her hips upward, silently begging for more. The whole bed moved as he thrust, and Greer's fingers fisted in the sheet so tightly that she pulled it off of the mattress.

Damon kissed her neck, using his lips, tongue and teeth to bring her pleasure. The only sounds in the room were their heavy breathing and the noise produced by their bodies moving together. Her body began to clench and release around him, signaling that she was near orgasm. He stilled within her for several moments, enjoying her whimpers and the movements of her body as he held climax just out of reach. He released her hip and reached between their bodies, rubbing her gently. Her head thrashed on the pillow, and she clamped down on him like a vise.

He was balancing on the edge of his own orgasm and slipped from her slowly. He was wet and slick from the moisture of her body, and he teased her entrance with the head of his penis, rubbing her with the hardness before slipping the tip inside again. He eased his hips back and forth, slow and easy, making them both groan as they tried to hold back. Greer rolled her hips to give her friction where she needed as she bucked them, trying to take him deeper.

Damon gripped her hips harder to hold them still. "You're fucking gorgeous right now. Hot and horny and about to come."

He pulled her forward until she slipped completely down on him and her legs were fully around him. He leaned over her until he clamped his mouth on hers in a deep kiss. He drove his hips into hers twice, planting himself as deep as possible before again reaching between their bodies and pressing his thumb against her clit. With a muffled yelp, she flew apart.

He rode her through her orgasm, until her muscles went limp and she was spasming around him from ecstasy before he gave in to his own and buried himself to the hilt, his release overtaking him. He wrapped his arms around her and rolled, dragging her onto his chest as he collapsed to the mattress. He flailed one arm, grasping the blanket in his fingers and dragging the quilt over her shaking, sweaty body.

Greer lifted her head and clawed her hair out of her face. Damon's chest heaved as he tried to catch his breath. She grinned down at him, her cheeks rosy red and her face betraying her satisfaction. He dragged her down for a kiss.

"Yours is the face of a woman who has been well fucked, babe."

She giggled and nestled her head on his chest. "You're amazing."

"I know." He grunted when she elbowed him in the stomach. "Hey! What was that for?"

"Cocky much?"

He wiggled his eyebrows. "I don't know, you tell me."

He laughed when she smacked him again. Gently, he lowered her to the bed next to him and rose. He yanked off the condom and tossed it into the trashcan before striding into the bathroom and returning with a glass of water. He drained half of it and offered the rest to her.

"Thanks." She took the cup and finished it, stretching to the side to place the empty cup on the bedside table. Damon climbed back into bed and stretched out next to her, his big body dwarfing her much smaller one. She scooted toward him, wrapping one arm around his waist and resting her head on his shoulder. "Did you enjoy yourself?"

He gaped at her. "At what point did you wonder if I was enjoying my-self?" He ran his fingers up her side. "The part where I was tasting every glorious inch of you? Or maybe the part where I finally got inside you?" He kissed the side of her head. "Or was it when I came so hard I thought my dick was going to shoot off my body?"

Greer flushed deep red and closed her eyes. "Stupid question, huh?"

"Just a bit." He kissed the side of her head. "Chill, babe. Not one damn thing is going to change between now and an hour ago."

"Except for your need to give me pet names."

They were both still giggling when Gabriel appeared at the foot of the bed in a flash of light. Greer yanked the blanket over her chest as Damon sat up. "Don't you know how to knock?"

Gabriel snapped his fingers and Greer was wearing one of Damon's shirts and a pair of underwear. "I need you to come with me right now. The life of Braxton's sister hangs in the balance. I don't know if she can be saved."

Greer looked down at herself and back up at Gabriel. "What hap-pened?"

Gabriel sighed in annoyance. "The Devils found where they were hid-ing. Samantha was taken to Abalam and tortured. Braxton and Alaria are there now. I need you to come with me right this instant if she is to have a chance at being saved."

Greer held out her hand. "Take me to her."

Chapter Twenty

August 18th, 2030 - Colorado
SAM'S CHEST WAS barely rising when Greer appeared in the cave. She raced across the chamber and dropped to her knees. Braxton moved back to give her more room to work, his eyes worried and his face strained. She laid her hands on Sam and immediately dove into the act of Healing. Her eyes went white and a soft blue light emanated from her hands. She reached inside Sam's body and searched desperately for any flickers of life. She knew the instant she entered Sam that there was little to no chance of reviving the woman.

Her heart was still beating. Greer focused on that and initiated small shocks to the vessels to help it beat stronger. A glimmer of hope formed when the organ pumped more blood and the chambers opened and closed regularly. She found the deepest wounds and sealed them shut, creating new skin and weaving new veins and blood vessels. Before she could move on from the deep gashes in Sam's back, her heart stopped beating.

Greer raced back through the vessels and into the struggling organ. She searched wildly for the injury. Finding none, she used the shocks to stimulate the heart into beating again. It beat four times before stopping. She knew that if there was no specific defect in the heart it was either a problem in the brain or there was not enough blood left to pump effectively. Desperate to save the rapidly waning life, she reached into the brain, looking for activity. She found darkness.

She searched for any flickers of light that would show her where there was still some neurological activity. She saw one synapse fire and rushed to it, working to fan it into flame. It flickered and wavered, bursting into life for the span of a heartbeat before slipping away into darkness. Three more times she tried to stimulate the synapse before giving up on it and continuing her search. She found a vessel bleeding near the stem of the brain and worked on repairing it, hoping that it would help fan the brain back into activity. It sealed easily, but there was no resulting increase in light.

It was getting harder to focus. Darkness threatened to overtake her field of vision, and she knew that staying much longer without progress was going to risk her own life. She forced herself to concentrate. Her work on the brain done, she went to the heart again. The organ was black. Dead. Swearing, she raced back to the brain, trying desperately to find a flicker of life. Nothing. Black encroached on her, and she scrambled to find anything that she could work with.

It was a fight that was lost before she'd arrived; she knew that unequivocally. Yet Greer still fought for any movement, any signs of life. Pain closed in on her, and she knew she was pushing too hard. It was beyond her ability to bring the dead back to life. The black closed in on her faster. She tried to pull out of Sam's body as it shut down, but she was too late. Death was coming.

It enveloped her, heavy and hot. She struggled to fight through it, the light that told her how to leave getting smaller with each passing second. She battled toward the light, following the sound of voices back into her own body. She snapped back into herself and fell to the floor, blood trickling from her nose, ears and eyes as a seizure wracked her body.

Alaria grabbed Greer and held her head to keep it from smacking on the stone floor. Her muscles contracted and became rigid as she shook. Gabriel rushed across the room and laid his hand on her forehead. The seizure stopped, and she collapsed into Alaria's lap, her breathing ragged and her eyes barely open. After several moments of panting and blinking, Greer managed to meet Braxton's gaze.

"I'm sorry."

Braxton bent over his sister's body and sobbed, his shoulders shaking with the force of the cries. Alaria helped Greer sit up before going to Braxton's side and taking one of his hands in both of hers in a small gesture of comfort. Gabriel sighed.

"Braxton, I cannot apologize enough for what has happened. I swear to you that they were fine when I left them."

Braxton rubbed his eyes and lifted his head, anger melding with grief in his expression. "It's not your fault." He shifted his gaze to Greer. "I know you did your best. She was too far gone when we got here. Even she knew it." He climbed to his feet and stared at Abalam, who was still confined in the Devil's trap. "He's the one responsible. He's the one who's going to pay."

Alaria cleared her throat. "I think we need to figure out what to do with the baby."

Gabriel took the infant off of her mother's still chest. "I will take the child to Heaven. She will sleep peacefully until this is over and will then be returned. There is no other safer place available for her."

Braxton nodded. "Do it." He waited until the Angel had disappeared. "Are you hurt, Greer?"

Greer shook her head. "I was weak, Brax. Maybe if I'd been at full strength..." She trailed off. "I was attacked on the dream plane. It took everything I had to keep myself alive tonight. I didn't have much left to work with. I'm sorry."

He shook his head and reached out to squeeze her hand. "Anyone could see how hard you fought." He turned to Alaria. "Do you think he knows where Laelia is?"

Alaria walked to the edge of the trap and studied Abalam. "I don't know. Do you know where Laelia is?"

Abalam glowered at her. "You're a traitor to your own kind. How do you live with yourself, rubbing elbows with them? You had the throne on the left hand of Lucifer! You gave it up for humans? You're a disappointment to Hell."

Alaria smiled. "Good." She strode to the tray of instruments and studied it. "This is a nice array you've got here, Abalam. How much thought went into figuring out which tools you wanted to use to kill Sam?"

He chuckled. "Standard tools. I use the same ones on souls every day down under."

She glanced over her shoulder, her hair streaming down her back and tight leather accentuating every curve. "I know." She chewed on her lip thoughtfully. "I'm going to give you one chance here. Tell me what I want to know and I'll let you walk out of here alive. If you refuse to tell me, I'll kill you. If you don't know what I want to find out, you're of no use and I'll kill you. Sound simple enough?"

"You can't kill me. The Jesus knife has been used."

She stooped to pull out a sharp knife from Braxton's knapsack. "You're right on both counts, brother. I can't kill you. What I can do is make you wish you were dead." She ran her fingers over each item on the tray reverently, almost lovingly. "Where is Laelia?"

Abalam laughed again. "Good luck."

Alaria clucked her tongue. "I don't need luck, sweetheart. I've got skill." She glanced at Greer. "Paint me Devil's traps under that chair. We're going to give Abalam here a little taste of his own medicine. He's going to tell me everything I need to know about Laelia. We don't have long before the idiots will be here, so there's no time to waste." She looked down at Braxton. "We need to give her a Warrior's sendoff. We can't leave her body to be possessed."

"I know." Braxton stroked his hand over Sam's hair. "I want to do it for my parents, too. I'll ask Gabriel to take them to Gage's. It'll be safe there." He stood, carefully placing Sam on the floor. "What can I do?"

"Get me some holy water and sterilize these things. They'll sting a bit more if they're blessed."

"Coming right up."

Alaria snapped her fingers and Abalam was bound, hand and food, with a gag stuffed in his mouth to keep him from abandoning the body as soon as he was free from the trap. She cocked her head to the side. "I can see that you're curious. I'll explain. When God made me human, He couldn't separate me from some of my talents. I got to keep some of the fun stuff. I'm finding a myriad of ways to make use of the abilities." She jerked her chin at Braxton, who had finished pouring holy water on the tray. "Head up top and release the jackass. I'm going to strap him into his seat."

She waited patiently, tapping her foot absently until she felt the protections drop. She strode to Abalam and seized the binds holding his wrists in one of her hands. She dragged him across the floor and shoved him into the chair. With efficient movements, she shackled his hands and feet and fastened the leather straps around his chest and forehead to hold him upright in the chair.

"I spent thousands of years learning how to torture from him. It was never my thing, but since I wanted to stay in Hell, I had to earn my keep." She smiled brightly. "Let's see if the student has surpassed the master yet, shall we?" When Abalam didn't answer, she completed the conversation on her own. "I think we shall."

Braxton reappeared in the door. "What are you going to do to him?"

Alaria clapped her hands. "I'm going to do to him everything he did to Sam and then some. He's going to be begging to tell me what I want to know before I'm done." She lifted her eyebrows at Braxton. "Do you want a crack at him?"

Braxton shook his head and circled the chair. "I'll let you do your thing. I want it to be as effective as possible."

Abalam chuckled. "You're stupider than I thought you were, Alaria. Lilith, Abaddon and Azazel will be here any second, and they'll tear your head off your shoulders. I can only hope you're headed to Hell so I can spend the next ten million years carving you to pieces."

She leaned close to whisper in his ear. "Not. Gonna. Happen." She straightened and studied her choices for several moments. "I forget, Abalam. Do you normally start with the drill or the scalpel?" She picked the drill up in one hand and applied pressure to the trigger, the mechanical noise of the electric tool filling the chamber. She looked at Greer and Braxton. "If either of you get queasy easily, you might want to wait outside."

Braxton sat down on the floor. "I want a front row seat to this."

Greer squared her shoulders. "I'll stay, too."

Alaria turned back to Abalam. "See that? They've never even met you and they want to hear you scream. Imagine how I feel having known you for millions of years." She giggled happily. "There's enough Devil left in me that I am going to enjoy this." She placed the scalpel on the tray deliberately, then carefully chose a bit for the drill. "How did you start with her? Did you pull her fingernails off? Or did you burn her? Maybe you sliced off tiny pieces of meat with that scalpel?" She pulled the trigger on the drill again. "Which is it, Abalam? This is an easy question."

The Devil snarled and bared his teeth. "I carved off her nipples and removed a few extra toes."

Alaria smiled. "That sounds like a good place to start to me." She looked over her shoulder at Braxton. "Any objections?"

His mouth was set in a thin line and his eyes blazed. "None at all."

Alaria replaced the drill on the tray and chose a scalpel, the blade gleaming in the light of the lamp. She held it up and examined it, running her fingers along the handle lovingly. She laid it back down and repeated the ritual with a pair of pliers. The blade of the scalpel was razor sharp, and the pliers gleamed ominously. She selected a rubber band and tied her hair away from her face.

Alaria smiled grimly and decided on the scalpel. She used the blade to slice his shirt off. "This is gonna be fun."

Chapter Twenty-One

Skin had some elasticity. It fought the scalpel briefly before succumbing to the cut. Once the blade reached muscle, there was more resistance. It was surprising how difficult it was to guide the edge through it with enough force to cut. Once removed from the body, flesh took on a slightly rubbery feel and made a slippery plop onto the floor when it was tossed.

Alaria bent her head over her task, carving Abalam's small, hard nipples from his chest. She held the scalpel in one hand and a cloth in the other to keep the blood out of her way. The Devil clamped his mouth shut and swallowed scream after scream. Alaria smiled when she heard the muffled noises deep in his chest.

"It's different when you're human. There are pain receptors in the skin that tell you how bad it hurts. There are nerves that will keep firing for a long time after I pull this knife out of you. Everything is diluted when you're not in a corporeal form. You can't control it when you're in a human body." She snarled at him. "I can't kill you, but I can make you die a thousand deaths before I'm done."

"I'll carve you apart in Hell, Alaria." Abalam spat the words violently, the veins in his neck straining against the skin. Alaria briefly considered slicing into one of them but decided that would cause too much damage to the body Abalam inhabited.

"We'll see about that." She stepped back to study her work—the two round meaty chunks missing from his chest. "Toes next, is that right?" She exchanged the scalpel for the pliers. "Do you want to tell me where Laelia is? Or do we keep going?"

Abalam glared at her. "Do your worst."

Alaria stooped to remove his boots and socks. "You're going to regret saying that."

She positioned his smallest toe between the grips of the pliers. She staunchly ignored the wave of nausea that was moving through her stomach and clenched the handles of the pliers together. There was a loud pop, a ripping sound when she jerked the pliers, and the toe fell to the floor. Blood streamed out of the wound on his foot, and Abalam threw his head back and screamed.

"I've always heard the saying that there's more than one way to skin a cat. I wonder how many ways there are to skin a Devil?"

Abalam laughed psychotically. "I don't care what you do to me, you bitch, but for the love of Satan, shut the fuck up while you do it!"

Alaria cut off another toe. The resulting screams echoed off the walls and filled the chamber. Greer was turning green and looked as if she would throw up at any second. Braxton's eyes never left the grisly scene, his expression betraying the dark pleasure he received from watching Abalam be tortured.

Alaria picked up a pair of scissors and laid her hands on his thighs, the metal blade cool against her hand. She leaned forward until her nose was barely an inch from his. When she spoke, her voice was low and intense. "Did you rape her?"

Abalam remained silent. Alaria opened the scissors and lopped off a piece of his ear carelessly. Blood sprayed the wall and coated her face. Silently, Braxton climbed to his feet and got her a wet cloth. She dabbed at the blood delicately, wiping both cheeks and her forehead to remove the red drops.

"I'll ask again. Did you rape her?" She picked up the speculum laying on the tray and shoved it under his nose. "Did you use this on her? Did you put your hands on her?"

Abalam took a heaving breath and smiled at her. "One question at a time, darling. Torture is only effective if you're consistent with the information sought."

Angry, Alaria removed another chunk of his ear, snapping the blades of the scissors together and ripping the cartilage from his body. He bit down on his tongue so hard that blood spurted from his mouth and dribbled down his chin, mingling with the blood still seeping from the holes in his chest where his nipples had once been.

She pressed her mouth against the bleeding ear. "I don't need your advice on how to make you talk." She stepped back and raised her voice so that everyone else could hear her. "Even if you don't give us what we want, Braxton is going to be very happy to see you suffer for what you had done to his family, aren't you, Braxton?"

Braxton nodded, his face grim and his eyes lit with fury. "I'm giddy with happiness at the thought of it."

Alaria used the scalpel to slice away pieces of denim until Abalam was naked. "If I cut your dick off, you'll bleed to death. I don't want that. I'm going to save that part of your body for the unlikely event you don't give me what I want." She picked up a wicked- looking piece of equipment. "Dentists use these, don't they?" She turned it over in her hand. "I think you use this to pull out teeth." She shrugged. "We'll find out. Brax, come hold his head still for me."

"Gladly."

Braxton climbed to his feet and crossed the room to stand at the back of the chair. Even with the strap around his head, Abalam could move several inches from side to side. Braxton seized the Devil's head in both his hands and held him still by wrapping one arm around his forehead and gripping Abalam's chin in the other, forcing his mouth open.

Alaria studied his teeth for ten seconds before reaching into his mouth and clamping the extractor around a molar. She gritted her own teeth and closed her eyes for a split second before jerking her hand back and tearing the tooth from the jaw. There was a sucking noise as the roots struggled to hold on to the bone and the tooth left a gaping hole in its wake. She threw it onto the floor carelessly and twirled the extractor in her fingers. Abalam spat mouthfuls of blood.

"Where is Laelia?"

His voice was thick from swallowing blood and spit. "You're not tough enough for this. You're already getting green around the edges, and I can tell you're about to vomit. You don't have the guts to do this. Not anymore. I can practically smell the fear and the nausea."

Alaria swallowed hard and grabbed his chin to hold it still. "I'll cut you into a thousand tiny pieces if I need to. You will tell me where Laelia is."

Gabriel appeared in the chamber with a crack of thunder, Damon on one side and Gage on the other. He surveyed the situation carefully, his nose wrinkling when he saw Abalam in the chair and the extractor in Alaria's hand. He stepped forward, purposely standing between Alaria and the Devil.

"What is going on?"

Alaria tried to side-step him before huffing and placing her hands on her hips, everything about her stance defiant. "He has information we need. I'm going to get it out of him." She crossed her arms over her breasts, the ample curves straining against the leather bustier. Gabriel couldn't help glancing at the ivory globes. Alaria smirked. "What are they doing here?" She nodded to Damon and Gage.

"They were on their way to the airport and Gage's private aircraft. I decided it was more effective for all of us to be present in the same place." Gabriel glanced around again, taking in the other four people in the room. "May we speak for a moment elsewhere?"

Alaria shrugged. "Sure." She tossed the extractor to Braxton. "Don't kill him while I'm gone." She smiled saucily. "Might as well keep going. We don't want to lose ground while I have a chat."

Braxton clamped the extractor on Abalam's left pinky. "I won't."

She reluctantly followed the Angel outside the cave. His gait told her he was upset and the rigidity in his shoulders told her he was worried. She laid a hand on his shoulder. "What is it? Has something happened?"

Gabriel whirled to face her, his eyes filled with fear and apprehension. "I leave to care for an orphan and when I return you're ripping a man's teeth from his skull." He held out his hands, palms up. "What could possibly be wrong with this situation?"

Alaria blinked several times, struggling to understand. "He knows where Laelia is, Gabe. I can make him tell me."

"At what cost?"

"At what cost? What the hell does that mean?" She gestured wildly toward the cavern. "He's a fucking Devil! It's not like I'm in there torturing a person! You saw what he did to Sam! He killed her, Gabe. He tortured her to death. He deserves everything he's getting. The only cost I see is that he's getting some well-deserved pain for what he did to Sam."

"Is this about information or retribution?"

Alaria glared at him. "I don't see why it can't be about both." She sighed when he stalked away from her. "Don't walk away from me, Gabe! I wouldn't do it if there was nothing to be gained from it. He knows what we need to know."

"Exactly how long do you anticipate Laelia will still be there once he tells Lilith and Azazel what you've procured from him?"

"I don't know! It's better than nothing! If we don't stop this soon, there's going to be no point in stopping it at all. You preach about preventing Greer and Damon's world, and then you balk at us doing what is necessary to prevent it. You have to pick a side here, Gabe. You can't have it both ways. Sometimes we're gonna have to do bad things for the greater good." She jabbed her finger toward the chamber where screams were still echoing as Braxton continued torturing the Devil. "We need to make progress. Getting information is how we do it." She narrowed her eyes. "I've known you since the beginning of time. You've never had a problem with a little violence before."

"I only condone it when it is ordered by God and justified by the circumstances."

Frustrated, Alaria groaned and stared up at the sky. "What part of this isn't justified?"

"I'm not sure the information you will get is going to be information that we can use. Laelia is likely protected by Angel wards. I am not going to be able to take you to where she is. If Abalam gets back to the others before we get to her, all of this will have been for nothing. How can you not see that?"

"It'll give us a starting point. It's better than nothing, which is what we have now." Getting angry, she paced. "Do you have a problem with what is being done, or that it's me who is doing it?"

Gabriel didn't respond. He averted his eyes from her and deliberately arranged his face into one of neutrality. Alaria laughed bitterly and clapped her hands, the sound echoing through the clearing. The Angel looked embarrassed.

"It's because it's me. You self-righteous asshole. How dare you judge me!"

Gabriel looked pained. "I fear for what these actions will do to you. As a human, you're intrinsically weaker than you were as either an Angel or as a Devil."

"Weak?" Alaria gaped at him. "You think I'm weak? These actions aren't going to do anything to me! I'm not going to revert to being a Devil just because I have to make some hard choices. Someone has to make the hard decisions. This needed doing, and we both know it!" She stalked toward him until they were toe to toe. "You want us to save the world?" She poked a finger into his chest. "Answer me, damn you. Do you want us to save the world?"

He nodded. "Yes."

"Then this is how it gets done." She stomped back inside. "Do us both a favor and mind your own damn business. I don't need your input on this."

Gabriel was gone before Alaria had taken two steps. She ignored the pangs in her chest and strode purposefully back to where Abalam was restrained. The light in his eyes told her he'd heard every word. She picked up the scissors.

"I'm sick of playing games. You're either going to tell me what you know, or you're going to get cut apart. I don't care if the skin suit dies, I don't care if you go back to Hell and have to claw your way out of the Lake, and I don't care what the fuck happens to you aside from you telling me what I want to know."

"Fucking an Angel." Abalam chuckled. "I always thought you had the hots for brother Gabe. Though I had always suspected he had his cock removed to make sure he'd never use it."

Alaria ignored him and drove the scissors into his thigh. Braxton and Gage exchanged a concerned look. She grasped both handles of the scissors and wrenched them apart, splitting muscle and skin and opening a six inch hole in Abalam's leg. He screamed and wailed, his head slamming against the restraints. She yanked the scissors out and let them clatter to the floor.

"Where is Laelia?"

Abalam laughed hysterically. "Angels and Devils. I never thought I'd see the day Gabriel fucked a Devil. Oh, how the mighty have fallen. You, I get. You never were one of us. Weren't one of them, either, but that's beside the point. I wonder how horny that Angel had to be before he'd stick his dick in you."

Alaria sighed. "Where is Laelia?"

"I should tell you just so you'll all die when you storm it like the beach at Normandy. How many demons do you think you can take on? How many witches?" He lifted his lips in a snarl. "What're you going to do when another group of demons comes through that Gate? They're angry and strong, and they'll burst through those protections and gobble you all up before you have a chance to fight them off."

Alaria picked up the drill and pressed the trigger twice. "You're not attached to those eyes, are you?"

He was screaming before the drill even touched him. Blood and vitreous fluid burst from the eyeball as it popped and drained down his face—a wet, sticky trail tinged with blood. Alaria picked up the pliers again and gripped one of Abalam's fingernails in it. She pulled, the nail peeling from the finger with a sucking noise. It held to the digit with strings of flesh and skin before snapping completely off. Blood welled where the nail had covered, and Alaria poured holy water on it, watching as the skin sizzled and burned.

"Where is Laelia?"

Abalam stared at her with his one eye. "If I tell you, will you send me back?"

Alaria took a step back and wiped her hands on a cloth. "Yes."

"I want your word."

"You have it."

He smiled evilly. "She's in Hell."

Alaria blinked. "What do you mean, she's in Hell?"

"Exactly what it sounds like."

Braxton climbed to his feet and crossed to stand next to Alaria, their shoulders touching. "How did she get there?"

Abalam laughed, his teeth bloody and his one eye alight with glee. "Lilith chopped her head off. We beat you to it!"

Alaria grabbed a screwdriver and plunged it into his other eye with a furious shriek. She ripped it out, the eyeball on the metal staff. Abalam screamed, his eyelids closing to cover the wide holes where his eyes had been only minutes earlier.

"You're a fucking liar!"

"Why? Because now you've lost before you've begun! Do you think we don't know what goes on in Heaven? That we had no idea how the Gate could be closed? There are some Angels who stayed with God for information, not because they wanted to. We knew what you had to do, and we got to her first. Once she knew what was going on, Laelia was happy to give up her head. To us, death is just a change in scenery and there's plenty for her to do down there."

There was a stirring sound, and Michael appeared in the chamber. He took in the situation with one glance and smiled smugly. "They've certainly got you by the balls, don't they?" He didn't wait for an answer before turning to Alaria. "I'm sure you're having a wonderful time, but one of the demons has alerted Lilith to what is going on. You're about to have way too many Devils on your hands to handle. Since Gabriel is being a whiny baby, I've come to return you to Gage's estate."

Gage bit his lip to keep from laughing. "What do we do with him?" He jerked his head toward Abalam.

"I'll be taking him somewhere safe. Don't worry. I can't hold him indefinitely, but it should be enough time for you to formulate a strategy without the others knowing what you were told. Get in a circle, please. It'll make it easier and faster to send you all at once."

Braxton hesitated. "I want to bury my family."

"You'll be given an opportunity to do so. I'll make sure that the bodies are returned to you within minutes after your arrival back in Scotland, but I must prioritize getting you all out of here safely." He waited impatiently while they arranged themselves in a circle. Michael reached out to touch each forehead before snapping his fingers. In the time it took to blink, they were standing in Gage's kitchen.

Damon dropped onto one of the bar stools. "What the hell do we do now?"

Greer lifted her head and cleared her throat. "I know exactly what we do." She waited until the other three were looking at her. "I go get Laelia."

Chapter Twenty-Two

THE UPROAR WAS instant. Four voices fired words at Greer at the same time. She let them rant for thirty seconds before slamming a coffee cup down hard enough to make a loud noise, getting their attention. Once all four mouths were shut, she took a deep breath and spoke.

"It's the only thing that makes sense. I'm the only one who stands a chance. If they can come out of the Hell Gate, I can go into it. I'm the only one with a prayer of coming back out." Braxton put his hands on his hips. "How the fuck do you figure that?"

Greer pulled a knife out of the block and dug it into her palm. She held up the bloody wound and concentrated on it. Within seconds, the skin pulled together and sealed shut. "Because I'm the only one who can do that." She sighed deeply. "We all know we're here for particular reasons. Even if Gabriel doesn't know why, God does. This is obviously my part in it. I'm going to have to drag that bitch out of Hell so we can kill her again. If anyone can get out of there alive, it's going to be me. One of you gets hurt, and there's nothing to do but pray. I get hurt, and I heal myself."

Damon shook his head. "You can't continually do that. You'll wear yourself out, and any serious injury will take a lot of energy out of you."

"I would still get another shot at it. You'd be dead. It's the best chance we've got."

"She's right." Gage's voice was low and raw. "I don't like it either, but she's right. We can work on her healing. We'll make her stronger. We can train for it. We'll need something to tie that bitch to, anyway. It's only her spirit in Hell. Her body was destroyed when they chopped her head off. In order to force her out, we have to anchor her to something in order for her to take a corporeal form. It's the only way we get her blood." He thought briefly. "I'll have to figure that out."

Damon shook his head again. "I don't like the idea. What are the odds that she makes it back out of Hell alive?" He held up his hands.

"Don't get me wrong, I want to kill the bitch as much as anyone else, but we can't send anyone to Hell without a pretty damn good chance they come back."

Braxton's mouth was set in a thin line. "As much as I hate to admit it, she's right. She's got a better shot than any of us do. If we can strengthen her ability to heal herself, we'll buy more time for her and give her an even bigger advantage. If we can keep the Devils from going in after her, we might be able to get it done, but it's going to require all of us working together."

Damon looked between them. "I think we need to think long and hard about this before we just let her traipse into Hell and go after Laelia."

Gage laid a hand on Damon's shoulder. "Son, before this is over, we're all going to have to take our turn. We need Greer to finish this, so trust me when I tell you that no one is expecting her to die doing this. We have to maximize our chance at success, and as much as you might hate it, letting her go is the best shot we've got."

Greer reached out and covered Damon's hands with one of hers. "I'm not lookin' to die. We all have to take chances. It's my turn."

Braxton cleared his throat. "I'm going up to bed. I have to bury my sister and my parents tomorrow, so if it's all the same to you, I'm going to drown my sorrows in some of your awesome bourbon, Gage."

Gage nodded. "I'll send up a couple bottles to your room."

Braxton grinned and headed up the stairs. "See that you do."

Alaria watched him ascend the stairs with regret in her eyes. She stood as well. "I'm calling it a night, too. We've all had a long day, so I suggest you get some sleep. Tomorrow is not going to be easy on him, and when something isn't easy on Braxton, he makes damn sure that it isn't easy on anyone else, either." She brushed her hand over Greer's shoulder. "You did good today, kid."

Greer watched as Alaria descended the steps into the basement. She wondered briefly why the woman never stayed on the second or third floor with the rest of them before she turned to Damon, who was still pacing the kitchen, his expression dark and angry.

"I'm not doing this because I have some sort of a death wish." She slipped off the stool and stood directly in front of him to stop the pacing. "It has to be done, Damon."

Damon nodded. "I know that. I just don't like the idea of you going in there alone. Alaria lived in Hell for ten million years. Let her go."

"They could kill her. It's harder to kill me. Besides, don't you think they'd know the second she got there?"

He snorted. "As opposed to you sneaking in, finding this vampire and getting out undetected?" He leaned against the island. "The odds of that aren't good, babe."

"I have a better chance than Alaria does of making it work." She reached out and took his hand, unreasonably hurt when he pulled it from her grasp. "Don't be mad at me."

Damon reached out and squeezed her hand quickly. "I'm not mad at you. I wish you'd have talked to me about this before making a decision to do it. We're supposed to be in this together, Greer."

"Are we any more in it than they are? We have to do this together. If it's me and you, and Gabe and Alaria, and Braxton all by himself, we're all going to end up dead. We have to trust each other and work together. That means making decisions as a group instead of just the two of us."

Damon glared at her before stomping to the stairs. "This will be over eventually, Greer. When it is, it's going to go back to being you and me. We've always been in it together and we always will be. This is just temporary. We need to be together on stuff, not sacrificing the trust we've spent fifteen years developing just to be a part of this. It's not worth it." He paused at the bottom of the stairs. "In all the time we've known each other, I've never stopped you from doing what needed to be done. That's not going to stop now. If this is the way it needs doing, fine. I just wish you would have discussed it with me before throwing it out there for the rest of them."

Greer flipped off the lights and followed him up the stairs and down the hall. She reached for the knob on her door across the hall, still not ready to go into the room where she'd been attacked. Damon opened his door, looked at the bed—still rumpled from the lovemaking that suddenly seemed like it had taken place a life time ago—and stalked across the hall. He laid his hand on hers, stopping her from turning the knob. She turned her head slightly to look at him.

"What?"

Damon brushed his nose against her cheek. "Just because I'm pissed off doesn't mean you get to hide out and pretend what we did earlier didn't happen."

Greer forced herself not to lean into his touch. His body was close enough that the heat he put off was seeping into her chilled skin. She shook her head. "We need to get some sleep."

"We will. Together. In my bed. You made your decision, Greer. I'm not going to let you walk away from this now."

Greer closed her eyes in defense against the tears that threatened to spill over. "Damon, we both know we shouldn't have done what we did. It was impulsive and stupid and the timing is all wrong—" Her words were cut off when Damon spun her around and slammed her back against the wall, his mouth covering hers in a searing kiss. Her head ground against the door frame, and her knees buckled as desire rose up and engulfed her.

"Don't tell me we shouldn't do this. We both want it. We've both wanted it for years. Dammit, Greer, you're my best friend, my family—you're everything to me. We've kept each other alive, and I would lay my life down for you. Why are you so scared of this?"

Damon's voice was tinged with desperation. His eyes betrayed the hurt he felt—the hurt she had caused. Greer couldn't stop the tear that slipped from her eye and trailed down her cheek to drip off of her chin. She sucked in a breath and forced herself to lift her eyes to meet his gaze.

"Because neither of us have ever been good at relationships, and we both know this isn't about the sex. I'm afraid we'll ruin each other."

He braced his forehead against hers and pushed into her mind almost before she allowed the access. "*Silly woman. Hasn't it crossed your mind that the reason we screw up relationships with other people is because we wanted each other instead?*" He kissed her again, and she was shocked when she felt the kiss from her perspective and from his at the same time through their mental link. He pulled back, his gaze intense. "*You can't tell me you didn't know we'd end up together in the end. We live in each other's heads, Greer. No one else can come close to understanding what we share. Like it or not, we're meant for each other.*"

Greer spoke out loud. "The problem is that I like it."

Damon shook his head. "That's not a problem. A problem would be if you didn't." He bent and scooped her up into his arms.

She squealed and smacked at him. "What the hell are you doing?"

He bumped open his door with his hip and carried her through it. "Taking you to bed and reminding you why this is such a good idea." He kicked the door shut. "We're not sleeping, babe. You'd better resign yourself to being tired tomorrow, because as long as my body cooperates, we're gonna watch the sun rise."

Greer wrapped one arm around his neck to balance herself. The sky was inky black and the moon had descended below the horizon. She knew it would still be several hours before dawn. The dream that had led to her being hurt seemed like days earlier but had, in fact, only been four hours before. Four hours. In four hours she'd nearly had her heart ripped from her chest, gone to bed with her best friend, failed to save Braxton's sister, and watched Alaria torture a Devil. It had only been fifteen minutes since Michael had dropped them off at Gage's estate.

Lives could change in an instant. Greer pondered what she had gone through as Damon carried her across the room. He lowered her to the bed, his big body pressing her back into the mattress as he braced his arms on either side of her and stared into her eyes. She locked her eyes onto his, brown to blue, and arched upward, claiming his mouth with her own.

She pulled back, shaking her head. "This is a mistake."

Damon shook his head. "Not doing this is the mistake." He lifted himself on his arms and stared down at her. "Greer, you've got to stop reading so much into it." Frustrated, he flopped next to her on the bed. "A guy can only take so much before he gives up, and you telling me this is a mistake while we're fucking in bed together is not doing good things for my ego."

Greer couldn't help the giggle that burst from her lips. She clapped her hand over her mouth and stared at him in shock. Sobering, she rolled onto her side and nestled her head into his shoulder. "You know I love you."

"If I didn't know that, we wouldn't still be here. I've never expended this much energy on a woman before." He turned his head to look at her. "How do you not understand this? We're lying here the same as we always have. We had sex, Greer, and we're still talking like normal. That is never going to change between us. Nothing could ever change that."

"Relationships change things, Damon. Sex changes things."

"What has changed between eleven o'clock last night and now?"

Greer looked pained. "Everything."

Damon reached down and took her hand in his. "I can't make you do this, Greer. I want to. I know you want to, and I think we'll both regret it if we don't. I want you to trust me. Trust me when I tell you that we will always be how we are."

Greer blinked back tears. "What happens if I die? Or if you die? The thought of losing you tears me apart. It'll only be worse if we do this."

"Babe, we've already done it. It started the night the city fell. This is how it was always supposed to go. Keeping our hands off each other isn't going to make loss easier to handle. I'm scared, too. But I want this, with you, more than I have ever wanted anything else. We have a chance to make a future for ourselves here. I don't want it with anyone else." He sighed. "But if you want to leave, I won't stop you."

Greer was silent as she stood. She looked down at Damon, who was lying silently on the bed. Emotions flooded her eyes as she struggled to make herself leave. Hours before, she'd been wrapped around him in that bed. She closed her eyes against the maelstrom of memories and feelings. Desire and pleasure wrapped up with a deep feeling of safety and love.

She forced herself to walk to the door. Damon stood but remained next to the bed, waiting to see what she would do. She knew, beyond doubt, that there would be no more chances. Damon had made his wants clear, and Greer knew that her indecision and fear was hurting him. Her fingers clasped the knob then released and gripped again. She pulled the door open.

The noise as Greer slammed it closed shook the room. She couldn't hold back the tears. Sobs tore out of her, one after the other, driving her to double over in an effort to catch her breath.

Damon was there in seconds. He lifted her again, cradling her against his chest as he would have a child. He crossed to the chair in the corner and dropped into it, settling Greer into his lap gently.

He smoothed her hair away from her face and gently wiped the tears off of her skin. Framing her face in his hands, he lifted her chin, forcing her to look at him. "Talk to me. Why are you so scared to just let me love you?"

She took in a huge, trembling breath. "I don't want to lose you! I'm terrified that we'll start this and we'll get each other killed or that we'll do to each other what we've done to every other person we've ever tried to be with."

Damon chuckled. "Where have you been the past few days? We're practically tripping over ourselves trying to keep each other from getting killed." He lifted her to place one of her knees on either side of his thighs. "Whether you want to admit it or not, the only thing that is changing is that we're giving in to what we've wanted for a long time. We've been a couple without having sex for years, babe. It was only a matter of time before we did this." He laid his hand on her neck and rubbed the skin there. "Just let me love you."

Greer's eyes closed, and she wrapped her fingers around his wrist. "I never saw this coming."

"Yes, you did."

"You weren't surprised by the kiss in that apartment?"

"The only thing surprising is how long it took us to go there." He tugged on the bottom of her shirt, smiling when she lifted her arms above her head to let him remove it from her body. "I gave you an opportunity to leave, and you're still here. Do you love me, Greer?"

She nodded immediately. "You know I do."

"Are you in love with me?"

Her eyes snapped open. His expression was serious, his eyes burning into her. She stared into them for a long moment, wracking her brain for a way out of the question without tearing them both apart. She couldn't lie to him. Slowly, she lowered her head. "I really think I might be."

Damon chuckled. "I don't need to think about it. I want this—I want you. I want it all, babe. No games, no fear, no going back and forth. I love you. I'm in love with you." He gripped her upper arms in his hands. "I want to spend the rest of the night making love to you. We'll go back to work tomorrow, and we might die before the day is out, but tonight is ours."

Greer leaned forward and kissed him. She placed her hands on his face and crushed her mouth to his. Her tongue swept into his mouth, tangling with his. He gripped her at the waist, his skin searing hers. Their breath meshed together, and Greer pressed her hips against his to maximize contact. Panting, he tore his mouth from hers.

"This is no joke. I want you to be sure."

She met his eyes with hers. "I'm scared. I'm going to stay scared until this is done. I want you, and that scares me. I don't want to leave. I want to feel you inside me. I want to love you." She laid her head on his shoulder. "I'm just not sure I know how."

Damon pressed into her mind, engulfing her with his strength. *"Just go with it, babe. We'll figure it out together, just like we've always done everything else."* He skimmed his hands up her sides. *"Do you trust me?"*

The response was immediate, both out loud and in his head. "With my life."

His lips were warm and firm on her neck, his voice low and silky in her mind. *"Let me take you like this."*

Greer wrinkled her nose. "In the chair?"

He ran his mouth over her throat. "No, silly. Connected. I want to be inside your mind and your body. I want to feel you and what you feel."

Greer's head rolled to the side. The sensation of feeling what he was doing from both her perspective and his was overwhelming. She sucked in a deep breath when he dragged his teeth across the tendons on her neck, and the flavor of her own skin burst inside her mouth, sweet and slightly salty.

She gripped his hair in her fingers and yanked, feeling both the silky strands and the sharp tug. Their mouths fused together, tongues mating almost violently. Greer scratched her nails down Damon's chest, sweeping down his skin to his belt. What had started off tender and slow ignited into a firestorm of desire.

She rolled out of his lap and braced her hands on the arms of the chair to continue the kiss while undressing him. Slowly, she tugged the belt from its loops, the leather cracking sharply as she jerked it through the air. A wicked smile gracing her lips, she slipped the button on his jeans from its hole and eased the zipper down. His lack of boxers was evidence of the hurry in which he had left the room after Gabriel had taken Greer.

His erection filled her small hands, long and thick. They both groaned when she stroked her fingers over the bulging length. A single droplet formed at the tip, and she spread it over the head with her thumb while stroking her other fist up and down. She grinned at him and stood upright, sweeping her hair up into a messy bun before slowly dropping to her knees.

Damon sucked in his breath when her tongue, small and pink, darted out and touched him. She dragged it along the length of him before swirling it around the tip and lowering her head to engulf him in wet heat. His hands tangled in her hair, and his head fell back onto the chair, his eyes closing tightly. She sucked strongly and bobbed her head up and down, using her lips and tongue to bring him pleasure.

His hips jumped when she swirled her tongue over the tip and wrapped her fist around the base. He groaned when she ran it up and down, her grip tight and his cock slick and gleaming from her mouth. She alternated between sucking vigorously and lapping with her tongue.

"Oh God, baby. You've gotta stop." He groaned and surged up, his hips moving of their own accord. He tugged on her hair. "Greer, stop. You've gotta...oh my God."

Greer laved attention on his penis until he trembled from the effort to withhold his climax. She felt the experience through him, the warm lips and soft tongue. She felt pleasure rise within her as it did him and continued until they were both on the edge of climax, though he had yet to touch her. She released him with a pop and stood, her lips red and swollen and a cocky smile on them. Her heart was pounding in her chest, its rhythm in sync with Damon's. She could hear and feel his breath, and she felt her own orgasm settle deeper down within her as the desire retreated from boiling level.

Damon stood deliberately. His gaze was hungry and hot as he pursued her like a big cat stalked prey. She met his gaze with her own, confident and sure. She backed slowly toward the bed, seeing the way through his eyes. He followed her, his eyes hot, and energy crackling between them so strongly it was almost palpable.

The end of the bed pressed into the back of her knees. She dropped, sitting on the mattress and sliding backward until she was holding herself on her elbows. Damon followed her, crawling onto the bed, his bigger body pressing against hers. His legs were rough with hair and hers were smooth and bare. He slipped his fingers into the sides of her panties and drew them down her hips.

Her nipples were tight and hard. Damon lowered his head and stroked his tongue across one before blowing on it, the cool air making her groan. His tongue was just slightly warmer than her skin and she groaned at the contact. She dropped her elbows so that she could lie back on the bed, her body completely exposed to his touch. He eased his fingers between her thighs and pressed against her center. He sucked one of her nipples into his mouth and rubbed it with his tongue.

Her hands clenched his hair. She dragged him to her, her mouth clamping on his, hungry and hot. Her hands skimmed down his back, and she gripped his ass, pulling him into her. He kissed her deeply, the tip of his erection resting heavily against her entrance. He tore his mouth from hers and fumbled for the night stand.

"Dammit, one second." He groaned when she wrapped her legs around his hips and lifted hers up, tying to take him in. "I'm trying to be good. Fucking things, where are they?"

"Don't bother. It's fine." She pistoned her hips against his. "No one back home has condoms."

"Which is why you either don't have sex or you get knocked up." He yanked the whole drawer out of the nightstand and rifled through the contents until he grasped the condom wrapper. "Ten seconds, Greer, fuck."

He ripped it open with his teeth and reached between their bodies to roll it on. "How have you managed to avoid babies with that attitude?"

She swatted at his hands and finished rolling the condom onto him herself. "This is not my normal attitude. Fuck, Damon, I can feel what you feel and what I feel. I think I'm going to explode if I don't get you in me soon."

He shoved into her with a powerful thrust, surging all the way in and seating himself deep inside of her. They both went absolutely still. Her muscles clamped down on him in undulating spasms. She wrapped her arms around his neck and pressed her face against his throat, overwhelmed both by the desire coursing through her and by feeling his desire magnified through their link. Silently, she begged him to move. Without a word, he answered and gave her what she needed.

He knew where she needed pressure as soon as she felt it. He moved to give her the most pleasure possible. Almost before the thoughts formed, he changed the angle of his hips or moved deeper, thrusting harder until she was wrapped around him, panting and nearly sobbing from the want. She begged him to stop and to keep going at the same time. He held her on the edge of orgasm until she thought she was going to die before letting her drop over the edge.

He rode her through the climax, never letting her come back down. She clenched at his arms and gnawed on her lip, her back arching to offer up her breasts to him. He leaned down and stroked one nipple with his tongue before scraping his teeth over it. A shallow scream wrenched from her chest, and she sank her teeth into his shoulder in an effort to muffle it. The pain muddled with the pleasure, and Damon growled, driving harder.

His own orgasm was building, fueled by hers, and he braced his hands on either side of her head, allowing himself to press harder against her. She thrashed on the bed beneath him, her thighs wrapping around his hips to hug him closely and her nails digging into his arms as she desperately careened toward release. He thrust into her one final time, the veins in his neck bulging as he came. She exploded around him as his orgasm traveled through their mental link and engulfed her. She was shaking and covered in sweat when he rolled off her and fell to the mattress, retreating from her head in the same moment he left her body.

Greer struggled to find words. Her breath heaved, her chest rising and falling quickly as she forced air into and out of her lungs. She turned her head to look at Damon wildly. He grinned at her, the expression more than a little rakish.

"Enjoy?"

She nodded mutely, still trying to decide whether or not she was going to be able to talk. After seven more breaths, she managed a sentence. "No one, at any point in time, has ever had sex that good."

Damon reached out to tuck a strand of her hair behind her ear. "Only if they were a Healer and a Hunter." He flopped onto his side and stroked a hand along the curve of her jaw. "Are you okay?"

"Yeah, why?"

"That was pretty intense."

Greer giggled. "If by intense you mean the best sex that has ever been had by any person at any point in time, then yeah, it was intense." She rolled to her feet, wobbling for a moment before her legs steadied underneath her. "I'm going to get a shower." She grabbed the glass on the sink and filled it with water. She reached into the shower and turned on the water before draining the glass and refilling it. She walked to the bed, took one last drink, her throat working as she swallowed; one lone drop sliding off her chin and trailing down her chest to splash against one still-hard nipple. She handed the glass to Damon.

He drained it in one gulp and reached out to swat her ass as she retreated to the bathroom to shower. Stretching, he reached down and yanked off the condom, depositing it in the trash before forcing himself to stand up. Before he could do anything, Greer's voice drifted out of the bathroom.

"You could grab one of those condoms and come fuck me in the shower."

Damon spent one heartbeat wondering if he had the energy for another bout before his body informed him that it did. Grinning, he snagged another foil packet and hurried to the bathroom. Greer was standing beneath the spray, water running down her body. He stepped into the shower, snapping the curtain closed behind him. She squirted body wash into the loofah and handed it to him, turning so that her back faced him.

Slowly, he drew the sponge over her skin, slicking suds over her wet flesh. He covered her back, swept it down to her ass, then worked his hand between her legs, washing gently. He dropped the loofah to the floor and ran his hands up her stomach to cup her breasts, his chest pressing against her back and her front against the wall of the shower. The contrast between the cool tile and the hot water made her nipples harden until they pressed into his hands. He leaned forward until his lips were pressed to her ear.

"Tell me now if you want anything other than hard and fast."

Greer slipped her hand back and gripped his dick in one hand, her fingers encircling him and pumping up and down, slow and snug. His eyes nearly crossed. She arched her back to press her bottom against him more fully. "I wouldn't have invited you in if I didn't want hot and hard shower sex. I've been showering with you in the dorms for years. I can admit now that I imagined more than once that you would just slam me against the wall and screw me senseless."

Damon laughed, his chest rumbling against her back. "Ask and you shall receive."

She turned to face him, reaching around him to grab the condom he'd placed on the shelf. She tore the wrapper into two pieces and used two fingers to position the latex shield over the head of his penis. Efficiently, she rolled it down his length, running her fingers up and down the shaft reverently before grinning up at him.

"You sure you can hold me up?"

Damon glared at her and stooped to grasp her thighs in his hands. With no more effort than it would have taken to lift a child, he hiked her up to waist level and slammed her back against the tile wall. His fingers dug into her flesh almost painfully, and he spread her thighs wide. She grabbed his shoulders for balance.

"Hold on tight. This is gonna be one helluva ride."

He slammed into her, spearing up into her body, stretching her to the limit and filling her completely. He didn't give her time to adjust before he was moving, pumping his hips to drive his dick into her over and over. She was wet and tight and felt like a hot fist wrapped around him. Her head ground into the tiles, her eyes tightly shut as she reveled in lust.

His thrusts were slow and heavy, driving himself completely into her with each one before withdrawing so that only the first inch of his penis dipped into her body. Her little gasps and moans made his gut tighten with desire, and he thrust harder and faster. By the time she collapsed into his arms ten minutes later, her body was shaking and spasming from orgasm and she breathlessly clung to him, her legs too weak to stand.

Not in much better shape, Damon carefully washed her hair and spent three minutes scrubbing his own body before grabbing two towels from the hook. Greer managed to work the knobs to turn the water off and took one of the towels gratefully.

They dried off in silence, Greer wincing when she realized how sore she was. It had been years since she'd had sex so many times in so short a period. She didn't bother to get dressed as they headed to the bed together. No sooner had they lain down than Damon was reaching for her, drawing her to him. As promised, by the time they fell into an exhausted sleep, the first tinges of purple and pink crept through the sky.

Chapter Twenty-Three

August 19th, 2030 - Scotland

"What is he doing?" Greer whispered to Gage from across the kitchen island, her expression conveying her concern. Gage looked at where she was gesturing to Braxton, who was standing over the bodies of his family.

"He's giving them a Warrior's burial. He's preparing the bodies. When they have time, there are certain rituals that they do for their dead. I'm sure they'd given most of that up by the time you knew any of them. There would have been too much death."

"I get that. I want to know what he's doing. I've never seen this."

Gage chuckled. "He's making sure that they can't be possessed or used by anything. Normally this is done immediately after death. At this point, there's no way a demon could get in there. They've been dead for too long. The mouths are filled with salt and herbs are placed in the clothing. The bodies are wrapped in fabric soaked in oils, and then they'll be burned. The herbs and oil help with the smell, but it's not a ritual of the funeral. It's a ritual done by Warriors for hundreds of years."

"He's going to cremate them."

"Basically."

"Braxton doesn't seem like the superstitious type to me."

"He's not, but his mother was. Miranda took the old routines very seriously. She would have wanted this for them, so he'll do it. I think it means something to him, but if it were anyone else, he'd dig a hole and dump in the gasoline."

Greer took a deep drink of her coffee. "Should I maybe offer to help?"

Gage shook his head. "I wouldn't. Alaria is helping him. Those two have a special relationship. She's the only one who can handle him when he's in a difficult mood."

"I thought she was with the Angel?"

The vampire laughed into his mug of blood. "Did I say it was romantic?" He waited until she shook her head. "There isn't anything between Alaria and Brax. I don't think either of them would ever go there. They understand each other. In a lot of ways, they're the same, and they're both trying to heal from the Choosing. It's only been nine months since Griffin died. Alaria switched sides about three months beforehand. It was the only reason they survived. She nearly died trying to protect them. Brax developed a grudging respect for her. She can get through to him when no one else can."

Greer smiled as Damon came down the stairs wearing sweats and a wife beater, his hair still mussed from sleep. He poured himself a cup of coffee and peered into the living room where Braxton was wrapping his father's head in a sheet. He quirked an eyebrow and looked at the other two.

"Do I even want to know?"

Gage rinsed his mug out in the sink and patted Greer on the shoulder. "I'll let you explain it to him. Just be aware that the funeral will begin at dusk."

Greer wrinkled her nose. "Is that another Warrior tradition?"

"No. I just don't want anyone to see the smoke. The last thing I want to explain to the police is why we're burning bodies in my backyard." He chuckled as he strode to the doorway. "Given that the two of you slept until well past noon, I think it goes without saying that you've addressed all of your issues and we can concentrate on the task ahead of us." He smiled at them both. "I know this is hard, and the two of you have done well, but this is going to get super intense super fast. There's no more time to deal with personal issues. If you don't have it figured out, either do it now or put it on hold. Tomorrow morning, we start training for you to be able to survive in Hell, Greer. It's going to be long, and it's going to be brutal, and I can't have your relationship shit in the way."

Greer nodded. "We're good. Promise." She turned back to the scene in the living room, where Alaria had just entered the room. The former Devil wore yoga pants and a tank top and her feet were bare. Without a word, she went to Braxton and took one of the sheets, helping him wrap his father. Greer leaned her head on Damon's shoulder. "I'm glad the two of them get along. It would suck for him to go through this alone."

Damon stroked his hand over Greer's hair. "Babe, I don't think any of us are going to be alone for a long time to come."

Michael appeared on the mountaintop in a flash of lightning. The sky was dark gray with swirling clouds, making it seem more like a living creature than refracted light. He glanced around, taking in the scraggly grass and the dark rocks. Nestled into the side of the mountain was a small thatched hut. He sensed movement inside and smiled grimly as he strode into the structure.

Lilith was standing in the middle of the room. She wore a white lace corset and thong. Her hair, white blonde and curly, fell down her back and over her shoulders in a silky curtain. Her breasts strained the thin fabric of the lingerie and her nipples were clearly visible through the lace. Her legs—long and tan—were spread, her feet encased in spike heels. She lifted one eyebrow at him when he entered the room.

"I didn't think you'd come."

Michael scowled. "I very nearly didn't."

"You haven't missed a single appointment in three thousand years."

"You stole a baby and had Braxton's entire family killed when you damn well knew they had nothing they could have told Abalam."

Lilith crossed the room and ran her hands up his lapels. "Darling, I'm a Devil. What do you expect me to do?" She brushed her lips over his jaw. "I'm evil."

"I don't know why I continually think there's something left of the Angel you used to be in there."

Lilith smiled sweetly. "Michael, you and I both know that I'm the same now as I was back then."

"You haven't always been this evil."

She caught his bottom lip between her teeth and tugged it into her mouth to suck. She released him and wiped away the droplet of blood with one finger before sticking it in her mouth. "I owe you quite the thank you for slipping up and letting me know you'd taken his family into protection. Once I knew that, it was pathetically easy to find Uriel and Raphael. They've always been Gabriel's guards of choice. Too bad neither had fought anything since the Fall."

Michael grabbed her arms roughly and shook her. "You have no idea what you've done. I have kept your confidences for millennia. I suppose I was naive to believe that you felt as strongly about our arrangement as I."

She quirked one eyebrow at him seductively. "That's where you're wrong. I enjoy our little arrangement more than you can imagine. I want it to continue, but I won't ever keep your secrets at the expense of Lucifer.

The only secret that is safe is that we're here. We'd both be strung up and quartered if we were found out."

Michael grabbed her wrists and jerked her against his body, his wings spread wide behind him. "I should have chained you in Azazel's prison. The Choosing showed me just how unredeemable you truly are."

Lilith chewed on her bottom lip, her teeth straight and white. "You fucked me harder than I can remember the first time we met after that battle. I wondered if you'd be able to turn off your anger at me long enough to come here." She tugged her wrists free and unbuttoned his suit coat. "We've always fought so viciously, in and out of bed. I have to say, lover, I enjoy your cock more than that of any other I've had." She tilted her head to the side. "Though the human Warrior you call Braxton was quite close. His stamina transcended any other human I've known."

"Shut up." Michael shoved her back harshly. He deliberately folded his wings against his back before toeing off his shoes. He shrugged out of his suit coat, folded it and laid it on the table methodically. He unbuckled his belt and slid his zipper down with a hiss. Lilith watched in anticipation, her gaze hungry and her nipples jutting against the lace of her corset—physical evidence of her desire. He stepped out of his pants, gave them the same treatment as his coat, and stood before her, naked from the waist down. "Get on your knees."

Lilith blinked rapidly and looked at him in mild confusion. "What did you say?"

Michael strode forward, seized her by her wrists and dragged her to him. "I said, get on your knees." His voice was low and angry. "If you want this, you do it my way. You want fucked?" He sneered at her. "Then you get on your knees and you wrap that mouth around my dick."

Lilith shivered as his words rolled over her and desire pooled deep inside her. She twisted her hair into a knot on her head, using a pin to secure it. She met his eyes and didn't look away as she lowered herself to her knees. She laid her hands on his hips, her fingers gripping the muscles tightly. Her tongue darted out and touched the tip of his pulsing erection. Michael reached down, grabbed her hair, and forced her head down, shoving himself into her mouth. She nearly choked as he impaled her and coughed twice before closing her lips around him and sucking.

Her head bobbed back and forth, his dick gleaming from her mouth. He kept one hand in her hair, controlling how fast she moved. She wrapped her tongue around the head, rubbing it against the sensitive flesh. He groaned, and his head fell back. He braced himself against the wall and let himself drift away on the pleasure that was Lilith.

She pulled one hand from his hips and reached between his legs to wrap her first around the base of his penis. She moved her hand up and down quickly, slickened by saliva, and concentrated her oral ministrations on the head. Michael groaned and jerked his hips, driving himself into her mouth deeper.

"Get up." His order was rough and his voice grainy.

Lilith grinned up at him. "What's the matter? Can't take it?"

Michael glared down at her. "If you want me to blow in your mouth, keep going. If you want me to fuck you, stop."

She ran her tongue down his length one final time before climbing to her feet. She smoothed her hands over his dress shirt, slipping the buttons loose and easing the fabric off his shoulders. She folded the garment carefully and laid it on top of his pants before stepping back to stare at his naked body.

He was fabulous. Broad shoulders, narrow hips and a bulging erection. His eyes were ice blue and burned into her, magnified in intensity by his pitch black hair. His jawline was sharp, and his cheekbones were a dramatic slash across his face. His hands were big and wide, with long fingers and scarred knuckles. Michael wore his war wounds proudly. He was an Angel who led his troops into battle and fought alongside them.

Lilith reached out and stroked her finger down a scar on his side. "I did that."

"In the battle at the Choosing." He glared at her darkly. "Remove your clothing."

"No foreplay for me?" She batted her eyelashes at him and smiled innocently. "You're normally so giving."

"You're normally not so disgusting to me." He shoved her toward the bed roughly. "We both know the score, Lilith. It's sex. You want it. I want it. We don't like each other—we use each other to satisfy a physical need." He shoved her onto her hands and knees. "What do you want?"

Her voice quivered. "You."

"Beg me."

She glanced over her shoulder, her eyes alight with surprise. "What?"

"You heard me. If you want it, beg for it. I want to hear you plead with me to fuck you."

"You're bossy tonight." She crawled onto the massive bed and slowly untied the lace on her corset, revealing her flesh inch by inch. "I think I like this side of you. There's something so sexy about a man not afraid to take what he wants." She tossed the lingerie aside, leaving her clad in nothing but her lacy thong. "Come over here and fuck me."

"That's not begging." Michael reached out and twisted her nipple between his fingers almost hard enough to hurt. She groaned and pressed her breast into his hand.

"Fuck me, baby, please."

He pressed her back onto the bed and ripped her underwear from her body. "Say it again."

She repeated the request when his mouth closed over her breast and his teeth scraped over her sensitive skin. She pressed her mouth to his neck and ran her tongue along the curve of his throat. "How are you going to fuck me this time?" She arched her back to press herself against him more firmly. "Are you going to take me hard? Or maybe soft and slow?"

The smack of his hand against her ass reverberated throughout the room. Lilith gasped and moaned as a bolt of pleasure speared through her. Michael flipped her over onto her stomach and stroked the reddened skin. He filled his hands with her flesh, kneading and massaging it. She squirmed against him, desperate for more.

"Spank me."

Michael smiled darkly. "Beg me."

"Please, Michael, spank me. I want it." Her voice was a whispered plea.

Michael almost believed her. He drew back his hand and slapped her ass sharply. She pressed her face into the sheet to muffle the groan. Her hips leaped in his hands and a rush of moisture pooled between her legs. He used one hand to stroke himself gently, wrapping his hand around his penis and rubbing it up and down as he studied Lilith.

With one movement, he gripped both of her hips and dragged her back against his body. He parted her thighs with his knee and used one hand to guide himself while gripping her hip with the other. He drove into her with a single hard thrust, spearing up into her and seating himself deeply. He didn't give her but a breath to adjust to his girth before he began thrusting.

Her ass filled his hands, and he squeezed the handfuls as he fucked her. Michael held her hips still to allow him greater access, and he pushed her face into the sheet to change the angle. Her moans turned to muffled screams as she climbed the crest of orgasm. He slammed into her over and over, with no regard for her pleasure, though she derived plenty. He rolled his hips against her and rocked into her, his eyes closing tightly as he felt his own climax threaten.

He reached around and grabbed both her breasts, pinching her nipples between his fingers and tugging on them. His huge body dwarfed her petite one. He slid his dick in and out, enjoying her wet heat and the feeling of her breasts in his hands. He squeezed them and rubbed the nipples against the palms of his hands.

His orgasm close, his thrusts became hard and staccato. Lilith moaned with each thrust, on the edge herself. He held still and jerked on her hips, dragging her down on him. His release bubbled up and streamed out of him. He gritted his teeth and groaned as he came, his fingers biting into her painfully, his cock twitching inside of her.

Without a word and without giving her an orgasm, Michael stood and strode to the dresser where his clothes were folded. He dressed in silence while Lilith stared at him, her body flushed with want and her thighs sticky and wet with fluid. After two minutes of deafening silence, she spoke.

"You've never done this before."

Michael wiped himself on a towel before pulling on his pants. "I've never been this fucking mad at you before. Even with the damn Choosing, I could comfort myself that you were just following orders. There's no excuse this time, Lilith. You betrayed me personally. You took what you learned here, in the place where there is no one other than us, and you used it to take lives. I'll not forgive you for that."

"I don't give a fuck if you forgive me. I never have. I want you to fuck me."

"I did."

"Then do it again. Get me off. Do it right." She screeched in frustration. "You can't just storm out of here."

"I can do as I please. I owe you nothing, Lilith, and I take from you whatever I want." He grinned at her harshly. "Any favor you had with me is gone. Our little arrangement is over. I can get pussy anywhere."

"It's not about the pussy." She stood and strode across the room, gloriously naked. "If it was, you wouldn't have been meeting me here for all of these years. You come because being with me here, like this, reminds you of how it used to be and how you wish it still was." She bared her teeth in a dangerous smile. "I don't share your sentimental bullshit. I fuck you because every time you come inside me, it's me flipping off God. He cast me down and I fuck His Angels." She looked him up and down. "If you leave like this, I'll never let you have me again."

Michael shrugged on his coat and buttoned it. "I don't want you, Lilith." He looked her over with an appraising glance. "The pussy's good, and you've got the best tits I've ever seen, but I'd rather fuck a human than wait for you to stab me in the back. After what you did with the Winslows, I know it's only a matter of time. I'm not interested in waiting around to see what you're going to do." He twisted the doorknob and pulled the door open. "Have a nice existence."

He was gone before she could find a response.

Chapter Twenty-Four

BRAXTON TOOK A long drink from the bottle of bourbon. His vision was slightly blurry and sweat beaded on his forehead. The sun was setting over the horizon, pink and purple fingers stabbing through the sky in one last effort to fight off night. He looked down at his left hand and the cigarette clenched between his fingers. He lifted it to his lips, inhaling the burning tobacco into his lungs. It had been over five years since his last cigarette. He scowled at the burning stick and tossed it to the ground, grinding it out under his heel.

He'd never liked the damn things anyway.

"If you don't like them, why do you smoke them?"

Braxton whirled around and found Alaria standing next to him. He glared at her. "You could at least pretend to be normal."

She leaned against the porch pillar. "Everyone knows I'm not normal. No use pretending if no one around is gonna buy it."

"This whole human with- Devil powers thing is weird."

"Imagine how I feel. I thought I was going to get to live. Find someone, have babies, grow old, and die. I didn't imagine taking up the cause and risking my neck again."

Braxton briefly considered trying to relight the cigarette on the ground. "None of us did." His eyes trailed across the yard to where Gage and Damon were building a pyre. "At least you and I got into this by choice. They were dragged into it. They didn't get a choice." His voice was thick with tears. "I pulled Sam into it, and she died because of that. It's cold comfort that Dad was dragged into it by God, but the rest of it is on me."

"None of us had a choice." Alaria reached over and laid a hand on his arm. "All we can do is try to survive. We're not all going to make it through this."

"I know." He covered her hand with one of his. "We just have to all get through until the last trial. We can't do the first two without everyone."

She tipped her head back and stared up at the sky. "We need that damned witch. Gabe is dragging his feet bringing her forward because he's afraid Lilith and Azazel will come after us in force. He doesn't seem to realize that she could help. If she's the most powerful witch that's ever lived in any time, we need her sooner rather than later."

Braxton dug through his pockets for another cigarette. Coming up empty, he settled for a deep swallow of bourbon. "Since when does Gabe do what's good for anyone other than him?"

Alaria winced. "That's not fair."

"How isn't it? Even with this fuck fest the two of you have going on, it's all on his terms. He disappeared when he saw you peeling Abalam like a banana. Weak stomach?" He pinned her down with an angry stare. "Or is it ruining the innocent human image he's trying to put on you?"

"It's none of your business."

"I don't want to know the intimate details. I'm not your fucking girlfriend." He twisted the cap back onto the bottle and dangled it from his fingers. "We aren't going to stand and gossip about your sex life, but I am your friend or something."

Alaria lifted her brows. "Or something?"

Braxton sighed deeply. "I don't think we're friends. It's not like we want to be working together, but here we are, and for better or worse, we're stuck with each other. It started the minute your heart started beating. That means that I have to care about what happens to you, and I don't want Gabriel to hurt you. I don't want him to make this harder than it has to be, and I'm afraid that if you continue down this road, it's going to bring nothing but pain to anyone."

"It was one argument. He'll come around."

His head fuzzy from bourbon, Braxton tore his eyes from the pyre to stare at Alaria, his eyes locking onto hers. "In all seriousness, before I'm too drunk to think straight, if he doesn't accept you for all that you are, he doesn't deserve you." He turned back to the yard and squared his shoulders. "Let's get this show on the road."

Greer stood back, unsure how to proceed as she watched the somber procession. Braxton carried Sam, Damon held Miranda gently, and Gage, the strongest, carried Allen's body. All three were wrapped in sheets that were tied tightly at the foot. Once the three men had laid the bodies on the pyre, she walked next to Alaria when the raven-haired woman held out her hand, her eyes locked onto the three simple wooden platforms on top of a bonfire.

"What's going to happen?"

Alaria turned to face Greer, her expression one of sadness. "Once they place the bodies on the platforms, Braxton will light them on fire. It's not like a regular funeral. No one is going to say a few words or whatever else it is that you humans tend to need. You don't have to be here if you don't want to be. This is for Brax. He needs to give them a Warrior's send-off."

"Kinda feels like we should stay." Greer looked around with a pained expression. "If I'd been a few minutes earlier, maybe I could've saved his sister."

"The only one who could've saved Sam was God Himself. She was dead long before we got to her. No one has ever survived Abalam." Alaria drew to a stop and watched the men place the bodies on the wooden slabs.

Gage handed Braxton a pack of matches and retreated several steps as the other man stood and stared at the small box in his hand. With slow, deliberate movements, Braxton withdrew a match and struck it. There was a hiss as fire erupted. His stony expression wavered, and his eyes moistened as he stared into the flames. Only when the fire had reached the tips of his fingers did he toss it into the prepared pile of gasoline-soaked wood.

Red and orange rose up to engulf the bodies. The oils that the sheets had been soaked in filled the air with the scent of lavender and citrus. Braxton took three steps back, bringing himself in line with the other four. Alaria patted Greer's arm gently and moved to stand next to Braxton, reaching down to twine her fingers with his in a gesture of support. A moment later, she extended her other hand and took Gage's, mirroring the grasp.

Greer watched the smoke fill the sky for several moments. Braxton lifted the bottle of bourbon to his lips and drained it. She took it from his hand and placed the glass gently on the ground before sliding her small hand into his larger one. He looked down at her in surprise when he felt her hand and returned the gesture when she smiled softly.

"We're in it together. All of it."

The only response she got was the slight tightening of his fingers. She reached for Damon, shivering when his body pressed against her back, one hand resting lightly on her hip.

After several moments of silence, Braxton cleared his throat. "I want to make something clear." He looked from side to side to include them all in what he was saying. "We all know some of us probably won't survive this. Some of us already haven't, and it's just now beginning. I never wanted this. I've been dragged into it from the beginning, and I don't want to be part of some grand scheme to save the world. This is not about that for me. I don't know if it is for you, but for me, this is about vengeance. I don't care about anything else other than making the bastards that did this to them pay. If we save the world along the way—great, but that's not the fucking point anymore. It stopped being the point when Griffin's death became for nothing."

Gabriel appeared with a rustle. His expression showed that he was upset, and he started to speak, but was cut off by Braxton.

"I suppose you're here to argue with me?" He snapped the words, only slightly drunk. "Are you going to tell me I'm wrong and this is all worth it?"

Gabriel shook his head. "Your feelings are not unreasonable given your loss. I've come to pay my respects."

Braxton tore his hands free and gestured to the fire. "You've got a lot of nerve, I'll give you that. You promised me they'd be safe!" His voice rose to a yell and tears made his vision cloudy. "You swore to me that you would keep them safe! You asked me to trust you with them, and you killed them!"

Gabriel lowered his gaze and stared at the grass. After several moments, he spoke. "I understand that you are upset and grieving. I do not hold that against you."

Braxton laughed bitterly. "How fucking noble of you." He stormed past the Angel and across the yard toward the house, his next words carrying back to them. "You're such a fucking saint, Gabe, really." He turned around and spread his arms, walking backward, just a bit wobbly from alcohol. "You basically abducted Greer and Damon, kill my whole family, fuck Alaria and then make her out to be a monster, and now you crash a fucking funeral. You couldn't even let me lay them to rest without interrupting, could you?"

When Gabriel started to follow Braxton, his face twisted into an expression of regret and guilt, Alaria held up her hand to stop him. "Don't. I'll handle him." She dashed after Braxton, wincing when he slammed the door several steps before she got there. She yanked it open and caught up to him halfway down the hall. "Brax!" She grabbed his hand to stop him.

Braxton moved faster than he should have been able to given his inebriated state. He whirled Alaria around and slammed her back against the wall. Before she could so much as suck in a breath, he clamped his mouth over hers in a searing kiss. He grabbed her wrists when she tried to strike him, pinning them above her head and pressing his body against hers, molding her curves to him.

She fought him, biting at his mouth and thrashing her body in an attempt to break his hold. Of their own accord, her nipples tightened and unwanted tremors of excitement jolted through her from the struggle and his dominance. His tongue forced its way into her mouth and he jutted his hips into hers, his erection pressing into her hard. She struggled against the feelings of desire, fighting to get free of his grasp.

Braxton wrenched his head from hers, panting for breath. "The fucking asshole doesn't deserve you. He can't give you what you need. I know you think you love him, and I know he might even think he loves you." He bent his head and ravaged her again. "The next time he fucks you, you're going to think about me. I heard you the night he came to you." His eyes bored into her. "I don't need to ask how to make a woman feel good, and I don't sneak out in the middle of the night. You deserve better than him, Alaria. We all do."

He released her as suddenly as he'd grabbed her. Before he could stomp off, a stream of light struck him and sent him sprawling. Alaria whirled and found Gabriel, one hand extended. She stared at him in shock, her lips swollen and bruised, confusion and fear evident in her face. Braxton remained sprawled on the floor, though she wasn't sure if he couldn't get up or had just decided moving was a bad idea.

"He's drunk and he's grieving, you jackass!" She stalked to him and jammed her finger into his chest. "What the hell do you think you're doing?"

"He had his hands on you."

Alaria snorted. "That had nothing to do with me and everything to do with him being pissed at you. He isn't interested in me! He just lost his wife and family! What do you expect, Gabe? He has no idea how to deal with this, so he's trying to punish you." Her voice softened. "You need to try to understand human emotions some before you punish someone for having them."

Gabriel stared down at her. "Only in the mind of a human could this become my fault."

Braxton began laughing from the floor. "That's where you're wrong. That's not a human thing. That's a woman thing." He heaved himself to his feet, wobbly and unsteady. "I'm going to continue to drink until I pass out." He glared at Gabriel. "Do us both a favor and stay the hell away from me. Do something like that again and I'll see whether or not it's possible to kill an Angel."

Gabriel struck out again, his expression dark with anger. Braxton slammed into the wall and fell backward, hitting his head on the stairs. Before Alaria could move, Gage was between Gabriel and Braxton, his eyes glowing red and his fangs bared. Gabriel tried to sidestep the vampire, but Gage held his ground.

"This is *my* house." His voice was a growl, low and threatening. "I can add in Angel wards to the other ones if you want to cause problems, but you are not welcome to come in here and pull this shit, Archangel or not. I won't have it." He shoved Gabriel back, passing Greer and Damon, who were standing in the entry. "You're better than this, Gabe. I've known you a long time, and I've never known you to act like a jealous teenager before. He may have been stupid, and he'll answer for that, but it is not your place to interfere. The first I'd have let you get away with because he deserved it, but not the second." He pushed Gabriel out into the yard. "This is your one chance. Do something like this again and you won't be able to come back."

Gabriel was gone before the door slammed. Gage turned the lock and looked at Braxton, who was unsteadily climbing to his feet, Alaria supporting some of his weight. He exchanged a worried look with her before retreating to the kitchen for a wet towel to mop up the blood spurting from Braxton's nose.

Greer trailed after him, worry evident on her face. "He could have killed you."

"Gabe isn't going to kill me. I've known the man ten centuries. I can't have him here acting like that. We're a tenuous enough group as it is. We don't need people not a part of this projecting their emotions and hurt feelings onto the rest of us." He gave Greer a dark look. "I think everyone other than Alaria would be happier if she were banging Brax instead of Gabe. It would make things a lot less tense around here."

Greer leaned against the counter and watched him pull a cloth from a drawer and hold it under the faucet. "Even they know it's a bad idea."

"It's a horrendous idea, and it's going to get people killed. You and Damon are used to each other, Brax and Alaria know the score, but Gabe and Alaria? There are millions of years of hurt feelings and anger there.

Nothing good is going to come of this." He patted her shoulder as he passed in front of her. "Don't feel like you have to stay for the show. I'm going to help Alaria pour him into bed, and then we all need to get some sleep. Your training starts tomorrow morning."

Gage was still muttering under his breath about idiot Angels when he handed Alaria the cloth. He watched as she wiped blood from Braxton's face and tipped his head back to inspect the damage done to his nose.

"It's broken."

"Go figure." Braxton pinched the bridge with two fingers to staunch the flow from his nostrils. He stared intently at the ceiling, his head still foggy from pain and booze. "I'll apologize to you in the morning, Alaria."

Alaria dropped to the stairs next to him. "Just don't do it again and we'll call it even." She patted his knee. "We'll figure it all out, Brax. Gabe knows you're drunk. He'll come around."

Braxton glared at her. "I'm not apologizing to him. I meant every fucking word I said. I'm sorry for what I did, not what I said. I've never put my hands on a woman who didn't want them there, and I'm not going to start doing it now. I shouldn't have grabbed you, and for that, I am sorry, but he isn't treating you right."

Alaria sighed deeply. "I thought you were gonna wait to do this until tomorrow morning?"

He laughed drunkenly. "No time like the present. Gage, help me to bed before I do anything else stupid."

Gage gamely heaved the other man to his feet. "That's the smartest thing you've said all day, my boy."

Alaria didn't move. She watched the men disappear down the hall before speaking. "If you've something to say, Greer, come out here and say it."

Greer appeared from the kitchen with a glass of water in one hand. "I don't, really."

"Spit it out."

Tucking her hair behind her ears, Greer sat next to Alaria on the stairs. "There's nothing I really want to say about it. They're both idiots, and they both care about you. From where I'm sitting, you're a very lucky woman." She was quiet for several moments. "Sometimes, you just need another woman, and since we're the only two at the moment, if you ever need to, you can talk to me. I can only imagine how difficult this must be for you."

Greer had climbed to her feet and was almost halfway up the stairs when Alaria spoke, her voice barely more than a whisper. "Braxton is right about a lot of stuff. Gabe and I are complicated. We always have been, and we always will be. You and Damon have a future together, and it still took you fifteen years to see what I knew the first time I saw him with you. The two of you are meant to be together. It's obvious to anyone who looks. Gabe and I have no future, and yet we can't stay away from one another. If we're going to be in the same room, this is going to keep happening. I can't help it. I wanted him as an Angel, I didn't want to want him as a Devil, and I can have him as a human, if only for a while."

Greer offered a small smile. "I don't think you're doing anything wrong. I think you have to give yourself a break, Alaria. You're learning to be human. All of the emotions and feelings and crap that comes along with it can be overwhelming and hard to understand. My only advice would be to figure out what feelings are from the past and which exist in the present."

"I don't have feelings for Braxton."

Greer smiled again. "I wasn't talking about Braxton."

Chapter Twenty-Five

ALARIA CLOSED the door to her room softly. She flipped on the light and stood, leaning against the door and staring at the room. The bed looked comfortable and inviting, but she had no desire to cross the swatch of carpet and climb into it. Moonlight streamed through the thin curtains, and stark white light came from the bathroom.

She smelled of smoke, bourbon, and Braxton. She didn't want to smell like any of those things. Emotions constricted her chest, unfamiliar and strong. She jerked her shirt over her head and threw it in the trash. Her boots joined it one by one, shortly followed by her pants. She twisted her arms behind her back to slip the hooks on her bra from their enclosures. The scrap of lace and underwire drifted to the pile soundlessly. She bent and hooked her fingers in the straps of her panties and lowered them, stepping out of them and casting them aside.

Naked, she straightened and strode into the bathroom. She stood in front of the mirror, staring at her reflection without paying much attention to it. She hadn't ever paid much attention to the reflection. Clenching her teeth, she forced herself to really see what was looking back at her in an attempt to understand what Gabriel and Braxton saw.

She was tall and thin. Her hair flowed over her shoulders and down her back in a curtain of blue-black silk. Her skin was tanned and exotic; her eyes were dark brown and just a touch too big. Her nose was small and rounded, her lips were lush and full, and her cheekbones were a dramatic slash across her face. Her lashes cast shadows on her cheeks, and her brows were dramatically curved. She was gorgeous. There was no pretending otherwise.

She had a classically beautiful face and a body built for sex. Her legs were long and slim, her hips flared out wide, sloping down gently into the perfect curve of her ass. Her breasts were large and high, tipped with dusky, pinkish brown nipples and slightly darker areolas. She hadn't ever met a straight man that didn't want to bed her.

Unreasonably angry at her reflection, Alaria slammed her fist into the mirror with a pained yell. The glass cracked and her reflection fractured into pieces. Frustrated and furious, with tears stinging the inside of her eyelids, she stomped to the shower and jerked the handle to turn on the spray of water. She stepped under the stream and slammed the glass door shut behind her. She slapped the tile with her palms and shoved her face into the water.

Still angry, she scrubbed her skin until it was pink and the whole room smelled of grapefruit. She washed her hair until her scalp was sore and then let the water rinse her until she was as warm as the water. Jerking the faucet again to shut it off, she stepped from the shower and wrapped a towel around herself, knotting it at the side.

Dripping water, she walked into the bedroom. Gabriel was sitting on the side of her bed, his hands clasped in his lap, looking embarrassed. Anger bubbled up in her as she stared at him, and she put her hands on her hips.

"What do you want?"

"To apologize to you. I acted irrationally and for that, I'm sorry."

Alaria snorted. "I'm not in the mood, Gabe. Just go away and let me get some sleep."

Gabriel sighed. "I am truly sorry, Alaria. I don't know what has overcome me recently. Never in my life have I struck out with so little forethought."

"You were jealous. It's an emotion."

"You're angry with me."

"I'm angry in general." She yanked clothes out of the dresser, her movements jerky and staccato. "You had no right to come here and do what you did."

Anger sparked in Gabriel's eyes. "He had no right to put his hands on you when you did not want him to." His eyes narrowed when she turned around to pull her shirt over her head, shielding her breasts from his view. "You did not want him to place his hands on your body, did you?"

Alaria whirled around. "What do you think, Gabe? That I'm fucking every guy who thinks I'm pretty? Or any guy who's drunk enough to think they can get in my pants? Give me a little credit here!"

"I think that your heart rate increased and your breathing became erratic four seconds after his mouth made contact with yours."

"I was fucking trying to fight him off! Of course my heart rate went up and my breathing became erratic!" She slammed her hands into the top of the dresser. "I told you I didn't want to do this now! I don't want to fight with you, I don't want to listen to excuses, and I don't want to hear all your reasons why I'm a whore and Braxton is a rapist."

Gabriel looked pained. "I don't want this to come between us."

She barked a laugh. "You're the one who's been telling me that there's no future for us. Why don't I save us both a lot of time and heartache? Go away, Gabe."

"No."

Alaria picked up her hairbrush and began raking it through her hair. "Don't pick now to grow a pair of balls on me. You've been a pushover for eternity. Don't stop now."

Gabriel stood and crossed the room to place his hands on her shoulders. He met her eyes in the mirror. "I don't want to leave. I don't want to be in this situation. I want us to be together."

"We both know this is just a 'for now' thing."

"I know, Alaria. I'm not as dense as most of you humans tend to be. I understand the limitations to our relationship."

Tears stung her eyes and she sniffed them back. "It hurts, Gabe. I'm not used to feeling the things that I feel. I don't like it."

"This is the curse of being mortal. It is what you have wanted for so long. Do you regret your decision to become human?"

She was shaking her head before he finished the question. "No. This is what I have always wanted, and it's what I still want." She leaned her cheek against his hand. "We're doing nothing but hurting each other. You hurt Braxton. He's getting protective of me, and it's going to cause friction with the rest of the group. The way you acted about Abalam hurt me, Gabe. You looked at me like you used to before I switched back to your side."

Gabriel kneaded her flesh in his hands. "Momentarily, you reminded me of when you enjoyed those types of activities."

"I nearly puked. I don't have the stomach for it that I once did. It was all I could do to keep going. I did what I did because it needed doing, not because I wanted to or enjoyed it."

"It's hard for me to believe that. I've seen the joy you derive from causing pain to others."

Alaria's eyes registered hurt. "Derived. Past tense. As in not any longer."

"That's what I intended to say."

She turned to face him. "Was it? Or did you say exactly what you meant?" She spread her arms wide. "You hated me as a Devil. You wouldn't love me as an Angel. Now I can have you, but you look down on me as one of 'them.' What do you want from me, Gabe? What do you want me to be? What version of me do you want?"

Frustrated, he shoved his hands through his hair, leaving it disheveled and messy. "I don't know!"

Alaria crossed the room to sit on the bed. "At least that's an honest answer."

Gabriel turned his back to her and braced his hands on the dresser. "What do you want?"

"I don't know."

"Me?"

She nodded. "You know I do."

"For how long?"

"I don't know." She wiped tears from her cheeks and stared at the floor. "This is more than I ever thought I would have, but the closer we get and the more involved we become, the harder it's going to be to make this work in conjunction with my being with everyone else."

"They don't care for my presence."

"They don't like that you pop in long enough to tell us what to do and then disappear while we risk our lives."

"It is not my job to fight on the front lines of this war."

"I'm fighting. They think you should fight for me."

Gabriel turned and met her gaze. "Is that what they think or what you think?"

"Does it matter?" She returned the look defiantly. "Would it make a difference? Would you stay and fight if I said it was me? If I asked you to?"

The Angel shook his head slowly. "No. It wouldn't make a difference. My role is to guide, not to battle."

"Not even for me?"

"It is not my role." He looked sad as he spoke. "I am already doing so much that I should not. I can't disobey my direct orders, too."

"What now?"

He crossed the room to sit next to her. "I can leave if you want me to. I don't want to stay if it would cause you more pain. I would like to stay if you'll have me."

Alaria leaned her head on his shoulder. "This is the last time, isn't it?"

Gabriel ran his hand over her hair. "I wish I could lie and tell you no. The truth is that I don't know. I don't want to go. I don't want to be apart, Alaria. I want you to know that beyond doubt. The circumstances in which we find ourselves are difficult."

Her tears fell freely down her face and dripped off her chin and onto her shirt. She looked up at the ceiling and stared at the tiles. "I feel like it's over before it started. We never even got a chance."

Gabriel awkwardly draped his arm around her shoulder. "It doesn't have to be over. Not tonight, anyway. I have a few hours before I'll be missed. There may be other times that I will be able to come to you. We have some time left before there can be no more."

Alaria took a trembling breath. "I don't know how much longer I can do this. You stayed away from me for months, Gabe. We had one night, and I thought it would go back to the way I wanted it, and then all of this. You hurt me. The way you looked at me...it was like you still see me as a monster. Then tonight with Braxton. I just don't know what to think."

"I'm sorry for my behavior. I should not have struck the boy. I'll apologize to him if that is what you desire." Gabriel sighed deeply. "I fear you are developing feelings for the human."

"I have feelings for you."

"I do not doubt that." He leaned over and pressed a kiss to her shoulder. She shivered involuntarily, and he smiled against her skin. "You asked twice to have me for as long as you could or for a night. I'm asking you the same tonight. Let me have you, Alaria. If this is to be the last time that we have or if it's the first of a hundred more, I want you."

Alaria closed her eyes, and for the first time since the Fall, she sent up a quick prayer. She prayed for strength and for the fortitude to get through the broken heart she knew she was going to have without making a mistake that would get someone killed. Her eyes opened, tear-filled and darkened with grief to nearly black. She reached out and took Gabriel's hand in one of hers.

"I don't care if we have one night or a thousand. I'm yours if you ask."

The first time had been born out of desperation and the second out of desire. The third was born of despair.

Sex had always been a weapon for Alaria—one she wielded with deadly accuracy, using it to get whatever she wanted. It was different with Gabriel.

He was the one with the weapon, pulling her in with his love. As she stood and pulled her shirt over her head and dropped it onto the floor, she knew that he was going to break her heart. Until that happened, she would cherish every moment she had left with him.

She took the lead. Her fingers were nimble as they unbuttoned his shirt and slid it off his shoulders. She trailed her fingers over his skin, igniting tiny fires wherever she touched. Her touch was soft and warm when she placed her hand on his stomach and used the other to unzip his pants, easing them down his legs until they hit the floor, and he stepped out of them. He toed off his shoes and tugged the white dress socks from his feet.

Alaria gently nudged him back until he was sitting on the edge of the bed. Silent, she straddled him and pushed his shoulders until he was lying flat on the mattress. She wiggled forward on his thighs until his erection was probing the entrance to her body. She lifted herself up, supporting her weight on her knees, and used one hand to hold him steady while she sank down. He stretched her body with his girth, making her feel deliciously full and content.

She rocked her hips back and forth, her motions slow and easy. She took his hands in hers and lifted them to her hips, placing them on her skin. She glided her own hands up her body and over the sensitive globes of flesh that were her breasts. Her short nails scraped over her nipples, and she kneaded the mounds in her hands. Her head fell back, her hair streaming down her back, wet and silky. Her eyes drifted closed, and she tried to focus on the feeling of Gabriel—anything other than the doubts and hurt.

His fingers gripped her hips gently, rubbing her skin and urging her to move. She leaned forward to press her mouth to his in a desperate kiss that tasted of fear and tears. He stroked her hair back from her face and held her to him. Their breath meshed as their bodies moved together, and Alaria fought tears as desire rose within her. She didn't want the orgasm, didn't want to derive pleasure from what was an act of desperation that would accomplish nothing other than delaying the inevitable.

A low groan rolled out of her chest before she could stop it and was absorbed into his mouth. Her body hugged his tightly, her thighs clenching around his hips as she rode him. Her hips rose and fell, driving his pulsing erection into her body over and over again. Her nipples rubbed against his chest, the friction sending spears of pleasure through her. With a muffled cry, Alaria toppled over the edge of orgasm and into ecstasy. Her hips jerked against his several times, and she sank her teeth into his lower lip hard enough to draw blood, the tangy taste of it blooming on her tongue as she came.

The pain mixed with the pleasure and Gabriel flung himself over the edge with her, his body pulsing inside hers and the tendons in his neck standing out as his body surged into hers one final time. Alaria collapsed onto his chest, hers heaving as she gasped for breath. His big hands came up and spanned the width of her back, rubbing up and down gently as she came down.

When she would have lain and cried, Gabriel effortlessly rolled her onto her back. He took her mouth with his and parted her thighs with one hand, sliding into her with a long, heavy stroke. Her body betrayed her and responded to the penetration. Damning both herself and his Angelic stamina, she lifted her legs to wrap around his waist.

Their lovemaking became increasingly desperate. They clung to one another, his arms braced on either side of her body and hers wrapped around his neck. She buried her face in the curve where his neck and shoulder met and let his lovemaking carry her away. They slipped over the edge together, collapsing into relaxation.

Gabriel's head lifted after less than a minute. He looked down at Alaria guiltily. "I have to go. They're calling for me."

Alaria opened her mouth to answer. "It's—" She trailed off as he disappeared, his clothes fading from her floor in the same instant that he did. "—okay."

She stretched out one arm to turn off the lamp and yanked the covers over her naked body. She stared at the ceiling, her arms over her stomach. She fought tears for several minutes before turning her face into her pillow and giving in to the sobs that had been threatening to tear out of her since she'd first stepped foot into her bedroom nearly an hour earlier.

She knew there was no future with Gabriel. She'd known that from the first kiss the night before the Choosing. She also knew that no matter how many times he came to her, if he wanted her, she would always give in, regardless of how bad an idea it was. She sobbed for the life she had dreamed of and would never get, for the future she wanted that was out of reach, and for the past that she had chosen in a moment of weakness that had cost her the other two.

They were both being selfish. They were taking advantage of one another and using each other in the worst way because they loved each other.

They were worse than Romeo and that weeping flower Juliet. Alaria smiled at the thought and dashed the tears from her cheeks. She took a deep breath and forced herself to choke back the next wave of grief. It was the time to be strong. There was no other choice.

She climbed out of bed and pulled on her pajamas. Tying her hair back from her face, she headed up the stairs and wound her way through the house to the kitchen. Gage was sitting at the island reading a book with a cup of cold blood near his elbow. He glanced up when she entered the room.

"Gabe leave?"

She didn't bother to deny it. "How did you know?"

He rose to get her a glass of wine. "I may not be truly immortal like the two of you, but I've been around plenty long enough to know the score. I've known the both of you for more than a thousand years. Did it help?"

She drained the glass in one long gulp. "Not even a little bit."

"Wanna talk about it?"

She looked pained for a moment before nodding almost unperceptively. "Have you ever done something you knew was a bad idea when you were doing it but wanted it so fucking bad you convinced yourself it would be okay?"

Gage took a drink of his blood. "Can't say I have. I avoid relationships, Alaria. If anyone around here knows what it's like to be a monster and try to come back from it, it's me. I've done shit the same as you have. Is this about Gabe, or is it about you?"

She poured another glass and sat down. "What do you mean?"

"I mean, are you so upset because you're desperately in love with Gabe and would give up anything to have him even one more time? Or are you this upset because you *want* to be so desperately in love with Gave that you would give up anything to have him even one more time?" He paused to give her time to think. "Eternity is a long time to work yourself up into thinking it's some epic love story when what you really had is some mutual crush that never worked itself out. Just because you felt one way then, or thought you did, doesn't mean you have to feel it now, and it certainly doesn't mean you have to let it hurt you."

She stared into the glass of wine. "I don't know."

Gage patted her hand gently. "That's an honest answer, and it gives us a good starting point. What exactly don't you know?"

"I don't know what I want or how I feel or what I feel or even who I am. This—" Alaria waved her hands wildly. "This is what is defining me.

Saving this God-forsaken planet *again*. I don't want to be here. I want to forget Gabriel exists and find some human and marry him and have lots of babies. It's what I've dreamed of for millennia. And then he comes off his self-righteous horse and makes me wonder if there's some sort of future there. He slipped, and I liked it and now neither of us wants to let it go because we finally get to feel what it's like to really be together."

"You're both smart enough to know that what happened with Abalam cannot happen again. We're going to have to do some unpleasant things to survive this, and that was the first of many. We can't have him yanking you out into the hallway for a lecture every time he doesn't like a decision."

"I know. He knows." She drained the second glass and poured a third. "I haven't told you the worst part yet."

Gage closed his book. "Spit it out."

"Braxton kissed me earlier." She lifted her shoulders and shrugged. "I'm pretty sure you know what happened. Brax was drunk and stupid and he didn't mean it, but he said that the next time I let Gabe have me, I'd be thinking of him instead."

"And?"

She took a deep drink. "I don't know if it's just because he put the idea in my head, but he was right. I was fucking Gabe and seeing Brax."

Gage stood and went to the cabinet to withdraw another bottle of wine. "You're gonna need this."

Chapter Twenty-Six

August 20th, 2030

Greer woke up before dawn. The sky was gray and dotted with clouds. Fog covered the grass in a thick layer. She wiggled out from under Damon's arm and walked to the window. Casting a quick glance over her shoulder to make sure Damon was still asleep, she pressed her hand to the glass and stared out. The crushing August humidity made the panes foggy and warm, and she rubbed the moisture between her fingers.

The door opened slightly, and she jumped, turning quickly to look. Braxton motioned to her with one arm, silently asking her to come out. She tugged the sleeves of her thin hoodie down over her hands and slipped from the room quietly, sneaking one look back to make sure that Damon hadn't been disturbed by the slight squeak of the door.

She crossed her arms and leaned against the door. "Is everything okay?"

Braxton smiled sadly. "You looked like her just now." When she looked at him blankly, he chuckled. "Griffin. When the end got close, I'd find her with her hands and face pressed to a window and her socks off so she could feel the cold. She said texture and temperature helped remind her that she was still alive."

Greer ran her hand over her hair self-consciously. "You aren't going to kiss me, too, are you?"

The moment shattered, and Braxton laughed warmly. "Good God, no. I wanted to get you away from Damon for a bit to talk to you about what is going to happen. I know you'll fill him in so that he's on board, but I don't think we need the overprotective drama any more than we've already had."

She pinned him down with a hard look. "How did you know I was going to be awake and not Damon?"

"I took a guess." He put a hand on her shoulder and led her down the stairs. They walked through the main level and into the kitchen. He lifted his eyebrows at the four empty wine bottles and one glass left sitting on the island. "Looks like someone is going to have a headache when she gets up."

"How do you know it's Alaria?"

"Because you're not hungover and Gage and Damon don't drink wine." He cleared the bottles. "Are you ready to start this?"

Greer took the carafe from the coffee pot and filled it up with water. "As ready as I'll ever be. There isn't another choice. We just have to get me to the point that healing myself is as easy as healing someone else."

"I wasn't here when Gabriel dropped you off, but Gage and Alaria have said you nearly didn't survive. I think this is the best shot we have, but I need to know that you can do it."

Greer pushed the button to start perking coffee and got two cups out of the cabinet. "I have some ideas to make it easier, but I think I need to run them by Alaria. She'll know better than anyone else whether or not they'll work."

"Let's hear it." Alaria shuffled into the kitchen, her hair frizzy and dark circles marring the skin under her eyes. It was obvious to both Greer and Braxton that she had been crying. "I could use something to focus on other than this headache."

"When Javal attacked me, somehow I tapped into Damon through our psychic link. It let me borrow some strength from him to heal myself. I've been thinking that maybe we need to approach it as a tandem thing. If I can learn to find that link and use it, you could help me find Laelia and bring her out from somewhere not in Hell. If I get hurt, I can borrow from him instead of using my strength. It would give me a better chance of finding Laelia before I have to expend too much energy on keeping myself alive."

Alaria moaned when Braxton handed her a cup of coffee, grabbing it and drinking deeply. "It's a hell of a good idea. If you can maintain that link to Damon, I could guide you to where you'll need to go and help you back out. Is there any way to forge a link to anyone else?"

"I don't know. I've never tried."

Braxton dumped sugar in his coffee. "You're going to. We need to know whether or not something like that is even possible. We also need to know how far the limits of that link are. Can Damon do anything else while he's connected to you?"

Greer giggled. "He can do anything you could do while having a conversation. It's not like the link is the only thing there. We share a space in our minds. It's not all-encompassing."

"Let's test it with Damon before we go on to other people. I agree with Braxton that it's important to know your limits, but I think it only comes into play if you've used more of Damon's energy than he can spare. It's going to mean we all have to work together and that's going to be hard. This is going to be training for you more than anyone else, and Damon more than us, but we need to find your limits, his limits, your limits together, and then how much the rest of us can offer."

Greer stared into her cup. "Why does this sound like I'm going to be tortured? How hurt are you expecting me to get?"

Alaria covered the other woman's hand with one of hers. "I don't want you to think that we're sending you in there to die. There is a good chance that you might get to Laelia without being seen. On the other hand, they could be there waiting for you when you go through. We have no way of knowing. If you have to fight your way through, the odds are that you won't come out. If we find a way in and you can sneak through, we'll bring you home safely. The simple truth is that we don't know what you're going to find."

Greer slid her coffee mug back and forth across the granite countertop. "There isn't another good option. I'm the only chance we've got." She sighed deeply. "I know this is going to be painful. The only way to work on my healing is to make me heal." She met Braxton's gaze. "Someone is going to have to hurt me over and over again."

He returned the gaze without wavering. "I know what it means, Greer. No one is going to enjoy it, but we will all do whatever is necessary. I don't like that this is gonna hurt you, but you're right when you said there isn't another choice. Has Alaria told you what you're going to have to do to get Laelia out?"

Greer shook her head. "No."

Alaria snorted. "That's because I haven't figured it out yet. I still need to go over everything with Gabe before we have a working plan. I suspect we're going to need a spell." She glared up at the ceiling. "Having our witch would make that easy. Without her, we're going to have to play it by ear."

Damon stumbled down the stairs sleepily, wearing sweatpants and a wife beater. His hair was standing on end and his jaw was darkened by two-day-old stubble. He lifted his eyebrows when he saw them circled around the island and ran his hand over Greer's back on his way to the coffee pot.

"No one invited me to the party."

Greer smiled. "Just talking about all the different ways they're going to have to hurt me in order to get me to where I need to be so that we can go find this Laelia chick and kill her."

Damon's expression darkened. "I still don't like this idea."

"There isn't another choice. I have to do it."

He sipped his coffee. "I know. That doesn't mean I have to like it." He laid one hand on Greer's shoulder. "I don't know which idea I like less. Letting you go into Hell to drag out a vampire or torturing you for weeks on end to make you get used to healing yourself." He drained the cup and smacked it down. "How are we going to do this?"

Alaria waved her hand to get his attention. "We were just discussing that. I think we've decided that the best course of action is to start by testing your link with Greer. We need to find out how much stuff you can take. One step at a time. Strengthen the link, test the boundaries, find the breaking point and then work on extending it. Gage and Braxton will keep their ears open for information. If they can't find it out, it doesn't exist. We need Gabe to send some Angels down below to get me some intel on where Laelia might be." She grinned viciously. "God can offer free passage to a soul to go to Heaven and they'll tell us anything we want to know. If He won't agree to it, I'll do to some demon what I did to Abalam. One way or the other, we will know exactly where that vampire bitch is before you go down there."

Greer rifled through the cabinets for pans. "I'm making breakfast. I at least want to eat something before you start torturing me."

Alaria turned her attention back to her coffee. "That way there'll be something to throw up when you start heaving. Stomach acid burns and food will delay it."

"You ready for this?"

Damon's voice resonated throughout Greer's mind. She glared at him, speaking out loud. "I'm ready. How do you want to do this? Test my abilities or the link first?"

"Let's work on the link. Relying on your ability to heal yourself is a last resort." Alaria pulled off her hoodie to reveal a tank top. "I'll let you choose. I can either beat you or stab you."

Greer laughed nervously and looked around the basement at the thick padded floors and equipment they used to train with. "What a choice." She giggled again. "Let's start small and work our way up to the bigger stuff. I was able to draw from him when Javal tried to rip my heart out, but I was panicked and dying and the power took over without my consciousness. I need to be able to use it for anything, not just stuff that would kill me." She looked at Damon. "You might want to tie him up. He isn't going to be able to stop himself from trying to keep you from hurting me."

Damon shook his head, his eyes dark and angry. "I am not going to be tied down like an uncontrollable child. We all know this is the way we're doing this. I want you to be as prepared as you can. Besides, if this works, I'll be the one feeling the pain, not you."

Gage leaned against the door and crossed his arms. "I'll handle Damon if he can't control himself."

Greer sat down in the chair Braxton had carried down from the kitchen. She planted her feet securely on the floor and gripped the armrests tightly. "Let's get to it."

The first punch stole her breath and left her seeing double. She searched for the link to Damon and held it, reaching into him and trying to steal from his strength. She hadn't figured it out when the second punch broke her nose. She snorted and spat blood and tried not to fall out of the chair. The third knocked her to the floor.

Alaria didn't ease up. She kicked Greer and sent her flying two feet. Greer grunted and fumbled for Damon's strength. She almost had it. She concentrated on the tether that connected her to Damon and slid down it, looking for the door. There. Another kick distracted her for three seconds, but it took much less time to find her way back. The pain dulled as she got closer. She lunged forward and latched onto it, wrapping her mind around that core of Damon's that would allow her to leach his strength.

Her nose cracked back into place and the blood stopped flowing. There were loud snaps as her ribs realigned and grew back together. Alaria hesitated to watch the healing before reaching down and grabbing Greer by the arms. She heaved the other woman to her feet and shoved her roughly back down into the chair.

"I'm sorry, sweetheart, but that was just the beginning."

Greer wiped the blood from her face and smeared it on her pants. "You're a bitch, Alaria."

Alaria smiled grimly. "I'd tell you this was hurting me more than it's hurting you, but it would be a lie."

"Keep going. I've got the link now, so we can fully test it. You okay, Damon?"

Damon nodded. "So far I feel a little sore but no real pain yet. I'll let you know if it's too much."

Alaria braced herself and swung, her fist colliding with Greer's face. Skin split and blood flowed for several seconds before the skin closed and the blood stopped. She shook her head before punching Greer again. "This healing thing is just weird."

Gage chuckled. "Effective for what we need, though. Let one of us know if you need a break."

"I'm good."

She broke Greer's nose for the second time, opting not to wait for Greer to heal before continuing to strike her. When Greer fell to the floor, she kicked her several times. After a three minute assault, Alaria stepped back. Greer rolled onto her back and coughed. She swiped blood from her eyes and climbed to her feet. Gage tossed her a wet cloth which she used to wipe away dried and drying blood, revealing a face that was nothing more than mildly bruised. Damon was more bruised, but wasn't bleeding.

Greer looked him over and then walked to the mirror to study her own face. She looked over her shoulder at Alaria, who was nursing bloodied knuckles. "Either you're a lightweight, or this might actually work."

Alaria glared at Greer. "I'm no lightweight."

"I can fix your knuckles so we can keep going."

Gage cleared his throat. "How do you feel, Greer? Are you weak? Do you need a break?"

"I feel a little weak, but nothing that I can't keep going through. How are you, Damon?"

Damon nodded. "I'm fine. A little sore, but fine." He rubbed his jaw. "I've been giving some thought to why this is working and I think I may have figured it out." He paused to take a drink of water. "Greer has always been able to heal others one right after the other, almost constantly. It would make her a little tired and a bit sore but nothing awful. When she's healing herself, she's using only her energy, whereas with other people, she is manipulating the energy of whomever she is healing and adding a little of her own where it's needed. By using the link between our minds, she's manipulating my energy to heal herself, so it's leaving her healed and me with her normal burnout."

Gage considered. "That makes a lot of sense. I think you're probably right. What we need to know is if she can use your energy to heal herself as much as she could heal others and if she can then heal you after she's done. If this works the way you think it will, it may be a way to make her healing ability almost limitless."

Greer mulled that over. "I don't think it's going to be limitless. I run out of energy fast when I'm healing myself. When I'm healing other people, I'm using their own energy, so it doesn't take a lot of mine. To use Damon's to heal myself, then his to heal him seems like it would honestly be too easy."

Alaria smiled grimly. "There's only one way to find out." She strode to a cabinet and pulled out a wicked-looking buck knife. "Let's take this up a step."

Greer ignored the waves of nervousness that coursed through her. She sat down in the chair and gripped the arms again, her fingers turning white from tension. She looked to Gage with eyes wide from fear. He lifted one eyebrow in a silent question. She shifted her eyes downward in embarrassment.

"You might need to tie me down for this. I don't relish sitting here and letting her stab me over and over again. I'm not sure I could make myself sit here and take it without fighting her off."

Gage nodded. "I'll get the ropes. Damon, I think you might want to consider the same. This is not going to be pleasant for you to either watch or experience if she's able to pass it along to you."

Damon looked around the room reluctantly. "This is fucking crazy. You expect us to voluntarily let you tie us up and stab her God knows how many times just to see if she can heal herself using my energy?" He shook his head. "We're all out of our damn minds. This is beyond crazy."

Greer giggled nervously. "You don't have to tell me how crazy this is. It's just going to get crazier. Let's get this done, Damon. The sooner we find the limits, the sooner we can plug up that exit out of Hell."

Damon shook his head again before looking at Alaria. "The second she says stop, you stop."

Alaria glared at him. "I'm not going to kill either of you. I don't enjoy this, Damon, and I don't want to have to do it. I'd much rather that there was a way for me to go get Laelia, because then I'd know my way around and exactly where to go to get her. It would be faster and easier and the risks would be less, but they'd know the second I went down there and they'd swarm me. There would be no sneaking—not even a chance of it. I would have to fight from the second I landed and I don't have the luxury of being able to heal myself if I get hurt."

Greer perked up. "What if there was a way to take you with me?"

Braxton pushed off the wall, his curiosity piqued. "What do you mean?"

"What if, instead of trying to strengthen my abilities and whatnot, we tried to connect my mind with Alaria's? When Damon and I are connected, we can see through each other if we want to. If she could see through my eyes, she could guide me and it would make the trip less risky. If I can draw from her energy to heal myself, that addresses both concerns. If she gets too weak, I can link with Damon and continue that way, and he can be the relay station between the two of us."

Alaria placed the knife on the table. "That might actually work. We still have to keep doing this because we need you as strong as possible, but that might just fucking work. How can we link your mind to mine?"

Greer sighed. "That's the tricky part. I've never tried to link with anyone other than Damon. I wouldn't even know where to begin." She perked up suddenly. "But I think I might know who does." She looked at Gage. "You wouldn't happen to know how to access the dream plane, would you?"

Alaria laughed. "That, my dear, is my specialty." She rubbed her hands together. "Where are we going?"

Chapter Twenty-Seven

Aradia stood in the clearing, her white gown billowing around her as she stared in shock at the two women in front of her. "Let me see if I understand this correctly. Greer, you're going to willingly go to Hell in order to find Laelia and somehow drag her out so that you can kill her again during this ceremony in order to put a plug in the Gate? And Alaria, you want to know if it's possible to link your mind to hers in order to what? Be her tour guide?" The redheaded priestess spread her arms and threw her head back. "You're planning a siege on Hell and I'm stuck ten thousand years in your past! Why in Zeus' name has that infernal Angel not come to bring me forward to you yet?"

Alaria's mouth quirked into a small smile. "I'll ask him the next time I see him. You've got it right as far as the general plan goes. We need to know if it can be done and how to do it."

Aradia tugged on her hair sharply in a sign of frustration. "Oh, I can help you accomplish your goals, all right. It isn't going to be easy, and I suspect it's going to take some time for the two of you to learn to control the link. Not so much you, Greer, since you already share a link with Damon, but for Alaria, this is going to be new and likely frightening. It may take some time before she can choose what to show you. It may be very painful for the both of you at first."

Alaria's smile faded. "She'll be able to read my mind?"

Greer was shaking her head before Alaria finished the question. "No. I don't read your mind. I would never intrude like that, even if I could. What she means is that you'll be able to project thoughts to me through the link. If you're having problems controlling it, you might show me more than you mean to. It's a learning process. At first, Damon and I couldn't even be in the same room together because we would fill up each other's heads, and it was like drowning in each other. I can probably help you control it once we're connected. I remember how we did it the first time."

Alaria mulled it over hesitantly. "How do we do this?"

Aradia closed her eyes and two beds appeared. "The trick to this is going to be getting what we do here to translate into the real world. Typically, what happens on the dream plane is dulled when you wake. That's how you're still alive." She looked at Greer pointedly. "I need for the two of you to prepare your bodies for what your consciousness is going to do here. You'll need to be in the same room—in the same bed would be better. There's an herbal tea that I want you to drink before you return here. It will help relax your psyches and allow for easier transmission of realities from the dream plane to your reality."

Greer nodded. "What's in the tea?"

"It's a combination of mint, lavender, jasmine, valerian, chamomile, kava kava, and passionflower. Steep the ingredients for thirty minutes and drink it hot and black. It will be strong and taste absolutely disgusting. Follow it with a sleeping tea in order to help your bodies relax into a deep sleep. The deeper the sleep, the easier it will make our work here. If you're struggling to wake up or going in and out of deep sleep, that will lessen the chances of success. I want you to put herb bundles in your pillows and surround the bed in salt. You should protect the room in which you are laying as well as you can in order to keep Javal and Garrick out. While you are gone, I am going to do everything in my power to make this place as secure as it can be. With any luck, we will be safe here for the time that we are working."

"Okay. It sounds like it might take us a couple of hours to do that and get back. You'll be here waiting for us?"

"I'm not going to leave. I can move fairly freely between my body and the dream plane. No harm is going to come to me. Go, now. The longer you dally here without appropriate safeguards, the higher the risk of Garrick or Javal sensing our presence."

Aradia flicked her wrist casually and sent both women hurtling back into their bodies. Greer woke a split second before Alaria and sat up blinking. Damon was at her side almost instantly.

"That was fast."

Greer swung her legs around and placed her feet on the floor. "We haven't even started. Aradia needs us to take a few steps here to get ready for the tethering process." She stood and leaned her forehead on his briefly. "I'm a little worried about what this is going to do to our link. Can I be connected to more than one person at a time?"

Alaria rolled out of the bed. "Believe me when I tell you that I don't want to be connected to you for any longer than I need to be. As soon as this is over, if we have to, the two of you can go back to the witch and she'll walk you through this process all over again to get your mojo back. I don't think this is going to affect anything permanently." She opened the door and stepped into the hall. "Let's go make some disgusting tea. I have a feeling we're going to have to send one of the boys out for some of these herbs. They aren't normally found in the kitchen."

Greer followed Alaria. "I don't even know what the hell kava kava and valerian are."

Gage appeared in the hall, emerging from his study. "They're herbs typically used in witchcraft. Why? And why are the two of you awake? I thought it would take most of the day to get that done."

"We don't know how long it'll take. We've been sent to drink tea and add extra protections to the room." Alaria descended the stairs quickly. "Do you happen to have said herbs on hand?"

Gage shook his head. "No, but I can send for them. There are a few Wicca supply stores in Glasgow. It'll take an hour or so for it to get here."

Alaria went to the pantry and withdrew an armful of supplies. "We'll get the room protected while you're taking care of that." She glanced to where Greer was tearing apart a pillowcase to make the bundles. "If you've got this, I'll go salt it."

Greer waved carelessly. "Go for it. I'm fine." She sprinkled lavender and mint leaves into each of the squares of fabric. She added three basil leaves and a sprig of sage before tucking a garlic clove in the middle. After that came agrimony on top of the garlic and she carefully placed a star anise in each bundle. Once she'd tied them all with twine, she got a bundle of aloe leaves from the refrigerator. She scored the leaves to get the liquid flowing and dripped aloe onto each bag. That done, she rinsed her hands in the sink and gathered up the finished products. She turned to leave the kitchen and squealed when she collided into Damon.

He grabbed her by the shoulders to steady her. "I didn't mean to scare you."

"I guess I was just zoned out. I was trying to get these ready so I can put them in the pillows and under the mattress so we're protected."

"There's a little time while we wait on Gage." He took the herbs from her and laid them on the sink. "Can we talk for a minute?"

She leaned against the counter. "What's up?"

"Did the witch know what this is going to do to our link? I feel silly even being concerned, but I don't think anyone wants Alaria in our heads all the time and I certainly don't want to have our link severed to make room for her. I don't think this will work unless you're connected to us both."

Greer lifted up to her tiptoes and pressed her mouth to his in a gentle kiss. "I promise you that I will make sure this is not going to affect us. We aren't going to lose our connection. It's the biggest thing that we have to offer." She laid her head on his chest. "I need you to support me in this."

He wrapped his arms around her and drew her close. "I do. It's hard for me to watch you put yourself through so much pain, but trusting you and supporting you has never been the problem. I hate seeing you in danger, and I'd do anything to keep you safe. That typically doesn't include helping you dive head first into dangerous situations." He kissed the top of her head. "I love you too much to be okay with that."

Greer smiled into his shirt and tightened her arms around his waist. "I need to get upstairs and help Alaria." She brushed one final kiss over his mouth. "I love you, too, Damon. But you're gonna have to back off a bit with this protective stuff. I'm a big girl, and I can handle myself."

Damon picked up the bags of herbs. "If I didn't know that, you'd be tied up in the basement." He started up the stairs. "Let's get this done."

Alaria glared at Aradia. "Just for the record, that tea was disgusting."

Aradia glanced up from where she was preparing a pallet of thatched leaves. "I never told you it would be pleasant. Are your bodies sufficiently protected?"

Greer nodded. "We've done what we can."

"Greer, this is going to be more work on your part than it will be for you, Alaria. Greer is more familiar with the mind and how the links work so I'm going to teach you how to open yourself to her. Your only job will be to hold still and not struggle while Greer forges the cord that will join your minds. Once that is complete, I will assist you in learning to control it. Once you've become familiar with it, you'll be able to choose when to share thoughts with one another." She smiled and pushed her mind into both of theirs, speaking inside their thoughts. *"Eventually, you'll learn to forge temporary bonds to communicate with."* She withdrew and spoke out loud. "The mind is an amazing thing, and learning how it works and how to control it will be extremely beneficial to our cause."

Alaria tapped her foot impatiently. "Let's get this show on the road. The longer we stand around talking, the more likely it is that one of those demons or that damn wizard are going to find out we're here and ruin this."

Aradia spoke sharply. "I need you both to lie down, side by side. If you're amenable, I'd like for you to also hold hands. A physical touch between the two forming the cord is helpful."

Greer flopped down on the pallet and waited until Alaria had joined her before reaching out and grabbing the other woman's hand. "What now?"

Aradia laughed softly. "Don't be impatient, Greer. This will take time. I want you to close your eyes. Alaria, this next part is for you. I want Greer to remain quiet and still and for you to follow my instructions."

Alaria nodded. "What do I do?"

"Breathe deeply and try to relax. No harm can come to you here. Concentrate on your breathing. Let your lungs fill as full as they want to and then control the release of the air, exhaling slowly. Let your limbs be heavy. Concentrate on nothing but the breaths. I want you to let your body go limp and sink into the leaves. Breathe in the aroma of them, let it surround you. Feel it seep into your pores and flow over you."

Alaria listened to the witch with half of her concentration. The whole prospect of opening herself to Greer sounded a hell of a lot more sexual than she ever cared to get with the Healer. She breathed deeply and inhaled the annoying scent of the leaves, earthy and rich. One of them had slipped between her shirt and pants and was prickling her skin. She wiggled her butt slightly to relieve the discomfort and moaned in relief when the leaf shifted enough that she was more comfortable.

The scent of the leaves grew stronger. It filled her nose and traveled down her throat and into her chest. Her head became fuzzy. She shook it to clear the fog and felt momentary panic when the movement had the opposite affect and instead dispersed the fog so that it filled every inch of her head. It smelled of lilacs and greenery. She tried to stop it from deluging her, but it seeped into her pores and surrounded her with its aroma. Aradia's voice lulled her to drift away on the waves of scent.

"Let it take you away, Alaria. Don't fight it. Float on the waves of relaxation. Let yourself go. Sink into it."

Aradia watched Alaria for several moments. Deciding that the other woman was where she needed to be, she turned her gaze to Greer, who laid quietly, her breathing deep and even. She didn't move when Aradia spoke, didn't open her eyes, and didn't twitch one single muscle.

"Greer, I need you to go inside your mind. I need you to find your link to the Hunter. Find it and follow it back into your mind until you can't follow it any further. Find the end of the link, deep within the recesses of your mind. Tell me when you have found it."

Greer knew exactly where the link was. It was a constant rope through her mind, connecting her to Damon in the most intimate of ways. She soared through her memories to the link and wrapped her fingers around it. Sliding down, she let herself fall deep into the recesses of her own mind. She followed it deeper than she ever had before, the colors and lights of synapses firing distracting her momentarily as she marveled at them. She couldn't remember having seen the inside of her own brain before. Finally, once she was below the synapses—the colors flashing and snapping wildly above her—she spoke.

"I found it."

Aradia's voice sounded distant and far away. "Good. I want you to picture a thread. A silver thread that branches off of where the link to the Hunter is anchored in your mind. Imagine it stretching out, winding its way through you. Can you do that?"

Greer concentrated briefly and grinned jubilantly when a silver twine rose up and shimmered in front of her. "Got it."

"Now imagine many more threads. Weave them together until you have a rope. Once you have the rope, you're going to thread it as a string through a needle until you've reached the surface of your mind. Take your time."

Greer wove threads together into a complicated braid. She knotted the end and grabbed it with both hands. She leapt through the synapses, watching in wide-eyed wonder as they showered her in color and energy. She ascended through memories and consciousness until she surfaced through the deep pool of her subconscious and into her body. She struggled to teeter on the edge, neither ascending into consciousness, nor diving back into the recesses of her brain.

"I'm there. It's hard to maintain, though."

"Then you're at the right place. I need you to stay in the in-between there. Awake enough that you can turn your head and see Alaria and submerged enough that you don't lose your grip on the rope. Can you do that?"

Greer struggled to maintain her position. "I think so, but it isn't going to be easy."

"It shouldn't be. Take the rope in your hands and reach out with your mind in the same way you would to share thoughts with the Hunter. I want you to feel for Alaria. Open your eyes and look at her. Reach toward her with your mind and push into her. Her mind should be open to you. Can you press in?"

Greer struggled to maintain her grasp on the cord and reach to Alaria at the same time. She had to stop several times and balance herself before continuing. After what seemed like an hour, she reached Alaria's head and slipped inside.

It became more comfortable once she was inside the other woman's mind. It was familiar. She pushed deep within the recesses of the brain and dove past the synapses to the subconscious. She took several deep breaths and tried to surface enough to speak to Aradia. Her voice was little more than a whisper, but she managed to form the words.

"I'm here."

"I need you to anchor the rope. Imagine that there is a loop through which you will thread it. The strands are delicate, so don't yank on them. Thread it gently through the loop and tie a knot. You want it to be tight but not so tight that it puts strain on the braid."

Greer followed the directions and pictured the loop. She gently pulled the rope through it and tied it into a knot. Stepping back, she surveyed her work with an appraising eye. The rope held strong, and it shimmered from the flashing colors above. She slowly retreated toward the surface.

"I got it. I'm coming out."

"Before you withdraw, can you feel Alaria in your head? Can you see her thoughts?"

She paused and reached for the familiar link with Damon. She found two links, one the strong, red link that was the familiar one, and the other silver and thinner, but just as strong. Alaria's link.

"Yeah, it's there. The only way to thoroughly test this is going to be once we're both awake."

"Come on out, and I'll wake Alaria."

Greer withdrew swiftly and emerged into consciousness. She sat up and rubbed her hands over her face before offering Aradia a smile. "That wasn't as hard as I thought it was going to be."

"When you know what you're doing, there is very little that is hard." Aradia bent to murmur in Alaria's ear. "I want you to come through the fog. See the light in the mist and go toward it. The scent of the leaves is lifting. Allow yourself to ascend into consciousness. You are slowly waking up in three, two, one. Open your eyes."

Alaria sat up, blinking rapidly. "Did it work?"

Greer pushed into Alaria's mind along the link. *What do you think?*

Alaria jumped, surprised when her head filled with Greer's voice, though the other woman never moved her lips. "How did you do that?"

Aradia laughed softly. "The link is working. Good." She glanced around. "We haven't been detected, but each moment you stay here runs a higher chance of Garrick sensing our presence. You should return to your bodies now. If you need other assistance, you need only ask."

Chapter Twenty-Eight

September 12th, 2030 - Scotland

Greer gritted her teeth as the blade of Gage's knife sliced through her skin and tore through muscle. She felt Alaria brace for the impact of the pain as she sent it hurtling down the link and into the other woman. Her skin closed, forming a pink scar that would fade within the hour. It was the same thing she'd done ten thousand times since Aradia had helped them form the mental bond. There was only one difference.

This time, Alaria was thirty miles away.

They'd slowly increased the distance over the last three weeks. At first, it wouldn't work it they weren't touching. After a few days, they were able to stand on opposite sides of the yard. At the week mark, on opposite sides of the property. Two weeks later, they were strong enough to be a half an hour car ride away from one another. Damon was a three hour flight away. Whether or not she could reach him would be the final test.

Gage tossed down the blade and put his hands on his hips. "I'd call that a success."

Greer nodded. "I think this is a manageable distance. If I get too far into Hell, I'll just switch to Damon and use him as a relay station. Our bond is stronger and more reliable anyway." She waited while he unlocked the handcuffs that had been holding her to the chair. "Let them know they can come back."

Gage picked up the phone and dialed. "All that's left is developing a plan for getting you into Hell and finding out where Laelia is." He turned his attention to whomever had picked up the phone. "Yeah, it's me. We're done. Head home." He hung up and dialed again, relaying an identical message to a second person. Once the phone was back in the cradle, he addressed Greer again. "Alaria will have a better idea of how to do that." He patted her back gently. "Let's get this last one out of the way before the plane takes off and Damon's closer to home." He picked up the knife and twirled it. "Ready?"

Greer braced herself and clenched her fists at her sides. "Ready as I'll ever be." She screamed when he stabbed the knife into her shoulder, burying it to the hilt in flesh and bone. Tears sprung into her eyes, and she dropped to her knees, her left hand coming up to pull the blade from her right shoulder. She grasped for the red cord connecting her to Damon and flung herself onto it, ignoring her natural instinct to heal herself. She latched onto his energy and molded it into new muscle and bone, sealing the wound shut and forming another scar.

She stayed on her knees for close to a minute as the pain ebbed. Gage watched her with concern in his eyes. "It took longer that time."

Greer glared at him. "Combination of distance and me not being ready, I'd bet." She climbed to her feet. "The important part is that I'm healed and fine." She started for the stairs. "I need to get dinner started for those of us who eat. They'll be hungry when they get home."

Gage followed her. "Do you think it could have something to do with switching back and forth so quickly?"

"Could be. We haven't really tested that part of it. There isn't time to work through everything."

"How are you handling having two people in your head?"

She laughed. "It's damned annoying. Alaria doesn't know how to filter. Damon and I had problems with that at first, too. But she really doesn't know how to filter. I can block her most of the time, but if she's thinking super loud or gets mad about something, there isn't anything I can do to keep her out. She's a bull in a china shop when she's bashing around my brain." She sobered. "She worries me."

"What do you mean?"

"That is one supremely confused woman. She has no idea what, or who, she wants and has no clue how to deal with it. Being human is new to her, and she doesn't know how to handle all the emotions that are flooding her. I'm living it with her. She's desperately in love with Gabriel, but so completely torn because he hurt her. She feels used, and she knows that there's no future there. It makes things difficult for her."

"Maybe you should talk to her."

Greer goggled at him. "Are you out of your fucking mind? She'd slit my throat if I brought it up!"

"How bad is it?"

She went to the refrigerator for an armful of food. "I'm not sure. I'm trying very hard to respect her privacy and not learn things she isn't trying to send me, but it's hard when she's so new at the whole thing. Like I said, I can generally shut it down pretty quickly, but some stuff has trickled through. What is consistent in what I'm getting is how much pain she's in."

"All of it revolving around Gabriel?"

She lifted her eyebrow in his direction. "You don't like him much, do you?"

"I like Gabe just fine. I've known him for more than a thousand years. What I don't like is that he picked now to discover his dick and that he's sticking it in a woman who has had exactly eight months' experience being a human and who has absolutely no idea how to handle all of the emotions that she is suddenly feeling. I don't think for an instant that he intends to be taking advantage of her, but that's what's happening. His emotions are dulled. That's the curse of being an Angel or Devil. They don't feel things like humans do. He doesn't feel pain and guilt and love in the same way. It's like touching things through a glove."

"Her heart's on her sleeve, and he's wearing a bullet proof vest."

Gage grinned. "That's a hell of a cliche, but it's pretty accurate. Eventually, he's going to have to make the decision to let her go. She deserves to be happy with someone who can actually give her a future." His smile turned to a frown. "Don't get me wrong. I'm not sure she should bang Braxton either, but that's an infinitely better choice than Gabe. The two of them can at least be on an equal playing field. Braxton is damaged and in love with his dead wife, and Alaria is struggling to find her footing. They would at least both be struggling. As it is, Braxton only wants her because he's trying to bury grief and guilt, Alaria wants Gabe because she's always wanted him and Braxton because he's human and someone she should have, and Gabriel wants Alaria because he loves her the best way he can, which is not half as much as she needs."

Greer shook her head as she dumped hamburger into a pan to cook. "Suddenly my life seems boring and normal."

"Better boring and normal than a ticking time-bomb. Because that's what this is. We can only try to mitigate the damage. Which is why we're having this conversation. If anyone can assess the situation, it would be the person in Alaria's head. If you get a chance, make sure she's okay. It'll benefit all of us."

"I'll see what I can do, but I'm making no promises. I have no relationship with Gabriel, and the one I have with Alaria is pretty strained. Besides, there are more important things going on than who Alaria is screwing."

Gage dumped tomato sauce into a pot. "If it were just the sex, I wouldn't even be interested. It's what it's going to do to Alaria that worries me. That, and how personally Gabe will take it. He can be jealous and judgmental. If he feels slighted or like things aren't on his terms, he may just disappear and leave us to muddle through this on our own."

"Do you really think he would do that?"

"Yes." Gage crossed his arms and leaned against the counter. "He's experiencing new things as well, and he's trying to mold Alaria into what he thinks she should be in order to be worthy of him. If she falls below that standard or appears to be too human or too Devil, he'll leave her. Whether he truly loves her or merely thinks he does, he'll leave because of his millions of years as an Angel. For all that he is, he'll never be able to shake off being an Angel."

"I hope you're wrong."

"Believe me, so do I." He glanced toward the door. "Sounds like Alaria's back. Brax and Damon will be another forty minutes on the plane." He held up a hand when the door opened. "We're in the kitchen, Alaria."

Alaria walked into the room, her face drawn and hollowed from stress and a lack of sleep. There was a tear in the thigh of her jeans where Greer had been stabbed. She slid onto one of the stools and folded her arms on the island. "What's up?"

Gage slid a cup of coffee across the island to her. "We need to figure out how we're going to get the information on Laelia that we need."

She stared into the cup. "The only way is to get a demon out of Hell that has knowledge of where she is and get that information out of them. I have some guesses about where she'd be, and I'm eighty percent sure she's going to be in the castle, but there's no way to be positive without firsthand information. The problem with that is if we capture someone too high up on the chain of command, they'll be missed. If we shoot too low, they won't know anything."

Greer stopped stirring the pot of spaghetti sauce. "That sounds like a whole hell of a lot of hassle. How many places could she be?"

Alaria laughed. "A thousand. I'm relatively sure she'll be in the castle, but that's the most dangerous place for you in all of Hell. It's where Lucifer lives and where the Devils come and go. They don't like to be out where the demons are or near the Lake where the souls are. There are chambers there, rooms for all sorts of things. Sex, torture, interrogation—that sort of thing. She'll probably be there, but being a vampire will put her at the bottom of the food chain. It's not likely she'll have free reign, which means you're going to have to find her." She took a deep drink of black coffee. "I think we need to get ahold of one of the guards. They have shifts, so if we can catch one off shift, they won't be missed for at least a few days. That'll give us time, and they'll probably have information."

Gage put his hands on his hips and mulled the information over. "Do you have a plan in mind?"

She stretched her arms over her head, cracking her back. "Michael! Get your ass down here!"

There was a quiet rustling and Michael appeared. He cocked one eyebrow, a ghost of a smile barely turning up the corners of his lips. "You bellowed, your highness?"

Alaria tried, and failed, not to chuckle. "Smartass."

He grinned. "You know me so well. What do you require?"

"I need you to fetch me a castle guard."

Michael looked at her blankly. "From Hell?"

"Preferably Jesslyn if she's not on duty, but any will do. We require some information."

He flicked his wings in annoyance. "How do you intend to extract this information?"

Greer couldn't help the giggle. "I don't think asking nicely is going to work." When the Angel glared at her darkly, she shrugged. "Just sayin'."

Michael crossed his arms over his chest. "I am not suggesting that you are incorrect. However, by specifically requesting Jesslyn, I believe that my former sister does not intend to torture the information out of this particular demon. What do you have in mind, Alaria?"

"I want you to get permission to offer her free passage."

"You're not serious."

Alaria shrugged. "I'm very serious. I can torture her until she spits it out, which could take hours, or it could take days. She's a demon, so she's been through Abalam's racks. She can take a hell of a lot more than he can. If I kill her, we're done, and our plan will be public knowledge, which none of us wants. If you bend the rules a teeny bit, she gets to go to Heaven, where her memory will be purged once she's inside the pearly Gates, and we get the information that we need. It's a win-win as far as I'm concerned."

Gage pushed off the island. "What makes you think this demon would even take a deal?"

Michael sighed. "Because she's tried to make it before. Jesslyn is a sore subject all the way around. She died five hundred years ago. She was a prostitute in medieval England. She died of some venereal disease. She didn't have a family, so they weren't able to meet the Church's price to prepare the body correctly and she was left hanging. When Death came to retrieve the soul, she was in the process of repenting but did not complete the process before death occurred. It was determined that Lucifer owned her soul. There was almost a second war over her. It would have been just as big as when Lucifer took up arms against God. It has been a point of contention ever since. Lucifer keeps her in the castle as a guard to keep an eye on her and because he likes to parade her around. It's really quite pathetic. She was tortured for two hundred years before her soul was twisted enough to be a demon. Since that point, she has lived almost exclusively in the castle and on Earth. She has a habit of pretending to be human."

Greer cocked her head to the side and studied Michael. "Why don't you want to do this? It seems like it's the easiest way to get what we need."

"Because Lucifer is not going to let her go without a fight. The fallout could be massive."

"But isn't there already a fight? You're trying to keep the demons in Hell, and they want out. How can this possibly make it worse?"

"There are very few things that Lucifer takes personally. Losing the Choosing was one of them, and these are the ramifications of that. Hell on Earth. Jesslyn is another personal pet of his. If I were to allow her passage into Heaven, I would not be surprised if Lucifer himself tried to burst out of Hell, if only to get her back. It is possible that there could be a siege on Heaven."

Greer nodded thoughtfully. "I understand that, but isn't the whole point of this to close the Gate and keep the demons in Hell? If we spring this one and move quickly once we have the information, then wouldn't the Gate be shut before Lucifer would even know about it?"

"Hypothetically, that is correct. However, the task you are now completing is merely a stopgap in order to stem the flow of demons until we can close the Gate. If Lucifer were to throw his power against the temporary door, I have no idea how long it would hold. It is the power of God holding Lucifer in Hell, but God is not directly involved in what is currently going on. He is ready to just clear off Earth and start again. If Lucifer has the right amount of human magic on his side, it is not unfathomable that he could burst forth onto the Earth."

Alaria sighed. "We don't have another choice. We can't send Greer down there unprepared, and she can't stay long enough to go on a wild goose chase. We need the information. If you want to bring me another guard to slice to pieces, we can try that, but I don't know how long that will take. I'm leaving it up to you. If you want us to do this now, bring Jesslyn and make her a deal. If you're fine waiting, bring me someone else."

Michael's wings fluttered in annoyance. "I'm going to give this some thought. I'll return shortly with a demon."

"When is shortly?"

He glowered at Alaria. "By your next morning."

Alaria's eyes darkened. "Do me a favor? Don't let Gabriel find out if you bring me something to torture."

Michael smiled. "I can't promise that, and you know it. I'll do my best to withhold the information if it comes to that. For what it's worth, you did what I would have, and I think you made the right decisions. My brother is short-sighted in his obedience. He always has been. I believe the humans have an expression. He cannot see the shrubbery for the bushes."

Gage bit his cheek to keep from bursting into laughter. "Something like that."

Alaria smiled. "Still, I don't want to make things worse than they already are."

"I'll do my best." He offered his arm to Alaria. "Walk with me for a moment before I leave. There is something I wish to discuss with you."

Alaria slid off of the stool and laid her hand on Michael's arm. With nothing more than a thought, he transported them to his hut on the mountain. She held out her hands to steady herself from the sudden trip and looked around curiously.

"I haven't been here before. Where are we?"

Michael led her into the house. "This is where I come to be with Lilith."

Alaria whirled, her face betraying her shock. "Why in Hell's name did you bring me to your love nest?"

"Because I wish for us to be frank with one another and for there to be no filters on this conversation. Bringing you here is a sign of good faith on my part. I am trusting you not to betray my confidence and therefore hoping that you will trust me to not betray yours."

"You're still sleeping with her?"

"No. After Braxton's family was murdered, I ended things. I'll not meet her here again. It was my slip that allowed them to be found, and I am not going to forget that betrayal."

"Even after the Choosing? You were still fucking her?"

"Yes. I am not in love with Lilith. We enjoy one another in a sexual manner. There are no feelings between us, and it has never spilled outside of this structure." He sat in one of the chairs. "Have a seat."

She gingerly perched on the edge of the bed. "I really hope you washed the sheets." She crossed her legs. "What do you want, Michael?"

"I know of you and Gabriel."

"I'm sure you do." She ignored the fluttering of her heart in her chest that betrayed her nervousness. "Why do you care?"

"I believe that everything occurs for a particular purpose. However, I have concerns about your relationship with my brother."

Alaria laughed in a thinly veiled attempt to mask her pain. "Ya think?"

"What do you intend to do?"

"I don't know." She stared at the floor. "Does He know?"

"No. I don't want to discuss the ins and outs of the relationship. That is not important. You may do what you wish with whomever you wish to do it. That is the joy of being a human. However, my concern is that this may affect Gabriel's ability to remain involved in the tasks that you face. It seems obvious to me that Gabriel does have some issue with certain tactics that may be necessary. How do you intend to handle that?"

"I don't know. I don't know what to do or how to do it or even what I feel. Things were going so well and then the torture thing happened, and he hasn't been the same. I know we're running on borrowed time."

"I didn't bring you here to hash out your personal life or have you cry on my shoulder. I want you to know that if Gabriel is not meeting his responsibilities to you or to these tasks that I am willing to step in whenever and wherever it becomes necessary." He smiled. "I've always had less respect for the rules than Gabe."

She spoke slowly. "What do you think?"

"You want my opinion?"

"Yes."

Michael shrugged. "I think the heart sometimes wants multiple things and that sometimes it wants unattainable things. The problems come in sorting out what you can have, what you want, and how to get it. Trust your gut, Alaria. It's gotten you this far." He held out a hand. "Ready to go back?"

She placed her hand in his and surprised them both when she stood and wrapped her arms around him in a hug. "Tell Him I'm going to make Him proud."

Michael touched her forehead and sent her back to Gage's kitchen, his words a whisper in her ear. "You already have."

Chapter Twenty-Nine

Jesslyn was a small woman with dirty blonde hair and pixie-like features. Her eyes were big and her nose was small with her mouth slightly lop-sided. In other circumstances, she would have been pretty. As a demon, anger and pain simmered just below the surface and mixed with the confusion and apprehension she obviously felt at Michael snatching her away.

"You're not idiots. You know I'm not one that'll go unmissed. When I don't show up for my shift, they'll know something happened to me, and you'll have all out war on your hands." She paced the kitchen—securely inside a trap—and glared at Michael and Braxton, who sat at the island.

Braxton twirled a dagger between his fingers. "Play your cards right, and nothing is going to happen to you. We need information on a certain vampire, and from what I understand, Michael here can give you something you've wanted for centuries."

The demon's eyes narrowed, and she looked pointedly at the traps on the floor and ceiling. "If this is a negotiation, why am I locked up?"

"Just in case Alaria is wrong about you and you're not what we think you are. Here's the deal—you tell us everything you know about Laelia and where she is. If what you tell us is true, when we find her, Michael grants you a one-way ticket to the streets of gold. Interested?"

Jesslyn's eyes lit up for a brief moment before she was able to smooth her features into a mask of neutrality. "What makes you think I'd even be interested in going to Heaven?"

Michael crossed one leg over the other. "Because I heard you scream for God for nearly a century while Abalam carved you to pieces. Because I can look into you and see that there is still humanity left in your soul. You are not yet twisted into what they have tried to turn you."

"I would want a contract."

Michael laughed. "You can't make a deal with an Angel. You know that."

She looked at Braxton. "I can make a deal with him. Or with Alaria. Or any of the humans that are involved in this. If you betray me, the world ends, because I will own their soul, and this little group you've got will be fractured. That's the only way I do it. I want the security."

Braxton and Michael exchanged a long look. After several seconds, Braxton jerked his head. "Fine. Eventually Hell is going to run out of demons to make deals like this with. First Alaria, now this chick. Who next? Lilith will want her wings back?"

Jesslyn giggled. "There aren't many down there, but there are a lot of souls that are in Hell that don't want to stay there. My circumstances are different in that God and Lucifer had a pissing match over me when I died. They both claimed me. So, in the same way that Alaria is unique because she was tricked into fighting with Lucifer, I'm unique in that I was a con-solation prize to Lucifer to keep him from slaughtering people."

Michael smiled ruefully. "Jesslyn wanting out is no surprise, and I'm not shocked by Alaria suggesting it. It was Alaria who was the surprise. Re-gardless, the task at hand is the contract that she requires in order to make this deal. I loathe asking one of you to put your soul on the chopping block, but there's no other choice that I can see."

Braxton shrugged carelessly. "I might hesitate if it were Gabriel mak-ing the deal. He'd betray it just to be rid of me, but you, I trust."

"Your confidence in my trustworthiness is overwhelming." Michael's voice was dripping with sarcasm. He gestured to Jesslyn. "Draft your con-tract. There is to be a provision within it that if your information is inac-curate, the claim on his soul is to be released. If your information leads to the location of Laelia, then your soul will be wiped clean and taken to Heaven. Should I betray the deal, Braxton's soul will be collateral."

Jesslyn snapped her fingers and a piece of parchment appeared in front of Braxton. She extended her hand to give him the pen she held. He took it and read through the contract. Without a word, he scribbled his name on the line and tossed the pen onto the table. He stood abruptly.

"This feels an awful lot like last winter." He glared at Michael. "Let's hope I'm better at keeping people alive than God."

Greer sank deep into the bubbles and let them slide up her body to cover her shoulders. Her toes peeked out of the other end of the tub, and she closed her eyes. It was her last night before she went to Hell.

She was as prepared as she could be. They had all of the information they needed, and Michael was off making sure that the backdoor to Hell that Alaria had told them about was unguarded. With any luck, she would be in and out of Hell within a few hours and the first task would be over.

"It could be that easy."

Greer shrieked and jumped when Damon spoke from the doorway. Her head disappeared beneath the surface of the water and she came up sputtering. "You nearly gave me a heart attack!"

He sat on the closed lid of the toilet. "I could hear you worrying from downstairs. You're giving Alaria a migraine."

She spent fifteen seconds closing off both links before speaking. "It's getting harder to keep them both under control. I don't think my mind was meant to maintain more than one link at a time."

"It'll be fine as long as you can keep it stable until after tomorrow. The plane takes off at six in the morning. Apparently this back door is somewhere in New Zealand. Quick in and out and we're back home within thirty-six hours."

Greer reached for the razor and propped one leg on the edge of the tub. "Can we please talk about something else?"

"I never thought shaving your legs was sexy until right this minute."

"You'd think it was pretty unsexy if I stopped shaving my legs." She lifted her eyebrows when he stood. "What're you doing?"

He drew his t-shirt over his head, revealing tan skin and rippling muscles. "I don't think I've ever taken a bubble bath." He bent to shuck off his pants and boxers. "And you're all naked and wet and alone in there."

Greer giggled and threw her loofah at him. "You're a goof." She squealed when he stepped into the water and sat down across from her, sloshing water onto the floor.

He grabbed her wrists in his hands and tugged her into his lap, bringing their chests flush. He wrapped his arms around her and nuzzled her neck with his nose. "I'm going to make love to you until we're too tired to keep going. I'm not going to let you keep worrying yourself sick over this. We will get through it." He kissed her throat and slid his hands over her back to press her closer to him.

Greer draped her arms around his shoulders. "I love you, Damon." She smiled against his mouth as he kissed her. "I love that we don't need big declarations and gestures. You always know what I need."

He pulled back and stared into her eyes. "That's because we were friends first." He tugged her hair to make her look up before he closed his mouth over hers. "I think I like bubble baths."

Greer leaned forward and pressed her mouth to his ear. "If you run into your bedroom and get a condom, you can find out how much fun sex in the tub can be."

Damon slid out from beneath her and dashed into the other room without so much as grabbing a towel. He reappeared thirty seconds later, a condom already rolled onto his erection. Greer stood on her knees to make room for him to climb into the tub before she straddled his lap.

Their skin was slick from the water and bubble bath. Greer's nipples rubbed on his chest as she slid against him. She braced her hands on his shoulders, pressed herself upward, and sank down on him, taking him into her body and lowering herself into his lap. Her body hugged him tightly as she rocked back and forth.

Damon's hands swept down her chest to cup her breasts. He lifted them out of the water and blew on them, the cool air tightening her nipples to hard little beads. He rubbed his thumbs over the nubs, drawing moans of pleasure from her. He pressed his mouth to hers, crushing their lips together as he banded his arms around her to hold her against him.

They moved together slowly, their chests heaving. Greer buried her face in his neck and muffled her cries of release against his skin. He followed her over the edge, dragging her hips against his and gripping her tightly. He grasped her chin in one hand and forced her to look at him, their eyes clouded with passion.

"Promise me you'll come home to me. We have a future together. I know this is dangerous and that you have to do it, but I need you to promise me that you are going to do everything in your power to come through this. Don't be a hero. I'd rather have you and the world we left than a perfect world and no you."

Greer kissed him gently. "I'll come back from this. I'll come home to you. This isn't some suicide mission for me. I fully intend to lay down in two nights and go to sleep beside you with all of my parts in the right place and the purge stopped." She slid off of his lap and stood. "I'll do my damndest to make sure I survive this, but we both know I can't promise you because a lot could happen down there."

Damon stood and snagged towels for them both. "If you get into something you can't handle, I will come and get you."

She wrapped the towel around herself and stepped out of the tub.

"It's not getting to Laelia that makes me nervous—it's finding a way to get her out. In order to yank her out, since she's technically just a soul left unchained, I have to have a body to put her into. I don't like the thought of cramming her down someone's throat and then killing them."

"Couldn't you heal them afterward?"

She sat on the edge of the bed to dry herself off. "Maybe. If I'm really lucky, I might be able to, but it's gonna be iffy at best. It would be best if Gabriel could snatch her body the moment before it bursts into dust and yank it forward."

Damon was shaking his head before she finished speaking. "You and I both know that isn't going to happen. He isn't going to mess with the past. There's no telling what any little thing could cause to happen. We don't want to go there."

"All I know is that if I go through all of this and drag her out, and there isn't a body there for me to stick her in, I'm going to be pissed."

"We'll find something. I wish we had more time to get ready, but I think we all know that there is a clock ticking and that we have to get the plug in place. As it is, I don't know how this is going to go." He pulled back the blankets and waited for her to slide between the sheets before turning off the light. "We've been working on you for more than three weeks, but we haven't done much preparation of anything else. It feels like we're walking into something without being at all equipped for it. I don't like that feeling. This seems too easy. We're not preparing for a battle or to be attacked or anything that could go wrong, and I'm not sure if it's that they're not thinking about it or if there's nothing we can do."

"As far as we know, they have no clue that we know where Laelia is. Abalam is being held hostage by the Angels, and Jesslyn won't be missed for a few more days. There's been no indication that they know what we're up to. All that they know is that we attacked the Gate to get Sam and that we were gone before they got there. They have no idea what we're doing. This isn't war, Damon. It's a deep cover mission."

Damon drew her against his side. "I feel uneasy about it. Maybe that's because there's something else going on that we don't know about, and maybe it's because I'm sending the most important person in my life to Hell on what is little more than a fucking suicide mission, but I do not feel comfortable about tomorrow."

Greer cuddled into his arms. "Are you getting premonitions along with being psychic now?" When he remained silent, she giggled and snuggled closer. "No one is pretending that tomorrow isn't dangerous, but neither are we borrowing trouble. I am quite sure that Gage's plane is going to be loaded with all sorts of toys for the four of you to use if you need to. We aren't exactly going in empty handed. I'm going to be fine, Damon. We all are. I don't want you to be so worried about me that you do something stupid to risk yourself. Gabriel and Michael will come through and find us a vessel to put Laelia's spirit in. We can't go into this thinking that something is going to go wrong."

He pressed a kiss to her hair. "I know you're right. I just can't help feeling like this. It doesn't feel right. I hate the thought of you going down there alone."

"I'll have you and Alaria both in my head. I won't be alone." She wrapped her arms around him and pressed her body to his. "Please, stop worrying." She ran her leg up his, his leg hairy where hers was smooth and silky. "I believe you made me some promises when you climbed into the tub with me a little while ago."

Damon couldn't stop either the smile that spread across his face or the hardening below his waist. "Did I?" He nipped her shoulder gently. "What is it that you think I promised you?"

Greer rolled onto her back, pulling him with her. She fumbled for the box of condoms on the nightstand and pressed one into his hand. "I seem to remember you saying that you were gonna keep fucking me until we passed out."

He rolled the condom on with a smooth motion and stared down at her. "Roll over and get on your hands and knees."

A bolt of excitement speared through her. She turned onto her stomach and lifted onto her knees. She balanced herself on her elbows and gasped as he gripped her hips and slipped into her in one strong thrust. When he slid almost all the way out and then back in, she couldn't help the whimper that escaped between her lips.

They lost themselves in each other, using their bodies as an escape from the reality they faced and the fear that threatened to overwhelm them. Damon didn't let her rest until he was too exhausted to move.

Braxton carried two glasses of whiskey into the library. Alaria was curled up in one of the chairs, her knees drawn up to her chest and her chin resting on top of them. She glanced up when she saw him and offered a half-smile. He held out one of the glasses before dropping onto the couch.

"You should be asleep." He adjusted the pillows on the couch so that they weren't poking into his side. "For such a man's man, Gage certainly loves his throw pillows."

Alaria's mouth quirked into a real smile. "He's something else." She sipped the liquor and savored the harsh burn as it slid down her throat. "Why aren't you in bed?"

"Too much going on to sleep. Tomorrow's a big day." He took a sip of whiskey and rattled the ice cubes in his glass. "It feels like all we're doing is getting from one fight to the next. I tried to log some sleep, but I just kept thinking about Griffin and the Choosing."

"I know the feeling." She balanced the glass on her knees. "Is there anything I can do?"

"No. I actually came in here to check on you. You aren't looking so good, Alaria. What's going on?"

She sighed. "I was dealing with things okay when it was just me and Gage here. He was helping me process things, and I was making progress. There hasn't been any time for dealing with my feelings since Greer and Damon got here, and it's making things harder for me."

Braxton leaned forward and braced his elbows on his knees. "What do you mean? The guilt?"

"A lot of it is guilt. I have millions of years of bad things to feel now. I could remember something new every minute for the next thirty years if I wanted to. It's inevitable that some of it is going to leak out. Griffin is the worst. Especially tonight, right before we're getting ready to do something similar to Greer. Griffin's granddaughter being sent off to the slaughter just like she was."

"Only she might make it through alive. Greer has a chance, and you can help her through it." He reached out and took her hand in his. "It feels the same, but it isn't. It might be a totally different outcome this time."

"We're all fucked if she dies."

"Then keep her alive." He rubbed her skin with his thumb. "You can save her, Alaria. You know Hell. You can keep her safe. Is this all it is? Nerves and fear about tomorrow?"

"Mostly. Tomorrow is the immediate concern."

"What's the other concern?"

She looked guilty and pained. "Gabe."

Braxton leaned back, though he didn't release her hand. "He hasn't made an appearance since the funeral?"

She shook her head. "No."

"And you want him to?"

Alaria stared at the carpet. "I don't know. Yes and no." She blinked back tears. "This is so human of me! I don't know what I feel and what I want! I want him here and I want him to stay away. It's easier and harder at the same time. I love him, and I hate him."

"Do you want some advice?"

She shrugged. "Might as well. Enlighten me, oh wise one."

He chuckled at her wry tone. "Cute." He patted her hand. "Humans love their cliches, though the problem with something becoming a cliche is that it's normally right. I can think of two that might help."

Alaria was trying not to giggle at the serious look on his face. "Shoot."

"Distance makes the heart grow fonder."

She snickered. "Lame. Try again."

"If you love something, let it go."

She sobered. "That one might be a little closer." She closed her eyes for several seconds. "This is so not important in the grand scheme of things, but I can't help but dwell on it." She rubbed her chest. "My heart hurts, and it's not something I've ever felt like this. I've felt pain before, as an Angel, and stirrings of things as a Devil, but nothing has ever been as intense as this. I didn't realize how much more humans feel all the time than I used to. It's hard to deal with, and it makes it hard to focus."

Braxton chuckled. "It's hard to deal with for those of us who have never been anything but human. You're doing remarkably well, and if you need to talk, I'm here. I know I was a jackass before and that I did stuff I shouldn't have for reasons that were mostly wrong, but I do consider you to be my friend, and anything you need, you only have to ask. I never thought I'd say this, but I kinda miss how you used to be. Even when you came to get me, you were so bossy and pissed off, and that's you. You're a force of nature, Alaria. This isn't you. I hate him for doing this to you."

Alaria wiped tears from her cheeks and shook her head when he shifted off of the couch and onto his knees in front of her chair. His skin was warm when he brushed the tears away. He rubbed her arms and took her hands gently. A maelstrom of emotions whipped up inside her, nearly drowning her in feeling. She struggled to break free, holding on to Braxton tightly as she fought the tidal wave that threatened to sweep her away.

"I hate him too. I hate me and him and sometimes you. It makes me want to go back to the way it was before, when I could do anything to anyone and never feel more than a mild twinge over it."

"You don't mean that." Braxton released her hands to frame her face. "You're a good person, and you're doing just fine. No one expected this to happen. You were supposed to have all the time that you needed to work this through, and now that's been cut short. We're asking a lot from you, and you're sacrificing yourself to do whatever you can. You're amazing."

Alaria choked on a strangled sob and folded her fingers around his wrists. "You wouldn't think that if you knew what was going through my head right now."

"Sure I would." He smiled reassuringly. "Tell me."

She took a deep breath and blurted it out before she could stop herself. "I love Gabe, but I'm confused whether it's what I feel now or what I felt in the past and want to feel now."

Braxton sat back on his heels. "I think that's perfectly normal." He stared at her intently. "That's not all, is it?"

She shook her head. "I feel...things...for you." She looked down, a blush tinging her cheeks red. "I'm sorry. I shouldn't have said anything."

Braxton sighed. "I didn't mean to confuse you in my drunken stupidity." He rubbed one thumb over her cheek. "You never have to apologize for feeling things. I was stupid that night, but I didn't say anything that wasn't true." He brushed his lips across her forehead. "You aren't alone in this, and it sucks for me, too. I love Griffin. I think I always will, but I wanted to kiss you the night of the funeral, so I did."

Alaria opened her eyes and damned them both. "Do you want to kiss me now?"

He nodded. "Yes, but I don't want to confuse you more. I want to make things easier for you, not harder."

She leaned forward and pressed her mouth to his in a desperate kiss. She tasted of tears, fear, and need. Her mouth was soft and supple, and her tongue flitted against his almost nervously. He laved her mouth with his tongue, sucking her bottom lip into his mouth and banding her against him with both arms. He pulled back gently, kissing both of her eyelids and the tip of her nose. He lifted her easily and sat down with her in his lap. She settled into his lap and laid her head against his chest, the rhythmic beating of his heart lulling her into sleep.

Chapter Thirty

September 15th, 2030 - New Zealand

New Zealand was vibrant and green in the early fall. Greer marveled at the lush landscape as the plane landed. She hadn't ever seen so many trees. She looked around in wonder while descending the steps from the plane. Gage winced as he stepped into the sun. Greer lifted her eyebrows.

"How is it that you don't burn up?" She studied him curiously. "I've never seen you out in the sun before."

Gage placed a hand on the small of her back to lead her around to the storage container beneath the plane. "I spent four hundred years conditioning myself to it. A tiny bit at a time, body part by body part. Now it's just like a sunburn when I'm out, but it won't hurt me unless I spend days out here. It gets painful after more than a few hours at a time." He tapped in a code and opened the hatch, revealing an array of weapons. "Let's get you ready, shall we?"

Her stomach knotted with fear, she nodded. "I don't suppose guns work in Hell?"

Alaria walked up behind them. "I don't know what'll work and what won't. I don't think many modern weapons have been tested down there. You'll be best off with a shotgun and salt rounds. Those'll at least blast a demon spirit back to the Lake temporarily and give you a chance to get out of the area. Blades will work fine, but only if they're using their vessel and aren't just there in spirit form. Holy water will work either way. Rule of thumb—there are only a few fallen Archangels. Lilith, Azazel, Abalam, Beelzebub, Abaddon and me. They all have vessels, and blades will work. Demons are either inhabiting a human body or in their spirit form, which is what they looked like when they were alive. You'll need salt or Holy water for them in Hell."

Greer took the backpack that Gage held out and watched silently as he dumped in several boxes of shotgun shells and a dozen clips for her pistol. He fitted a holster around her hips and tucked a wicked looking knife into one side and the pistol into the other. The shotgun had a sawed off stock and barrel, making it a small weapon that fit inside the bag. A box of protein bars and four bottles of water went in next. She shook her head when he started to shove in a first aid kit.

"There's no reason for that. If I can't heal it myself, a first aid kit isn't going to do me any good. There's no reason to take up the space and increase the weight."

Gage tossed it to the ground. "Anything else you want?"

"Is all the water blessed?"

"Yeah. I figured you can drink it either way, and it'll be multi-use if it's all Holy." He cocked one eyebrow. "You sure you're ready for this?"

She nodded. "I'm as ready as I'll ever be."

Alaria picked up a crate of supplies and headed into the woods. "Follow me. We've got about a half mile hike to the entry." She led them through the trees to a small clearing bisected by a quickly flowing stream. She dropped the box and strode over to a group of boulders. "It's here. Brax, hand me that spray paint."

Braxton fished through the box he had carried for a can of paint. He handed it to Alaria and watched as she drew several unfamiliar symbols on the rocks. She pulled a knife from the holster around her thigh and sliced her palm open, letting her blood drip onto the dirt in the center of the formation. She murmured in Latin and slammed her bleeding hand against one of the symbols, smearing blood on the rock.

Wind rippled through the trees and stirred up dirt as it whipped through the clearing. The stones moved and shifted as the dirt dropped out from the middle, exposing a door. Alaria stepped back and waited for the wind to die down.

"Inside the door is a stairway. Take it all the way down to the bottom, and there will be a tunnel. You'll have to crawl through it. It'll dump you out near the beach at the Lake. Once you're there, you'll have to move quickly. If there is anything at the other end of that tunnel, come right back here. Once you're on the beach, I'll guide you to the castle. It'll take a few hours to sneak in or about a couple hours if you just charge through. I'll wait until I can take a look around to make that decision."

Greer shouldered her pack. "Are there other exits if this one gets blocked off?"

Alaria shook her head. "Just the main Gate. This is a back door that only a few know about, and as far as I know, they don't know I'm one of them. It's not guarded, and it's closer to the castle. If you have to make a run for the main Gate, it's going to mean that you're going to have a solid six to eight hour run if you do it straight. To get there without getting killed, more like a day."

Damon unzipped her backpack and stuck in a length of rope, a pair of handcuffs, a box of salt, a flashlight, and a small box filled with packets of herbs. "How are you going to get Laelia out?"

"I'm going to knock her out and drag her." Greer looked at Alaria. "Are you sure there's no way to dissolve her into her essence and stick her in a bottle or something?"

Alaria glared at Greer. "She's a vampire, not a genie."

"It's gonna be a tall order to carry out another human being, especially if she's bigger than me."

Alaria chuckled. "Once you're outside the castle, there is a spell to drag her through the Gate. That's what those herbs are for. You'll need to cram salt and herbs down her throat, and I'll do the rest. That won't go undetected for long, so once she's dragged out, you hightail it out of there as fast as you can."

Greer nodded. "Okay, let's get this done." She reached out and squeezed Damon's hand tightly. "I'll see you in a few hours."

He dragged her close for a searing kiss. "Come back to me."

She leaned her head against him for a brief moment. "I will. I love you."

Greer stepped into the portal before he could respond. The boulders shifted closed behind her, and she was engulfed in darkness. She opened her pack and withdrew the flashlight, pushing the button so that the thin beam illuminated the stairs enough for her to wind her way down them.

Her boots clicked on the stone as she descended the stairs, and she stopped every four steps to make sure there were no other noises. Once she determined that she was alone, she continued. It took her more than ten minutes to reach the end. Once she was at the bottom, she was faced with a choice of going back or laying on her belly and wiggling through a narrow tunnel. It wasn't large enough to fit her and her pack at the same time.

Greer removed the backpack and shoved it into the tunnel ahead of her, pushing it several feet in front, crawling to it, then repeating the process twenty-seven times until she reached the end of the tunnel, all the while clenching a flashlight in her teeth.

There was a small sliver of light that grew slowly bigger. She shoved her bag as far to the side as she could get it and spat the flashlight into the dirt so that she could fumble to turn it off. She craned her neck to look around, the harsh red sand and light painful to eyes that had grown accustomed to the dark.

There was no one around. Greer could hear water lapping against the shore close to her and saw the red earth fade into black beach. She squirmed out of the tunnel and crouched, one hand on her bag and the other on her knife. When no one approached after thirty seconds, she straightened and looked around.

The sky was red and dotted with black clouds that swirled and twisted as if they were alive. In the distance, she saw the peaks of an onyx castle jutting into the air. It was beautiful and frightening. The air smelled of sulfur—bitter and strong. The waves were inky black and lapped against the shore. Curiosity got the best of her, and she crept toward the waterline.

Once she was close to it, she realized the Lake was boiling. She peered into the water and leaped back, falling to the sand and scrambling away from it when she saw thousands of souls chained to the bottom. Their feet were wrapped in shackles that anchored them to the depths. Their eyes were wide and blind, the irises bleeding into the whites and their mouths were stretched wide in unheard screams.

Alaria's voice sounded in her head. *"This was the first thing I showed your grandmother when she was four years old. The first thing I asked her was if it was horrible."*

Greer scrunched her nose and stood. *"It's horrible, all right. Okay, tour guide, where am I going?"*

"Head to your right. I'm going to take you the long way around. It'll take us about five hours to get there, but it's going to be the safest route."

Greer glanced around one more time and began jogging. *"Is that time walking or running?"*

"Walking."

"I'm a soldier, Alaria. I can cut that in half." She picked up her pace and ran down the beach in the direction Alaria had pointed her.

The first thing Greer had learned as a soldier was to be aware of her surroundings. Her eyes were her best weapon, with her ears a close second. She continually swiveled her head to keep an eye on everything around her, and every fifteen minutes, she stopped to listen for anything out of the ordinary. Twice, that meant hiding behind rocks and in the shadows as demons drifted past her. One terrifying time a Hell hound got within inches of her before being called off by its master.

"*Quickest way to end a hound is to chop its head off.*"

Alaria's voice was almost singsong in Greer's head. "*Failing that, slit its throat.*"

Greer's chest was heaving as she sucked in air. "*Shut the fuck up.*"

She gritted her teeth and pressed on, digging her feet into the dirt to push off and run faster. "*The only thing I want from you is directions.*"

"*Hang a left at the next boulder.*"

Greer followed the instruction and turned sharply around the boulder. The castle was appearing larger quickly as she got closer to it. It had been nearly two hours since she'd entered Hell. Sweat ran down her neck and soaked into the cotton of her shirt. She pushed through the exhaustion and ran until her calf cramped and sent her tumbling to the ground. Gasping, she grabbed at the muscle and massaged it, her fingers biting into the seizing muscles and loosening the knot.

Alaria's voice was urgent. "*Get up and run. Now.*"

"*What is it?*"

"*I hear hounds coming up fast. If they've caught your scent, they'll be on top of you in a matter of minutes. Run!*"

Greer rolled to her feet and took off as fast as she could. Her heart thumped in her chest, a mixture of exertion and panic. Her feet struck the hard, cracked ground, and her blood pounded in her ears. The wall of the castle was getting closer and closer. She pushed herself harder.

Her shoulder slammed into the onyx and the pain jarred her whole body. She ignored it and ran along the wall until she felt the seam of a door. She bent her head and whispered the words Alaria was feeding her. The door slid open with a quiet swoosh, and she darted inside, pressing herself against the wall and holding her breath until the door closed.

The castle was gorgeous and glimmered with the shine of gems. There was a grand, sweeping staircase carved of rubies and floors made of black diamond. Everything glittered and shined. Greer looked from side to side, her eyes struggling to take it all in.

"*Why is it that Hell is so quiet?*"

Alaria chuckled. "*Most of the fun goes on down in the dungeons. That's where Abalam and his crew do the torturing. The clouds that you saw when you came onto the beach? Those are demons in their true form. They don't pay much attention to anything. They're waiting for their chance to cram themselves through the Gate and possess someone. The Devils hang out on Earth and in that castle, but neither Hell nor Heaven are nearly as crowded as you'd think. There are thousands of demons and thousands of Angels, but Heaven and Hell are big places."*

"What about the Angels that fell that weren't Archangels?"

"They're kinda in between. They have vessels if they choose to find them, but they aren't as powerful." Alaria's tone darkened. *"Enough chitchat. You need to go up those stairs and take a right. Follow that hallway to the end and turn to the left. There'll be a set of double doors. Go through them and cross the ballroom into the back. There, you'll find a staircase that leads down into the dungeons. Laelia is down there."*

"Where souls are being tortured? How in hell am I supposed to keep from getting caught?"

"Jesslyn said that all of that has ceased since the Gates opened. Abalam was working on Earth, and the dungeons are being used to hold Laelia. They don't want her getting back out onto Earth somehow."

Greer jogged up the stairs and down the hall. She followed Alaria's directions as quickly as she could. She yanked open the double doors and stared at the throne room. There were three gilded gold thrones in the center of the room surrounded by onyx and silver. She gaped at it for several seconds before shaking her head and racing through the room.

It took several minutes to get down the stairs. They were narrow and slippery, and she was forced to use her flashlight to see the way. The door at the bottom was rusty and shrieked when she opened it. She went absolutely still, holding her breath and listening intently for any footsteps. After thirty seconds without a sound, she crossed the threshold and began checking rooms for Laelia.

Greer got lucky on her sixth try. She opened the door to reveal a slim blonde laying on a mattress, her bare feet on the floor and her arms crossed on her stomach. When the woman heard the door open, she sat up, stretching.

"Is it time for my breakfast? I think I'd like to feed on a man today. I'll fuck him before I kill him. It's been weeks since I've had a cock in me." She trailed off when she saw Greer. "Who are you?" She sniffed the air. "You're human!" She clapped her hands. "Oh, they've sent me a present." She dashed across the room and pressed her nose to Greer's neck. "You smell tasty."

Greer fought the urge to shiver. "Are you Laelia?"

The woman absently made an affirmative noise and licked Greer's neck. "Yes, why? Do you want to play for a while before I eat?" She dragged her fangs down Greer's throat, inhaling deeply. "It's been decades since I took a woman lover, but I'm horny enough that you'll do nicely. Take your clothes off."

Greer closed the door and sat her pack on the floor. She grabbed the handcuffs off the top and waited until the vampire got close. Moving as fast as she could, she grabbed Laelia by the hair and slammed her face into the stone wall. She repeated the motion until the woman went limp and unconscious.

Working swiftly, she tied Laelia's arms to her trunk and fastened the cuffs on her wrists. Greer ripped off one of the sleeves of her shirt and tore it into strips. Yanking out the box of salt and the herbs and preparing the mixture quickly, she pried Laelia's jaws open and poured the herbed salt in, mashing it down her throat and then using the strips of fabric to gag her.

She lugged Laelia to the bed and used that to get the leverage she needed to drape the woman over her shoulder in a fireman's carry, grunting under the weight. She struggled to balance the load, but eventually straightened her back and left the room.

It took four times as long for her to climb the stairs with an extra hundred and thirty pounds. She walked through the throne room as fast as she could and made her way into the hallway before descending the stairs as quickly as she could. She was at the bottom of the ruby staircase and halfway across the entry when she heard footsteps.

Greer hit the wall and crouched into the shadows. A man in a white suit with slicked-back blond hair and rings glittering on both hands walked into the entry, whistling. The door was less than ten feet away. Alaria's voice filled her head.

"That's Lucifer. Do not move. Whatever you do, do not make a sound."

Greer concentrated on keeping her breathing quiet. Lucifer started up the stairs and disappeared down the hall. She let her breath slip out between her teeth on a sigh of relief. She reached out to Alaria.

"Run?"

"Run. He's probably headed for the dungeon. Get out of there as fast as you can."

She stepped out from the wall just as shouting started. Alaria began screaming in her head.

"Run! Run! Get out of the castle! I'll do the spell and drag Laelia out. Run as fast as you can!" Alaria swore when Greer burst through the door and saw a squad of demons heading her direction, blocking her escape to the back door. *"Turn left and run. You need to go northwest about fifty miles. You have to head for the main Gate. We'll get on the plane and meet you there."*

Alaria snapped out of Greer's head and began chanting, the words of the spell slipping from her lips. The air filled with the scent of sulfur and the rocks began shifting, making room for Laelia's essence to come out. She turned to look at the three men.

"The vampire bitch is on her way out, and Michael still isn't here with a vessel. We need to cram her into something."

Braxton swore. "It's gotta be one of us. Where's Greer?"

"Running from demons toward the main Gate. She's been spotted. Gage, fire up that damn plane. How fast can you get us to Colorado?"

There was a rustling as Michael and Gabriel appeared. Michael strode forward. "Not as fast as Gabriel can. He will take you to the main Gate."

Alaria gestured to the three men, who began loading up with weapons. "We need a vessel. Laelia is going to come pouring out that hole in about two minutes and we don't have anything to put her in."

Michael looked between Damon and Alaria. "It has to be one of you. You're connected to Greer, so you could contain her essence without being completely overtaken."

"I'll do it." Damon stepped forward. "Alaria still has some of her Devil abilities, which makes her more valuable if I'm out of commission. Just put her in me."

Alaria began chanting again. Within a minute, a black cloud swept up through the entrance, and Alaria directed it into Damon. Damon shuddered and shook for several seconds before his eyes cleared from black to their normal color.

"This feels fucking weird. She's bashing me up from the inside."

Michael stepped forward. "Open the Gate again, Alaria."

"What? Why?" She blinked rapidly. "There's no telling what could be trying come out it and we need to get to the other Gate to get Greer when she comes out."

"It's not a matter of what is coming out. It's about who is going in." He drew his sword and spread his wings. "I'm going to get Greer."

Chapter Thirty-One

GREER RAN AS fast as she could. Sweat dripped off her nose and stung her eyes. Her lungs struggled to take in enough air to fuel her escape. Her shirt stuck to her body and her fatigues were growing damp with perspiration.

She heard barks and growls behind her that told her the hounds were getting closer. There was no way she could outrun them for fifty miles, but she knew she needed to get as close to the main Gate as she could. She dared to glance over her shoulder and swore. If they kept up their current pace, they'd be on her in another twenty minutes. She dipped her head and ran faster.

There was a shriek of pain from behind her and a high-pitched yelp from one of the dogs. She risked another quick look, turning her head to see what was going on even as she continued to run. An Angel had snatched one of the Hell hounds from above and ran it through with a sword. When the Angel turned, she caught sight of massive red wings. Michael.

Greer skidded to a stop and dropped her bag to the ground, grabbing the shotgun from inside and snapping a shell into the chamber, all the while keeping one eye on the large slavering beast that was charging toward her. She dug her feet into the ground, brought the gun to her shoulder and fired. The hound that had been nearly upon her fell to the ground, blood pouring from its neck and bits of bone and gray matter littering the dirt. She snatched a fistful of shells from the bag at her feet and loaded them into the gun with ruthless efficiency. She pumped the gun again and fired.

That time the shell hit the dog in its chest, blowing a hole the size of a grapefruit. She got one glimpse of intestines and organs before it collapsed at her feet in a dead heap. She stepped over it, her boots covered in blood, and loaded another shell. She had three more shots before she would have to reload.

Greer used two of those shots on demons that raced at her. Michael was slicing through the horde of hounds, blood coating his sword, his shirt torn open to reveal deep cuts in his alabaster skin. She loaded her last round and blew the head off of a hound about to fasten its powerful jaws on the Angel's neck.

"Cover me! I have to reload!"

Michael shifted to block the swarm from getting to her as she grabbed six shells from the bag and loaded them into the gun. She was efficient, and the entire process only took thirty seconds, but even that was long enough to have Michael surrounded. She checked to make sure the pistol was still strapped to her thigh and charged into the fray.

Six shells didn't last long when there were a hundred demons. Twice they grabbed her, one snapping her arm before she managed to shoot them. She grabbed to the link with Alaria and healed herself as quickly as she could, her concentration split between keeping herself in one piece and killing monsters.

The shotgun clattered to the ground, and she drew the pistol in one smooth motion. The rounds didn't pack the same amount of punch, but there were more of them and her accuracy was better. She fired the twelve shots in the clip and the one left in the chamber in rapid succession, blasting eight demons and a hound before she was forced to reload.

Michael stood in front of her, blood dripping from his wings and sweat gleaming on his face. He used his wings to shield her on both sides and his sword to hack through the rush of demons. She took the extra time to reload the shotgun before standing and pressing her back to his, both to protect him, as he was her, and to use his wings as a shield.

They moved together, both fighting for their lives. Greer gasped when claws sliced into her thigh, and she nearly fell to her knees with the strain it took to find the link and use Alaria to heal herself. Even the link to Damon was hard to grasp. She switched to that one, knowing it was stronger, and pulled the trigger yet again.

The horde was getting thinner. Her eyes moved across their enemies, counting. Ten hounds and thirty-two demons. They had cut it in half. Two against a hundred, and they were still standing. Michael tensed and turned his head so that she could hear him.

"The Gate just opened. Lilith and Azazel have come inside. We need to go. Now. Is there anything in that bag that you need?"

"Weapons. Ammunition for my guns."

"Grab it. I'm going to fly us out."

Greer swooped down and grabbed her satchel. Before she could strap it onto her back, Michael grabbed her around the waist and took off, his wings propelling them high above the mass of creatures. She locked her arms around his neck, trapping the bag between them, and wrapped her legs around his.

"The demons in their true form will be on us in minutes. I can get us to the main Gate in less than ten. Gabriel has transported your companions there. I'm sure they'll be fighting to clear it in order for us to emerge and finish this. Are you wounded?"

"I'm fine. I've been using Alaria to heal myself. She might be pretty sore though. I don't think it was anything bad enough to put her out of commission."

"That is beneficial. You fight very well."

Greer giggled hysterically. "I'm in Hell, flying with an Angel, getting ready to blast my way out, and you're giving me a compliment!" She couldn't stop the laughter. "This can't possibly be my life!"

Michael looked down at her in concern. "I need you to be strong, Greer. We may not get out of here yet. This is not the time for you to have some mental breakdown. Our lives are dependent upon each other. Do you understand?"

Greer nodded, still not trusting herself to speak without giggling. There was a black mass moving closer to them, and she peered at it almost curiously, trying to make out one demon from the rest. Michael saw her looking and spoke.

"They can't hurt you in that form. They have to take a corporeal form in order to cause you harm. Don't be afraid of them yet. It's what awaits us on the ground that you should be scared of."

"I think we killed off most of the hounds."

"Hounds are Lucifer's pets. He makes as many as he wants." Michael began to descend. "Do you have projectiles in your weapons?"

"Bullets." She counted quickly. "Two in the shotgun and thirteen in the pistol."

"How many more are in that bag?"

"A lot. I think about forty for the shotgun and seven clips for the pistol."

"You will likely need them. Do you have a sword?"

She shook her head. "I have a knife and four bottles of Holy water.

There's a bit of salt left, too."

"Useful bag."

Greer tried not to laugh. She glanced down, and the laugh slid back down her throat. "Fuck, fuck, fuck!"

"What?"

"There are like fifty dogs beneath us!"

Michael glanced. "So there are. Are you prepared to fight again?"

Greer ignored the knot of panic that clamped down on her chest. "I don't think I have much of a choice." She let go of him with one hand and swung slightly to the side, allowing enough space between their bodies that she was able to free the bag enough to get her hand inside it. "Do we have a strategy for this?"

"Stay close and stay alive."

She shoved the pistol into her waistband. "That's as good as any, I suppose. How do we get through that Gate?"

"When we get to it, I will open it. I have the key. As it is, it opens twice a day to allow demons out. Without the key, it will never allow access more often than that. I can open it for several seconds in order to allow us to exit."

Greer didn't have a chance to respond. Her feet hit the ground, and she was immediately surrounded by demons and hounds. Her heart pounded in her chest, and she struggled to contain her screams of terror. They were too close to use the shotgun. It clattered to the dirt with a thump as she fumbled for her knife, hacking her way through.

Several times, a demon got hold of her. She stabbed one in the eye, spraying herself with vitreous fluid as the eyeball popped, leaving a gaping, bloody hole where it had once been. Another got so close that she was able to cram the barrel of the gun into its mouth before pulling the trigger. The back of the skull exploded, spraying the crowd with brain and bone fragments. The body collapsed to the ground and disappeared. She knew it would have to climb back out of the Lake before it could come back.

"This is like a fucking video game! They die and respawn somewhere else."

Michael spared her a split second glance. "I have no clue of what you speak. I suggest you stop talking and start killing."

Greer lashed out, kicking a hound back and pumping three rounds into its head. "What does it look like I'm doing?" She crouched and popped in a new clip. The three seconds it took was enough to let one of the hounds get too close.

Powerful jaws closed on her, and she felt her skin pop where the teeth broke through and tore into her muscles. She couldn't stop the scream of pain. Her blood spurted from between its teeth, and it shook her violently. Her head collided with the ground, and her gun skidded out of her grasp. She felt and heard her ribs shatter from the pressure of the bite.

Hurt, nearly dying, she gripped the knife as hard as she could and stabbed it into the roof of the dog's mouth. Blood poured from it and covered her arm, soaking into her clothing and covering her in sticky, red liquid. The dog fell to the ground, releasing her as it howled. Its chest rattled as it attempted to breathe and couldn't. After several moments, its powerful body went limp, and the life seeped out of its eyes.

Greer fumbled for the link to either Alaria or Damon and found them both weak and distant. She latched onto both, careening down the links and seeking energy. She grabbed onto their energy as fast as she could and brought it back down the cord and into her own body. She felt her ribs snap back into place, and the holes in her abdomen began to close. Still healing, she crawled to her gun and rolled onto her back, firing twelve shots into the demons that surrounded her.

Michael was there before they were on top of her, slashing through them with his blade and brushing some aside with his powerful wings. Blood matted his feathers, and he was covered in cuts and bruises. He stood over her, using his body as a shield while she struggled to reload her weapons and climb to her feet.

Again, the mass was thinning. They were making progress. Greer grabbed the barrel of the shotgun with her fingers and dragged it to her, cramming six shells into it and pumping it to load one into the chamber. It only took forty-two seconds for her to expend all nineteen bullets. She loaded another clip hastily, panic rising in her throat as she saw that there were only three left. Every shot had to count. Soon, she would be resigned to pouring Holy water on them and using her knife.

Greer wrapped both hands around the butt of the pistol, her shotgun between her feet, loaded and waiting. She concentrated on leveling the gun, finding her target and applying the right amount of pressure to the trigger. At that moment, she'd have given anything for high ground and a sniper's rifle.

But there was no high ground, and there was no rifle. She had to make do with a pistol and a shotgun, and each shell had to be a kill. If it wasn't, she would run out well before they had hacked their way through the sea of demons and hounds. Michael's sword wouldn't run out of ammo, but without her taking out as many as she was, it would lessen both their chances of survival.

The bullets hit their targets almost every time. Greer was very fast at pushing the button to release the empty, stooping to grab a full, and snapping it in, all in a matter of less than ten seconds. Michael stood to her back, and they hacked their way through the crowd.

The sky was darkening to nearly completely black, and it was becoming hard to see. Michael threw out his arm and grabbed her by the wrist. He dragged her in the direction of the Gate, plowing through the demons and ignoring the nicks and slices of their knives and swords. He shoved Greer behind him and plunged one hand into his pocket, withdrawing a slim, silver key. He pushed it into her hands.

"There is a lock on that Gate. Turn it to the left, to the right and left again. Symbols will pop up. Press every third one moving from left to right, then every fourth going right to left. Once that is done, there will be a yellow light. Reach into it and you should feel a handle. You need to pull it open. I'll hold them off while you do that."

Greer ran to the Gate and shoved the key in the lock, turning it as quickly as she could. The dark was becoming deeper, and it was nearly impossible to see. She was forced to run back to her bag and get her flashlight. Wind rushed through Hell and whipped her hair around her face. Michael's wings spread wide, and he hovered several inches above the ground, slashing at anything that dared get too close.

She had to yell to be heard over the sound of the wind. "What's going on?"

Three people walked through the crowd. One, a woman, wore a white gown that billowed out behind her and bared long, tan legs. Her golden curls blew off her shoulders, and the wind plastered her gown to her body, revealing every curve. One man was shirtless and wore only a pair of leather pants. He had long curly hair and a broad, sculpted chest. The third had dark brown hair slicked back from his face and wore an expensive Italian suit with a blue silk shirt, a pinstriped tie and shiny leather shoes.

"Get that Gate open. Those are Devils." Michael wielded his sword and spread his wings to offer Greer some protection as she worked before turning to speak to the Devils. "You're too late. Laelia is on Earth."

Lilith lifted one shoulder in a shrug. "Good for her. There are so many demons on Earth that it doesn't matter if you close the Gate."

Michael looked to the man in the suit. "You're supposed to be dead, Beelzebub."

Beelzebub smiled. "Dead for us means in the Lake. After that bitch stabbed me with the Jesus knife, I found myself chained to the Lake like a human. It boiled off my flesh, and there was no relief from the heat and pain. It gave me a new appreciation for what we do to souls when they come down here. There was not a second that I was not experiencing agony. Time is so different down there. For every day here, it's a hundred years down there. Luckily, my Father cares for me so much that he dove into the Lake and yanked my chains from the bottom, freeing me. I've been recovering in the castle since then, but when this human infiltrated today, I knew it was time to jump back into the fun." He formed a ball of fire and stared into it. "You're not supposed to be here, Michael."

Michael shrugged. "I was retrieving a soul that belongs to me. We're on our way out."

"You've left a trail of dead hounds in your wake and sent hundreds of my demons back to the Lake. Do you really think you're going to get through that Gate alive?"

"We've done pretty well thus far. Don't start something, Beelzebub. I can have legions of Angels upon you in minutes."

"If that was the case, you would not have come for her alone. I suspect God isn't all too interested in this fight. From what I hear, He's sending Angels to Earth, but getting Him to send a squad down here would be stretching you a bit too thin."

"You hear a lot for a dead man. This is correcting things, and you know that. Had your side lived up to their part of the bargain, Angels would be contentedly walking the Earth, and you would all be here, wallowing in your own filth. You violated the sacred agreement between Lucifer and God."

Azazel laughed. "What did you expect? This is Hell, Michael! We're Devils! Did you really think we'd abide by your stupid fucking rules?"

Michael sighed. "I suppose not. Which is why I'm no longer playing by them, either." He struck out with the sword, lighting it on fire and slashing at them. He threw out a stream of fire and grabbed Greer, leaping through the Gate and slamming it shut behind him.

Greer waited several heartbeats before whispering. "How do we get out?"

"We follow this to the end and climb out the other side. We must be very careful of what we emerge into. It all likelihood, Gabriel is leading your friends in battle to clear that cave again. How many bullets do you have?"

"Nine. My bag got left back there. All I have is my pistol with nine shots and my knife."

Michael frowned. "It will have to suffice. If you are overwhelmed, yell for me. I will attempt to stay as close as possible to you should we emerge into a battle."

Greer huddled close to his back as he reached for the door that would lead back to Earth. She could feel both Damon and Alaria in her mind, though something was different. Concerned, she held her breath while Michael turned the handle and pulled the door open.

Chapter Thirty-Two

Damon felt sick. He could feel Laelia inside him, tearing at him, trying to force her way through to the surface. She was evil and strong, and every time she threw herself against the doors to his mind, she very nearly forced them open. He closed his eyes for a moment and forced her back down.

Gage was next to him when he opened them, pressing a rifle into his hands. "Are you okay to help or do I need to tie you up and leave you here?"

Damon shook his head. "I'll manage. She's not strong enough to surface. Vampires aren't really meant to possess people, so she's not as strong as I imagine a demon must be. I don't think there's a risk of her taking over. If I start to feel differently, I'll let you know."

Gage studied him for another long minute before nodding. "See that you do." He crawled up the hill and peered over it to get a gauge of the threat they faced. Sighing, he slid back down the hill. "There are twenty demons and about half again as many hounds. I see Abaddon down there, but none of the others." He looked to Gabriel. "You still have Abalam in custody, yes?"

"He has not yet freed himself from Azazel's prison. As far as I am aware, he is not being missed by the Devils. There was much dispute over him being placed in charge. Lilith and Azazel are glad he is gone, and Abaddon is solely focused on his own task. It is not a permanent solution, but it remains secure at this moment."

Alaria's breath hissed out between her teeth. "We need a plan of attack here. We can't just charge in and hope for the best."

Braxton snapped a clip into his pistol and tucked it into his waistband before grabbing a machete and twirling it. "Yes, we can, and that's exactly what we're going to do. Michael could already have Greer and be waiting for us to clear the entrance before he brings her out. Every minute we're waiting here is a minute that she could be dead."

Alaria gasped and dropped to her knees, grabbing her arm with both hands. Tears welled in her eyes, and she bit her lip until it bled to keep from crying out. Gabriel was immediately at her side.

"What's wrong? What's happening?"

Alaria waved her hand and brushed him off. "I linked myself to Greer. Wherever she is, she just broke her damn arm and used me to fix it." She rubbed the appendage and scowled at the darkening bruise that marred her skin. "That fucking hurt."

Damon laughed wryly. "Imagine how it felt first hand." He glanced around. "Okay, here's the plan. I'm going to head up to that ridge line on top of the cave and pick them off. I'll start with the hounds since they're the most dangerous. Gabriel, you get inside and guard that Gate. The most important thing is keeping it clear so that we can do the ritual as soon as they're out. Alaria and Braxton, you get down there and start hacking. Let me get a few shots off before you go in. Hopefully, some of them will scatter once I start blowing their brains out."

Alaria nodded. "I'll hang back a bit to make sure that they don't just charge up the hill and tear you to pieces. Brax, can you handle being front line?"

Braxton grinned. "It's been too long since I've had a good fight." He clapped Damon on the back. "Get up there. Pick off as many as you can, but your main task needs to be giving us cover once we're in it. You have the best vantage point from up there."

Damon grabbed several clips of ammo and headed up the hill. "On it."

He climbed the hill slowly, taking care not to make enough noise that he would draw the notice of the demons below. The wind was in his favor, carrying his scent away from the clearing. He found two rocks high enough to give him some cover from return fire and with a crevice between them that was large enough to balance the barrel of his rifle. He screwed on the scope and lay on his stomach.

Sharpshooting required concentration and awareness. He had to take the wind shear, distance, angle and movement of his target into consideration. He pressed his left eye to the scope and closed his right. The crosshairs were thin black lines across his field of vision, and he angled them down until they were pinned right between the eyes of a Hell hound. He held his breath, said a quick prayer and squeezed the trigger.

The gunshot was like a crack of lightning in the clearing. The hound's head exploded, spraying the demon next to it with blood and bits of bone and brain. There was one second of confusion and silence as everyone tried to take everything in.

After that one second, chaos erupted.

Damon pulled the trigger four times in rapid succession, one bullet tunneling into the dirt and the other three finding homes in the skulls of three more hounds. He saw Braxton, Alaria and Gabriel charge into the clearing, and he focused on keeping them safe. Gabriel worked his way through the clearing quickly and disappeared inside. He saw a flash of light that told him the Angel was doing something very violent.

Damon saw Alaria hit the ground, writhing in pain a moment before it hit him. His ribs broke and his skin ripped, blood flowing from the wounds and soaking through his clothes, dripping to the ground and leeching into the dirt.

They were healing almost as soon as they ripped through him, but it was enough. He felt Laelia rise up in him, taking advantage of the pain and his lack of concentration to wiggle her way into his consciousness. He struggled to fight both the pain and the vampire but found that she was stronger than he was when he was injured.

The vampire took hold of him, battering him back down and forcing her way up. She closed in around him, smothering him into the deep recesses of his own mind. She stood and shrugged, stretching her arms over her head and surveying the body she now inhabited.

"Well, I've never worn a man before. This is quite interesting." She cracked her knuckles and bared her teeth, the canines extending into fangs. "This is going to be fun."

"Not so fast, Laelia."

She whirled, Damon's body bigger than what she was used to, and faced Gage. She smiled. "Gage, darling. I haven't seen you in centuries. I had heard that you were on the wrong side of this fight, but I didn't believe it until right this very instant."

"Wrong side is a matter of perception. I happen to think I'm on the right side of the whole thing. Regardless, that's not important, because we're going to win, and that starts by killing you."

"Killing me requires killing this body. From my brief time in here, I think he's rather important to this whole thing."

Gage sighed. "Leave that to me, love. Right now, there are bigger things to worry about." He didn't move when he heard Alaria sneaking up the hill from the other side. With any luck, Damon's body was taking time to adjust to being inhabited by a vampire and didn't yet have preternatural hearing. "Like dragging you down that hill and draining you dry on that Gate."

Laelia laughed. "Good luck with that, darling. In case you haven't noticed, I'm stronger than you. I'm your sire. You owe me your life, Gage. The least you can do is help me win this. You'll be banished to Hell when this all goes south anyway. Is that what you want? To rot in Hell for eternity?"

"I'm aware of my fate, Laelia. I chose it willingly. Just because I'm a monster doesn't mean that I'm incapable of deciding for myself. I'm going to stop you and the Devils and everything like you, and if I have to be chased off the Earth too, then I consider that a small price to pay for getting rid of everything else evil."

"Don't be such a martyr. It's very unbecoming."

Alaria stepped up behind Damon and swung the heavy branch she held in her hands against his head. His body collapsed to the ground in a heap, unconscious. She stepped over him and looked down. "Night night, bitch."

Gage laughed. "You like your theatrics, don't you?"

Alaria cocked one eyebrow. "All girls do. Let's get him downstairs and wait for Michael and Greer to come through that Gate."

Gage stooped and lifted Damon onto his shoulder. "What the hell are we going to do about killing Laelia while she's in Damon's body?"

"Not a fucking clue. Hopefully Gabe will have a better idea." She paused and looked at him. "Is it true, what Laelia said? About you going to Hell with the rest of the creatures at the end of this?"

Gage smiled sadly. "Yeah. I don't have a soul, and I'll be banished with the rest of them but that's not important now. We've got plenty of time before it becomes an issue. Let's just get him down there and get this ritual ready. We don't know how much time we have before we get more company."

Gabriel stepped out of the cave and into the clearing. "Are you three coming down here, or are you going to continue to discuss things that have not yet been decided?"

Braxton laughed from where he was inspecting all of the hounds to make sure they were truly dead. "Give it up, Gabriel. People are always going to have conversations that you don't think are necessary. Did you stop Damon from killing us all?"

Gage carried Damon's unconscious form down the hill. "Did you doubt that I would?"

Braxton jerked his chin toward Gabriel. "He did."

Gabriel looked incensed. "I have never expressed anything aside from my utmost confidence in your abilities to carry out these tasks."

"Not out loud, anyway." Alaria sauntered past him and into the cave. She saw the dark look on Braxton's face when he peered into the chamber where Sam had died and reached for his hand, squeezing tightly for a long moment before releasing him. She jumped when the Gate began to glow and stepped back. "Guys! It's opening."

Gabriel stepped in front of her, shielding her. "We do not know that it is Michael and Greer coming through."

Michael's voice drifted out. "Don't be overly dramatic, brother. We both know that Gate only spits out demons twice a day, and the last was eight hours ago. We have four hours before the next group of demons will come through."

Greer stepped through the Gate and stared at Damon lying on the floor. "What happened to him?"

Alaria laid a hand on her shoulder. "That isn't Damon right now. We didn't have a vessel, so he volunteered to house Laelia. When you used us both to heal yourself, it was too much, and she was able to overcome him. He's possessed."

Michael and Gabriel exchanged a dark look. Michael stepped forward and placed his hand on Greer's other shoulder. "We have been unable to find a vessel in which she could be placed without ending a human life, which we cannot do. We have a very short time in which we can perform this ritual before Azazel, Beelzebub, and Lilith are upon us. I'm afraid that we must proceed with Laelia inside of Damon."

Greer shook her head violently, tears stinging her eyes. "No. No, no, no. No. I won't let you. You can't. He'll die!" Tears trailed down her cheeks and dripped off her chin as she cried. She surprised Michael when she turned and buried her face in his chest, her shoulders shaking with sobs. He closed his arms around her and rubbed her back soothingly.

Gabriel, however, had focused on what Michael had said. "Beelzebub is dead."

Michael shook his head and spoke over Greer's head. "He was placed into the pit when Griffin stabbed him with the consecrated blade. It seems that Lucifer has immersed himself into the Lake and dragged our erstwhile brother out. He is as annoying as ever, I'm afraid."

Braxton laughed bitterly. "She can't even have that. Griffin risked her life to kill Beelzebub, and he gets to come back like nothing ever happened?" He shook his head. "Nothing about this is right." He tossed up his hands, palms up. "I swear to God, after this is over, I'm done. He doesn't get to ask another thing out of me for as long as I live."

Gabriel glared at the Warrior. "This is neither the time, nor the place for your emotional human nonsense. We have a ritual to perform. I suggest you begin preparing the ground for it."

Greer lifted her head and wiped her face. "I can heal him. Whatever we have to do, I can heal him. This isn't like the Choosing. There's no need for him to die. I can heal him. If there's anything left when we're done, I can bring him back. I will bring him back."

Alaria looked at Gabriel. "She's right, isn't she? We need all of us to complete the other tasks, so he can't die."

Gabriel shrugged. "It's unfortunate if he dies, but I can find another Hunter to take his spot. The other tasks cannot be completed without this one, and I would rather try to do those with five than leave that Gate open another moment." He looked guilty when everyone glared at him. "Just because your human emotions get in the way of your logic does not mean that I have the same problems. I believe that Greer should do everything in her power to save Damon's life, but if it is a choice between failing this task and his life, I'll snap his neck myself."

Greer's hand went to her throat and tears filled her eyes again. "This isn't some random human we're talking about. It's Damon! He's one of us. He's my best friend! He's risked his life to save all of ours. The least we can do is return the favor."

Alaria slipped her arm around Greer's shoulder. "We will. You can use all of my energy that you need to for him. We'll do all that we can, and no one is going to let him die." She led the other woman several steps away. "Let's get things set up. I'm going to get the ritual started while you go salt the entrance to the cave and paint some traps in that clearing out there. It'll help keep any unwanted guests out."

Greer nodded slowly. "I can do that."

Chapter Thirty-Three

Symbols had power. If drawn one way, they would repel a demon. Drawn another, that same demon would be trapped. A third would keep Angels from finding a location. It was hard to believe that lines and shapes drawn in red paint were so powerful. Alaria pondered that as she shook the can of spray paint and coated the walls of the cave. She heard Gage and Greer outside doing the same thing. Braxton worked next to her, pouring a salt circle then lining it with a smaller circle of gun powder.

"How exactly is this going to work?" Alaria glanced at Gabriel as she spoke. "You've been suspiciously short on details."

"There is a spell. It is a human-created spell to counteract the ones used to open the Gate. It inserts a break between Hell and the entrance to the Gate that will stop more demons from coming out. The ones already here will still have the ability to go back to Hell, but no new ones will emerge. It will allow us to seal the Gate once the warlock holding it open is dead."

Alaria tapped her foot impatiently. "We know that. We've been told that a thousand times. What we need to know is how we do the spell. What are the words?"

Gabriel snapped his fingers and a piece of parchment appeared. "They are written here for you. I will not utter words of witchcraft."

Alaria snorted. "God created it, y'know."

Braxton looked up from placing Damon's prone body into the center of the circles he had made. "Last time I checked, Gabriel here doesn't like a lot of God's creations."

Gabriel's eyes snapped with anger. "Your input is completely unnecessary and not at all appreciated."

Braxton laughed. "Do you really think I give a rat's ass about whether or not you want my opinion?"

Alaria stepped between them. "That's enough from the both of you.

We have too much going on for the two of you to get into some sort of a pissing contest."

Michael stood at the back of the cave, watching the exchange with his eyebrows raised. He exchanged a look with Gage, who shook his head and rolled his eyes toward the ceiling. The vampire stacked candles around the salt circle and lit them, one after another. The sky outside was rapidly darkening with swirling storm clouds as nature reacted to the magic charging the air.

Greer came back in, her eyes rimmed with red from tears and her hands shoved deep into her pockets. "I think we're ready."

Michael's eyes narrowed, and he strode across the cave quickly. He went outside and then ducked back in. "We have a problem."

Alaria's head snapped in his direction. "What is it?"

"Vampires. A few werewolves. They're smart enough to know that we'll have the place coated with traps, but the lesser creatures can still get in." Michael looked at Gage apologetically. "No offense meant, of course."

Gage chuckled. "None taken. Did you get a count?"

"I believe there are a dozen vampires and twice that in werewolves."

Braxton bent to dig through their crates of supplies and came up with silver bullets and stakes. "Then it's a good thing Gage packed us enough stuff to fight a war from right here in this cave." He tossed Gage a stake. "Alaria and Greer need to stay in here and work on that ritual. The four of us will hold off our unwanted guests."

Michael drew his sword and waited while Gabriel did the same. "That is an acceptable plan."

Alaria shook her head. "There is something that feels so sexist about this. The men charge out into battle and we stay in the cave working spells."

Greer couldn't help the giggle that bubbled out of her. "You know this isn't that. I have to heal him once we slaughter the vampire, and I'll need your energy to do it. If you fall over in the middle of fighting a werewolf, it might bite your head off before you can get up." She loaded the silver bullets into a pistol and strode to the entrance. "I'll make sure nothing comes in the door while you're working, but hurry up."

Alaria dumped leaves of oregano and sprigs of sage into a pestle and used a mortar to grind them into a fine powder before adding lavender and aloe. "I feel like I'm making some very strange spaghetti sauce. What's going on out there?"

Greer peeked out. Gage's eyes were glowing red and his fangs were fully extended. He was circling with two vampires, both much larger than him. They charged at the same time. Gage dipped his shoulders and rammed one, using the monster's momentum against it as he flipped it over his shoulder. The second was a heartbeat behind him. Gage reared up and plunged the stake into his chest, and the vampire disappeared into a pile of dust. He lashed out with his foot, pinning the first to the ground and stooping to execute him efficiently.

Braxton twirled a stake in his hand, a gun stuck in the waistband of his jeans. He blocked a punch, returned it—a hard uppercut that snapped the vampire's head back so hard Greer wondered briefly if he broke its neck. When it continued to charge him, Braxton grabbed it by the wrist, whirled it around so that its arm was pinned and delivered a sharp kick to the back of the knee. The sound of breaking bone echoed through the clearing. Braxton placed both hands on the vampire's head and jerked sharply, breaking its neck. He jammed the stake into its chest before the body crumpled to the ground.

The Angels were working a bit harder. Michael twirled his sword and whirled to the side, dodging a werewolf. His blade flashed in the moonlight as he swiveled and slashed. The sword sliced through flesh and bone with a wet sound and blood splashed on the ground. The wolf looked at him in shock for several moments. As if in slow motion, the wolf's abdomen split open, and moonlight gleamed off a river of blood flowing into the dirt. Inch by inch, a mass of organs and intestines spilled out and landed on the forest floor in a shining, greasy pile. Another wolf, on the tail of the first, barreled after Michael. It slipped in the entrails and crashed to the ground, trying and failing to get its footing three times before Michael ended its life with one slash of his sword, severing its head from its neck.

Greer looked over her shoulder where Alaria was standing over Damon's body, one spiked heel on either side of him and a can of spray paint in her hands. The mist of paint was forming complex symbols on the roof of the cave. Greer turned back to the fight just in time to shoot a wolf that was charging toward the entrance to the cave. She pulled the trigger twice more before darting back into the cave to stand next to Alaria.

"They're fine. We need to get this going. You know the Devils are watching, and they'll keep sending in vamps and wolves until they kill us all."

"I'm ready." Alaria picked up a dagger and sliced deep into her hand. Blood welled in the cut, and she clenched her fist, increasing the flow of blood. It dripped onto the ground, droplets splashing before they soaked into the dirt. She glanced at the parchment Gabriel had handed her and shook her head in disgust. "Why do fucking spells always have to be flowery and rhyme?"

Greer shrugged and crouched next to Damon, ready to heal him as soon as the vampire was out. "Maybe it makes them stronger. Just do it already, Alaria."

Alaria began reading the words, her voice rising to fill the cavern. "The price is paid in blood for access to the magic of the Earth, and I command it to rise. From the streets of Heaven to the bowels of Hell, I seal the door for all Angels who fell. Demons, Devils, hounds of Hell, I bind thee. Souls of the damned, souls of the cursed, I bind thee. I bind thee to the Lake of Fire. I bind thee to the onyx walls. The doors will close, the locks shall turn, forever in Hell, your spirits shall burn." She looked around, her eyes wide, when the flames on the candles leapt three feet into the air and her blood on the ground began to sizzle. Greer jumped to her feet.

"What the hell?"

Alaria turned in a circle as the salt circle ignited into purple and blue flames. "Holy shit." She looked at the parchment again. "To consecrate this ground and refuse the passage of all who seek to leave the pit, I offer up the life's blood of the first vampire—the first creature borne of Hell." She stepped into the circle, knife in hand, and crouched next to Damon. "Only with her death, can Hell on Earth be ceased." She exchanged worried looks with Greer, and with a strangled yell, she yanked Damon's head back and slit his throat.

The wound was deep and long. His throat split open, and blood poured down his shirt like a waterfall poured over a cliff. It soaked into the cotton, staining it red, and pooled on the ground beneath him. Laelia's essence tried to escape, surging from Damon's mouth in a cascade of black and red. It was trapped by the circle. As Alaria and Greer watched, the smoke formed into a transparent woman with fearful eyes and her mouth open in a silent scream. The fire from the circle and the candles leapt up and ignited the smoke.

Flames filled the cavern, though when they brushed against Greer's arms, they weren't hot. They incinerated the vampire and drove into the Gate. It swung open, and for one terrifying moment, they saw into Hell and saw the legions of demons fighting to escape. The flames formed into a door. The demons charged it and were tossed back, one by one, over and over again. The Gate slammed shut and the vision disappeared.

Greer hit the ground on her knees, her hands ripping Damon's shirt to spread on his chest. She found their link and followed it into his mind. It was turning black and eroding even as she descended. She went straight for his throat.

The easy part was the skin. She stitched that closed in a matter of heartbeats. The trachea and vocal chords took longer to reconstruct. She could feel the heavy weight of death encroaching on her, and she struggled not to choke on it. She would not lose again. She couldn't. Not with Damon.

Once his throat was closed, Greer descended further into his chest and went to the heart. It wasn't beating, though electric pulses still moved the organ. She reached for Alaria, relying on their connection to give her more strength. She applied a stimulus to the heart muscle and watched it jump. Blood pumped through the veins and poured from one ventricle to the next. The beat was slow and irregular but there.

She raced through his veins and into his brain. Most of the synapses were dark but several still flickered. She reached out and touched each, urging them back to life. There was damage done there. She worked at it, painstakingly trying to heal every nerve ending and connection, knowing all the while that it was impossible to reverse all of the damage.

Greer stopped to listen several times for his heart, and each time, it grew stronger. She was winning. She spent several more minutes working on his brain before going back to the heart to repair and reinforce all of the muscle that had been damaged by the lack of blood. That done, she knew the one thing left was to replenish his stores of blood. His organs were slowly dying, and the synapses she had fired were already flickering as his body struggled to function with nearly no blood.

She pictured the cells in her mind, red and round. She had to form them one by one. Red, then white, then clear plasma. Cell by cell, she replenished his blood. She had no idea if it took her seconds, or if it took her days. The exertion was too much. She reached again for Alaria and found the link weak and eroded. She tried to grasp it and felt it give, snapping back into Alaria's mind and leaving her alone inside Damon's. Tired and weak, she had no choice but to proceed with only her own strength.

It was too much. Too much work, too much time, too much damage. Greer tasted blood in her own mouth and was thrown back into her own body. Her eyes snapped open, and she got one glimpse of Alaria's concerned face before her whole body seized and she collapsed to the ground, the cool blackness of unconsciousness rising up to embrace her as she fell.

Alaria lunged and caught Greer, guiding her to the ground as gently as possible. Gage and Braxton came back into the cave, bloody and bruised but relatively unharmed. Gage looked over the situation and met Alaria's gaze.

"It's done?"

She nodded. "It worked. I saw the new door. It was fucking awesome."

Braxton crouched next to Damon and pressed two fingers to the other man's throat. "He's alive. Is she?"

"Yeah. She knocked herself out." Alaria smiled when Damon's eyes flickered. "He's waking up."

Gage helped Damon sit up, patting his back gently and supporting most of his weight as he blinked blankly. "You missed the party, son. We're glad to see you back in the land of the living."

Damon turned his head, taking in the situation. "What the fuck happened? I remember Greer smacking me with some healing shit and then it all goes blank."

Gage chuckled. "You died. Well, kind of. Laelia was possessing you and took over when Greer used you to heal herself. We had to drain all of your blood during the ritual. Greer managed to fix you up." He cast a look to Greer, still unconscious. "I thought you told us that she could basically heal other people all day? Last two times I've seen it, she's ended up passed out on the ground."

Damon struggled to stand, thought better of it when his knees buckled, and sat back down. "The last two times you've seen it, she's been trying to bring people back from the dead. Last I knew, that was something even God did only rarely."

Michael entered the cave. "Your threats are eliminated. Gabriel is going to transfer you to Gage's estate. Should you need more assistance from me, you need only yell."

Before any of them could talk, Michael disappeared. Gabriel entered the cave a moment later. He surveyed the situation and nodded. "The first task is completed. If you'll stand in a circle, I'll send you home."

Braxton stooped and picked up Greer, while Gage helped support Damon's weight. Alaria reached out and laid a hand on each of their arms. Gabriel stared at her for a long minute with sadness in his eyes before he stretched out his hand and laid it against Greer's forehead. He whispered something no one heard under his breath, and they all disappeared.

Several hours later, all five sat at the dining room table, staring at Gabriel, who was sipping a cup of coffee gingerly. His suit was pristine somehow, though it had been muddy and in tatters after fending off werewolves, and not one hair was out of place. After several minutes of silence, he placed his cup deliberately on the table and cleared his throat.

"I'm sure you have questions about the next phase in this trial. What would you like to ask me?"

Greer spoke before anyone else. "When are you bringing Aradia forward?"

"It will be several months before her presence is required here. In order to kill Garrick and close the Gate, you will need the natural power of the Summer Solstice, which occurs in June. As it is currently September, this is far too soon to bring her here. She will be here when she is needed."

Braxton's voice was incredulous. "You're telling me that we're just going to sit on our asses for nine months before we can continue?"

Gabriel sipped. "That's the basic premise, yes. Do not think you will be doing nothing. The witch will be preparing, and the other side will be preparing, but both sides need the power of the solstice. They will be trying to cast a spell to keep the Gate open permanently, which would allow them time to find a way to break through the door you just placed, and we will be preparing to kill Garrick. Javal is a powerful demon who has been at Garrick's side for millennia. Theirs is a dangerous, powerful combination. You will need the time to gather information and to plan a strategy. The witch will be here with enough time."

Alaria's voice was slightly annoyed. "What do you propose that we do for the next nine months, Gabe?"

Gabriel shook his head. "It is not my job to give you tasks. I suspect that you'll find ways to occupy your own time."

Alaria leaned forward and braced her elbows on the table. "You don't think they're going to try to kill us between now and then?"

Gage shook his head. "No, they're not. It would be stupid of them to, wouldn't it?" He narrowed his eyes at the Angel. "What do they have to do to keep the Gate open for good?"

Gabriel averted his eyes. "That isn't important."

Alaria scowled. "Stop avoiding. What's going on?"

Gabriel sighed. "Not that it's any of your concern, but in order to cast the spell to hold the Gate open permanently, they must sacrifice the witch who could close it."

Gage chuckled. "They aren't going to come for us, because they're going to be too busy trying to kill Aradia. Unless they've gotten new powers since I was involved in Hell spawn society, time travel is still a bit beyond even Devils. They can't get her until she comes here, and if they kill any of us, she won't come here and they'll be stuck as they are forever." He glared at Gabriel. "Do I have it about right?"

Gabriel looked almost embarrassed. "You are not far from the truth. I do not yet know where this next phase will take place. God does not reveal everything to me at once. It is possible I will have to transport the five of you to her, though I suspect I will bring her forward. Things will unfold as they are meant to. We're in uncharted waters. The Choosing was supposed to be the end of this. Neither God nor Lucifer anticipated anything past that one event. This is not predestined, and God is not taking much interest in it. We are feeling our way along and doing the best that we can with the information we have. I do not enjoy dallying in the realm of magic and witch craft or of leaving things to nature and chance. I prefer operating within the framework of God's plan."

Alaria laughed. "This is your way of saying you don't have a clue why, isn't it? God isn't telling you what to do, and you're having to play on Earth more than ever before, following our rules and messing with things you think are beneath Angels."

Gabriel looked uncomfortable. "I wish I had more guidance is all. Regardless, all that we can do now is wait. There is no choice about that."

Damon yawned. "Well, that answers the what we do question. I don't know about the rest of you, but I'm damn tired. I'm going to grab some sleep. Greer?"

She took his hand. "Yeah, me too. Night."

Gabriel waited until both Gage and Braxton had left the room before turning to Alaria. "This is confusing for me and extremely difficult to deal with. I don't like keeping you in the dark, but I have no guidance on what I can reveal and when I should reveal it. I hope that you can understand that."

Alaria sighed. "I understand that you believe that. Gabe, we're trying to save the world, and from the way you're talking, God has gone on hiatus."

"Unfortunately, that's not a bad word to use for it. Michael is commanding the Host, and I am in charge of dealing with this. Nothing has changed in Heaven except that God has gone quiet. He has no interest in knowing what is going on, and He has not given any guidance about what should happen. We were given fifty years to fix the error, and if it's not done by then, Earth will be destroyed. Without the involvement of God, we have no choice but to rely on human inventions such as magic and weapons."

"I know it's scary for you, but just because you aren't getting orders doesn't mean that it's right for you to leave us hanging for weeks on end about what we're doing."

"I don't know how much I can tell you."

Alaria stood and crossed her arms. "We're either a team or we aren't. If we aren't, we don't need you, and if we are, we need to know everything. It's your choice, Gabe, and you need to make it."

Gabriel looked at the floor and studied his shoes. "I want us to be a team."

"Then you need to consistently share what you know with us."

"I'll make more of an effort." He reached out and stroked one hand down her face. "I have missed you these past days. May I stay with you tonight?"

Alaria very nearly gave in. His gaze heated her down to her core, and his touch ignited small fires on her skin. Her body responded to his suggestion in a primal way. She laid her hand over his and leaned into his touch for three seconds, relishing the feel of his skin on hers. She shook her head.

"No. You've been an ass, you've left us high and dry, and the last time you left me like a john leaves a hooker. I know you're confused, and I know this is hard, but I need more than that. Until you make some decisions, you can stay in Heaven, and I'll buy a vibrator." She stalked down the stairs to her room, her final words trailing back up them to his ears. "Get some rest, Gabe. We've got a lot of work left to do."

END

Enjoy this Sneak Preview of *Devil's Redemption,*
Coming in April 2015!

Prologue

Amaya was awake. She lay in the dark, staring at the ceiling, listening to her parents. Their phone had rung several minutes earlier, and she knew by the hushed voices and whispered urgency that they were leaving again. She heard the flutter of wings seconds after the door slammed and she turned on her bedside lamp. Gabriel turned when the light came on and wagged his finger at her.

"You, young lady, are supposed to be sleeping."

"So are Mom and Dad, and they just went down the stairs. What's going on?"

"They've been called away."

Amaya huffed. "No shit, Sherlock. I'm not an idiot. I'm twelve years old now. I hear them when they leave and I see how they always come back bloody and bruised. What are they doing when they sneak out in the middle of the night?"

Gabriel crossed the room and perched on the side of her bed. "Your parents are helping people. There are wars being fought, and they are doing everything within their power to keep those wars away from you."

"It's drugs, isn't it? They're drug dealers?" She threw back the covers and climbed over him to stomp to the window. "Why won't they tell me anything? They sneak out in the middle of the night and leave you to watch me. They come back with cuts and bruises and don't talk about it. They call each other 'Mom' and 'Dad' but never by their real first names. When I ask, they just tell me I'm not old enough to know. I'm twelve! What is old enough?"

Gabriel stood and reached out to lay a hand on Amaya's head. "Your parents are not dealing drugs." He sighed deeply. "This is not a conversation that I should be having with you."

"You tell me stories that would make an adult blush." Amaya crossed her arms and glared at him. "Seriously, Uncle Gabe, I learned what sex was from your bedtime stories."

Gabriel made a strangled noise. "It would seem my storytelling may leave much to be desired. Does your mother know?"

Amaya couldn't help but giggle. "No, silly. She hasn't talked to me about that yet." Her face fell into another glare. "That would mean they would have to let me in the same room as a boy, and God knows that isn't ever going to happen."

"You're smart enough to realize by now that the stories are more than stories."

"Duh. I know that demons are real. You have wings." She lifted her eyebrows and stared at him as if he were a very simple child. "I'm also smart enough to figure out that some of these 'characters,'" She made air-quotes with her fingers, "are my parents, though we both know you aren't about to tell me which ones, or even if those are their real names."

Gabriel was silent for several moments. "You will eventually know everything, Amaya. It will not be tonight, and it will be left up to your parents to choose when they reveal things to you about themselves. It is not my place to make that decision or to provide you with that information. I cannot do that, no matter how much you desire to know."

Amaya tugged on her curly hair in frustration. "I'm not a little kid anymore, Uncle Gabe! I'm old enough!"

He reached out and cupped her cheek gently. "It is not my decision to make, child. I wish that I could give you what you ask, but I cannot. I can only promise you that the time will come that you will receive the answers that you seek."

"When?" She squealed in frustration. "Seriously. I wake up in the middle of the night to my literal Guardian Angel standing in my room, which has been happening since I was three! This is creepy! You're an adult, and a boy, and I'm a girl."

Gabriel's eyebrows drew together. "Do I make you uncomfortable?"

Amaya shook her head so hard her curls bounced. "No, you don't make me uncomfortable, but it still seems creepy. Do you spend time in many girls' bedrooms?"

"No. I watch over you because your parents are my friends and because they need to be certain of your safety while they are doing their jobs." He looked at her with a long-suffering expression on his face. "I fear you are beginning to enter puberty."

Amaya shuddered and blushed. "You're so gross, Uncle Gabe." She stared out her window for a long moment. "You promise they aren't criminals?"

Gabriel chuckled. "I promise that your parents are not criminals." He efficiently made her bed and drew back the blankets. "Back into bed with you. It's much too late for children to be awake."

She slipped between the sheets without argument. "I'm almost too old for stories."

He looked at her fondly. Amaya was beautiful, caught between being a little girl and a young adult, wanting a story and unwilling to ask for it lest it make her seem younger than her years. He toed off his shoes and climbed into the bed with her. "Would you like me to tell you a story, Amaya?"

She pretended to think it over before nodding slowly. "Maybe, if it's a good one."

"I haven't yet told you what happened after Laelia was killed." He smiled when she snuggled against his side. "Do you remember what the six were to do after killing Laelia?"

Amaya yawned. "They had to kill Garrick. He's the wizard that got the gate open."

"Very good. Garrick was a very powerful wizard. He was human long, long ago and made a deal with Beelzebub that he would serve Lucifer for eternity in exchange for immortality."

"Where did Garrick's magic come from?"

"Magic is energy. It is in and around everything and everyone. It can be good or bad, the same as people can be good and bad. In the purest sense, God created magic when He created Earth, and He created witches and wizards when He created Adam and Eve."

"How do people use magic?"

"They learn to find the energy and manipulate it to do what they want. That is how Greer heals people and it is how Aradia helped Greer and Alaria form their link. Magic, in and of itself, is neither good nor evil. It simply is. However, when those who sought to use it for evil did so, eventually magic twisted and became black. Black, or evil, magic is almost limitless. It is what Garrick uses. Aradia uses white magic, or magic from nature. She is only allowed to access as much as she can handle."

"Can she kill Garrick using white magic?"

Gabriel patted her knee. "That's a huge part of the story, my dear. You don't want me to ruin it for you, do you?"

Amaya giggled and shook her head. "I guess not." She snuggled down into the blankets. "Will you tell me one thing?"

Gabriel leaned back against the headboard and draped the blanket over his legs. "Maybe. It depends on what that thing is."

"Does Alaria ever figure out what she wants? She just seems so torn between the two men." She looked up at him. "I'm assuming the Gabriel in the story isn't you."

He didn't respond to the statement. "Alaria finds her path. That is not the story for tonight. Tonight I am going to tell you about Aradia and the power that flows through her and how she used that power in an attempt to stop Garrick."

"What about Javal?"

"Javal is a powerful demon. His ability, which stems from his existence as a human, is that he can take on any form that he wishes to. He can appear as a child or an old man, a dog or a dinosaur. He has the ability to change what he looks like to fool those he wishes to kill. When not inhabiting a body, however, he is weaker and able to more easily be killed. In a corporeal form he is nearly as strong as the Devils, and his abilities made him one of the most feared in all of Hell."

"Did Aradia have to fight them both?"

"Aradia was not fighting on her own. Remember, there were six, and they would either succeed or fail as one. She had plenty of help."

Already interested in the story, Amaya pushed herself to sit back up. "I think I'm going to like this one. How does it start?"

"It starts as all good stories start, my darling girl. Once upon a time, in a land far from here and in a time long forgotten, there was a magnificent Queen who was also a very talented Dreamweaver named Graciela..."